Columbus Day

Expeditionary Force Book 1

Craig Alanson

To Tom Duckhorn
from David Dempster
I hope you like it
as much as I Did!

Contact the author
craigalanson@gmail.com

Cover Design By:
Alexandre Rito
alexandre@designbookcover.pt

Table of Contents

CHAPTER ONE COLUMBUS DAY

The Ruhar hit us on Columbus Day. Every country had a name for the day the Ruhar attacked; the common name that stuck, after a while, was Columbus Day. I guess that makes sense. There we were, innocently drifting along in the cosmos on our little blue marble, like the Native Americans in 1492. Over the horizon come ships of a technologically advanced, aggressive culture, and BAM! There go the good old days, when we humans only got killed by each other. So, Columbus Day. It fits.

When the morning sky twinkled, with what we later learned were Ruhar warships jumping into high orbit, we were curious. When power plants, refineries, factories and other industrial sites around the planet started getting pounded from orbit with hypersonic railgun darts, we were shocked. For me personally, when a Ruhar combat transport dropped out of the sky and skidded across a potato field outside my tiny hometown in northern Maine, that was when I became Officially Alarmed. It was a Monday morning in early October, the Columbus Day holiday in America. I was home on leave from the Army, visiting my folks. Taking a break after my battalion got rotated home from peacekeeping duty in Nigeria. What a shit job that was, I was happy to be home in the States. My leave was ended by a burning streak across the sky, as the Ruhar transport came directly over my truck. It arced over the lake and crashed in the Olafsen's potato field, plowing up dirt and potatoes until its nose was half submerged in a pond. It wobbled side to side for a minute, with a screaming sound coming from its engines, then it took off and flew low and unsteadily over the tree line toward the center of town, trailing smoke from its underside.

Our supposed allies, the Kristang, think that Ruhar assault transport was damaged during the drop from orbit, and fell short of its intended target, since that is the only possible reason the Ruhar would have invaded Thompson Corners, Maine. Hell, I didn't want to be there anymore, that's why I joined the Army in the first place. My hometown is nice enough, it's simply nothing special. There's potatoes and cattle and sheep and other farming, of course, and some people like my Dad had jobs at the big paper mill down in Milliconack. You could get by with some lumbering, working as a hunting or fishing guide, a little welding on the side, whatever. Nobody in northern Maine relies on one job. Anyway, Thompson Corners is not the sort of vital strategic target that military planners would think of, when deciding where to drop from orbit a combat transport, with a dozen or so heavily armed troops. The Ruhar troops, cute and furry bewhiskered bastards that they are, no doubt waited until their transport finally skidded to a stop on the front lawn of the elementary school in the middle of town, popped the door open, gazed in awe at the magnificent vista of Thompson Corners, and asked the pilot where the hell they were. Soldiers are soldiers, whether they have fur, skin or scales. So, logically, the Ruhar lobbed a missile at the most imposing structure in the area, the potato warehouse, and took it out in impressive fashion. I mean, they blew the hell out of it, those soldiers must have had something against potatoes. Next they destroyed the two bridges across the Scanicutt River; the railroad bridge and the old concrete highway bridge that's been there since it was built by FDR's Works Progress Administration in the 1930s. We'd had a lot of rain, and the river was running high, so with the bridge out, the only way for me to get into town was to drive all the way to Woodford and cross the river there. Like the old New England joke; you can't get there from here, right? Nice idea, if the roads hadn't been clogged with panicked traffic, and a hundred other people didn't have the same idea I had, at the same time.

When I saw that assault ship coming in, trailing smoke behind it and headed for the center of Thompson Corners, I was already in my parent's pickup truck, on my way into town to pick up my sister from her friend's house. It was ten minutes after the first sites got hit, the radio said the governor had just declared a state of emergency, urged everyone to remain calm, then all communications went out. No radio, no cellphones, no TV, no electricity. I didn't need to wait for instructions, I was going to pick up my kid sister, get back home, and hunker down with my family until I figured out what the hell was happening. Behind the seat was my father's bird hunting shotgun, and a box of shells that were good for quail and not much else. Shows how clearly I was thinking that morning. All my Army gear, including my rifle, were back at Fort Drum in New York State. I was, after all, on leave. Coming over the hill, I saw the ruins of the bridges, and nearly crashed into a line of traffic that was trying to get into town like I was. Bill Geary, a volunteer firefighter and a retired captain from the Maine National Guard, was getting people organized to drive over to Woodford and come into Thompson Corners using the old fire road. I, like a dumbass, shouted that my truck had four-wheel drive. Almost everybody in northern Maine has four-wheel drive, even if it's only a beat-up old Subaru. Since I was last in line, I got turned around first, and three guys whose car had gone in a ditch jumped in my truck. We roared off like the cavalry coming to the rescue in a movie.

By the time we fought through outbound traffic to get across the bridge in Woodford, and bounced along the poorly maintained fire road halfway toward town, the Ruhar had already secured the center of Thompson Corners. The town was empty because no humans had waited for an engraved invitation to get the hell out of there. One sheriff's deputy panicked, and fired off a couple shots with his 9MM service weapon, until the Ruhar got annoyed and took out the Shell station he was hiding in, with what looked like an antitank rocket.

I've seen Ruhar up close since then, plenty of times. No, they don't eat humans. And, no, they don't kill babies. Believe the propaganda if you want, I know what I've seen. If that sheriff's deputy hadn't opened fire, the Ruhar might not have killed a single person in town. I couldn't blame the Ruhar; if some idiot was taking potshots at me, I'd light him up with a rocket, too. I know, because I'd done the same thing in Nigeria.

Anyway, the Forest Service gate across the fire road was locked, we wasted five minutes while a guy three trucks ahead of us tried blasting the lock with a shotgun. Surprise! The Forest Service had anticipated somebody trying that, and that lock wouldn't budge. A guy rammed the gate, and busted both the gate and the radiator of his truck, which then needed to be pushed off the road before the rest of us could squeeze by and drive through.

Yeah, yeah, everybody has a story from that day, this is my story, so shut up and listen. One thing I've learned is that Ruhar Army grunts are like grunts across the galaxy; they want to get the combat over with and get back to their barracks, or dens, in their case. Did I hate them? Hell yes, but I don't think they meant to kill people, at least, except as collateral damage. Whatever their objective was on Earth, these troops had missed their landing zone, and were making the best of the situation. Everybody would have been better off if those Ruhar had sat in their busted transport with their thumbs up their asses, called the Ruhar version of AAA, and waited for a tow truck. Combat ops don't work that way. Something gets screwed up on every mission; you adapt and do the best you can to accomplish your objective. This group of Ruhar decided their objective was to secure Penobscot County, whether that made sense or not. The Kristang told us that the Ruhar's most likely plan was to destroy our industrial infrastructure, and knock us back into the stone age, so we'd be no threat to them. If that was their original objective, they missed it by a couple hundred miles, when they landed in Thompson Corners. The Kristang were mostly telling the truth about why the Ruhar hit us, although they lied about everything else, which I'll get to eventually.

We shouldn't even be fighting the Ruhar, they aren't our enemy, our allies are.

I'd better start at the beginning.

My name is Joe Bishop, I was twenty years old on the day the Ruhar attacked Earth, a Specialist in the US Army. Before the Army cut it, I had slightly longer than medium length hair of an indeterminate blonde-brown color, which I got from my mother. She called the color 'mouse fur brown' and had dyed her own hair a golden blonde for as long as I could remember. Blue eyes I got from both my parents, and my height at six feet three inches definitely came from my father's side, my mom barely stands five-four in her stocking feet. In high school I played third base on the baseball team, wide receiver on the football team, and was a backup shooting guard on the basketball team, although I didn't play basketball my senior year. Truth is, I wasn't a star athlete at baseball or football either. I worked hard, put the team first, and we won our share of games. When it came time to send out applications to colleges, I didn't know where I wanted to go to school, or what I wanted to be when I grew up. Other than knowing that I didn't want to sit behind a desk all day. And that I wanted to get out of Thompson Corners. My father had been in the Air Force for a couple years, then he went into the Reserves as a mechanic. Same type of job he did at the paper mill. He liked working with his hands, fixing stuff, and I kind of did too. Money was tight, and I didn't want to bury myself in debt with student loans, so the military sounded good to me.

When I'd signed up for the Army, I did it because I wanted to serve my country, and because the Army would pay for college. The life also appealed to me, I loved the outdoors; camping, hunting, fishing, hiking, canoeing. The training was tough, sure, nothing that I didn't expect, and I was proud to get through basic and be assigned where I wanted: the 10th 'Mountain' Infantry Division, in Fort Drum, New York. Peacekeeping duty in Nigeria wasn't what I would have wished for, but we got orders, and I went. I was surprised that peacekeeping involved killing so many people, but it is what it is.

So, now you know why I was laying under a bush atop a small ridge that overlooked the center of my hometown, staring at that busted Ruhar transport ship. Laying there and trying to figure what, if anything, we should do.

"That is one big damned hamster, Bish, you ain't lying." Tom Paulson said as he handed the binoculars back to me. "What're we gonna do?"

"I don't know yet. Let me think." There were plenty of military veterans around my hometown, I had one of them with me, but Tom had been a Navy supply clerk twenty years ago, and I was Army infantry with recent combat experience and on active duty. I guess it made sense the others were looking at me for ideas. They knew I'd been in combat in Nigeria, but fighting disorganized home-grown militia fanatics in the bush was totally different from tangling with giant space hamsters in my hometown in northern Maine.

"Goddamn, where are all the gun nuts when you actually need them? Is this all we got?" I looked in dismay at the collection of hunting rifles, shotguns and the odd 9MM handgun. Everybody in Thompson Corners had a gun, because everybody hunted, or at least needed to keep bears away from their backyard bird feeders. "Come on, nobody has an old M-60 in the attic? Maybe an AK?"

"Hell, Bish, I want to kill a moose so I can eat it, not vaporize the damned thing." Tom said. "Hunting licenses ain't cheap."

"All right, all right, me too." I looked through the binos again, at the hamsters patrolling the streets of my hometown. At the dark smoke coming from the potato warehouse, across town by the railroad tracks, which was still burning. At the hamster's shuttle, or landing craft, or infantry assault ship, or whatever they called it; squat and ugly and powerful looking, with a banged-up nose and a bent wing, and a thin stream of white smoke coming from the belly, as it sat on the front lawn of the elementary school.

Hamsters. We have other names for them; rats, weasels, rodents, but with their fine, golden fur, round faces and whiskers, what they most look like are hamsters. Except hamsters aren't six feet tall, standing on two legs, wearing body armor, helmets and goggles, carrying evil looking rifles, and coming down from orbit in an assault ship. That I know of, I mean, I never owned a hamster, so what do I know? We didn't know they were hamsters, until one of them in the doorway of their ship, maybe the pilot because he didn't have a rifle, took his helmet off, got something from his pocket, and started eating it. He got yelled at, and put his helmet back on, but not before we saw his furry head and hamster ears. They weren't exactly hamsters, but close enough.

Susie Tobin lifted her eye from the scope of her .30-06 hunting rifle. "What about the quarry? They have dynamite, right?" Susie was about five feet nothing, her day job was a teacher at the regional middle school, and looking at her, you wouldn't think she could even lift her old Army surplus rifle. But I'd seen the racks of deer antlers, tacked up on the south side of her barn, so she sure knew how to use it.

"What're we doing with dynamite?" Diego scoffed. "Run up to that ship of theirs, and throw it through the door? You wouldn't get within a hundred yards, before they cut you down."

"She's right," I said, thinking of the hell that IEDs caused us in Nigeria. They were a problem on the roads, but especially dangerous when we were patrolling a village, where sightlines were limited and there were plenty of places to conceal a bomb. Patrolling, like the hamsters were doing right now. Pairs of hamsters were checking out buildings in the center of town, which, considering it is Thompson Corners, isn't much. You may think that, being the Columbus Day holiday, there would have been lots of tourists in town when the Ruhar dropped in for a visit. If you think that, you've never had the good fortune of visiting my home town. Columbus Day is a big leaf-peeping holiday in New England, a weekend when city folk from down south drive out to the country, to see the colorful foliage on the trees, stay in quaint little inns and bed and breakfast places, and take lots of pictures. We do get tourists in our part of the Great North Woods, but not for leaf-peeping. By Columbus Day, a lot of the trees around here had already dropped their leaves, and our part of Maine is pretty flat anyway, plus the pine trees don't turn color. People come here for canoeing, fishing, hunting and snowmobiling. There isn't a whole lot of that going on the first part of October, so the town was pretty empty when the Ruhar crash-landed, the day being a school holiday and all. Damn good thing, too, I couldn't imagine what would have happened if the elementary school had been full when the Ruhar took control of the town. I didn't have to imagine that scenario, since I'd already seen that in the movie *Red Dawn*. The good one made way back when Reagan was in office, not the crappy one they made later.

Anyway, I had an idea. "Susie, your father works at the quarry, right? You and Tom get us dynamite, detonators, wires, whatever we need to blow something up remotely." I had no idea how to do that, having never even seen a stick of dynamite. "Diego, stay here and watch the hamsters, see where they patrol, especially how often they go by the old town hall." Which was now home to the town's only diner, and an insurance agency. "Stan, Deb, see if you can find a truck or van down there that we can get started, big enough to fit a couple people in the back, something covered, not an open truck bed. Keep to this side of town, you don't want to cross Route 11, or the hamsters will see you. If you find something, drive it over to Red Brook Road and leave it there. We'll meet back here."

"Ok, Bish." Tom nodded. "What're we going to do?"

I took one more look at the Ruhar, noting the disposition of their troops without even thinking about it, seeing where they were patrolling through the town, and where they had defensive positions around their ship. "We're going to the dentist."

"You have *got* to be kidding me." I blurted out.

"Bish," Stan said defensively, "this is the best we could find. It's either this, or an old Dodge Neon."

"Most people got in their cars and left in a hurry, it looks like, there aren't a lot of cars left on this side of the river." Debbie added.

"Yeah, but-"

Tom shook his head. "There is no freakin' way we can drive this. We're fighting an alien invasion. We can *not* drive this, this, thing."

I had to agree. Except for one thing, it was a perfect truck. They'd found a delivery van, like a FedEx truck, it was in pretty good mechanical condition; the tires weren't bald, there was some rusted-out spots around the wheel wells but nothing serious, it had big back doors so several people could get in or out fast, and they reported that it ran and shifted well, with no squeaky belts or squealing brakes. They'd found it behind the Davis Brothers garage, where it must have been getting the interior rebuilt, because the inside was stripped other than the driver seat. It was a good truck, except for that one thing.

Barney.

Barney, the big purple cartoon dinosaur with the perpetual stupid grin. Barney, and Smurfs, Mickey Mouse, unicorns, and a lot of other fictional characters were painted on the truck. Whoever decided which characters to paint on the truck had made interesting choices, like, why was Iron Man waving to the Smurfs? And, was that Darth Vader down near the right front fender, or had someone started painting black primer to cover up a rust spot, and decided to get creative? Most of the characters were poorly painted, it took me a minute to realize that what I thought was a sitting Buddha, was supposed to be Winnie the Pooh. Winnie the Buddha? It was an ice cream truck; in case you hadn't guessed yet. A ridiculous ice cream truck, that I was fairly certain didn't have permission to use any of the trademarked characters painted on the side. Also, instead of the familiar 'Mister Softee' logo, this one had a poorly stenciled 'Super Softic' logo. How could ice cream be super soft? Was it melted?

This was clearly a bandit ice cream truck, the kind that I pictured furtively roaming suburban neighborhoods of a big city, selling expired ice cream and trying to avoid local authorities. The giant purple Barney plastered across both sides, and the stuffed Barney strapped to the hood, were impossible to avoid. Whoever owned this truck must really, really, like Barney.

"We could throw a quick coat of paint on it." Stan suggested.

"We are not taking time to repaint the damned thing," I growled. I didn't like the idea either, but this truck is what we had. To go into battle with. "Besides, the hamsters won't know who Barney is, they may think he's a fierce predator." Even I didn't believe that one.

"Oh for Christ's sake," Susie was exasperated. "You idiot men are afraid to ride around in a truck that says 'Softie' on it? Get over yourselves. I'll drive the damned thing. Joe, what's the plan?"

"GO GO GO!" I shouted along with Stan, as we jumped in to sprawl on the floor of the ice cream truck. Susie didn't need to be told twice, she hit the gas as we were still in the air. Stan would have slid right out the back of the truck if Deb hadn't gotten hold of his shirt collar. Tom kicked Stan's feet inside and slammed the back doors shut, just as the truck bounced over a big pothole, and Tom landed on his ass on top of the Ruhar soldier. The hamster grunted, which told us it was still alive, I hadn't been completely sure of that when we grabbed it.

Looking back, it was a stupid plan, and we got lucky. I'd noticed the hamsters went through the alley between the diner building and the hardware store next to it. While the rest of us were off gathering supplies, Diego had watched and confirmed the hamster patrols went through that alley regularly, looking in windows and knocking open doors to look inside. They were doing that all over town, I chose the diner because there was a short dirt road that led from the river right to the back of the diner. The road went through woods and had good cover most of the way. We'd had a lot of rain from a nor'easter the week before, so the river was almost at spring flood stage, and was really roaring as it went over the rocks and under the bridge, it made enough noise to cover the sound of the truck backing up behind the diner. Dynamite was placed inside the diner, up against the brick outside wall, we blew it up as the hamster soldiers got halfway down the alley.

None of us knew how much dynamite to use, so we used too much; it collapsed most of the wall into the alley. Even the ice cream truck got hit with stray bricks. No matter, our improved bomb did what it was supposed to do; it knocked those two hamsters silly and buried them under bricks. Tom, Stan and I grabbed the hamster that was closest to us, it also was least covered with bricks. Debbie covered us with a shotgun, as we hauled it out of the alley, Tom and Stan each got hold of an arm and I held its feet, we scrambled down the alley, tripping on bricks, and tossed the hamster in the back of the ice cream truck.

It was a stupid plan. Diego was watching from the hill, with a walkie talkie that Susie got from the quarry, she had the other unit in the truck. Diego reported that as soon as the dynamite exploded, a half dozen hamsters sprinted from their spaceship, another thirty seconds and they would have caught us. And if for some reason, like none of us really knowing how to use dynamite, our bomb hadn't exploded, those two hamsters would have walked to the back of the alley and seen the truck that wasn't there before. I didn't like our odds, against alien soldiers with body armor and advanced weapons.

Luck was with us that day, even as Tom fell again; this time into the button that controlled the ice cream truck's music system, and 'Turkey in the Straw' blared out of the rooftop speakers as the truck bounced and skidded down the gravel road along the river. "Shut that damned thing up!" Susie yelled at Stan, she had enough to do driving the truck. There was no seat belt for the driver, that was one of the items removed when they stripped the interior, and Susie's feet barely reached the gas pedal. Still, she had that sucker on the floor, and we were *moving*.

Stan punched buttons, and the music changed to 'Camptown Races', then 'Pop Goes the Weasel' then a couple video game theme songs I couldn't name, before Stan finally got the stupid thing to stop. I never felt like such a total idiot in my life, trying to hold down an alien soldier in the back of an ice cream truck, my chin getting bashed into the metal floor of the truck as moronic music blasts out of speakers and Barney's evil twin grins maniacally from both sides.

Our truck shot through a gap in the trees along the river, a clear space of about fifty yards. This is where I figured the hamsters were going to shoot us, they had a clear shot for a couple seconds at least. Why they didn't shoot, I think, is by that time the hamsters who reached the bombed-out alley realized one of their own was missing, and guessed it was in our truck. Anyway, we made it, the truck flew across the gap, then the land rose slightly between us and the center of town, and then Susie was standing on the brakes to slow the truck for a curve. After that, we bounced up onto a paved road, and Susie put the pedal to the metal. While on pavement, with a smoother ride, Tom and I got the hamster's hands tied behind its back, tied its legs together, and I started pulling off its gear. We had it under four lead vests, the kind dentists use when they give you X-Rays, that was my idea to block the signal of any location device the alien soldiers may have. The body armor around its torso had a quick release mechanism, as I expected, because human or alien, a soldier needed to get gear off and on quick. I also popped the latch for the chinstrap of its helmet, and for the first time, got a good look at the enemy. One of its eyes was open, there was blood from a cut on its cheek but I didn't think it was badly hurt, mostly stunned and disoriented. It was wearing an earpiece and microphone, which I tore off, and on its belt was what looked like some kind of radio. I told Tom to throw all of it out the window, we could come back to get it later if we had the opportunity, our priority then was to capture an alien soldier so our military could study it, see what kind of enemy we were facing.

Per the plan, Susie drove us a mile down the road to Tom's place, he had a barn, and she drove the truck right in through the open door, skidding to a stop. We all shared an 'oh shit did that really happen' moment. None of us could believe it. The hamster was moving about, so Tom sat on it, and I pointed a handgun at its face. That calmed it right down. It had probably never seen a Sig Sauer before, but it recognized a projectile weapon when it saw it.

"I can't hear Diego anymore," Deb reported, holding up her walkie-talkie. "The last thing he said was the aliens were running around, but their ship isn't moving." My last instructions to Diego had been to get out of town, in the opposite direction, as soon as he lost sight of our truck. I'm sure he was safe; he knew his way around the woods.

"They're waiting for a tow truck." I guessed.

"What?" Susie asked, like she hadn't heard me right.

"A tow truck," I explained. "Their ship is busted, they must have called upstairs to their fleet, and they're waiting for someone to come fix their ship, or pick them up. Let's get Fuzzy Face here into the root cellar, before his friends get organized and come looking for him."

Tom's place had an old root cellar, when I say old, I mean his house dated from 1848, and the root cellar belonged to the house before that. The root cellar had been expanded and converted into a bomb shelter, by the family that owned the farm back in the 1950s, now Tom and his wife Margie used it for storage. We got the hamster down the stairs and cleared space in the middle of the shelter for it, Tom padlocked a chain around its ankle, with the other end of the chain around a pipe sticking out of the floor. With the hamster comfortable in the center, there wasn't much room for the rest of us, because of all the shelves. Did I mention that Tom's wife Margie liked to can fruit and veggies? The woman had a bit of a canning problem, the whole place was stacked with jars. Most people in this neck of the woods can stuff, it's a way to have good food through the winter, and a lot cheaper than buying food from the store. My folks made applesauce, and jams, and canned tomatoes, beans, whatever we got from our garden. Tom's bomb shelter looked like Margie was planning to invite the entire 10th Division over for supper, and wanted to have plenty of food left over.

"What now?" Stan asked, while looking hungrily at a jar of blackberry jam.

"Now we wait. The military has got to be here soon." We'd all been surprised not to see any fighter jets or helicopters in their air, which told me the enemy had total air supremacy. "Hopefully, this guy's buddies," I pointed to our captive, "will be leaving soon. When our cavalry gets here, we hand him over."

"What makes you think they're going to leave?" Deb asked.

"Because no way would alien invaders have Thompson Corners on their initial target list. These guys are here only because their ship is busted. My big worry is if they stick around to look for Fuzzy Face, after the tow truck gets here. I'll stay with him, the rest of you better head south, see if you can find any National Guard, or even state cops."

Susie was indignant. "You're sending the womenfolk away to safety?" She had her hands on her hips, I knew what that meant.

"You have a family-"

"So does Tom." Susie pointed out.

"Tom got a text from Margie," I said defensively, "she and the kids are all right, heading to her mother's place. And Stan's wife is in Portland."

"And my husband is down in Milliconack and my kids are in Bangor with my sister. I'm staying here." Susie said empathetically, and held up her rifle for emphasis.

"Fine." I conceded without much fight, I really didn't want to be alone. "You and Stan have rifles, you get up in the woods behind the house where you can cover the road. Deb, get up to the rock ledge behind the house, you know it, right? Tell Susie and Stan if you see anything coming this way. Tom and I will stay here with Fuzzy Face."

Fuzzy Face wasn't talkative. Tom and I tried communicating with gestures, and pointing to ourselves, the hamster sat there stone-faced. Except when it shifted uncomfortably, then it grimaced. There was blood, red blood, on its hip. At least alien blood was red, and not green or blue or something really weird like that. I approached slowly, hands open to show I didn't have a knife. "We need to look at where you're hurt." I can slowly and loud, which is always the best way for foreigners to understand. Remember, foreigners are stupid, so you have to talk loud and slow so they will understand you. The hamster shrank away from me as far as it could, backed up against a shelf on the outside wall. I gestured to my hip, then his, then put a finger into the blood on the floor, holding my finger up so he could see the blood. Shaking my head and waving my bloody finger, I spoke slowly to the hamster. "You are hurt. This is bad."

"Bish," Tom said uncertainly, "you sure you should be touching that thing's blood?"

"It's got to be safer than touching human blood. You got bandages down here?"

"Yeah, first aid kit's in the cabinet. We got paper towels, too, Margie buys them by the gross at a warehouse store."

The hamster wasn't hurt badly, I blotted the wound clean, washed it with sterile water, which made it wince again, then slathered antiseptic lotion on the cut, and applied a bandage. It looked at me different after that, like it hadn't expected humans to be civilized. It made a sort of kissing gesture with its lips.

"I think it wants water?" Tom guessed. Margie had also bought bottles of water by the gross, we got out three bottles, Tom and I both drank from our bottles, then I opened another and held it to the hamster's lips. It downed half the bottle steadily, while looking me in the eye, that kind of freaked me out. Then it looked down meaningfully at its left front pocket, gesturing with its nose. Very carefully, I opened the pocket flap, which was a kind of magnetic thing, I think, and pulled out what looked like an energy bar. It didn't have bright packaging like the Hooah! bars I knew from the Army, just a green plastic wrapper with white writing in an alien script. I pulled the end of the plastic wrapper open, facing away from me. Which was stupid, what if it was some kind of explosive, and pulling the wrapping just pulled the pin on the grenade? Nothing happened. I sniffed it carefully, it smelled like sugar and nutmeg mixed with sawdust. It was an energy bar for sure. I broke off a piece and fed it to the hamster, it chewed for a long while, I guess their energy bars are as tough as ours. In about ten minutes, it ate half the energy bar and drank more water, then shook its head when I offered another piece. I felt the same way about our energy bars, half of one was usually enough for me before my jaw gets tired. In a further attempt at interspecies cooperation, I held the bar up in front of the hamster as I folded the wrapper over it, and tucked the remaining half back in its pocket, next to another two full energy bars. It smiled, or tried to. Smiling, without understood context, could be viewed as baring teeth in a threatening manner. The hamster had teeth that weren't much different from human teeth; white enamel, it looked like, the two upper front teeth were bigger than in humans, but not comically large like a beaver's teeth. Now that I was closer, the fur on its face was fine, it covered all its skin, but the fur was finer and shorter than a human beard.

"You hear that?" Tom asked. "Sounds like someone's shouting." We had kept the door to the bomb shelter cracked open so we could hear if Susie saw anything, but mostly closed so any radio signals from an implanted transmitter in our hamster would be blocked, I hoped. Tom stepped outside, I could hear him shouting with Stan. He stuck his head in the door. "They say the tow truck is here."

We left our hamster captive in the combination bomb shelter - root cellar - warehouse, and hustled across Tom's backyard into the woods. "It came from the Northwest, I saw the contrail first," Deb reported. "It flew right into the center of town. I think you're right, Joe, the hamsters here called for a ride."

"I hope whatever their mission is, it's more important than finding one missing soldier." If the new alien ship picked up the stranded hamsters and left the area, my plan was to load Fuzzy Face back into the ice cream truck, and race south on the highway until we found a military unit, probably National Guard, that could take custody of our prisoner. "Let's go up to the rock ledge where we can see."

What we saw wasn't good. The new alien ship, same type as the first one, was circling around the town at about five hundred feet. It appeared to be flying a search pattern, and pods on the side of the ship had opened, exposing racks of missiles. There was a flash of light, a rumble of thunder and a column of smoke from the center of town. "They blew up their busted ship." I announced, as if everyone hadn't guessed that. "That's interesting."

"Why?" Deb asked.

"I think it means they don't plan to stay here, at least, not *here*," I pointed toward the town. "And they don't want us poking around their technology while they're gone. If they planned on staying here, they would have brought a repair crew."

The ship climbed, hovered, then slowly headed toward us. Not toward us, exactly, but east, then it flew along the river. "Shit." Stan spat on the ground. "They must have a signal from that stuff we threw out of the truck."

I tried to assure people. "Nobody panic. That's why we threw that stuff out of the truck, and that's why our hamster is under concrete and earth right now, behind a steel door." After our captive was in the root cellar, Stan had thrown the lead blankets over the hood and tailpipe of the truck, to reduce the heat signature. "Unless they can somehow track us into Tom's barn, it will take them a long while to search everywhere, and they don't know we're not already ten miles down the road." Stan and Deb had argued for us to keep driving, rather than stopping at Tom's place. To put as much distance as we could between us and Thompson Corners before an alien rescue ship arrived. I had vetoed that idea, because we didn't know how soon another alien ship would arrive, and because I didn't entirely trust the lead blankets to block a tracking signal. We didn't even know whether the aliens used radio, they may have some more exotic technology. If the aliens could track a signal, it didn't matter whether we were one mile or fifty miles away, they were going to find us. Tom's combination root cellar - bomb shelter - whatever was perfect to hide a technologically advanced alien. Whether my plan was any good depended on what the aliens did.

The alien ship slowly made its way along the river, then sped up and followed the highway south, toward us. After circling twice, it descended out of sight below the tree line. For a moment, just a peaceful moment, things looked almost like a normal October day in rural Maine. Tom and Margie's house was tidy, he had a couple cords of firewood nicely stacked in a line behind the house. Margie had cornstalks tied around the lamp post in the front yard, getting ready early for Halloween like she always did. In the backyard, she had the bathtub Madonna decorated also, with a-

Oh. I'd better explain what a bathtub Madonna is to you uncultured types. You take an old bathtub, set it on end half buried in the ground, paint the outside white and the inside a light blue, and then you put a statue of the Virgin Mary under the arc, like a grotto. It's a homemade shrine of sorts. These days, you can buy ones already made out of concrete, but that's cheating, and God certainly knows if you did it the lazy way. Most people put stones or flowers around it, Margie's shrine was surrounded by brightly colored mums. Or I thought they were mums, I'm not a flower expert. The Madonna had been there when Margie and Tom bought the house, and Margie spruced it up with the flowers. She also decorated it for the seasons. At Christmas time, Mary had a little Santa hat. Right now, for Halloween Mary was wearing a Jedi knight outfit, complete with glowing lightsaber that Tom had hooked up. I sure hope God had a good sense of humor.

Across the road, there were pine trees, lots of pine trees, and then flat fields, a glimpse of the river. It was a nice sunny day. Except for the pillars of smoke coming from town, from the smoldering potato warehouse, and the burned-out alien ship. And except for the other alien ship now climbing back into the sky, it zoomed up to a thousand feet and hovered. "Yup," I said, "they found that alien stuff we threw out of the truck, and dropped off some guys to check it out. That ship up there is providing close air support to the guys on the ground. Tom, there's," I counted on my fingers, "six, no, seven, houses between here and where they are?"

"Ten," Tom corrected me, "you didn't include the McDonald and Burgess places, back off the road. And the old gas station fruit stand that's been abandoned for twenty years. That's ten places, with multiple structures like barns and garages. They'll be thorough searching each one, right, and that takes time."

I bit my lip, which is a thing I did when I was thinking. "The alien commander up there has no idea where we took his soldier." What would I do, in his situation? "We could be in any house or barn around here, we could be in a cave in the woods, we could be ten miles down the road. He has no idea." Unless our captive had some sort of transmitter that could be detected even from the bomb shelter. They did, after all, have technology to travel between stars. I tapped my chin, that's another thing I did when I was thinking. "They only sent one ship. If this was a search and rescue mission, they would have sent several ships. This guy started down from orbit before we grabbed fuzzy face, he only planned to pick up hamsters from the first ship."

"What does that mean?" Susie asked.

"It means the next five minutes will tell us what their orders are. If that ship recovers the guys on the ground and flies away, then they're sticking to their original mission plan, and they'll handle search and rescue later. If that ship hangs around, then they've scrubbed the original plan, and they're waiting for reinforcements to sweep the area."

"That's what you'd do?" Susie asked.

"That's what we'd do, the Army."

The alien ship descended again, then climbed and resumed hovering, closer to us. "Damn it! It's Option B. He just dropped off more guys to start searching buildings." I saw Susie check her rifle again. "Susie, forget about any cowboy Alamo last stand shit. All we've got is three rifles, a shotgun and two pistols. If they get close, we head east through the woods. The missiles on that ship could kill all of us from ten thousand feet."

"We're going to give up?"

"We're not giving up, we're being realistic." I couldn't believe I was arguing with Susie about this. "We can't use the ice cream truck again, it's too distinctive, and that alien ship is too close."

"Fine!" Susie shot back. "We wrap our Fuzzy Face in lead blankets, and carry him into the woods here. It's only a mile to the river from here, we can-"

"Hey!" Deb shouted. "The sky! More lights!" We looked up to see the morning sky twinkling again. There were a lot of lights up there. "Oh, damn it. They're bringing in more ships?" Deb asked. "That can't be- WHOA!"

We looked away, spots swimming in our eyes from a searingly bright explosion in the sky right above us. I blinked, staring at the ground, my shadow flickering as more explosions lit up the sky.

"Yeah!" Stan pumped his fist. "We're hitting back! Nuke the bastards!"

"No way." I shook my head. "Our nukes don't have seeker warheads, they can only hit a preprogrammed targets, on the ground." Unless the Air Force had some amazing toys I didn't know about. There were still spots in my eyes, I shielded my eyes and looked toward the horizon. More explosions in the sky, farther away. "That's not us." Was that an EMP blast, the aliens setting off a nuke high in the sky, to knock out our electronics? We didn't know it then, but the second set of lights in the sky was a Kristang battlegroup jumping into orbit, then attacking the Ruhar.

"Then who is it?" Tom asked.

"Hey, look!" Debbie pointed up the road. The alien ship that was tracking our captive was descending again, fast. It was on the ground only a few minutes before taking off again, and this time, it stood on its tail and went straight up, fast. We heard a sonic boom, and it left a contrail behind. Wherever it was going, it was in a hurry. "Whatever is going on up there, that ship just got new orders. Let's get Fuzzy Face in the truck again, and bring him to the National Guard armory, before they come back."

"Then what?" Tom asked, as we scrambled down the trail, all of us glancing at the sky. We needed to get Fuzzy Face away from the area, before the aliens changed their minds again.

"Then, I see what my orders are." If I couldn't contact the 10th Division, I'd hook up with a local National Guard or Reserve unit for now. "And we survive. I have a feeling Margie's warehouse of canned goods is going to be more important that these guns, with winter coming on."

CHAPTER TWO   DEPLOYMENT

Late the following spring, I was in Ecuador, about to be shipped off-world, to fight hamsters in outer space. Ain't that a kick in the ass? I was surprised how cool it was in the mountains of Ecuador, my mental images of South America always involved suffocating heat, like I'd experienced in Nigeria. It had been a cold winter in Maine, not cold in terms of temperatures and snow, which was about average for recent years. Cold in terms of, no electricity for a long time, and gasoline and heating oil in short supply. My hometown, and my folks, were better equipped for the winter than many others across the country; my parents had a wood stove in the house, and another out in the garage/workshop. A family from down state, who'd been frozen out of their apartment building, came to live in the garage after Christmas, my father bartered repairing a tractor engine for bales of straw that we packed into the garage walls as insulation, covered by canvas tarps. I visited my parents a couple times, the garage was cozy and warm, and smelled like new-mown hay. There was another family of three, plus a single woman, living in my parents' house, as part of a government resettlement program.

Everyone was on their best behavior, all winter.

The state and federal governments in the US had a rough start dealing with the crisis after the Ruhar attack, fumbling around uselessly, then they got their acts together and focused simply on getting people through the winter. The Ruhar attack hadn't been what we expected from watching sci fi movies, instead of hitting military bases and major population centers, they had mostly destroyed electric power plants and industrial facilities. It was weird, I saw satellite pictures of New York and DC after the attack, and other than lack of lights and traffic on the roads, the cities weren't touched. After the Kristang kicked the Ruhar out of our solar system, the US of A didn't have much working electric-powered infrastructure left. Phones and the internet were down, electricity was spotty if you got power at all, the radio only broadcast emergency messages a couple times a day, TV stations and cable were out. The Navy brought nuclear submarines and aircraft carriers into port in major coastal cities, and hooked them up as floating power plants to provide electricity to critical facilities like hospitals. We were slowly regaining electric power across the country, the key word being slowly. When I left for Ecuador, my parents still didn't have power, other than the generator my father hooked up from the tractor's power takeoff. He ran the tractor on a 50/50 mix of alcohol and gasoline, with the alcohol home-brewed. The alcohol ate up seals in the engine, so my father and the guy living in the garage replaced the seals every month. They only ran the electricity in early mornings and evenings, anyway, there wasn't fuel available for much more.

The biggest problem facing America wasn't lack of electricity, it was the economic crash that followed the attack. My father lost his job when the paper mill shut down. Loggers didn't have enough gasoline to run their trucks or even their chainsaws. Without wood pulp, the mill couldn't produce paper. The market for paper had collapsed anyway along with the rest of the global economy. Industrial nations like the US, Japan, China and across Europe were hurt much harder than lower-tech areas of the planet, which was ironic. The greater the level of a nation's technology, the worse it was hit by the crisis. The value of technology companies went straight into the toilet, and not just due to lack of demand from the overall economy. Who wanted to invest in Silicon Valley, when our new allies the Kristang were going to share incredibly advanced technology with us?

Except they didn't. The Kristang said we weren't ready, that we couldn't be trusted with their level of technology, and that we needed to focus on rebuilding our current infrastructure. Really, our new allies were a disappointment, other than chasing the Ruhar away. The bulk of the Kristang battlegroup jumped away within a week after defeating the Ruhar, because Earth didn't have space docks or warship servicing facilities, or pretty much anything else the Kristang needed. They didn't fight the Ruhar for the benefit of humanity, they fought to deny the Ruhar a base in our little corner of the galaxy. Earth was Guadalcanal in WWII, that's how one of the National Guard officers described it. Neither side cared about the place, except as a steppingstone to somewhere more important. The US and the Japanese hadn't cared about the island of Guadalcanal or the natives living there, all either side had wanted was to use that island as a base to push on to the next conquest. The Kristang and the Ruhar felt the same way about Earth. Being American, the world's only superpower, strongest military force in history, it had been tough to think of ourselves in the role of the native primitives. We were watching the Kristang and Ruhar forces do battle over our land, with weapons we could barely comprehend.

"Hey! Bishop! Hey!"

I spun around, disoriented, to find myself face to face with a guy from my fireteam, a guy I never thought I'd see again. "Cornpone!" I shouted.

"Brown bread!" He responded, and we hugged and pounded each other on the back so hard it knocked the wind out of me. Jesse Colter, from Arkansas and a proud son of the South, which is what he'd told me when I first met him in basic training. I called him 'cornpone' because that was, I think, something people ate in the South. 'Brown bread' was his retort, referring to a molasses-sweetened raisin-filled bread in a can that is a New England tradition. I had served him a slice once; some people heat it in the can in hot water, but I prefer to toast each slice. You cut off both ends of the can, and push the bread out, with the rings from the can visible on the bread.

I know. Trust me, it's delicious.

"Or should I call you Barney now?" Jesse laughed.

Shit. The story had gotten around; I'd been teased all winter by the National Guard guys I was with. 'Barney and the Smurfs' is what people were calling me and the gang who captured the alien soldier. "Oh, man, does everyone know about that now?"

"With the internet kinda back up, the whole planet knows about it. Damn, man, good to see you!" Jesse said. "There's a few of the 10th here, but nobody else from our squad yet."

"You're the first person from the 10th I've seen." I admitted, looking around for other familiar faces.

"How'd you get here?" Jesse asked, as he bent down to pick up the duffel bag he'd been carrying before he saw me.

"After Columbus Day, I was going to try to get back to Drum, but nobody had enough gas to make the trip. So, I hooked up with the local National Guard, asked if they knew what was going on. The Guard colonel commandeered me, they'd been Federalized anyway. I figured what the hell, they gave me a rifle, a helmet and food, right?" Orders officially assigning me to the Guard came by shortwave radio later. "So, I played soldier in Maine, helped harvest crops, guarded fuel and food convoys. Then I got the call to come here, so I hopped a train to Boston." A freight train. Riding in a converted old boxcar, I'd felt like a hobo, even though I'd had a ticket from the US government.

"No, what I meant was, how'd y'all get *here*? You fly?"

"Oh, yeah, uh, they put us on a troop train from Boston, it took us five days to get to Miami. We flew in about two hours ago." We'd flown on a United 767 that had seen better days.

Jesse nodded. "I took a train to Dallas, and sat around there three days waiting for a flight, the damn Air Force couldn't scrape enough fuel together to gas up the plane. I hear some units are coming on ships, from New Orleans and Houston."

"You seen this tower thing?"

"The elevator? Just what you can see from here. I don't know about this, compadre."

We looked up the mountain, the summit was barely visible under an overcast sky. Shooting straight up from the top of the mountain was a ribbon of white light. When the UN agreed to provide troops to fight under Kristang command, the Kristang had constructed what they called a space elevator, built it in less than a month. They chose this mountain in Ecuador, because it straddled the equator. On top of the mountain, the Kristang had constructed a base station with a fusion reactor, and thousands of miles above was a station in geosynchronous orbit. What connected the two stations was a thin magnetic field, basically a stationary lightning bolt. We were supposed to go into orbit on an elevator car that rode the lightning bolt. One of the Air Force guys on my flight said he'd heard the Kristang sent pulses up the magnetic field, and the elevator car was pushed along by the pulse. This elevator in Ecuador was the first to be finished, the Kristang were talking about building two others, one in Africa and the other somewhere in Indonesia. I squinted and shaded my eyes with my hand, examining the thin beam of light. "I don't know about this either, man. One thing I do know is if the Kristang can do this, I'm glad they're on our side."

"I hear that, amigo." Jesse agreed.

Looking up at the sky, at the lightning bolt I'd be riding into orbit, I wondered what had happened to Fuzzy Face. We'd driven south in our ice cream truck, until we ran into a state police roadblock, and when the cops saw who was in the back of the truck, we'd been given an escort down to Lincoln, where a National Guard helicopter took Fuzzy Face away. After that, any information about him was classified, and I'd been discouraged from talking, or asking, about him. Wherever the hamster was, I hoped he was being treated well.

A buzzing sound caught our attention, we both turned to watch a group of grey-painted tilt-rotor aircraft, flying in formation and coming in from the West. As they approached, the lead planes slowed and swung their propellers up into hover mode, descending like helicopters. Before I could ask, Jesse volunteered "The Navy has two carrier groups off shore, the *Lincoln* and the *Reagan*. I met some of the Marines around here this morning."

"They coming with us?" Two carrier battlegroups would have sounded impressive, before the Ruhar attacked. Compared to alien militaries that could lift people into space on a lightning bolt, our nuclear-powered carriers were obsolete row boats.

"Some Marines units are, but these guys? Nah, they're here to provide security for the elevator."

I'd heard on the radio that the Kristang left security of the space elevator in Ecuador to the USA. I laughed. "Bet they're happy about that." No red-blooded US Marine wanted to be stuck on guard duty, while the Army went off into space to avenge the attack on our planet.

"Hell yes, man. They offered me big bucks for this patch." Jesse fingered the blue UNEF patch on his right sleeve, the logo of the United Nations Expeditionary Force, which is what they were calling us now. National patches, in our case the US flag, went on the left sleeve. "Like money means anything now." Jesse frowned and looked down at his clothes. "At least those Marines have real uniforms on. I got this at a surplus store in Arkansas." His pants fit, while his top looked to be three sizes too big.

My own 'uniform' was mismatched, the pants were from the Maine National Guard, while the top, which had been issued to me on the train to Miami, was in an old camo pattern, and looked like it had been in storage since the Iraq war, the first one. Or maybe the Spanish-American War. It still smelled faintly of mothballs. "Maybe the Army will issue us new unis here."

"Don't count on it." A familiar voice barked at us. We turned to see Lt. Amos Gonzalez, who had been a platoon leader in the 10th. Not our platoon, but a familiar face. Jesse and I snapped to attention and saluted. "At ease, men. Bishop and Colter, right?" His face broke into a grin. "It's good to see the two of you. Glad you made it to the party."

"Good to see you, too, LT." Jesse said. "Do you know how many of us are here?"

He shook his head, eyes down, as he kicked the dirt with his boot. "Communications are still spotty. We're putting people to work as they straggle in."

Jesse frowned at Gonzalez avoiding the question. "Hey, LT, all I've seen here so far is us, guys from the Belching Buzzards," he meant the 101st Airborne Screaming Eagles, "the 3rd Infantry, and Marines. We're not bringing any armor or cavalry?"

Lt. Gonzalez shot him a scornful look. "Colter, you really want to be in a tank, fighting against an enemy that can shoot down from orbit?" He didn't wait for Cornpone's answer. "That's a quick ticket to a long dirt nap. The Kristang said they needed infantry, so that's what we're sending. The armor and aviation boys are going to sit this one out."

"Pardon me, sir, but what the hell good is infantry going to do against the Ruhar?" I asked. "I don't even have a weapon."

Gonzalez nodded sympathetically. "The Kristang won't allow weapons on the elevator. We're supposed to get weapons, body armor and everything else we'll need, when we get to wherever we're going. Personally, I like my old M4, but I don't want to go up against the Ruhar with it."

"We're serving with Marines, sir?" I asked.

"A Marine brigade, yes. And, I hear, Brits, French, Chinese, maybe some Russians and Indian army also. You men checked in yet?"

"No, sir, I just got off the bus from the airport." I said. I could still feel the steel slats of the bus seat on my butt. We had come from the airport, and climbed the rough, newly cut road, in a convoy of garishly-painted old school buses that were probably the finest transportation this part of Ecuador had to offer, before the Ruhar attacked.

"Uh-uh." Jesse shook his head. "I've been here since this morning, and as soon as I got off the bus, the Marines had me moving food pallets."

"Better get checked in, then, you need a medical eval before you take the magic carpet ride up into space. You see that big circus tent over there, the one with the UN flags?" He wasn't joking, it really was a circus tent. "Get over there on the double, the elevator's leaving at 1700 hours."

The tent was a madhouse. Jesse and I weren't looking forward to getting poked and prodded by Army doctors, we needn't have worried. The medical exam consisted of standing fully clothed in a booth the size of a shower, and having a light beam run down, up, down and up again. When I stepped out, the doctor didn't look up from his computer.

"You'll live, Bishop." I could see a file with my picture on the computer screen, the doctor clicked a few buttons, and the file was replaced by some other guy's. "Next!"

"Excuse me, sir, is that it?" I asked, confused.

"That's it. You just got your first exam with a Kristang medical scanner, and it says you're healthy enough. Move along, people, we haven't got all day. Next!"

After the medical exam, we got showers, with honest to God hot water, although we weren't issued new uniforms so we put our old clothes back on, and then went to another tent for a hot meal, Army style. As far as I was concerned, Army-style was a good thing, it meant I got plenty of food. I went through the line, and was standing with my tray in hand, looking for a place to sit, when Jesse stood up and waved me over to his table. "This here's Gus, 1st Armored," Jesse said through a mouthful of cornbread, pointing to a guy sitting next to him.

"I thought only infantry was going on this trip?" I asked.

Gus shrugged. "I drove a Bradley; I guess they need drivers for whatever they've got up there." If the Kristang thought we needed drivers, then hopefully that meant the infantry wouldn't be walking every place we went.

Cornpone used a piece of bread to soak up gravy from the meatloaf. "I don't know where we're going, but if it means three hots and a cot, I'm all in. Things were pretty lean this winter at home."

I didn't know what I expected the space elevator to be, but it wasn't what I expected. It looked most like a waiting lounge at an airport. The huge disc-shaped elevator car had four levels, with the lowest level containing the machinery. Or so I supposed, since we were only allowed on the upper three levels. Cargo pods were slung below the bottom of the car. The habitable levels were each divided into eight wedges, containing row after row of thinly-padded plastic chairs. Chairs with seat belts. The trip up to the orbital station was scheduled to take nine hours, hours enlivened only by crowding around the viewports and looking down at our receding planet's surface. After a while, even that got old. The elevator was a no-frills contraption, designed to transport a maximum number of troops in a minimum amount of time. Comfort on the trip was not a Kristang priority. There wasn't even a snack bar built into the elevator, so the Army had set up a portable kitchen on each level, and the food was plentiful. I had my first decent cheeseburger in a very long time, then went back for another. Jesse and I explored the place, wandering around, meeting the soldiers we'd be serving with, swapping stories, listening to contradictory rumors. Since the elevator had a capacity of five thousand humans, a good part of a full army division was aboard on our trip. We wandered by one wedge that had been set up as an impromptu officers' mess, poking our heads in, before moving along to mix with the rest of the grunts.

After I'd downed three sodas, alcoholic beverages not being supplied by the Army, I needed to check out the bathrooms, which I had been dreading. What kind of plumbing had the Kristang provided? Either the Kristang had similar biological functions, or they had consulted human plumbers, because I need not have worried. It looked like a typical highway rest stop bathroom, only new, and cleaner. The dispensers even had soap.

The trip at first was slow, it really was like riding an elevator, there was a subtle pressure of extra gravity, and a faint vibration. As we climbed and the atmosphere thinned out, we accelerated, and the artificial gravity kicked on to compensate, at what we were told was about 85% of Earth normal. I talked to one of the Army cooks, who had been up and down on the elevator several times. As we approached the space station, he explained, we would slow down, but we wouldn't feel any movement because of the artificial gravity. I expressed doubts about the safety of riding a lightning bolt, especially with Ruhar raiders still harassing the Kristang, the cook told me not to worry. Earlier in the week, a Ruhar frigate had popped out of hyperspace while the elevator car was halfway to the space station, at its most vulnerable point. The frigate had fired off two missiles before it got popped by a pair of Kristang patrol destroyers, and defensive lasers on top of the elevator car took care of the incoming missiles. It was nice to know we weren't entirely sitting ducks, while we ate snacks and sat in uncomfortable chairs.

I managed to fall asleep, slumped over in a chair; I woke up when a Marine kicked my foot. "Rise and shine, sleeping beauty. This joy ride is coming to an end. Collect your gear, if you have any." The Marine moved away, kicking awake other sleepers.

Jesse had been asleep on the floor behind me, using his duffel bag as a pillow. I shook his shoulder. "Oh man, your ugly face isn't what I want to wake up to." He said grumpily. "What's up?" He managed to say through a jaw-stretching yawn.

"I think we're approaching the space station. Want to get a look-see?"

The station was a donut, with six arms radiating out. At the end of two arms were what I assumed were Kristang ships, resting what looked like belly-down on platforms. One of the ships was sleek and dark, the other much larger and not as powerful looking. While Jesse and I gawked, the cook I'd been talking to earlier came over and squeezed through the crowd to stand next to us. "That," he pointed to the smaller ship, "is a cruiser, and the fat ugly one next to it is the transport ship."

"You been on it?" Jesse asked.

"Nah, they only let us on the station while the elevator car is unloading, then it's right back down to Ecuador for the next group. I hear the transport ship can hold this whole group, as soon as you're aboard, they're leaving."

"Any idea where they're sending us?" I figured the cook might have heard something on one of his trips.

He shook his head. "I don't know, and if any of our officers know, they ain't saying. Personally, I think the Kristang are keeping it on a need to know basis, and we humans don't need to know." We watched silently, as the elevator car slowly approached the station, until the bulk of the station cast a shadow across the window, and hid the cruiser from view. "I wish I was going with you, tried to switch to infantry," his uniform patch said he was 1st Armored, "but the Army says my MOS is cook, so that's what I'm doing." He sounded bitter.

"Hey, you make a damned fine cheeseburger." I stuck out my hand.

He wiped his hand on his apron, gripped my hand fiercely, and looked me straight in the eye. "You guys are going to kick ass, right?"

"Damn straight." I answered with conviction. I didn't know if I was coming back, but I was going to kill as many hamsters as I could. Every soldier and Marine I'd talked to felt the same way, the same deadly sense of purpose. We'd been attacked, the very survival of our species threatened. Rage wasn't an adequate word to describe how we all felt. In the train station in Boston, I had been walking through with three other soldiers, headed for outer space and war, and the crowd noticed us. People stopped, spontaneously started saluting, then they applauded. It really touched me. I remember one old guy, must have been a grandfather, had his young grandson with him. He showed the little guy how to stand, and positioned the boy's hand to salute us. The expression on the grandfather's face, right then, told me everything about how people felt about us soldiers in the United

Nations Expeditionary Force. We were carrying all their hopes, and not only hopes for vengeance. Hope for survival, survival of the human species. That's what made this war different, for the first time we really were all in this together.

"Damn straight, man, we're going to kick ass." Jesse said with all seriousness, and we bumped fists. "Army strong, can't go wrong. Hooah."

Like the cook, we didn't get to see much, after we left the elevator car. US Marine guards directed us into the space station, which generated the lightning bolt we'd ridden up into space. We lined up single file, to do what, I didn't know. The station was big, I wondered aloud how they'd built it so fast.

"A Thuranin star carrier brought it here in sections, and they assembled it." A lieutenant in line ahead of us said.

"Sir?" I asked. "What is a Thuranin?"

"The Thuranin are the patron species of the Kristang." Reacting to the totally blank stares he got from me, Cornpone and everyone else, he stepped slightly out of line to speak to us. From his uniform patch, I could see he was with the 3rd Infantry. "Didn't they tell you people anything?"

"Sir, I'm from northern Maine, we first got the internet a week before the Ruhar attacked." I could see he didn't appreciate my attempt at humor. "I've never heard of the Thuranin, sir."

He twirled his finger in the air. "This station, the elevator, that's all Thuranin technology, the Kristang don't even have artificial gravity aboard their ships."

"Sir?" Jesse's face began turning green when he heard that. Everyone in the line was looking queasy at the idea of experiencing no gravity. "Zero gee? We haven't been trained for that, at all."

"That's why you're in line here, to get meds to prevent space sickness. We can't have humans puking their guts out, in a Kristang transport ship."

"We're not going on a Thuranin ship?" I asked, feeling queasy already. I was deeply regretting that second cheeseburger. The line moved forward, and we shuffled our feet along the deck.

"Thuranin star carriers rarely venture down into a gravity well, they stay well out in the Oort Cloud of any star system." Seeing more blanks looks, although I was feeling smug that I knew what an Oort Cloud was, he added "That means out beyond the orbit of Pluto, where spacetime is flat, and it's easier for their star carriers to form a jump field. Kristang ships can only jump short ranges, we guess six to eight light hours, which is about here to Neptune. They make a series of small faster than light jumps like that, out to where a Thuranin star carrier is parked. A star carrier is a big, long spine, with hardpoints for short range ships to latch on. The star carrier has an advanced jump drive, way beyond what the Kristang have, so the Thuranin carry Kristang ships between star systems. G-2 thinks the Kristang ships can't actually travel between stars; with their short jumps, and the need to recharge engines between jumps, overall they travel at less than the speed of light. It would take them more than four years to get to the nearest star from here. The Thuranin, we think, can travel something like three hundred times the speed of light, in jumps of about one lightyear."

I didn't like the math that was running around in my feverish brain. Three hundred times the speed of light was incredibly fast, but it also meant that if we were going to a planet that was, say, a mere hundred lightyears away, it would take four months to get there! Four freakin' months. Stuck on an alien ship. In zero gravity. And a hundred lightyears sounded like a lot, but the galaxy is huge. Somewhere in school, I'd learned that Earth is twenty seven thousand lightyears from the center of the galaxy, and the whole galaxy is something like a hundred thousand lightyears across. I hadn't considered any of this when I was so eager to get off Earth and fight the Ruhar. "Sir," I asked slowly, "where are we going?"

"That's not a secret. We're going to a planet the Kristang have set up as a training base for us, we're calling it Camp Alpha."

"And how far is that?" Cornpone asked as he shot me a look. He was doing math in his head also.

"The Kristang won't tell us, but people who've been there took pictures of the night sky, and from the position of stars, our astronomers have got it fixed at 1223 lightyears from Earth." Just then, one of the doors at the end of the line opened, and the lieutenant was called in.

Oh My God. A twelve hundred lightyear journey, aboard a ship that traveled three hundred times the speed of light, meant we were going to be stuck aboard a Kristang ship attached to a Thuranin star carrier, in zero gravity, for *four years*! I'd heard the troubles astronauts had aboard the international space station in zero gravity, how their eyesight deteriorated, their bones became brittle and their muscles wasted away after a couple months. What good were human soldiers going to be after four years in zero gravity? I was so shocked, it didn't even occur to me the lieutenant had said somehow humans had already gone to Camp Alpha and come back, obviously in much less than a year.

"Four years, dang! Is that right, twelve hundred lightyears away, at three hundred a year?" Cornpone's voice reflected the shock we all felt. "Maybe they're going to freeze us, make us sleep the whole way? They did that in Avatar, right, you saw that movie?"

People were grumbling, stunned at the implications of what the lieutenant had told us. Then it was my turn with the doctor, who was wearing civilian clothes and a white lab coat. She looked bored. "Do I need to take my shirt off, ma'am?" I was hoping I could keep my pants on. It was embarrassing enough standing around in my boxer shorts in front of a male doctor, with a female doctor it was worse. I mean, I didn't want my friend to be obviously happy to see her, if you know what I mean. But maybe it was worse if he didn't rise to the occasion. The doctor was cute, and I was a healthy guy, so I felt that out of respect for her I should at least have a semi-

"No, soldier, keep your shirt on. Lift your chin, please." She held what looked like a plastic and chrome gun under my left ear, and squeezed the trigger. I hardly felt anything. Same thing on the right. She put the gun down and checked a computer display screen, tapped it a few times, and said "looks good. You've been injected with Kristang nano machines, that will soon migrate to your inner ears, and prevent you from feeling nauseous in zero gravity. They will dissolve after a while, and you shouldn't feel any effects. If you do feel like your balance is off while you're in gravity, contact the medical staff aboard the ship."

"Ma'am, how long will we be aboard-"

"You will receive a full briefing aboard the ship." The door opposite where I'd come in opened, and I took a hint to leave. The gravity was working fine; it was the thought of being injected with tiny machines that was making me queasy. Microscopic alien robots were swimming in my blood. It was creepy.

Once our group was all done with the doctors, guards directed us to the transport ship, and hustled us along with no time for sightseeing. There wasn't much to see on the station corridors anyway, blank walls in a light blue color, with markings in several human languages attached to the walls. The Kristang ship was more interesting, lots of access panels, corridors going in every direction, pipes or conduits along the ceilings. The walls and floors had recessed handholds; I guess for when the ship was in zero gravity. No Kristang were visible, I still had never seen one of the lizards in person. A Marine took charge of our group, and directed the men into one compartment, women into another. The compartment I was in had row after row of bunk beds, stacked three high. Each group of three bunks was attached to an arm that could rotate the stack 90 degrees for when the ship was under thrust. The Marine told us this was a Kristang multi-mission pod, which was currently configured for troop transport. We were lucky, he said, that the bunks were sized for Kristang, who were slightly larger on average than humans. I shrugged and found an empty bunk, tossed my small duffel bag into it, and secured it with a strap that I figured was there for that purpose. The bunk wasn't bad, seven feet long, and about four feet to the bunk above it. It was almost luxury. Somebody already had a card game going, Jesse wandered over to the game, while I flopped on my bunk and pulled out a book to read on my tablet. I was getting anxious about the tablet, it was down to about 25% power, and there didn't appear to be an electrical outlet anywhere. It looked like I'd been stupid to bring the thing into space with me.

A sergeant came to stand in the doorway. He cleared his throat to get our attention. I was amused to see he was wearing the same out-of-date style uniform camo top that I had on. "I am Staff Sergeant Raynor, I'm in charge of this compartment, and the two on either side of you. In two hours, this ship will undock, and boost out of Earth orbit. You all need to be in your bunks and strapped in, ten minutes before departure. If you don't know how to work the straps, Specialist Edwards here will show you. After we depart from the station, the artificial gravity will cut off, so make sure you don't leave anything loose that can float around. This ship will boost for about an hour, the acceleration is only thirty percent of normal gravity, it's not like NASA rockets. Then the ship will make a jump through hyperspace. You will be able to get out of your bunks once the Kristang give the all clear, in about ninety minutes. After that, you're free to move around, keep in mind we'll be in zero gravity. I don't want any jackasses horsing around in zero gee! Once the ship gets far enough away from Earth, we will be making a series of hyperspace jumps, and you will need to be in your bunks for those also. Our ultimate destination is a planet the Kristang have set up as a training base. If you have any questions, you will get an opportunity to get answers later."

If I was going to be stuck in my bunk for over an hour, I decided to hit the bathroom first. I went back out the door and asked the Marine guard where the bathrooms were. He pointed down the hall, with a wry smile.

The restroom facilities were interesting. There were no urinals. You could sit normally, but the toilets were designed for zero gee, and there were straps to hold you in place and the seat formed a seal on your backside. And there was a flexible tube, with disposable cups, if a guy only had to pee. The stalls all had instructions plaques in several human languages, and it was not as complicated as it sounds, the toilet's computer took care of everything. Score a point for technology. Kristang also apparently had unisex bathrooms, so we took turns; five women, then five men. Damn, women take forever. There were a lot less women than men, so it wasn't a big deal. On my way back to my assigned compartment, there was an Army captain standing in the hallway, reading something on a tablet. I saluted, and stopped to talk to him, if I could. "Excuse me, sir, how do you charge your tablet?"

"In each compartment is a set of magnetic pads; set your tablet on it, and it'll charge. It's like a charging mat, and it senses what kind of juice your tablet needs, so it won't burn it out. Thuranin devices are smart."

"What's a Thuranin, sir?"

The captain shook his head. "The Thuranin are a very advanced race, they lead the coalition that the Kristang belong to. I'm told they look a bit like aliens in sci-fi movies; short and skinny, with big bald heads."

Now I was completely confused. "The Kristang aren't in charge?"

"As far as we humans are concerned, yeah, anything to do with Earth, the Kristang are in charge. The Thuranin are the Kristang's, patrons, is maybe the right word. Anyway, all you need to know is, traveling from one star to another is a slow process in a Kristang ship, so they latch onto Thuranin motherships for the big jumps. And before anyone asks, no, I've never actually seen a Thuranin, we stay aboard the Kristang ships."

"This is getting complicated, sir."

He nodded sympathetically. "Think of it this way; the Thuranin are the major leagues, the Kristang are, ah, the triple A farm team. And we, well, we're kind of the semi-pro local league right now. We're hoping to get promoted to single A ball, but we need to prove ourselves first, and we've got a hell of a long way to go. Get back to your bunk, soldier, we're boosting out of orbit soon. You'll get a briefing later."

After an hour of gentle acceleration, boosting away from Earth, and ten minutes of what I guessed was preparation for the jump, our transport ship jumped. I couldn't see anything, strapped into my bunk. When the ship jumped, it felt like static electricity crawling on my skin for a split second, then it was back to floating in zero gee. I kept track of time on my watch, it took eight hours, twenty one minutes between the first and second jumps. Later, I learned that Kristang ships are powered by fusion reactors, and their jump engines take about eight hours to build up enough power for a jump. That time lag between jumps can be a major tactical liability for an attacking force; the attacking ships, which have just jumped into combat, mostly can't jump away immediately if they get into trouble, whereas a defending ship, with fully charged engines, can pop to a different location, if it has a swarm of missiles incoming. In actual battle, the time lag between jumps is not so much of an issue. Warships always maintain reserve energy for a short emergency jump. Ships can't safely jump in or out of hyperspace near a large gravity field such as a planet, the jump field can get distorted and tear the ship apart. So an attacking force needs to come out of hyperspace away from a planet, and travel through normal space to get into orbit. Once the attacking ships get close enough to a planet to use weapons, they are so far within the gravity field that even ships with fully charged engines can't safely jump. Defending ships, which never know where an attacker is going to pop out of hyperspace, tend to hang close to planets, and then move out to intercept. If that sounds too much like a game with lots of rules to memorize, it is. Lucky for us humans, we don't have to think about it. We don't have any starships, and the Kristang aren't giving us any. We're infantry, we fight on the ground. The Kristang get us there, and we'll take care of the fighting. That's what we all thought then, anyway.

Between jumps, the ship boosted for about two hours, then we had free time, when we could be out of our bunks. Everyone experimented with moving around in zero gee, I could see after only a few minutes that we should have been issued helmets. Sergeant Raynor came in to yell at us for stupidity, but mostly let us get bumps and bruises. Experience is the best teacher.

One of the show-offs was Jeff Murdock, he came into our platoon in Nigeria halfway through my tour there, so I didn't know him that well, but, man, he took to zero gee like a dolphin takes to water. He was doing flips that would have made me dizzy, and he could push off a wall and float across the compartment to wherever he wanted to go, swimming through the air. He hung from a bunk upside down, using his feet to hold himself in place, with a huge grin. "Man, this is great! I can't wait to get some of that Kristang biotech. I'll be a super soldier, man!"

The rest of us weren't so enthused about watching him fly around like a giant squirrel.

"Murdock, you don't need advanced alien technology to be a soldier, you need a freakin' miracle." Garcia laughed.

"Yeah, man, what you need is a brain, and you better talk to the Wizard of Oz about that." Was Thompson's comment.

"Hey, fuck you guys!" Murdock shot back, and flew across the compartment, spun and landed gracefully on the opposite wall, he didn't even bounce. "You'll see."

We were brought to the Kristang version of a chow hall or Dining Facility, or maybe it's called a galley since it's on a ship? Our experience with zero gee in our bunk compartment helped, when we had to pull ourselves along corridors through the ship. The chow hall held almost a hundred people, and had tables and chairs, what made it different is those chairs were solidly attached to the floor, and had seatbelts. Lunch was MREs; humans couldn't eat Kristang food, and the Kristang didn't want us screwing with their kitchens in zero gravity. MREs reminded me of camping when I was a kid, and they weren't bad, but I'd eaten too many of them in Nigeria, and I glumly ate my food, swapping stuff with the people around me. Cornpone was extra hungry, he gulped down his MRE, and bummed a pack of crackers off me. Halfway through the meal break, an Army major came floating into the compartment, expertly flew across to the opposite wall, and hooked his feet to a strap. He made it look easy. "Is everyone enjoying their astronaut food?" That drew a laugh from the crowd. "I understand there is a lot of bad intel going around, so I'm going to set you straight. First, we will not be in zero gee the whole way. This Kristang ship will latch into a Thuranin star carrier for the majority of the journey. The hardpoints on the star carrier are platforms that have artificial gravity, so after we're attached, we'll have the eighty five percent gee that is normal for the Thuranin. Second, this journey will not take four years, and you will not be frozen. So, you'll have to listen to your bunkmates snore." Another chuckle from the crowd. "The Thuranin star carrier will be jumping to an artificial wormhole, and then passing through the wormhole to the other side, which is hundreds of lightyears away. The star carrier travels between wormholes, and lets the wormholes take us most of the way to our destination. It's going to be seventeen days from Earth to our first destination, a planet we're calling Camp Alpha. That's a training base where you'll receive your new weapons and equipment, and learn the rules of engagement. The Kristang are sticklers about us adhering to the ROE, so pay attention while you're there. We are not going to cause problems for our new allies. As for Camp Alpha, I have been there, and all I will say about it now, is that is an excellent place to focus on our training mission."

That drew a knowing groan from the crowd. We all understood that was Army speak for a hellhole where there was nothing to do but work and train. I looked at Cornpone, and we shrugged. We'd seen worse, and we weren't out in space for a pleasure cruise. The major didn't take any questions, and left the chow hall when he was done with his brief speech. I felt a lot better, knowing we wouldn't be stuck aboard the ship in zero gee for four years.

After the Kristang ship made a fourth jump, we had to stay strapped into our bunks, as the ship maneuvered to latch onto a Thuranin mother ship. There was a clanging sound, and a vibration, as our ship attached itself to the star carrier. Gravity slowly came back, to cheers from everyone I could hear. Especially when it was announced that we'd have hot food for dinner, now that the kitchens had gravity. It was beef stew, with a lot more potatoes and veggies than beef, but it was a promise that we wouldn't be surviving solely on MREs for the next three weeks. And the biscuits were hot and fresh. Good chow is important for good morale, the Army sure knew that.

I like fresh, hot biscuits.

In case you were wondering.

The Thuranin star carrier, mothership, whatever you call it, then went through a series of jumps I lost track of, because some of them happened while I was asleep. Some people aboard the ship were trying to keep amateur records of all the ship's maneuvers; jumps, time between jumps, time and force of acceleration. Personally, I lost track after the second jump, and I figured we had qualified people keeping track for us. The loudspeakers woke us up around 0300 one night, when the ship was approaching the wormhole, and I wished I had more warning, because my bladder already was sending me warning signals. The idea of falling into a wormhole, having my atoms ripped apart and reassembled, or whatever it was that happened, had me scared. I was laying rigid in my bunk, waiting for the unknown, when the loudspeaker announced "Wormhole transition complete. Secure for normal space maneuvering." Damn. Not only did I not need to have worried about the wormhole passage, I didn't even realize when it happened. There were more jumps, more waiting between jumps, and lots of boredom. We exercised in shifts, using equipment brought from Earth, including treadmills and exercise bicycles. I liked running, but hated treadmills, it was so boring. Even competing with the guy on the treadmill next to me didn't help, after the first couple days. We played games on our tablets, and exercised, and read books and watched movies. Being aboard the ship was kind of what it must have been like for soldiers in WWII, crossing the Atlantic and Pacific in slow transport ships. Except, on a WWII transport ship, those guys had been able to go up on deck, get fresh air, and see the sun, and the horizon.

We had decent chow, and enough room to move around on the ship, except for the areas off-limits to humans. What we didn't have was anything to look out the window at, if there had been windows. And we didn't have any news from, or contact with, Earth. In Nigeria, I'd been able to get onto the internet, and send emails, and video chat with my folks and friends, at least most days. Here, we were out of contact until we came back, a long, long way. One thing we'd learned, is that not even the technologically superior Thuranin had faster than light communications, except for drones which carried messages by jumping. Kind of like a high-tech carrier pigeon.

After a while, I felt like we were low budget tourists stuck aboard a crappy cruise ship, it didn't feel like being in the Army. After a bunch more hyperspace jumping, that I didn't even bother trying to keep track of, the star carrier arrived outside some star system, or so we were told. The Kristang ship went to zero gee again, detached, and jumped four times. Finally, we maneuvered into orbit at our destination. All in all, my first interstellar voyage consisted mostly of being stuck in a windowless compartment. I wouldn't recommend it for a vacation, unless you're desperate.

Columbus Day

We did get a look at the planet below, and it wasn't inviting. Earth from orbit looks blue, and green, and tan where there are deserts and grasslands, and white ice at the poles. This place looked brown, and red, and even the places that had water weren't a nice blue. The one pole I could see had an anemic layer of dirty white, like snow beside the road in April, when it's all dirty and crusty and everyone wishes it would just freakin' melt and go away, damn it.

In groups, we packed into the mess hall to get a briefing, Lt. Gonzalez stood on a chair, and waited until everyone got settled into the compartment. "Welcome to Camp Alpha! The Kristang didn't want to tell us their name for this planet, so it was just 'Alpha'."

Some guy at the front asked "But we know where we are, right, LT? I mean, somebody has figured it out?"

"Yeah," Gonzalez smiled, "the advance team took pictures of the night sky, and astronomers on Earth calculated where the view must have been taken from. I think the Kristang were having fun with us, keeping it a secret, they must have known we'd be smart enough to discover this planet's location. We are still in the Orion Arm of the galaxy, the Milky Way galaxy, about twelve hundred and twenty three lightyears from Earth. That's far enough that you can't see our sun from here, without a telescope. I'm told our sun is an unremarkable star anyway."

"Has everyone been to the window, and seen where we'll be training? Camp Alpha is not the kind of place you would go on vacation. It is the kind of place where soldiers are trained, and formed into an army the Ruhar will learn to fear. The Kristang have set aside this planet as a training and staging base for humans, for three reasons. First, nobody else wants this place. It's dry, I'm told that it can be 110 degrees in daytime, and down to 20 below at night. And that's the nice part of the planet, where the training base is located. The sunlight is a funky blue-white color, and it will peel the skin off your bones if you aren't protected. Second, because this place is so damned nasty, it's a great place to train. Not every planet we'll be going to is like Earth, here you will learn to use the equipment the Kristang provide, and to survive in harsh conditions. If you can't be combat effective here, we don't need you. And third, the Kristang chose this place because they think the Ruhar don't know about it. Yet."

"Sir," someone asked, "why is the planet all brown and burnt looking?"

"The star here is a slow variable, it hiccups every once in a while and increases its output. When that happens, it scorches the entire system, then it settles down again."

Hiccup? That sounded like one hell of a hiccup. The crowd of us shifted uncomfortably on our feet, and a low murmur went around.

"Don't worry about it, the Kristang know the star's schedule, it won't flare up again for another ten to fifty thousand years." Gonzalez added hurriedly. A range of ten to fifty thousand years sounded like the Kristang should have just told us they had no freaking idea when the star would next blow up. "Your briefing packets have all the info you need about this planet, so I'm only going to cover the high points. There is life down there, the biggest animal is an insect about three inches long. It has sharp pinchers and it's venomous, but the venom isn't fatal to human biochemistry, it only causes a mild rash sometimes, as an allergic reaction. Most people don't react to it at all. The only things that are dangerous to us down there are the climate, which can get really hot and really cold, and our own stupidity. Use common sense, remember you're here for training, and read the regs; they're written to keep you alive and combat ready. We will assemble into units when we get dirtside, until then, follow instructions."

CHAPTER THREE   CAMP ALPHA

There was no space elevator at Camp Alpha, so we made the trip to the surface on a Kristang shuttle. Only, I learned, it wasn't called a shuttle, or a dropship, or a lander, which were other terms I'd heard people use. The Army term was Surface To Orbit Craft, or STOC. In practice, we called such ships either dropships, or STOCers, pronounced 'stockers', like stock car, only one word. STOCers could reach orbit by themselves, not needing booster rockets, and some of the larger types were capable for interplanetary flight, if you had plenty of time on your hands and got along really, really well with the other people you were squeezed in with. The Kristang, and other species, did have craft they called something like 'dropship', but dropships were used for large-scale invasions, to ferry lots of troops and equipment down to the surface, a one-way trip. Technically, a dropship was like a WWII glider, they could survive entry into an atmosphere, maneuver a bit before landing, and land vertically, but once down, they stayed there. Dropships were one-shot craft, whereas a STOCer could climb back into orbit, and make the trip multiple times. The distinction didn't matter much to me, as I would only ever be a passenger, but it was cool knowing how our senior partners did things, it made me feel part of the team, not just a cog in a machine.

The dropship I squeezed into held 220 people and our gear, it was the size of a 747, roughly, most of it being engines and fuel tanks. The ride down was rough, we hit the atmosphere and it felt like I had a sack of concrete on my chest. Then it got worse. Man, I was glad when the ship leveled out and flew like an airplane for a short time. We all cheered when that happened. The actual landing was uneventful, I realized we were down only when the engine sound cut off.

Me. Landing on an alien planet. Who'd have thunk it, huh? "Lieutenant," someone asked, "do you know who was the first human to set foot on another planet?"

"Probably General Meers." A soldier behind me said. Meers commanded UNEF.

"Nope." Gonzalez shook his head. "It was a female British Army captain, part of the multinational advance team. It was supposed to be a Chinese Army colonel to go first, but this British captain was seated next to the door, and when they landed, the Kristang pilot told them to get out, pronto. The Kristang didn't see humanity's first landing on another planet as a big deal, they wanted them all off the ship quick so it could go back up and pick up the next group."

Damn. I'd been hoping the first person was an American. Well, we still had Neal Armstrong, and old Neal had done it with good American technology. This Brit only hitched a ride on an alien space bus.

My own first footstep on another planet was almost embarrassing, I was used to the 85% gravity of the Thuranin star carrier, and then zero gee again, and Camp Alpha's gravity was 107% of Earth normal. The unfamiliar weight caused me stumble down the ramp. Lt. Gonzalez hadn't been joking about the heat, when we got off the dropship, I was hit by a furnace-like blast of heat. And humid, too, none of that bullshit about it feeling cooler because it's a dry heat. And bright, I had to shade my eyes and squint to make it the hundred meters to where the transport vehicles were parked. Everything smelled burnt, like the aftermath of a fire. The oxygen content of the atmosphere was supposed to be only a bit lower than Earth normal, it sure felt like my lungs were sucking air and not getting a whole lot of benefit. Maybe the landing site was at high altitude. I had almost reached a transport truck, and was waiting in line to board, when a woman behind me swayed, and began to slump to the dusty ground. My own head was swimming from the sudden heat, like a head rush when you stand up too suddenly at the beach. She protested and tried to push me away, but it was clear her knees were wobbling. "Listen," I checked the name above her left pocket, "hey, Miller, we are Army Strong." I repeated a US Army recruiting slogan, "We don't let each other down, not in combat, and sure not in this stinking heat, you got that?"

She nodded angrily, and leaned on me breathing heavily, until she could stand up again. I could tell that needing assistance, even briefly, was killing her pride. "Thanks, uh," she glanced at my name tag, "Bishop. God damn it's hot here. I'm from Seattle."

"Ha! Northern Maine here. You don't know what cold is. " She let me hold onto her shoulders to steady her a few seconds, until her legs stopped shaking. Ten feet away, a guy's knees buckled suddenly, and he face planted in the dirt, another victim of the sudden heat. Miller recovered and climbed stiffly into the back of the truck by herself. Once the truck was loaded, we drove off to a tent city that was being built atop a bluff. I looked around, trying to savor my first moments on an alien world. There wasn't much to savor. It was dry, and dusty, and the air still smelled burnt, so the smell wasn't from the dropship's engine exhaust. Low vegetation clustered around rocks, it appeared to be a type of pulpy, fleshy lichen. I guessed the plant stored its own water supply, like a cactus. Bouncing around in the back of the truck, we looked at each other and grimaced knowingly. Camp Alpha was our first alien planet. And it sucked.

Sitting on the truck was my only time to savor the experience, as soon as we got to our assigned campsite, the Army put us to work setting up tents. The heat wasn't so bad, now that I'd had time to get used to it, but the extra gravity was a bitch, and the burnt smell had saturated my nose. A staff sergeant assigned me, Cornpone and five others to set up a large medical structure, made of prefab insulated wall panels. It was tougher than it looked. "Let's start with this side wall section," I said, hoping that the sooner the tent was complete, the sooner we could go for chow.

There was a muffled sound like a really long, high-pitched fart, then the moaning started.

"Is that, bagpipes? WTF?" Cornpone exclaimed.

"Yeah, there's a British battalion on the other side of the camp." I jerked my thumb over my shoulder, to where I'd seen the Brits building their encampment.

"And they play bagpipes? For real? I thought that was an Irish thing."

Garibaldi scoffed. "Scottish, not Irish, you bonehead. Damn, don't you know nothin'?"

Valdez said "hey, you hear the one about the Scottish guy? He's sitting at a bar, drowning his sorrows in whisky."

"Everybody got a good grip on it?" I asked "Lift with your legs, not your back."

Cornpone snorted. "Damn, Bish, you sound like my mother. We got this."

"So he says to the bartender," Valdez grunted with the effort, "he says, so, you build thirty houses, and when you walk down the street, do people say 'there goes MacDougal, the home builder? No, they don't'."

We got the wall up on top of our knees, and I told the team to get under it, and lift it to our shoulders. The extra gravity was killing me.

"Then he says 'you save five children from a burning building, and when you walk down the street, do people say there goes MacDougal, the rescuer'? No, they don't."

"Valdez, will you shut up a minute? All right, people, lift!" I said in my best US Army voice of authority.

We got that bitch of a wall unit up above our shoulders, and were winning the fight against gravity, when Valdez gasped "'Then MacDougal says, 'but you fuck *one* sheep'-."

We lost it. Men scattered as the wall unit came crashing down, and people were rolling on the ground laughing. I tried to bark an order, but I was laughing so hard that a snot bubble came out of my nose, and when people saw that, they fell over laughing again.

Lieutenant Gonzalez shot a dirty look at us, and a sergeant started walking in our direction. It was official, I had no business being in charge of anything, the Army made a huge mistake giving me even responsibility to set up a tent. I got the men back together, and we tried to lift the wall unit again, but every time we got it a few inches off the ground, Valdez started laughing at his own joke, and it cracked everyone up. Finally, I sent Valdez away to get us some water, called over a half dozen more guys, and we got the damn thing set upright and fixed into place.

"*One* sheep." Cornpone laughed, and I couldn't help joining him.

After we got the tent set up, Cornpone and I finally connected with the other two guys of our old fireteam; Sergeant Greg Koch, and Private Dave Czajka. We called Koch 'Sergeant', he had a nickname but you needed at least sergeant stripes to use it, unless you wanted a six foot three shaved head black man from Georgia glaring at you. You didn't. Dave we called 'Ski', because he was from Polish stock around Milwaukee, and even though his last name didn't end in '-ski', the rest of us figured it should have. Really, it was his fault for not having a decent nickname when he joined our unit. Damn, it was good to get the band back together! I had trusted all three of them with my life. We'd gotten into some hairy shit in Nigeria, we'd come through with nothing worse than some scars and bad memories. Before I left home, I'd sort of kept in touch with them by spotty emails, but I hadn't heard from them since then, and Cornpone and I weren't sure either of them had made the trip from Earth. They had, they'd been on a different Kristang ship, and arrived at Camp Alpha a few hours before us. Koch got us bunked into a tent, which we had to help set up, and he figured out where to go for chow. We were happy campers.

Sergeant Koch went off to do important sergeant things, and the dining facility wasn't opening for dinner until another three hours, so Cornpone dug into his pack for snacks.

"What you got?" Ski asked.

Cornpone winked. "Uh, let's see. Damn! I got a gen-u-ine smorgasbord of Hooah! bars."

"A smorgasbord?" I asked skeptically. "Really?"

"Oh yeah, a smorgasbord at least. Could be a plethora, maybe even, oooh, an honest to God, gosh-darned corn-u-copia of snack foods." It was funny to hear Jesse say 'plethora' in his deep southern accent.

"Cut the bullshit, man, you're making me hungry." Ski protested. "What flavors you got in there?"

"Well, I got Cinnamon Cardboard, of course, also Raisins 'n' Gravel, and, my personal fave, Original Sawdust."

Crap. I got stuck with Raisin 'n' Gravel. The raisins were harder to chew than the gravel.

The next morning, we were marched out to the shooting range after chow time. It was cold, the thermometer outside our tent said it was near freezing. Excitement was high; we all expected to finally get our hands on some incredible, super high-tech weapons from the Kristang. And maybe clothing that automatically heated and cooled you. I felt naked without a rifle. Standing in front of us was a Marine Corps gunnery sergeant with a crew cut so severe, it looked like it could cut your hand if you touched it. He wore combat pants and boots, but over his top was a red US Marine Corps sweatshirt.

"I am Gunnery Sergeant Cragen, of the United States Marine Corps." Cragen paused as shouts of 'Oorah' and 'Semper Fi' rang out from the crowd. "I am relieved to hear that we have a few qualified riflemen among us. Since the rest of you are Army, I'll try to talk slowly, so you can understand." The other Marines laughed at that remark.

"Listen up, people!" There was a gray box on a table in front of him, he touched a button on the side of the box, and it swung open silently. Everyone craned their necks, we were finally going to see the super high-tech weapons that we'd be killing hamsters with. So it was understandable to hear the grousing when Sergeant Cragen pulled what looked like a standard M4 rifle from the box.

"Oh, screw this!"

"You *got* to be kidding me!"

"This is bullshit, man!"

"An M Goddamn four?"

"Whiskey Tango Foxtrot?!" Which meant, of course, What The Fuck?

"Man, this is for shit," Ski whispered to me and Cornpone. Cornpone just spit on the burnt dusty ground.

Those were some of the milder comments. Cragen let the protests die down, rather than chewing us out for lack of discipline. "People, say hello to what we humans are calling the M4B1. The Kristang don't trust us with anything more powerful, and we won't need it for the missions we'll be assigned for the immediate future. The M4 *Bravo* unit fires ammo similar to the five point five six mike mike caliber, two two three long cartridge you're used to. The difference is this," he picked up a bullet from the table, and pointed to the tip. "This is an explosive charge. The Kristang assure us this ammo will penetrate the body armor that Ruhar soldiers wear, if you select the explosive option, because the explosive is a shape charge. Like a HEAT round our tanks use. You can also select to deactivate the explosive, which you will do, depending on the rules of engagement in effect at the time. The way you select the mode for the explosive tip is with this switch here," he pointed to a recessed button on the back of the grip, which was convenient for right and left handed soldiers. "You slide up this cover in the grip, to expose this recessed button. It is recessed, so you knuckleheads don't activate the explosive tip option by accident. After firing nine rounds, which you can do in standard single shots or three round bursts, you have to press the button again to select explosives."

Cragen went on at length about the M4 Bravo, but for most people, the thrill was gone. Where was the self-guided ammo, the lasers, the genetic enhancements to make us super soldiers, the bionic eyes, the mech suits that allowed us to jump thirty feet in the air and run a hundred miles per hour? Where was all the cool stuff we'd seen in sci-fi movies? This was bullshit! The Ruhar could pound us from orbit with masers, railguns and smart missiles, and all we had were Vietnam-era rifles with fancy firecracker bullets?

Total bullshit.

A couple hours later, I got an M4 Bravo in my hands, on the firing range. It felt exactly like my trusty old M4, which I'd left behind at Fort Drum when I'd gone home on leave. And I never went back to Drum, so my rifle might still be there. The Kristang supplied us with conversion kits for our regular M4s, and the ammo with explosive tips. We learned later that much of our ammo came straight from Earth, with no fancy enhancements, because the Kristang had a limited supply of the explosive stuff. Each squad would get Kristang clips equal to half the normal weapons load, the rest would be regular 5.56MM ammo. Our allies figured we wouldn't need fancy ammo for the missions they were assigning to us. It was a bit insulting; any tough jobs in this war would be done by the adults, us human soldiers were sitting at the children's table.

My M4B1 came with two clips of explosive-tipped ammo, I took my turn on the firing range, practicing using the button to select explosives or not. The explosive mode was impressive, there was much cheering along the firing line as we saw metal targets shredded. Our regular bullets bounced off the targets, leaving only little shiny dents. One advantage of Kristang ammo is that every cartridge was exactly the same, down to the nano level; even better than what our snipers called 'matched ammunition'. And Kristang ammo fired much cooler and cleaner, so you could rock 'n' roll without melting or fouling the barrel. We still needed to take our weapon apart and put it back together. Blindfolded. And clean it. I took one of the Kristang bullets out of a clip and examined it closely. Other than being a different color and being perfectly smooth with absolutely no scuff marks or scratches, it looked like the standard NATO ammo I'd been using for years.

We were going into battle with none of the hoped-for enhancements, having to hitch a ride to every planet, and we weren't entrusted with any important missions. It was like the Kristang were merely humoring our desire to get into the fight. This was the future.

It wasn't what I expected.

That first afternoon while we were on the firing range, a group of aircraft flew by, low and close enough for us to see them clearly. The aircraft circled around for hours, practicing landings, takeoffs and formation flying. I say aircraft instead of spacecraft, because the instructors on the firing range told us that's what they were, designed to fly in an atmosphere, and not capable of reaching orbit. What surprised me is they were Ruhar aircraft, not Kristang. Wherever we were going next, the Kristang wanted our pilots ready to use equipment captured from the hamsters, instead of the Kristang having to transport their own equipment across the star lanes. There were two basic types, known by the names given by humans; the Buzzard, which was a transport ship like a V-22 Osprey tilt-rotor, and a sort of two-person gunship like an Apache, that we called a Chicken. Just like the way we called the Ruhar hamsters, we gave disrespectful names to their aircraft. They were both vertical takeoff and landing craft like helicopters or tiltrotors, but they had jet engine pods at the end of their short wings, not rotor blades. We all had to admit they looked cool. And we were all proud to know humans were flying them, and would be flying them in combat. Soon, we hoped.

The next day, we got some of the other minimally upgraded toys the Kristang were allowing us to have. The most useful toy was a personal tactical radio that hopped frequencies, transmitted in encrypted bursts, and used wide-field white noise jamming in the background so their location was very tough to pinpoint. We all got a personal radio the size of a typical Earth smartphone, except it was thin as a credit card, with a touchscreen that couldn't be scratched, and you couldn't damage it unless you shot it with an explosive-tipped round. With the radio came an earpiece and microphone to wear under our helmets. Our helmet cameras transmitted video through the new radios, so squad, platoon, and company leaders could see what their soldiers were seeing. We could also take the radios off our belts, and use the screen to select cameras in our squad to view anyone else's camera. And, instead of one person in a unit being the designated radio operator, and lugging a heavy piece of equipment around, every soldier now had the ability to communicate to anyone else, across the planet. The touchscreen popped up a menu written in whatever human language you spoke into it. English, Spanish, French, Mandarin, Hindi, you name it, the radio understood it all. We all had to admit that was cool stuff. People who had a Military Occupational Specialty related to comm equipment were out of a job, since humans were not allowed to screw with the gear, and didn't understand it anyway. Personally, it was all magic to me.

The Army wanted us to call the new tactical radios 'TacRs', for Tactical Radios. Some jokers were calling it the 'zPhone', because Z was as far beyond I in the alphabet, as the zPhone was beyond the iPhone. I'm sure the Army had some official name like Radio, Tactical, Multipurpose, Kristang Supplied, in accordance with Mil Standard blah blah blah. Whatever. The coolest feature of the TacRs was they could be used as translators, which was great, because none of us spoke a single word of Ruhar. I spoke some broken Spanish, and had learned some useful phrases in Hausa and Yoruba when I was in Nigeria, but really, I wasn't even all that good at speaking American. Your and you're still got me confused, which drove my mother bananas when I sent her email with grammatical errors. We all got to practice with our TacRs in translator mode, what you did was put the earpiece in one ear, and speak slowly and clearly into the little boom microphone near your mouth. You had to speak a couple pages of your native language when you first used your TacR, so the translator could understand your particular speech pattern. Somehow, the thing was able to figure the difference between my Downeast accent and Cornpone's Southern drawl. That was impressive by itself. You spoke into the mic, paused, and your words came out of the TacR's speaker in whatever language you selected. It could even detect another language being spoken near you, and automatically translate that into your own language. The sound on either end was smoother than I expected, although it still was clearly a computer voice. What impressed me was that the TacR handled slang pretty well, even ubiquitous military slang. When it didn't understand something, it made a humming sound, the machine equivalent of 'uh'. There was a French battalion a couple kilometers away at Alpha, a couple of their squads came over to visit one day, and the Frenchies got bombarded with requests to talk, so we could both try out our TacRs in translate mode. It was great, they spoke their Frenchie babble into their mics, and I heard it in English. I learned, for one thing, that French toast is not called 'French toast' in France, it's called 'pain perdu'. Which makes sense, when you think about it, I mean, why wouldn't the French just call it 'toast'? Although, why did we call our cheese 'American cheese'? Why didn't we just say 'cheese'? Right? Maybe I'm getting off the subject. Anyway, it was weird to hear me speak, and the TacR repeat my words in French, especially since the TacR actually used a French accent. It was so funny, for both sides, that we had great fun saying stupid stuff, and hearing the TacR translate it. Probably that was not the training the Army intended, but we did get a lot of use out of the translator and got comfortable with using it.

Some people reported they had tried the translator with Chinese and Indian troops, on visits to their parts of the base, and it worked darn well. As for how it worked with the Ruhar, we practiced with a computer speaking Ruhar, and all I can say is, I sure hoped the darned thing worked as well in the field as it did in practice.

Another new toy drew more groans when it was shown to us. Gunny Cragen again was standing on a platform in front of us, this time he pulled a bulky tube out of a box. "Say hello to the FGM-148 *Bravo* Javelin missile."

Shit. The Javelin was a decent enough weapon, a man portable fire-and-forget antitank missile that I'd used in Nigeria, but it had some issues. For starters, the description of 'man portable' was pushing the practical limit, the damned thing weighed fifty pounds. Civilians may think a weapon that enables a single soldier to destroy a main battle tank is worth every one of its fifty pounds, but they haven't humped one through the bush day after day. And that's fifty pounds on top of your rifle, 180 rounds of ammo, radio gear, canteen, MREs and everything else the Army thinks you need to carry. So Javelins are assigned to two-man teams, at least. In battle, one man acts as a spotter while the other operates the weapon, then they both get the hell out of there as fast as they can. Shoot and scoot, we call it.

Anyway, Cragen was speaking. "You all know the strengths and weaknesses of the Javelin missile. Our allies have helped us with the main weakness; the infrared targeting system. The manual says the infrared seeker cools down in a couple seconds, but we all know that depends on the conditions you're in; when it's ninety eight degrees in the desert or jungle, it takes longer to go active. The Kristang have given us kits to upgrade the seeker on the FGM-148 Bravo, it now cools fully down in less than half a second. And it stays cool for up to half an hour, so you don't have to worry about using it right away. After half an hour, you have to turn it off, but ten minutes later, you can activate it again. Be aware that every time you do use it, it won't stay cool as long, that's all in the manual. The seeker's imaging system is also upgraded, so if you've ever had trouble, on a hot day, getting the weapon to recognize a target that is almost as hot as its surroundings, that is no longer a problem. Also, once you identify a target to the weapon, it will stay locked, even if you or the target move."

There was a scattering of slow, ironic clapping. Cragen gave us a sour look. "I know you people expected laser rifles, and nukes the size of a hand grenade when you came out to the stars. We don't have that, this is what we have," he hefted the Javelin Bravo over his head. "And we're going to fight to the very best of our ability."

What he didn't say is, our ability to fight would be greater if we had better weapons. Whatever. The Army says we fight with the force we have, not the force we'd like to have. Hooah.

After a mildly depressing and disillusioning week of training for space warfare, with essentially the same weapons I'd used in Nigeria, we finally got a truly high-tech new toy to play with. The Javelin Bravo antitank missile, like our original Javelin, had a minimal antiair capability, limited to use against low-flying helicopters. The Kristang must have decided that none of our MANPAD missiles, that is MAN Portable Air Defense, were useful in this conflict. I'd used our Stinger missiles in training, never in combat, and it was a damned good missile against helicopters, drones, slow fixed wing aircrafts, and even jets sometimes. That was only if you got lucky and the jet didn't cross out of range, before you got the Stinger set up and targeted. Against supersonic dropships that could climb vertically into orbit, I couldn't see a Stinger giving us any chance. I'd seen even our captured Ruhar Chicken gunships go from hover mode to zooming straight up at amazing speed. Everyone I knew agreed us ground pounders needed to do something serious against the air threat, or any combat situation would be game over before we got started.

The MANPAD missile the Kristang provided to us, we instantly named the Zinger, of course. It weighed about thirty pounds, not much different from a Stinger, the difference being the Zinger targeting system was built into the launch tube and was disposable, whereas with our Stinger, you had to attach the targeting system box to the disposable launch tube when you wanted to fire the missile. A Zinger could climb up to eighty thousand feet, it was hypersonic, and if it missed one target, it could look around and decide to engage another target on its own, or the user could redirect its targeting via zPhone, or it could talk to other Zingers in the area to get targeting advice. Its wings could also deploy wide so the missile could loiter in the area up to twenty minutes before its fuel was exhausted, that feature meant we could fire it ahead of time into an airspace before the enemy arrived giving the user time to get the hell out of there.

The Zinger got a genuine, enthusiastic reception when it was shown to us, and we got to use it for real against drones. Unlike practicing with Stingers, where the US Army mostly had us firing little flares instead of expensive missiles, the Kristang had no problem with us expending ammunition, even though our practice rounds had the warheads disabled. It was immensely satisfying for us grunts to see drone targets knocked out of the air.

Then it got tougher. The drones we fired at initially were dumb, they could maneuver a bit to avoid missiles, but had minimal defensive capability. Next, we practiced against drones that simulated Ruhar aircraft and dropships like Chickens, Buzzards and the nasty dropship gunship we called a Vulture. They all had laser or particle beam defensive turrets that could confuse, fry or outright destroy a Zinger, even with the Zinger jinking on approach to avoid the beam defenses. Zingers also had to deal with electronic countermeasures, and those weren't only in the infrared or microwave spectrum. Ruhar aircraft had an active stealth capability that made them difficult to see even in the visible spectrum. With active stealth engaged, the aircraft didn't become invisible, what happened was the air around them rippled, distorting their shapes, and multicolored lights blinked on and off in an envelope around the aircraft, making it hard to tell exactly where it was. The tactics we were taught to use by the Kristang was to fire multiple Zingers at a target. In practice, we could pick up a Zinger tube, unfold the targeting screen from the side of the tube, designate a target, and fire in less than a minute. One Zinger team of two people could carry and fire four Zingers, in theory, with one person operating the missile system and the other person acting as a spotter. Keep in mind, two Zingers weighed over sixty pounds, and while carrying a Zinger you were expected to still be loaded down with a rifle, ammo, canteen, zPhone, body armor, and anything else UNEF expected a sharp-dressed soldier to lug around with him or her. Of course, while setting up for a second shot, the enemy air would be looking for you and shooting back, which tended to shorten the user's life expectancy, and therefore combat effectiveness. That last comment wasn't a joke I made up, by the way, it was written right into the user manual we got from our patrons the Kristang. They needed to work on their public relations, big time.

Anyway, with the Zingers, for the first time us UNEF grunts felt we were being semi-properly equipped for the fight, and that we didn't need to only hunker down in foxholes and die in combat. We could shoot back. Shoot only up to eighty thousand feet, true, we couldn't do anything about ships in orbit. It gave us hope. If the Kristang trusted us with their toys, and supplied us plenty, they were planning for us to do something useful in combat. Wherever that would be.

Most of our training time at Camp Alpha wasn't spent learning to use our new or modified weapons. It was refresher training, for soldiers like me, who had been harvesting crops and helping civilians since the Ruhar attacked. The work I'd done with the National Guard in Maine had been hard, back-breaking labor, but hadn't prepared me for combat. Until I got to Camp Alpha, the last time I'd fired a rifle, other than hunting, was in Nigeria.

I was rusty and a bit out of shape. Hikes with hundred pound rucksacks, hand to hand combat training and running obstacle courses toughened me up quick, and I was glad for it. The Ruhar weren't going to take it easy on me, it was better to be sore and exhausted now, than not prepared when we went into action.

Running in heat beat the crap out of me. Running in extra gravity beat the crap out of me. Combine them, and my legs were shaking from exhaustion after only a few miles. Cornpone fell to his knees and puked his guts out three times on our first five mile run. After that, Sergeant Koch decided we'd be getting up extra early, to run before it got hot. On Camp Alpha, the temperature was like an On or Off switch, when the star came over the horizon in the morning, it got hot fast. At sunset, the temperature plummeted. The third morning saw us sliding out of our bunks to run in the predawn cold. A day on Camp Alpha was a bit over 28 hours, our schedule left time for seven solid hours of rack time, even with rising early.

Without the daytime heat, we only had to deal with the extra gravity. And the blowing, burnt-smelling grit. And the crushing disappointment that coming out to the stars hadn't meant we'd been transformed into super soldiers. We would become super soldiers the old fashioned way, Sergeant Koch announced, through hard work. Those were inspiring words until about the two mile mark, when we were gasping for breath.

Our fireteam wasn't the only group up early for exercise, the second morning we were running, we were about a mile from the base on the return leg when we came around the side of a hill and there was a half dozen people on the other side, also headed back to base. Without anyone needing to say anything, we picked up our pace. And so did they. And the other group upped the ante. Soon we were sprinting. I pulled ahead, I'd been a runner since I was a little kid and my mother brought me out running with her. The other group had two fast runners, then one. Ahead of us, the trails converged, I reached the intersection just ahead of the other runner, then he pulled even with me and we ran as fast as we could, while our teams behind us cheered.

Only he wasn't a he, he was a she, I would have known from the short ponytail bobbing behind her head if I'd been paying attention. Damn. I knew her sort of, she was in our brigade support battalion, her name was Shauna or something like that, but I hadn't seen her since like a month before I rotated home from Nigeria. Crap, I didn't know she was so fast. She pulled ahead of me, only a foot, two feet, but I could not catch her, no matter how much effort I put into it. She was struggling too, her footing was wobbly and her breathing was as ragged as my own. We shot past the two big boulders that marked the unofficial edge of the base and I collapsed to my knees, having to use my hands to push myself back to my feet to walk it off. She stood next to me, hands on her knees, gasping. "Damn."

"Shit yeah." I replied. "You trying to kill me?"

"Hey, *you* were pushing *me*."

I held out a hand. "Joe Bishop."

"Yeah, I know you, you're the Barney guy, right? Shauna Jarrett." We shook hands.

"You want my autograph?" I was only half joking. The whole Barney thing was getting really old for me.

She cocked her head. "Why, does the Barney thing get you laid a lot?"

A light bulb went on in my head. Yes, I know, every time a girl smiles at a guy, he's hopeful that she's interested, but this time I thought she really might be. "Not so far," I winked.

Columbus Day

She laughed, and it was beautiful. "You keep hoping, Joe." The other people in our groups arrived, and Shauna got backslaps for winning our impromptu race. Shauna and her group started to walk away.

If there was any sort of opportunity there, I wasn't going to let it get away. We were a long, long way from Earth, at war, and there weren't a whole lot of women within a thousand lightyears of Camp Alpha. "Hey, Shauna, I'll see you around?"

To my delight, she smiled at me back over her shoulder. "Maybe?"

Along with getting familiar with new equipment, and getting back into proper condition, we had classroom time, which was us sitting on the dirt floor of a tent, listening to lectures about the enemy, our allied command structure, and most importantly, The Rules. It all blew my mind when I first heard it, so I'll explain it slow. Best you get comfortable, because there will be a pop quiz at the end.

I'll wait while you get yourself a beer.

Comfy?

Ok, first, some background intel for you. The Kristang were not at the top of the allied coalition, which I already figured, from the fact they needed to hitch an interstellar ride on a Thuranin star carrier. What was news to me was that the Thuranin weren't at the top either. The allied coalition is led by cat-like aliens called the Maxohlx. Rumored to be cat-like, since no human, and very few Kristang, had ever seen one. As humans were unlikely to ever see a Maxohlx in my lifetime, all I'll say about them is they are an ancient species, with incredible technology. Surely when the Maxohlx fought, they were armed with something better than an M-fucking-4. And I know 'Maxohlx' is an odd name, it was the best our G2 people could think of to spell how the word sounds when the Kristang said it.

The home planet of the Maxohlx is two thirds of the way around the galaxy from Earth, if that means anything to you, which it doesn't to me. It's far, far away. The Thuranin, we learned, were themselves not unique, they were only responsible for a small slice of the galaxy under Maxohlx control, and the Kristang handled a couple thousand cubic lightyears under Thuranin control. The Maxohlx had other second tier species besides the Thuranin, and the Thuranin had two other species under their command, that we knew of, besides the Kristang. The Thuranin are sort of little green men, they are shorter than the average human, but humanoid, with two legs, two arms, two eyes and a bald head. Humans who had talked with the Kristang got the impression that the Kristang didn't like their 'patrons', and the feeling was mutual; the Thuranin are disdainful of any species with lesser technology. I wonder what they thought of pitiful humans.

On the enemy side, the situation was similar. At the top were the Rindhalu, who are creepy looking spider type things. Just thinking about it made my skin crawl. Their second tier allies, in this quadrant of the galaxy, are the Jeraptha, who are almost as creepy, being insects. The Jeraptha aren't a hive mind like bees, they are more like beetles. The Ruhar are a client species of the Jeraptha, the same way the Kristang were clients of the Thuranin. Based on some things the Kristang said, our G2 intel people speculated the Ruhar had slightly better technology than the Kristang.

Kristang propaganda, I say propaganda because that's what it sounded like to me, said the Rindhalu were older, much older, than the Maxohlx, and had tried to suppress the development of other intelligent species in the galaxy, until the righteous Maxohlx rebelled, many thousands of years ago. The allies were fighting for the right of intelligent species to develop on their own, while the enemy species were slaves of the creepy spider

Rindhalu, who wanted total control of the galaxy. For an advanced species, the Kristang had remarkably clumsy propaganda. Think Soviet Union, or North Korea, or Nazi Germany. We allies are fighting the evil enemy for the glorious and virtuous common people! Under the magnificent guidance of our supreme leaders, our righteous cause will triumph! Strength through unity! And so on. Anyway, that's what we were told. I'm sure the truth is more complicated, it always is.

The incredible technology of the Maxohlx and the Rindhalu did not extend to creating, or even operating, the wormholes that made long-range interstellar flight practical. Those wormholes were created millions of years ago, by a long-gone species that is unknown, other than what they left behind. The Kristang called the wormhole-builders the Elders. Wormholes didn't care who went through them, and there was no known way to control one, or shut it off. Or damage it, even a nuke had no effect. The wormholes worked, and that's all we needed to know.

Then we got to The Rules.

The Rules were the Rules Of Engagement for combat. They applied to both sides, and were strictly enforced by the Maxohlx and the Rindhalu. The Rules explained why the war had been going on for many thousands of years, why both sides hadn't wiped each other out a long time ago. The basis of The Rules was that the Maxohlx and the Rindhalu couldn't afford to seriously fight each other directly, in the same way that America and China couldn't fight each other. On Earth, countries with megatons of nukes couldn't fight without destroying their own countries. Out in the galaxy, species with weapons that made nukes look like firecrackers also could not afford to fight each other directly. So they fought through their client species, and those species also had clients, and so on. Most of the actual fighting and dying was done by third-tier species like the Ruhar and the Kristang. And by their clients. Like humans.

Anyway, here are The Rules.

You'd better grab a pencil and paper.

Rule Number One; no use of nukes, or other types of radiological weapons, on or near an inhabited planet, or even potentially habitable planet. No antimatter either, because such a weapon produces hard radiation even if it is short-lived. This rule was listed first, because the Maxohlx and the Rindhalu didn't want their grubby underlings contaminating a planet they may later want for themselves. Even in the vastness of the Milky Way, the number of habitable planets within practical range of a wormhole was limited, so both sides didn't want useful planets removed from productive use because some jackass went crazy with nukes.

Rule Number Two was no chemical weapons, for the same reason as Rule Number One. Nasty chemicals could linger in the environment for a long, long time. They didn't quite say that any species abandoning a planet was supposed to sweep up after themselves and take their trash with them, I figured that was implied.

Rule Number Three, no use of nano weapons. Nanotech was widely used to make things, but it could not be used as a weapon. Even the Kristang weren't sure of the basis for this rule, but ancient rumor held there was an incident where nanotech gets loose, and caused that entire star system to be quarantined, permanently. Hence, nano weapons were a huge November Golf in the war.

Rule Number Four, no biological weapons. This rule wasn't so much to protect the Maxohlx and the Rindhalu, because species were different enough that a pathogen deadly to one species mostly had no effect on others. This rule was more like a Geneva Convention sort of thing; where the combatants agreed not to do something to the enemy, so the enemy wouldn't do it to them. Otherwise, each side could simply drop stealth missiles with canisters of biological weapons into the atmosphere of enemy planets, and soon no one would be left alive on either side.

Rule Number Four was, we heard, a little sketchy in actual use, as viruses, bacteria and other biological hazards mutated over time, and if a known, natural virus became more contagious or deadly, who could say that didn't happen naturally? Rule Number Four was in place to prevent catastrophic biological attacks, but apparently a certain level of cheating was allowed, as long as it didn't get out of control, and no one got caught. The Kristang told us the Ruhar were notorious for pushing the limits on Rule Number Four. I'm sure the Ruhar would say the same thing about the Kristang. The bio weapons thing scared me, despite reassurance from the Kristang that the Ruhar didn't know enough about human biology to make a weapon effective against us. What scared me is the Kristang had medical technology far advanced beyond what humanity had brought to the stars, and they weren't sharing any of it with us. They said that without years of studying human biology, they couldn't safely apply their advanced technology to us. Which meant even a common flu virus, that some human brought with them from Earth, could be a serious problem for the Expeditionary Force. And that wounded troops had to be treated with whatever medical care was available on that planet. There would be no medivac flight back to the States on this campaign.

Rule Number Five was, simply put, no dropping rocks. No steering asteroids or comets so they impacted an inhabitable planet. This also meant no taking even a small rock, accelerating it to relativistic speed, and slamming it into a planet. Any planet with a decent population had systems that could detect and deflect rocks that were naturally on an impact course anyway, the rule was to prevent a combatant from saturating those defenses, or encasing a high-speed rock in a stealth field. What, you may ask, about railguns? Spaceships routinely used railguns to accelerate kinetic rounds up to relativistic speeds, and railguns were used for both space combat and planetary strikes. The key to using railguns for planetary bombardment was the effect on the planet; you had to limit the energy yield of a single kinetic impactor to less than a megaton, and you couldn't use so many railgun strikes that you affected the planet's climate. Pounding a planet with a lot of railguns could throw a thick dust cloud into the air and lead to rapid cooling, that dust could take a long time to settle out of the atmosphere, even leading to a mini ice age.

So, those were The Rules. I wasn't capitalizing those words on my own, that's the way they were on UNEF's PowerPoint slides. The point of The Rules seemed to be that inhabitable planets within practical range of a wormhole are rare and precious, and the Maxohlx and Rindhalu could not allow lesser species to damage valuable real estate. The Rules weren't focused on protecting soldiers or civilians on either side, there was no alien equivalent to the Geneva Conventions for space warfare. The Maxohlx and Rindhalu had put The Rules in place to prevent their ancient war from getting out of hand. As long as lesser species conformed to The Rules, they could kill each other all they wanted.

All of The Rules were Ok by me, especially as UNEF didn't have any nuclear, nano, biological, chemical or relativistic railgun weapons with us at Camp Alpha; The Rules meant such weapons wouldn't be used against us. Except maybe biological, if an enemy thought they could get away with it. There wasn't any point to us humans worrying about it.

I didn't see Shauna running again in the mornings, and I didn't want to be creepy by pinging her via zPhone. So I was thrilled when we ran into each other in the DFAC, which is what the Army calls a dining facility. It was a big tent, with tarps on the ground to keep dirt and dust out of the food, and the pervasive acrid burnt smell to a minimum. I had a tray of sandwiches, one peanut butter and one was some kind of mystery meat, with mashed potatoes and what was supposed to be gravy. And green beans. Real green beans, they looked like, they weren't cooked to death. And a roll. With butter. After busting my ass all day, I was hungry and all the food looked good. I turned around to find a table, and almost crashed my tray into Shauna's.

"Hey! Uh, Shauna, right?" I said as nonchalantly as I could.

"Hey yourself." She looked at my tray. Her tray only had a sandwich, green beans and an apple. "You want to grab a table?"

Did I? Not trusting myself to speak without saying something stupid, I simply nodded and followed her to a table that wasn't too crowded. "You know what I was doing on Columbus Day," I said as a way to open a conversation, only it may have come across as bragging so I added "did you do anything stupid that day?"

"I was with friends in Phoenix."

"You weren't out leaf peeping that day?"

She tilted her head and gave a me a sarcastic look. "People in Phoenix don't do a lot of leaf peeping."

"Got it. My family doesn't need to go looking for leaves, by Columbus Day they're covering the lawn two feet deep."

"You going to eat?" She looked at my still full plate.

"Oh, yeah. Don't want to talk with my mouth full." I bit into a sandwich and swallowed quickly.

"I went home first to make sure my mother was all right, my father was on a business trip in Houston, then I went over to check on my grandmother. She lives in a high rise, and without power she was stuck up there, I didn't think she'd be able to make it all the way down the stairs, she's got a bad hip. And she's, you know, old." Her voice trembled a bit, recalling that day was bringing up a lot of emotion for her. "She was so scared, she was so scared, and she told me not to worry about her, she told me that I was young and strong, and that I needed to get out of the city, get somewhere the aliens wouldn't find me. She kept saying it was the End Times, Judgment Day, and that I needed to leave her, and survive. In the city, we didn't have Ruhar assault ships landing in the streets, all we saw were lights and contrails in the sky, and pillars of smoke from sites they'd hit. The only way we knew there was an alien invasion were emergency announcements on the radio. And I didn't believe it at first. " She ate the last forkful of green beans, then pushed her tray away. "Those hamsters frightened my grandmother almost to death. I hate them for that. That's why I'm out here. I don't want my grandmother, or anyone else, to ever be scared like that."

"Yeah. I used to go out on clear nights, look up at the sky, and wonder what's out there in the universe. After Columbus Day, I look at the sky, and if the stars are twinkling, for a second, I think maybe it's an enemy ship jumping into orbit. "

"Yes! Exactly!" She slapped the table. "Because of the hamsters, nobody can look at the sky again without fear. I hate those MFers for that."

"They stole our innocence?" I mumbled over a mouthful of mashed potatoes.

"Yeah, something like that. Not you and me, we've seen combat, we saw some shit in Nigeria. But most people, just living their lives, they don't get to think they're safe again, ever." She looked away for a moment. "Ever. Now we know there's a whole galaxy full of enemies out there. Looming over our heads, all the time."

Columbus Day

We talked about what total bullshit it was, that we were expected to go into combat with basically the same gear the US Army had been using for decades, and exchanged rumors about what our first deployment would be, neither of us knew squat about where the Kristang would send us next. And we both wondered and worried about what was going on back home, while I finished my dinner and she ate an apple. Her family was much worse off than my folks; her parents had both lost their jobs and they, her young brother and grandmother had been resettled in east Texas, where her father was on a farm labor team and her mother was working at a day care. That was a big change for her parents, her mother had been a real estate agent and her father a sales rep for an IT company. Both of those jobs vanished when the economy crashed, and their condo in Phoenix had become unlivable without electricity to run air conditioners.

My father lost his job at the paper mill, but he got by for the first couple months on odd jobs, logging, welding and auto repair. My mother still had a steady job as a teacher, especially with so many families moved from electricity-starved cities to the countryside. Late in December, someone had the idea that the big paper mill where my father had worked, which had a 'cogeneration' plant that burned basically leftover sawdust to make electricity for the mill, could be started up again to produce electricity for the region. That brought my father back to work at the mill, with the only problem being that there wasn't enough lumber being brought to the mill because there wasn't enough diesel fuel for trucks to haul the wood. The Great North Woods had plenty of lumber, and no way to get it anywhere. There was barely enough diesel fuel around for trains. The solution was to bring old steam engines from a tourist railroad in New Hampshire, with guys who still knew how to keep steam engines running, and how to make them run on wood rather than coal or oil. Good old American ingenuity in action, with steam engines hauling logs out of the woods to a paper mill that was now a power station. The entire US electricity grid was being rebuilt, slowly, as the 'smart grid' we should have had decades ago, and lots of smaller local power stations rather than one giant plant for a whole region. The Kristang weren't helping much with rebuilding electrical generation around the planet, except in industrial areas they deemed vital to the war effort. Our new allies were disdainful that humanity still relied on fossil fuels for energy, and they set up a couple fusion reactors around the planet for their own needs, but even though they had explained their fusion technology to our scientists, it was going to be a very long time before humanity built a working fusion reactor on our own.

When I left, electricity was still spotty in my hometown, most of the power from the new power station in Milliconack went downstate to the Bangor area. My parents kept their house warm with wood stoves, didn't need air conditioning, and the garden we'd expanded over the winter should bring in plenty of crops to feed my family and the people living with them, plus food left over to sell. They had two cows now, and chickens for eggs, and when I left my mother had been bargaining for a pair of piglets. It was the same all over the world; people higher on the economic ladder before the Ruhar attacked were now sometimes worse off than those people who had been scraping by. If you were a farmer before Columbus Day, your life hadn't changed a whole lot, other than it being difficult to get fuel for tractors, since people still needed to eat, so there was plenty of demand. What did the Bible say, something like 'many who are first will be last, and the last, first'? Nobody ever expected scriptural prophesies to be delivered by alien invasion.

"I'm busting my ass to qualify for combat duty," Shauna explained. "Almost qualified when I signed up, I fell on an obstacle course and sprained my ACL with two weeks to go, pissed me off! So I went into logistics. I want combat duty, Joe."

Being in the infantry, and having been in combat, I wanted to caution her against too much enthusiasm. It wasn't any of my business how she wanted to serve, so I kept my mouth shut. We finished eating, people from her unit came over to talk to her, and then she left. If that could be considered a first date, it was a downer.

The first war game on Camp Alpha was Operation Valiant Shield. Code names for operations were ideally supposed to be selected at random, so as not to give the enemy an idea of your intent. Like 'Operation Desert Storm' was a cool name, but it had been pretty easy for the Iraqis to figure that op was an offensive in the desert. Not that it had mattered back then. The problem with random words is that you could end up with ops with unintentionally funny or lame names, like Flaming Bunny or Limp Justice, so really operation names were dreamed up, or at least vetted by, the UNEF PR staff. The name Valiant Shield was probably thought to be inspiring for the troops, when I heard the name all I could think was we were supposed to die valiantly. Like the old Roman saying, where a soldier was supposed to come home with his shield, or on it.

I wish I could tell you that during our first war game, I dreamed up some incredibly brilliant tactic that no one else had thought of, and it led us, or at least my platoon, to victory. I could tell you that, and it would be an awesome story, right? Maybe I will tell something along those lines someday to my grandchildren, when they're complaining how uncool old Grandpa is. Or maybe I'll tell a story like that someday when I'm drunk and I think it'll get me laid. The truth, unfortunately, is that me, and everyone else in two platoons of our company, were declared dead from an orbital railgun strike, less than an hour after the war game started. We were hustling across a shallow canyon, going from cover to cover, when my zPhone beeped, and a squawking voice announced that I was dead. Then my zPhone stopped working entirely. Crap. How the hell was two platoons of foot soldiers worth a railgun strike? The company had split up to avoid providing a juicy target, and that didn't work.

Protocol called for us to sit or lay down where we were, and wait for an all clear signal, which could come the next day, depending how the war game was going. The sun was over the horizon and it was getting hot already, our officers decided we could cheat a little and walk back across the canyon to shelter under a rock overhang. That's where I spent the rest of that day, all night, and half the next morning. We were running low on water, it was a six hour walk back to base, because we'd been dropped off by Buzzards before the start of the war game. Somebody at HQ took pity on us and sent trucks, they didn't have air conditioning and although we grumbled about that, we appreciated not having to walk the whole way.

One lesson that had gotten hammered into our heads by the war game is that the key to surviving ground combat in this war, in a situation where the 'high ground' is above the atmosphere, is like surviving combat in situations where the enemy might use tactical nukes. Avoid concentrating your forces, and keep cover as much as possible. In a potential nuclear war situation, do not give the enemy a target they might be tempted to hit with a nuke, like battalion-size forces, large ammo dumps, fixed airfields, vital bridges, that sort of thing. The Kristang didn't use nukes against ground targets, you might think that was a good thing, however it actually made the situation more dangerous. Deciding to use a nuke requires a whole lot of high-level leadership handwringing over an enormous nuclear escalation of the conflict, an escalation you can't step back from, a genie you can't put back in the bottle. Using railguns, which can accelerate rounds to a significant percentage of lightspeed, and can have the destructive energy equivalent of a tactical nuke, is so easy that it's a given in interstellar warfare. To us grunts on the ground, that means getting hit with a railgun from orbit is a matter more of when, not if.

Overall in the war game, UNEF Blue forces got crushed by the opposing simulated Ruhar Red force. The Kristang were reportedly very pleased with the outcome. Not pleased that UNEF troops had 'died' by the thousands, pleased that UNEF troops had held on long enough to delay the Red force's occupation of the surface. Scattered UNEF forces had used guerrilla tactics to attack Red forces after they landed, and our Zinger MANPAD teams had 'shot down' an encouraging number of Red dropships. And our Airedales had done well for themselves, too. Sure, by the time the Kristang halted the war game, the UNEF Blue force had less than a hundred aircraft capable of flying. If you think that's bad, the Kristang had expected all our air assets to be depleted within the first twelve hours. Modern combat is high intensity, especially once your feet get off the ground.

Two days after the war game, my fireteam was watching a basketball game in the evening, our battalion against a British Army team, us enjoying hot dogs and popcorn, when an Army lieutenant still wearing a flight suit sat down next to us in the bleachers. "Hey, you're a pilot, sir?" I asked, stupidly.

"Uh huh," he said over a bite of hot dog, "used to fly an Apache, now I fly a Chicken."

"How'd you do in the war game?" I asked eagerly. I'd heard a lot from ground pounders, but nothing from our Airedales so far. In my enthusiasm, I didn't consider the guy might have just finished a long flight, and wanted to relax and watch a ball game instead of telling me the same story he'd already told a hundred times. There wasn't need to worry, because a pilot never got tired of talking about flying.

"Did all right," he said while watching the game, "shot down a Dodo and a Vulture."

"Damn, sir, you Da Man!" I offered him a high five, and I was thrilled when he slapped my hand.

"Thanks, soldier. Course, I got popped by a missile from a Ruhar cruiser two minutes later. Felt good anyway, I lived longer than I expected."

"You shot down a Vulture?" Ski asked. "That's a gunship?"

"Yeah, it is. The Dodo had landed troops, a formation of six Dodos with Vulture escorts, they were headed back to orbit when we attacked from two directions, came in fast and low, right on the deck. It was a massive dogfight, a real furball, we got all the Dodos, simulated, of course, and we lost half our aircraft. That last Vulture, I had to chase the stinking thing up above seventy thousand feet, that's the max altitude for a Chicken, we're not rated to operate out of the atmosphere, I was on internal reaction mass and was barely able to control the ship with the secondary thrusters. The Vulture was way above me, it was pushing two gees and climbing away, while I was about to lose control and go into a flat spin. I ripple fired my last four missiles and my gunner hit the Vulture with the particle beam, the beam is defensive only, but it tied up the Vulture's defenses enough for one missile to get through." He turned back to watch the game. "Their active stealth doesn't work as well out of an atmosphere, they didn't tell us that, I figured it out." He took another handful of popcorn out of the paper bag and ate it slowly, thoughtfully. "You know, the sky up at that altitude isn't bright blue, it's almost black, and you can see the planet stretched out below you is round. That Ruhar cruiser that got me? I could *see* it. Not as a ghost on the headup display for the war game, this was a real ship, right there, hanging in the sky, it was spooky. The image on my HUD showed a Ruhar ship superimposed over the real Kristang ship for the game, when I clicked the HUD off, I could see the real ship. A real star ship, hanging in low orbit above me. It was awesome, for a moment, until it hit my starboard nacelle with the edge of a laser, I flew right through it. Put me into a spin, I was busy trying to hold the ship together when their missile crawled up my ass. Simulated, it felt real enough. I wouldn't have been able to recover, either, the autopilot took over and guided me down to angels thirty, that's, uh, thirty thousand feet."

"Shit," Ski said, "I thought us grunts on the ground had it tough."

"You do, for sure. We're more exposed up in the sky, we have countermeasures that help a lot with missile threats, it's funny, kind of, we're almost back in WWII days, before guided missiles took over air combat. The stealth and countermeasures mean getting a reliable firing solution on the enemy isn't a lock that it is in air combat on Earth, a missile only gets a hit maybe fifteen, twenty percent of the time, the Kristang aren't telling us for certain. We're guessing at the twenty percent number based on the tactics we're taught." He laughed. "It's funny, they sent me out here because they figured a helicopter pilot would have an easier transition to flying a Chicken or a Buzzard. When they're in hover mode, sure, true enough. Thing is, a Chicken can go supersonic, and climb higher than our jets. I wasn't ready for that; last time I flew fixed wing was a little turboprop in training. My Chicken can out climb and outmaneuver an F22 easy, most of the time you're flying it, the thing is a jet, not a helo. A Buzzard is more similar to a V22 Osprey, it isn't supersonic." He shook his head. "The techniques we learned flying rotorwings on Earth don't apply here, I have to keep reminding myself not to worry about dynamic stress on the rotor blades, and I don't need to keep the tail rotor clear when I land, because we don't have one."

"Sir," Cornpone asked, "we only have aircraft, right, and the enemy has dropships that can go into space. Do we really stand a chance in combat up there?" He pointed to the sky.

"Oh, yeah. I get your point. Yes, we do, we actually have an advantage in air combat over dropships. Dropships are big and heavy; they handle like a pig when they're deep in an atmosphere. With stealth and countermeasures, if your first volley of missiles doesn't hit, you close the distance to the target real fast, and then you're in air combat maneuvering, using your guns. The key to air combat is kinetic energy; if you bleed off too much speed in a turn, you're dead. Energy means you can engage and disengage a dogfight as you need. Dropships are ultimately much faster than our aircraft, they can reach escape velocity, but they don't accelerate as fast. We can get up to speed much quicker." He went on for a while about tactics of air combat, the three of us were enthralled, at that moment, I thought he was the coolest guy who ever lived. I left my seat and got another hot dog for him, so he'd keep talking. The game ended, though, the British team won by two points, and a group of pilots came by, so he left.

"Damn," Ski said wistfully, "wish I was a pilot. I thought about it, too, one of my uncles is in a flying club back home, the club has a single engine, uh, Piper, something like that. My uncle flew me and my father to Minneapolis once for a Bears game, that was great. Never had the money for flying lessons, though."

"That would be so cool." I agreed.

"Yeah, cool enough. He still died in the game." Cornpone pointed out.

"Uh huh, yeah." Ski said. "So did we, and we didn't do shit before we died. I'd rather die up in the sky doing something, than get vaporized in a railgun strike I didn't see coming."

Columbus Day

Inspired by watching the basketball game, Ski, Cornpone and I went to another court and found a pickup game we could join. Ski had a really good outside shot, I concentrated on feeding the ball to him and crashing the boards on defense. It felt good to play hard, to sweat out frustration. All of us were pissed that we'd died and accomplished nothing during Valiant Shield. Sure, us getting blown up from orbit was a realistic scenario, our question was what we were supposed to learn from it? And how were the Kristang supposed to evaluate our combat capabilities if all we did was get an unlucky roll of the dice by some Kristang computer in orbit? If those imaginary dice had rolled another way, some other unlucky bastards would have 'died' instead of us.

My zPhone on my belt vibrated during the game, I didn't check it until we took a break for water. It was a message from Shauna, she wanted to know if I was busy, and if not, did I want to get together?

Did I?

Did the sun rise in the East? On Earth, I mean.

Hell yes!

Here's a simple test to tell whether a guy wants to get together with a girl:

Step One- does he have a pulse?

Step Two- is he conscious?

There is no need for a step three.

Like the idiot that I am, I typed in <Is this a booty call? *smiley face with wink*>

Fortunately, my survival instinct caused me to erase that message before hitting send. Instead, I typed, as casually as I could <Sure! Playing hoops, we're winning. Be done soon>

And then caught hell from Cornpone and Ski because my head was clearly no longer in the game, I kept feeling phantom incoming text vibrations from my zPhone. We won the game anyway, not that anyone was serious about keeping score.

Damn. The game was over and no reply from Shauna. Had I been too eager? Too casual about it? Crap. My grandmother told stories about how she had sat by the phone at her house, this is before cellphones, sat by the phone, waiting for a guy to call. It sounded pathetic to me, back then. Sitting by the phone, instead of being out having fun, in case some loser guy decided to call?

Yet, when Ski and Cornpone suggested we go see what movie was playing in the big rec center tent, instead of going with them, I said I was tired and wanted to crash. They gave me a funny look, but left me alone. There I was, not with my buddies, not back at our tent in case they came back there, there I was, sitting alone in the basketball arena tent, waiting for a girl to contact me.

For all women who've waited for a guy to call or text them back, I know how you feel. It sucks.

And then my zPhone pinged with a text.

What I expected was for Shauna to suggest we meet somewhere, talk, maybe meet her friends, that sort of thing. She totally surprised me by meeting me at a gate to the logistics group motor pool, a fenced area for the Kristang trucks we'd been using. She had the code to the gate, and we slipped in, I followed her quietly as she put a finger to her lips. We weaved our way between the closely parked trucks, I didn't know where she was leading me, until we stopped behind a truck and she swung the back gate down. The truck had a canvas type roof over it, she pulled the flap aside and pointed a flashlight inside. For a second, I was afraid there were other people in the truck and Shauna expected me to get into some sort of sketchy activity that I was not interested in; my Army personnel file already had enough remarks about me getting into trouble.

There wasn't anyone in the truck. There was a thick pile of blankets.

My eyes must have shown my total surprise, because Shauna grabbed my shirt and kissed me passionately. "You Ok with this?" Her eyes were glittering in the dim security lights. "You're cute. Kinda dumb, maybe, but cute."

I nodded like a four year old being asked if he wanted a bowl of candy. "Yeah, Ok. Yes!"

For those of you who've had sex, I won't bore you with sweaty details of me and Shauna. You know what it's like, and I'm sure we didn't do anything you haven't done before. Or wanted to do.

For those of you who haven't, I won't spoil the surprise for you.

Hint: a-w-e-s-o-m-e.

Wow.

We took a break, some small talk, she was laying on her back, me next to her. After a while, I lightly traced my fingertips down from her neck, between her breasts and stomach, and down.

"What are you doing?" She giggled.

"Running my fingers through your hair." I said innocently.

"That's not what that means!" She laughed and slapped me playfully.

"This isn't romantic?"

"Yeah, like your friend here," she tapped my friend, "is all about romance, Joe."

"Hey," I said, with my friend waking up from her touching him, "he's very romantic."

"Mmm hmm, uh huh, I'll bet. He's into romance, if it leads to sex."

"Ok, I have to admit, he is a horn dog, I can't control him sometimes." Like right then, with Shauna continuing to encourage him.

"Oh, you have no control over him? Like you're not involved?"

"You have no idea," I shook my head ruefully. "Sometimes, I wake up at 4AM because he's forgotten a key to the front door, and I'm like, 'where have you been', and he's like 'nowhere, just out for a walk', and he smells like vodka and perfume, and I just know he's been roaming around getting into trouble."

"A key? Where would he put it? He goes out by himself?" She laughed.

"Well, he brings the boys along, the three of them are a posse. But, clearly, it's not my fault, the trouble they get into. My heart is pure."

"Your heart is pure bullshit, Joe, but you're funny." She laughed again. "I'm going to, uh, talk to your friend, see what he says about this. You don't mind, do you?"

"No, no, please, go ahead, you can, *talk*, to him all you want."

A couple hours later, Shauna said we needed to leave, because there was a security patrol coming through. The security people usually only turned on the big lights for a minute, to make sure nothing major was wrong. I could see their point, who would steal a truck on this planet? What would you do with it?

"I'll, uh, call you? Tomorrow?" Damn. Should have said that before I pulled my shirt and pants back on. In my defense, it was getting chilly in the truck, now that I was out of the bed.

"Call me? You'll call me?"

"Or, text you?" I said slowly, wary that I'd done something wrong.

"You'll *call* me? Huh." She was unhappy about something. "I'd like to be mad at you, but you're so darned goofy cute."

"True, it's a curse. You know, I don't want you to think I'm, uh, you know?"

"What? That you're using me for sex? Joe, I'm not some silly high school girl. *I'm* using *you* for sex."

"Oh."

"Is that a problem?"

"No! No, not a problem at all," I lied. It was, maybe, a tiny bit of a problem, for my ego. Yeah, I know, this would be a dream situation for most guys, unless they were completely honest with themselves about it. A guys likes to know that he meant something to a girl, even if she was a one-night stand.

Yeah, it's a male ego thing. Sue me.

"Listen, Joe, we're on an alien planet," she said, her voice muffled by the blanket over her head, as she wriggled into her pants while still nice and warm under the blanket. I wish I'd thought of that. "We don't know where we'll be going next, you and I could be posted to different planets next friggin' week. I'm busting my ass to qualify for combat duty, I want to make a difference in this war, that's what I'm focusing on now. I don't have time for a boyfriend. You don't have time for a girlfriend. I like you, you like me, girls get horny and you're pretty good in the sack. No commitments. Can we keep it uncomplicated?"

"Oh, uh," that brightened up my day again, now that I understood, "sure. Yes. Yes!"

"Great." She swung her legs out from the blanket, stuffed her feet into her boots, hopped to her feet, and kissed me on the cheek. "I'll call *you*."

That kind of freaked me out.

Then, she did call two nights later, and we wore out the truck's springs.

It was awesome.

Any thoughts I had, that my amorous nocturnal adventures had gone unnoticed, went out the window at breakfast the next morning. Sergeant Koch had run us ragged over an obstacle course in the dark, I hadn't gotten enough sleep and the three of us were ravenously hungry.

"What is that?" Cornpone mumbled over a mouthful of food, pointing at Ski's bowl with a piece of toast.

I looked at it too. "Damn, Ski," I said, "what are you doing?" Instead of eggs, French toast, hash browns or anything good, he had one lonely, barely buttered piece of wheat toast, and a bowl of what appeared to be plain oatmeal. Plain, as in oats soaked in water. No raisins, no brown sugar, no walnuts, not even any cream. The kind of thing you serve to horses. Yum. "That looks like a bowl of, like, soggy.... *sadness*."

"A bowl of sadness." Cornpone choked he laughed so hard, spitting eggs onto his plate. "That's funny. Is Soggy Sadness a Kellogg's brand?"

"Seriously," I added, as Ski sat there stone-faced, "eating that must be like being a Cubs fan. Sure, once in a while, the Cubs will luck their way into a win, and it's like you find a marshmallow in the bowl, but, come on, you *know* by the end of the season you'll be choking down a bowl of sadness."

"Shut up." Ski growled, but there was a twinkle in his eye.

Cornpone slapped the table. "Bish, damn, you're killing me here."

I offered a slice of French toast to Ski, but he waved it away with a frown. "No, man, that meatloaf last night had an argument with my stomach, I need something bland after that obstacle course."

"Oh, yeah, the meatloaf. What was that gravy?" Cornpone shook his head. "10W-40 motor oil, tasted like."

"No, I think it was hydraulic fluid hamsters use on those Buzzards. Yummy," I licked my lips, "mystery meat floating in an oily pool of hydraulic fluid."

"Uh huh," Cornpone agreed while spooning hash browns into his mouth. "And when the oily gravy starts getting cold, it gets that rubbery skin on top, and it-"

"Oh." Ski's face was turning green. He pushed the oatmeal away. "Guys, shut up, please, I'm gonna lose it."

Busting each other's balls was a key part of being in a fireteam, we also knew when to quit. Last thing Cornpone and I wanted was for Ski to ralph all over the breakfast table, that would make us real popular in the platoon. Not. "Here," I took two slices of wheat toast from Cornpone and put them on Ski's plate, "this will fill you up. We got a busy morning." The schedule called for an hour on the rifle range, then the platoon was hiking twelve miles, finding our way to five navigation points before a lunch break. This was part of our preparation for a major combined arms war game in a week, where we were hoping to show the Kristang what badass soldiers we humans were in simulated combat. Part of the war game scenario, which was still being developed, included simulated orbital bombardment, and humans flying captured Ruhar aircraft against Kristang dropships. UNEF would be the Blue team defending the planet, and the Kristang would be the Red team invaders, with the Kristang force playing the part of the Ruhar; using Ruhar tactics.

A couple slices of bland toast in Ski's stomach made him feel better, enough for him to steal a piece of French toast off my plate. He was feeling better enough to ask "hey, Bish, that girl Shauna, you hittin' that?"

"Yeah," Cornpone elbowed me in the ribs, "what's the deal?"

They almost made choke on a mouthful of hash browns. "The deal? The deal is, first, she's a woman, not a girl-"

"You know what I mean." Cornpone wasn't going to get distracted from the subject.

"-and she's none of your business. We bumped into each other at dinner, and we talked. It's no big deal."

"You talked with a real, live, actual girl. You may have *touched* a real girl. That is a big deal." Ski objected.

Cornpone "Bish, you know what? I heard that across UNEF, only sixteen percent of the force are women. Sixteen percent! That means for every guy, there's like, uh, for every girl, there's like, uh, four guys!"

"I think you need to check your math, there, Jesse," Ski cut in. "The point, Bish, is that with those odds, we're kinda desperate, and if *any* guy on this planet is getting laid, we at least want details."

"I am *not* giving you details."

"Aha!" Cornpone slapped the table, drawing looks from others around us. "There *are* details."

Shit. I'd screwed that up. "Guys, hypothetically, some guy on this planet is, let's say, enjoying the company of a lady. Do you think it will improve the odds of other guys getting lucky if he talks about it? Or if he keeps his mouth shut? Huh? You think the women on this planet would be happy about some guy bragging about the details?"

"Damn it," Ski groused, "he's right."

"You can brag about getting laid, or you can actually get laid. It's real simple." I concluded.

"Damn. Hell, in that case," Cornpone said grumpily and reached out with his fork, "I'm taking the rest of your French toast."

My zPhone beeped one morning while I was on the rifle range, it was a message from my platoon, ordering me to report to a Captain Andrews on the other side of the base. Andrews commanded a company in another battalion of our brigade. The message didn't say 'on the double', that was implied. When I found the tent Andrews was using as company HQ, I stepped inside and saluted. "Specialist Bishop reporting as ordered, sir."

"Bishop," he barely looked up from his laptop, "at ease. I'm sure you know we left Earth without a full complement; if people couldn't get to Ecuador by the departure date, they got left behind."

I nodded. Transportation to Ecuador had, ironically, been more difficult than transport up to orbit and across the stars. Because of manpower shortages, we had sergeants in charge of squads, staff sergeants filling in for first sergeants, lieutenants acting as captains, etc. The other fireteam in my own squad had only three soldiers, and the battalion had scraped together new squads from understrength units. Overall, the 10th Division had fourteen percent less manpower than authorized, and that didn't even count the field artillery battalions that had been deliberately left behind. Or most of the sustainment brigade that had also been left behind, so we didn't have our combat engineers with us. It was a big problem that Division was still sorting out.

"I've got your personnel file here," Andrews continued, and my face fell.

I'd seen my personnel file, the original one on paper, still in official Army triplicate. Coming out of Nigeria, it said 'bad attitude' on it, all capital letters, and it's underlined twice. There isn't even a smiley face as the dot over the 'i' in 'attitude', so you know it's serious. I hoped Captain Andrews wasn't going to underline it again, and circle it with a big angry face. Running frantically through my memory, I couldn't think of anything I'd screwed up more than usual since we left Earth. Balanced against my alleged bad attitude was a Purple Heart that explained the scars on my left arm, and paperwork started to award a Bronze Star. That paperwork had stopped at the brigade level, which I could understand considering the circumstances. I appreciated the gesture anyway.

"You know Staff Sergeant Agnelli?" He asked, and I nodded again, then he said something unexpected. "There's an opening for a sergeant in his squad, and you've been recommended." He didn't say who had recommended me. "It's yours if you want it. We don't have time, or resources, for a regular training program, so you'll learn on the job. If you're interested, report to Agnelli, and I'll handle the paperwork."

Shit. I didn't know if I was ready to command a fireteam, three guys I didn't know. Andrews cleared his throat. "That was me waiting for an answer, Bishop. I know this is unusual, we don't have time for the normal process out here."

"Oh, yes, sir. Thank you. I mean, yes, I'm honored. Yes." Promotions were supposed to be a more formal process; I was taken completely by surprise. The Division had holes that needed to be filled.

"Uh huh." He sounded less than convinced. "Agnelli will keep you out of trouble. And, Bishop?"

"Yes?"

"Stay away from ice cream trucks." He wasn't smiling.

Taking command of a new fireteam wasn't the most difficult part of my promotion, my three guys all had experience in Nigeria and knew what to do without me needing to tell them much. Staff Sergeant Agnelli was patient with me and, other than the administrative part of the job that was overwhelming at first, I didn't have much trouble adjusting. The Army didn't have time to put me through the standard training, which saved me from memorizing a bunch of crap, and I'm sure that would come back to bite me in the ass later. The most difficult part of being promoted was leaving my old unit; Sergeant Koch, Ski, and especially Cornpone. Cornpone had a tear in his eye, which he said was caused by blowing sand, and my eyes teared up too. "Damn," Cornpone said, "think how much stupid stuff you get into when I'm around. What are you going to do without me? And the Army put you in charge of a fireteam?" He shook his head sadly.

"If I see an ice cream truck, I'll run the other way."

He snorted. "Bish, that takes care of, like, ten percent of the problem. You get into a situation; you should think 'what would Jesse do'?"

"And then do the opposite?" I laughed.

He made an exaggerated shrug, then gave me a back-pounding hug. "Take care of yourself, and don't forget to write."

I pulled out my zPhone. "Write? With this thing, I can see your ugly face whenever I want."

"Oh, damn," he rolled his eyes, "I forgot about that." He pulled out his zPhone. "How do I block people from calling?"

The Kristang didn't have faster than light communication, but the US Army rumor mill did. "*Sergeant* Bishop?" Shauna was the first person to call me about my promotion. "Man, they'll promote anybody."

"True enough."

"Seriously, good for you, Bish."

"Confession? I have no idea what I'm doing."

"Bish, we'll be fighting *aliens*. Nobody knows how to do this. We'll make it up as we go."

Damn, it was good hearing from her. Which reminded me, I needed to review the Army regs about fraternization, Shauna wasn't under my command, she was in a different battalion. Did that mean I was Ok to continue being with her? I sure hoped so.

My new squad was led by Staff Sergeant Salvatore Agnelli, who despite the name had blonde hair and looked more German than Italian. In my fireteam, I lucked out, and both Agnelli and I knew it. Privates Chen and Baker, and Specialist Sanchez, were all veterans of Nigeria, and Sanchez had served briefly in Korea before that. Greg Chen was an ABC from suburban Maryland, he had to explain that ABC meant American Born Chinese, since I had no idea what he meant. Jeron Baker was raised on a farm in Alabama, which he was immensely proud of, and he was immensely grateful to get away from. And Pete Sanchez was from eastern Kansas, his parents had a small farm but his mother worked as a nurse and his father at a car dealership, their farm not being big enough to provide a living for a family. Their previous sergeant was now a staff sergeant, leading a squad in 2nd Brigade. We got off to a great start when none of them made a Barney joke, or asked about or seemed in any way curious about what I'd done the first time I saw a Ruhar. They'd read all about it, it was ancient history, and it didn't mean squat now. The four of us got to know each other in drills and combat exercises over the next week, I was collapsing in bed each night completely exhausted, and I hadn't been happier in a long time. I had a great team, and we were honing ourselves for battle with an enemy that had threatened our home planet. What we needed was a real mission.

Eight days after my promotion to sergeant, our brigade received orders to deploy. I'd been scrambling to get up to speed for the next war game, Operation Razor, in ten days. We got the news from Captain Teller, who assembled the company in an empty hangar on the edge of the base. He stood on a platform at the far end, with us crowding forward to hear him. "People, we have an opportunity."

Chen groaned and whispered "BOHICA, man." Bend Over Here It Comes Again was a popular saying in the Army, especially when an officer said we had an 'opportunity'. It usually meant we were getting screwed one way or another, hence the time-honored expression.

Teller waited a moment for the inevitable murmuring to die down. "We have an opportunity to put our new toys into action, and do something useful in this war. UNEF received orders, we move out in two days and a wake-up. First Brigade is going in with one British and one French battalion. UNEF is all in on this one, everybody's going. The whole force is bugging out over the next two weeks."

A guy in the front spoke up. "What's the mission, Captain, we gonna kick some rodent ass?" The question was asked with deadly seriousness.

Teller made a face like he'd just bit into a lemon. "No, the Kristang say we're not ready for that. I've seen Kristang battle simulations, and they're right, we're not ready. We'd just get in the way. Most combat happens in orbit, or further out, and since we don't have a space navy, we can't help there. The Kristang have retaken a colony world they lost to the Ruhar a while back, they're kicking the Ruhar off the planet. They've reached a truce, the deal allows the Ruhar to evacuate their civilian population over a thirteen month period, it will take thirteen months, because there are almost a million Ruhar there now. Our job is to occupy the planet, and facilitate the evacuation."

This news did not please the Company

"Garrison duty?!"

"Shit. We're gonna be peacekeepers."

"We have to wear freakin' blue helmets?"

Teller held his hands in the air, until we quieted down. "I came out here to fight the Ruhar, just like you, to kill those rat-faced MFers. I don't get to do whatever I want, I'm in the Army. Our job out here is to protect Earth, and since we sure as hell demonstrated we can't do that by ourselves, the best way for us to protect the folks back home is to work with our allies. The Kristang are stretched pretty thin right now, they don't have many troops to spare to hold the places they've captured. That's why they asked for infantry. There's some sort of biological hazard on this planet that prevents the Kristang from landing in force right away, the Kristang say the Ruhar are cheating on Rule Number Four. The Ruhar say the virus or whatever, is left behind from back when the Kristang occupied the planet. That's for them to argue about. Bottom line is the Kristang can't land their troops on this planet unless they're wearing full environment suits, and that ain't happening. Until the Kristang can develop an antidote to the virus and distribute it in quantity, UNEF is going to be fully in charge on the ground. This is a job we can do, and we're going to do it to the best of our ability. Those are our orders."

"What's the R-O-E, sir?" A loud voice from the back asked about the Rules Of Engagement.

"No shooting, unless they shoot first. Whether we like them or not, the Ruhar on this planet are mostly farmers, and that includes women and children. The Kristang tell us not to expect much opposition, the Ruhar civvies should be happy to be alive and allowed to go home." There was a lot of grumbling from Able Company. Teller didn't flinch. "This is a test; in case you haven't figured that out yet. So far, all the Kristang have seen from humans is us dying, without inflicting much damage on the Ruhar." He paused, frowned, and continued. "In double-U double-U Two," he pronounced the words precisely, "the US Army didn't hit the Normandy beaches in their first battle. We landed in North Africa first, and those of you who know your history, know that's a damned good thing. We were completely unready to take on the Germans in 1942, if we'd landed in Normandy first, we would have gotten our asses kicked back across the Channel. By fighting in North Africa, and Sicily, and Italy, we learned how to fight the Germans, learned what worked. The Kristang have given us a few shiny new toys to fight with, that doesn't mean we know the best tactics to use them against the Ruhar in ground combat. The Kristang have trusted us with what should be a simple job, we can *not* screw this up. We take control of the planet, we move the Ruhar civvies to the space elevators and get their furry butts off the planet, and we secure the place, until the Kristang sort things out upstairs and can land their own troops. We are going to show the Kristang that the United Nations Expeditionary Forces are disciplined, competent, and ready to take on combat operations in the future. Platoon leaders, I want your squads ready for departure inspection at 1400 hours the day after tomorrow. Are there any more questions?"

I spoke up. "Sir, where are we going, and what can we expect for conditions?" I wanted to know as much as possible about what my new fireteam would be getting into.

"The short answer is we're going to Bum Fuck Neptune." The smile only lifted one side of his mouth. "Oxygen-nitrogen atmosphere, a bit more oxygen than we're used to. Gravity was two percent heavier than Earth. The star is hotter than our Sun, but the planet is further away, so the climate is similar to Earth; hot at the equator, ice caps at the poles. It's mostly a farming colony, the Ruhar call the place Gehtanu, which translates roughly as New Grain Field, or something like that." That drew a chuckle from the crowd. "The Kristang call it Pradassis. We're calling it Paradise. It's got one big–ass continent, a couple island chains and big islands like Greenland size, the rest is ocean. Our PowerPoint Rangers put together a briefing deck, which your platoon leaders should have on tablets to distribute, it says the main continent is largely flat grasslands, like the US Great Plains, or the Russian steppes. Lots of big farms tended partly by robots, with the Ruhar clustered in villages. All the intel we have will be available on your notepads shortly, I need everyone to study up during the flight. The whole 10th Division, plus our British and French friends, will be loading on three transport ships, and the trip will take sixteen days. After we drop, the Kristang will keep a destroyer plus two frigates in orbit for fire support, but this is our show. General Meers has assured the Kristang that we can handle this, we are not going to prove him wrong."

Shauna pinged me before I could contact her. "You hear? We're moving out!"
"Yeah, we're going to Paradise."
"Paradise!" She laughed. We hadn't been together since my promotion to sergeant, we'd both been too busy and I was way too tired. It hit me then that I might never see her again, once we left our base on Camp Alpha, we'd probably be on different transport ships, then assigned to different sites scattered across the surface of Paradise.

"Hey, uh, good luck on qualifying for infantry." I didn't want to call to end, and I didn't know what to say.

"Thanks, that'll have to wait until we get there." There were loud voices in the background. "Joe, I have to go, let's keep in touch?"

"Sure." And that was it. At least we'd be on the same planet.

You might think that 'two days and a wakeup' means we had two full days, plus a luxurious full night of sleep, before we had to assemble for departure. You would be wrong. The 'wakeup' happened at zero dark stupid, it felt like my head had barely hit the pillow before lights snapped on in the tent, and my feet had to hit the dirt. Getting up at zero dark thirty was nothing new to me, and I didn't resent it even though I was not by nature a morning person. Or even a mid-morning person. My sister was an annoyingly cheerful morning person, and growing up I'd wanted to smother her with a pillow more than once.

Anyway, I had to get up at zero dark stupid, which meant I then had to wake up my fireteam. The difference between zero dark thirty and zero dark stupid, is that zero dark stupid means you rouse out of bed, get all your gear ready and assemble for departure inspection, only to stand around for *three Goddamn hours* when you could have used those three hours for something productive, like sleeping. As a sergeant now, I had to endure the resentful glares from my team while keeping a neutral expression on my face.

The whole departure was a clusterfuck. The Kristang wanted their dropships loaded as quickly and efficiently as possible, which meant cramming the maximum number of people aboard in a frantic rush, even if that meant splitting up platoons, squads or even fireteams. When we finally boarded a dropship, Baker and Chen had their feet in the door when the MP held out a hand to stop anyone else from boarding. "We're full, move on to the next ship," she announced.

I frantically yanked Baker and Chen back out by hauling on their packs, and waved another two guys forward. Hell, no way was I going to let my new fireteam get split up right after we'd met. You'd think we would be first in line to board the next dropship, but the MPs keeping us organized had other ideas, and several dropships lifted off before we were waved forward. Being aboard a dropship wasn't the last of the confusion, when our dropship docked and we got aboard the Kristang starship, we discovered we were not only aboard a different ship from the rest of our platoon, but most of the ship was occupied by the US Army 3rd Infantry Division, not our home unit the 10th. The ship had people from the 3rd, the 10th, most of a company of US Marines, more than a full company of Chinese, two squads of Brits and a scattering of Indian troops. Either the Kristang didn't understand the concept of combat loading, or they had so little regard for human combat capabilities that they figured it didn't matter whether our units were scattered all over hell and gone. Supposedly UNEF HQ was keeping track of who was where, but I had no way to contact anyone in my chain of command. I got us to bunk with some other people from the 10th. It was a lonely voyage, and I was grateful that my guys shrugged and took it in stride. If this was the worst screwup we got into, we'd be doing great.

CHAPTER FOUR   PARADISE

Unlike Alpha, Paradise had a space elevator. It looked a bit different from the one that hovered over Earth, someone told me this one was put there by the Ruhar. That surprised me, I figured the Ruhar elevator would have taken a hit during the battle when the Kristang had retaken the planet. Maybe targeting space elevators was against one of the unwritten Rules? Or maybe it was just practical; the people trying to conquer a planet wouldn't want to damage a valuable asset, and the defenders figured, even if they lost that battle, they could try taking the planet back again someday? The Ruhar elevator rode a lightning bolt like the one on Earth did, but whereas the Thuranin elevator 'cable' was pure energy, the Ruhar design had a physical cable, thinner than a human hair, in the center of the lightning bolt. Because of this, the Ruhar didn't have any vital facilities on the equator of Paradise; if that cable ever snapped, it could wrap itself around the planet several times, and crash down with a considerable impact despite the small mass. We were told the cable had explosive charges along its length, to make it less of a disaster if the cable ever snapped or was cut, but for sure I didn't want to get stationed on the equator, I'd spend half my time looking warily at the sky.

The trip down the elevator to Paradise wasn't much different from the trip up from Earth, except there was no smiling Army cook serving delicious cheeseburgers, we had to settle for MREs again. And this elevator car had more windows, and the passenger compartment was easily three times the size of the one at Earth, I guess this one was designed primarily for civilian use. We got a good look at Paradise as we descended, and we descended pretty fast, there was a lot more vibration than I remember on my one other space elevator experience. Paradise looked good, at least it had a lot of green and blue, not the star-blasted dead browns and tans of Alpha. As the elevator car got close enough so I could see the outlines of villages, it occurred to me that I would soon be setting foot on my third planet. And this would be my first planet that was enemy territory, even if that enemy had already surrendered to the Kristang. Getting low enough so individual buildings were distinctive, I touched the new sergeant's stripes on my sleeves. This place was a home of my enemy, the aliens who had attacked Earth. Not that I needed any extra motivation, but at that moment, I was filled with determination to do everything I could to get the Ruhar off this planet on schedule, and show our saviors the Kristang that humans could be entrusted with more important tasks in the future. And if any damned hamsters got in my way, well, I'd remember the rules of engagement, but I wasn't taking any crap from the hamsters. I would show them the same courtesy they showed us, when they sneak attacked Earth and destroyed much of our electric generation capability.

When the elevator car landed with a gentle thump, we were hustled off as quickly as we could move. It wasn't ten minutes after the last of us cleared the fence line around the elevator complex, that a series of alarm blasts rang out, and the car ascended again to pick up the next group in orbit. I watched it, craning my neck, still amazed, as the guards hurried us along to an airstrip, where there was a line of the biggest airplanes I'd ever seen. The guards called them 'Dumbos', because of their large body and relatively small wings. They had four engines, buried inside the wings near the roots, and they were probably six times the size of the US Air Force C-17s I'd gotten used to. Dumbos needed only a short runway, but they couldn't take off straight up, that took too much power to be practical in a heavy lifter. While I was watching, one lined up and took off, its engines screaming, and I swear the thing was airborne in less than four hundred yards. The engine exhaust could pivot down to help get it off the ground, then the wings took over to provide lift. Anything that big, moving that slowly through the air, made me think there must be an invisible string holding it up. Like Buzzards, Dumbos were leftover Ruhar equipment that we humans were expected to use, until the Kristang took over.

We were supposed to assemble by platoon, except my fireteam was alone. I managed to keep my fireteam together, it wasn't difficult, and after a while I learned where we were supposed to go to eventually link up with our platoon. Once staff sergeants counted noses in squads, then platoons and then at the company level, we waited. And waited. And waited some more, in the hot sun. We must have waited for an hour, as other platoons and companies marched past us onto Dumbos, and as Dumbos landed, loaded and took off again. I could see Chickens and Buzzards circling the airfield in the distance, they were already a familiar sight from Alpha. The blessing was whatever material the tarmac was made from was a light tan color, and didn't bake in the heat the way dark-colored asphalt would have on Earth. After an hour, with my fireteam being on their best behavior for their new sergeant, we finally marched halfway across the airfield, past a couple empty waiting Dumbos, to our Dumbo. It was good to see the US Army was just as awesomely efficient and organized on other planets as it was on Earth. We all crammed together on uncomfortable seats made of lightweight netting, and sat down to wait again. There was cool air blasting out of vents in the front of the cabin, by the time the air got to us in the back, it was as hot and humid like the air outside. Some kind of commotion was going on at the back ramp, with a captain pointing at a tablet and arguing with a lieutenant. The lieutenant shook his head at the captain, and walked toward us, clearly unhappy. He got close enough for me to read 'Koenig' on his name tag, and I stood up and saluted. "What's going on, sir?"

"Charlie Foxtrot." He muttered. Another typical Cluster Fuck. "They say we're on the wrong bird, we'll get it sorted out."

Whatever the problem was, five minutes later the doors slammed closed, and we started rolling. Everyone cheered. The word got passed down that we should relax, and get settled in for a two hour supersonic flight. The pilot made an announcement when we settled into cruise speed, which was around Mach 1.4. Even having traveled faster than light, going through wormholes, and going down from, and back up to orbit in a shuttle, that speed impressed me. Then it hit me that the announcement was a human voice. I leaned over to a second lieutenant sitting next to me. "Sir, who's flying this thing?"

He yawned. "Some Air Force pukes."

"Uh, how much flight training did they get?" I asked slowly, not wanting to hear the answer I expected. On Earth, C-17 drivers had years of training before they qualified for even the right-hand copilot seat. No way could these guys have more than a couple weeks flying time. In a totally unfamiliar, gigantic aircraft.

"Nothing to worry about, sergeant," he said, although I noted he wasn't looking at me when he said it. "There's a computer than does most of the flying, and a Kristang in orbit can take over and land this thing remotely if needed. The guys up front are there to make coffee."

I didn't laugh.

The flight was uneventful, except it ended in a landing so abrupt it made me think the pilot was Navy, not Air Force, and he was trying to land our Dumbo on an aircraft carrier. Then I saw the 'airfield', which was a dirt field, a field that had contained some sort of crops recently, before the land was cleared for airplanes. Without much waiting around, we were marched across the field to a rank of waiting Buzzards. I was excited, eager for a ride in the unfamiliar aircraft. Thirty of us crammed into a Buzzard. I wanted to sit in the doorway, legs hanging out into the air, rifle on my lap as the Buzzard roared low across the landscape. The copilot quickly straightened me out. "This bird isn't a Blackhawk, sergeant, we cruise around four hundred miles an hour when we get to altitude. If you want to hang out the door, go ahead, but shut it behind you."

I found a seat, a staff sergeant was grinning at me, but he later told me he'd been thinking of doing the same thing. The flight in the Buzzard was also uneventful, much smoother than any helicopter I'd flown in, and we flew across endless farmland and scattered forests and lakes, until we circled a village and set down.

When the door of the Buzzard popped open, we smelled it. You know the scent of new-mown hay, or, if you've lived in the suburbs, freshly cut grass? That clean, fresh, invigorating scent, a scent of nature that reminds you of childhood, of running barefoot across a field, under bright blue heavens, with big puffy white clouds piled high in the sky? Yeah? This was not like that. The scent wafting from the hamster's field of, whatever the hell they ate, smelled vaguely of-

Baker sniffed, and wrinkled his nose. "Damn. What is that?"

It wasn't right there, in your face, it was more something at the back of your mind, or the back of your nose, a scent that makes you stop and try to identify it. I had a good memory for scents, but it took me a moment to figure it out, because it was close, but not quite right. "Parmesan cheese." I announced.

Not parmesan cheese as in, a big hot bowl of spaghetti on a cold winter night, with a couple juicy meatballs on top, and you've been smelling that tantalizing tomato sauce simmering on the stove all day, and you're sitting down with a slice of garlic bread and a glass of hearty red wine, and you sprinkle fresh parmesan on top, and it kind of melts into the sauce? Not that. This was parmesan cheese as in, you're already sick with like the flu or just an epic hangover, and your stomach is already on the edge, and you smell parmesan cheese that's been out of the fridge too long, and you know you're going to hurl. That's the parmesan cheese we smelled, coming from the fields.

"Parmesan- goddamn, it smells like Sanchez's feet!" Chen said disgustedly.

"My feet? You ever smell your own?"

"I wash my feet!"

"Once a year, maybe."

"All right, pipe down, you two." I ordered. "Maybe it's a chemical they spray on their crops, and it'll go away. Or we'll get used to it, and not even notice it anymore."

"Shit." Chen spat. "I been bunkin' with Sanchez for weeks, and I ain't got used to his stinky feet yet. If this whole planet smells like that, this is gonna to be a long deployment."

The rest of our platoon was already there, they'd set up a base in tents around a barn, the hamster town was half a kilometer to the East. I got my fireteam sorted out, and the first sergeant of the platoon told me to report to Lieutenant Charles in a tent.

I saluted smartly. "Sergeant Bishop, reporting as ordered, sir."

"Bishop, I expected your team this morning." He gave me a casual salute back, he seemed to be distracted. Establishing a platoon base on an alien planet had to give a guy headaches.

"Charlie Foxtrot loading the dropships at Alpha sir, the Kristang put us on the wrong starship. We're all here now, sir, Sergeant Agnelli is getting us squared away"

"Yeah, UNEF is scattered all over this planet. You made it here, that's what matters." He pointed to a map laid out on a table, a real map, printed on some sort of plastic. It showed about a tenth of the main continent, the part where we were right then. It was mostly farmland, flat farmland, with some low ridges running north-south, rivers and lakes here and there. The seacoast was off to the West, the space elevator base station somewhere off the map to the Southeast. "We're here in this region," he circled a finger around a gray shaded area, "the Ruhar call it, some damned thing," he pointed to the markings, which were in Ruhar script, "but we're calling it Butt-scratch-istan."

"Buttscratchistan?" I laughed.

He smiled. "The region to the north of us is Back-scratch-istan, so, to the South here must be Buttscratch, right? Your fireteam will occupy a village about a hundred kilometers west of here," he pointed to a tiny dot on the map. "The hamsters there are all farmers, population around two fifty if you count the surrounding farmsteads. There's a school, barns, a grain storage building, some houses, and that's about it."

One fireteam of four soldiers against over two hundred hamsters? I didn't like those odds. A fireteam didn't usually operate alone, two fireteams belonged to a squad, with a staff sergeant in charge. "Sir, how is one fireteam supposed to keep control of that many hamsters?"

"You're not. This is an experiment," he grimaced, "a bright idea from Division. We have company-size quick reaction teams scattered around, with Buzzards and Chickens, backed up by Kristang firepower in orbit," he glanced at the ceiling of the tent. "There's plenty of firepower available if we need it, what Division wants is to avoid needing it."

My shoulders slumped. "Hearts and minds?" That was the Army term for attempts to get the civilian population to cooperate with us, or at least not actively resist us. It had started in Vietnam, and continued in various forms and terminology in Iraq, Afghanistan, Nigeria and pretty much every place the US of A had gotten involved. We built schools, roads, water and power distribution systems, and helped plant and harvest crops. Long-term, it was cheaper and more effective to avoid making more enemies, than it was to kill enemies. Especially since the enemy you killed was someone's relative, and they, and probably their entire tribe, then became your enemy. If you know anything about history, you know these kinds of hearts and minds campaigns have, let's say, a mixed record. A month after we pulled out of a third world area, the schools got burned out, the water system blown up, and the power lines stolen for scrap copper. Our politicians declared victory anyway, and moved onto the next crisis. Hooah.

"More like soft power, Bishop. We're not going to build schools for these hamsters, we just want to keep things peaceful until they take the trip offworld. Think of it as your own little slice of Paradise." He added with a grin.

"Sir, I'm a new buck sergeant- "

"You're also a farmer, you grew up on a farm. Sanchez and Baker did too. These aliens may be hamsters, but they work the land, I'm hoping that gives you an understanding that some of our city boys won't have. This region is in the middle of the line to be evaced offworld, so there's more time for things to go wrong." He put a hand on my shoulder and squeezed reassuringly. "You don't have to be nice to these hamsters, but don't try to intimidate them. They've already agreed to leave the planet, the deal they have with the Kristang allows them to continue raising and harvesting crops right up until the evac is complete; the Ruhar are paying the Kristang to transport their crops. I know, it sounds crazy, but the Kristang have been fighting this war for a long time, and they know what they're doing. The Ruhar here want to keep those food shipments flowing, they should be well motivated to cooperate with us. If you get into trouble, whistle us on your zPhone, and we'll bring in the air cavalry. If it gets bad enough, the Kristang can hit any site you want from orbit, and the hamsters know it."

Again, I wasn't filled with confidence.

"Agnelli will be taking the other half of the squad to a village north of where you'll be. You're not an occupation force, UNEF is calling these units Embedded Observation Teams. G2 wants to know what's going on with the hamsters, at the local level. All the satellite and airborne surveillance in the galaxy won't tell us what's really happening on the ground, and a recon team passing through once in a while won't tell us enough. We need people on the ground, living among the hamsters. There's a complete set of guides for EOTs on your tablet. It would be best to get you some training, but Division wants everyone in place ASAP to establish a presence, before the hamsters get any stupid ideas that UNEF can be pushed around."

"Yes, sir. We've got this." I didn't have to like it. That's why they are called 'orders' and not 'suggestions'.

When I got to the area the platoon was using as a motor pool, my confidence dropped even lower. "What in *the* hell is this thing?" I asked.

"It's a hamvee, Sergeant." The grinning mechanic announced.

"A what?"

"We call it a hamvee, it's like the old Humvee on Earth, only it's leftover hamster vehicles. We take any type of hamster truck, glue composite panels on for hillbilly armor, and you get a hamvee." He looked proud of the piece of crap he expected us to patrol around in. Barney's ice cream truck looked more capable. If you took an SUV, added big but flimsy looking tires, thick screens over the windows, and multicolor panels attached haphazardly here and there, you'd have something almost as ugly.

"Glue?"

"Yup. Can't weld it on, because it's not metal. We use this Kristang glue," he held up a caulking gun like you'd find at any hardware store on Earth, "apply the panels to the hamvee with this dingus, then use this fancy Kristang doodad," it looked like an iron, "to set the glue. Incredibly strong stuff."

"Dingus? Doodad? You're not impressing me."

He shrugged. "The Kristang have names for all this stuff, but it's hard to pronounce."

"Is there anything heavier?" I asked, as I skeptically ran my fingers over the farmer armor panel, which felt like Styrofoam to me. It was about four inches thick, tapering down at the edges of the doors, which had to be a weak point. If Styrofoam had a strong point anywhere.

"We have hamtraks, kind of like a Bradley, or a Stryker 'cause it has wheels, they're hamster military personnel carriers. Those are for company level use. Don't worry, I've seen a demo of this armor," he rapped the Styrofoam with his knuckles, "and regular bullets only dent the surface. You have to hit it in the same place a couple times, with an explosive round, to punch through. Tough stuff. We should bring some of this shit back to Earth with us."

"A demo? Are you joining us on patrol, the first time we get shot at?"

He shook his head and grinned. "Not my MOS, Sergeant. You guys have fun, and don't scratch the paint. Private Ringold here will show you how to drive them, and keep the powercells charged."

Columbus Day

After we picked up our pair of hamvees, we went over to the supply depot to get all the equipment we would need for our EOT assignment. The 'supply depot' was in what looked like, and smelled like, a former chicken coop. First, we got personal gear; extra uniforms, body armor, all the crap a well-dressed human soldier occupying an alien planet needs. Next, ammo and heavy weapons, which meant Javelin Bravo missiles, and our old familiar light unguided anti-tank weapon, the 84MM Swedish AT4-CS. Here we were, on an alien planet, bad-ass conquerors, and we were equipped with weapons I'd used against militia nutcases in Nigeria. This was unsat, in my opinion. Nobody asked for my opinion.

The next morning, we were ready to depart. First Sergeant Mitchell came to see us off. "You squared away, Bishop?"

"If I said this was November Golf," which was No Go in Army slang, "would it make any difference?"

Mitchell laughed. "The LT wouldn't send you out if he didn't have total confidence in you, Bishop. So, Alpha Mike Foxtrot to you." Adios Mother Fucker, is what he meant. I didn't reply.

We rolled toward our assigned village, trailing a cloud of dust that drifted high in the breeze, giving away our position to anyone who cared to look. As we approached the village, we came to a low rise, and I called a halt to our column. 'Column' was an exaggeration, we had two hamvees, me and Sanchez in front in a sort of SUV thing, and Baker and Chen behind in a pickup truck. Both vehicles were loaded with gear, including what the platoon thought was enough consumables (meaning everything from food and medicine to toilet paper) to sustain four men for a month. We also had a standard load of rifle ammo, both regular and explosive-tipped. Plus, two Javelin Bravos and a pair of AT-4s. No mortars; if we needed any sort of stand-off weapons, we were supposed to call the air cav. The first sergeant assured me we'd get regular visits from the platoon HQ, and supplies every two weeks. If the first sergeant was as skeptical about this 'soft power' concept as I was, he kept his feelings to himself. Personally, I gave this experiment less than a month before Division, or UNEF HQ, came to their senses. Having part of our forces thinly scattered across the planet was inviting the hamsters to defeat us in detail, which means each small unit could be overwhelmed piecemeal. If that happened, the hamsters would eventually get pounded from orbit by the Kristang, but that would be of little comfort to any dead humans.

As pre-arranged, a pair of Chickens flying overwatch buzzed the village low and fast, to get the attention of the resident hamsters. The Chickens had their weapons pods open, and after they buzzed the main street, they broke formation and climbed, with one providing cover to the north and one hovering over us. I glanced once more at the intel package on my lap. Satellite photos, reports from a recon column that had passed through the village two days before, and records from the hamster regional government. According to their records, the current population was 178 hamsters, down from the estimate of 250 I'd gotten from the platoon. Our arrival should have been no surprise, as the hamster government said they'd contacted the villagers to alert them to our approach, and to urge cooperation. We also had plastic-laminated sign boards, printed in Ruhar script, that we were supposed to post in prominent locations around the village. The signs, supposedly, listed regulations like curfew hours, prohibitions against carrying weapons, and what the hamsters were to do in order to accommodate us. The idea of putting up posters made me uncomfortable, it felt vaguely like some heavy-handed thing the Nazis or Soviets would do when they occupied a village.

I signaled the Chicken pilot we were ready, and told Sanchez to get rolling. Our bad-ass hamvees cruised into the village on nearly silent electric motors, tires crunching on dirt and gravel, slowing down as we reached the first building, the official start of the village. The village wasn't much to look at, although being from a small rural town myself, I appreciated that the buildings, both houses and barns, were neat and in good order. Houses had shade trees, shrubs and flowers, fences and barns were well-kept. I'd have expected the hamsters to let things slip, forget about maintenance and things like planting flowers, since they were all going to be evacuating the planet. I expected graffiti, like 'humans go home' or something like that. Instead, I saw signs the hamsters were planning to be here for a while, including a barn that was in the process of having the roof replaced. Were the Ruhar unable to accept that they'd lost the planet, or did they know something UNEF didn't know? Either way, it was going into my first sitrep back to platoon HQ.

Sanchez was from eastern Kansas, he remarked that the village, the fields and the countryside reminded him of home. It reminded me of small town home, too. The houses were neat but not fancy, each house had a barn or workshop behind it. Back home, such houses would have a sign out front advertising the hundreds of side jobs rural people did to make ends meet. Honest work like selling fresh eggs, welding, small engine repair, hair cutting, log splitting, child care. My father thought you could combine tasks, like log splitting and child care. No more lazy kids sitting around with coloring books or playing with Legos, my father would say "you kids better have those three cords of wood split and stacked by five o'clock, or no juice boxes for you. And no crying if you hit your foot with the maul, walk it off. It's just a flesh wound." I may be exaggerating a bit.

There were vehicles in the road or fields and, even though they were clearly alien, they also reminded me of home. Every vehicle had a dented fender, or a body panel that was a different color. These were working vehicles, for working people. My kind of people. Except they were aliens, and they had attacked Earth without provocation. Now that I thought about it, I hoped neither of our two hamvees had been commandeered from this particular village, that would make for an awkward situation.

A male hamster walked partly into the street ahead of us and waved, in what I hoped was a friendly, or at least non-threatening, manner. I could tell he was male, because the fur on his face was a light downy coat all over; females had facial fur almost too fine to see. Also, males had bigger whiskers.

He was wearing overalls. Blue, denim-type bib overalls, with patches on the knees, an outfit identical to several my father wore for working around the house. And a straw sort of baseball cap, with a wide brim. The hat had a logo, was it a hamster sports team, or a seed business, maybe the logo of the company that made the tractors in the fields? I called a halt, got out, and told Sanchez to stay put, with the engine running. My rifle was on the seat, I had my sidearm, but otherwise was unarmed. Hearts and minds, I told myself, hearts and minds. See if we can start things off peacefully; I could get rough later if needed, but a rough start was hard to overcome. Besides, the pair of Chickens, weapon pods bristling, were hovering in plain sight, ready for action.

My zPhone was already set for Ruhar, I held up one hand, and said simply "Hello."

The hamster spoke into his own sort of zPhone type device. "Hello. Welcome to Teskor. Teskor is our village."

Columbus Day

So the name of the place was 'Teskor', or that's what the translation sounded like. We hadn't been able to read the Ruhar script on the map. I pointed to my chest. "I am Joe Bishop." My rank I left out, not sure if 'sergeant' would be meaningful to aliens.

The hamster nodded. "I am called Lester Cornhut."

"Lester Cornhut?" I asked, surprised, I swear to God, that's what the translator said in my ear. We'd been told that names were not translated, so the sound of 'Teskor' and 'Lester Cornhut' came through just the way he said them, in the slightly squeaky Ruhar voice.

The hamster said "yes", and smiled.

Baker asked me on the tactical channel "Did he just say his name is Lester Cornhut, or Cornhole?"

"Cornhut," I replied, with the translator function paused, "there's a 'T' sound on the end of it." The four of us got a good chuckle, and agreed that 'Cornhut' was an excellent name for a hamster farmer. I turned the translator back on. "You are the leader of this village, the leader of Teskor?"

"No leader, no government here." He pointed from one end of the village to the other, I guess he meant a place that small didn't need any form of government. "I was chosen to speak with you. We will cooperate as instructed by," my translator made the humming sound it did when it didn't understand something, "and we hope your time in Teskor is pleasant. This is a good place."

Enemy species or not, Lester hadn't personally attacked Earth, may not have ever heard of our home planet. Hearts and minds, I told myself. We had a brief discussion, confirming he understood the date the people of Teskor would leave for the trip to the space elevator, and that we would be commandeering a farmstead on the outskirts of town. Lester told me they had already cleaned the place in preparation for our arrival, the family who had lived there lost a son when the Kristang took the planet back, and had moved away months ago to live with relatives. We put up our posters, drove to the other end of town and back, and then drove out to our makeshift Command Post. All in all, our entrance to the village was anticlimactic. After we got to the house where we'd be staying, I waved the Chickens off, and we started unpacking our hamvees. I left like we were children playing House. I sent a message to Shauna, but it didn't connect, possibly she hadn't landed yet.

That first night, I couldn't sleep much, I was too pumped up about my first command, even if it was only leading an experienced fireteam on a recon mission. Setting up our Command Post, I felt like a real sergeant, a leader. I took the first watch, and let the guys sleep, and toward the morning, I got up as sleep was elusive, and relieved Baker so he could get a bit more shut-eye. In addition to being excited, I was nervous; if the hamsters were going to do anything hostile, they were likely to do it our first night, before we got fully settled in with surveillance systems and ranged fields of fire around the CP. To keep watch, we had set up a ladder so we could climb up onto the roof of the house, that's where I was early that morning. The roof had the advantage of an excellent 360 degree view, it had the disadvantage that the person keeping watch was totally exposed to sniper fire. Our zPhones had a nifty feature that, if the person the zPhone was assigned to died, as in their heart stopped, the zPhone would alert anyone nearby. Which gave me the great comfort, as I sat exposed on the roof, that if a sniper picked me off, my fireteam wouldn't be taken by surprise.

UNEF thought Embedded Observation Teams of a four man fireteam, off by themselves in the middle of nowhere, were a great idea. Sitting on the exposed rooftop, in the wee hours of the morning, I was not so sure we weren't simply sitting ducks. In the early morning, when a person's thoughts can match the enveloping darkness, I wondered whether UNEF was hoping vulnerable EOTs would be attacked, as an excuse to show the Kristang what humans could do in combat. Lord knows the US Army had sent me out on patrols in Nigeria that seemed to have no point, other than exposing us to IEDs and sniper fire. It wasn't the Army family that I didn't trust, it was the politicians giving orders. Folks back home would be more excited hearing about humans in combat, than hearing about UNEF performing garrison duties that didn't generate headlines. Politicians certainly loved headlines.

Still, it was peaceful in Teskor. So peaceful, so quiet, sitting up there on top of the roof. Peaceful, and dark. With the planet so sparsely settled, there wasn't a lot of light pollution, Teskor seemed pretty dark at night, with no street lights, and only a single dim light here and there at the front or back of houses. I hadn't experienced darkness like this since I left electricity-starved northern Maine. Our base at Camp Alpha had been lit by floodlights at night, blanking out much of the sky. Here, sitting on a rooftop in the tiny village of Teskor, on the alien planet of Paradise, I saw the sky. The stars. The Milky Way. This far from Earth, the constellations were all wrong, but, man, the Milky Way was sweeping across the sky in all its glory. It was mesmerizing, I had to remind myself not to stare at it, that I was up on the roof to keep watch, not to gaze at the stars. I swept the horizon and the road from the village with an infrared scope, it was all clear. The eastern sky had just the faintest hint of pink from the approaching dawn, and insects began to buzz, or chirp, or whatever insects did on this planet. This time of morning is when, on Earth, birds would begin to sing, but Paradise didn't have any native birds. The guidebook said the biosphere wouldn't evolve flying animals other than insects for many millions of years, and since the planet was now occupied by aliens, Paradise probably never would get a chance to evolve birds on its own.

I sat on the roof, watching the eastern sky lighten, listening to the low buzzing of unseen insects, and felt homesick. I missed Earth. Mostly, I missed the Earth that used to be, before alien invaders, before electricity was a luxury, before we saw twinkling lights in the sky and thought of anything other than meteor showers.

Before Columbus Day.

While we were eating breakfast, I got messages from Cornpone and Shauna. Cornpone told me our old squad was part of a rapid reaction force base about five hundred miles north of Teskor, he sounded excited, it was a damned good assignment. Way better, he said mockingly, than babysitting hamsters. I had to agree with him. The fireteam had replaced me with a new guy, a guy from North Carolina, and Cornpone said the new guy was a huge improvement over me, since the new guy had a proper Southern accent, instead of my Downeast drawl. Shauna reported that her unit was temporarily at a logistics staging base almost a thousand miles to the east. I wrote three messages to her, erased them, then sent a simple note. The odds were that we wouldn't see each other for a long time, maybe never. I tried to respond in a way that was friendly but not too friendly, so she wouldn't feel she needed to make any special effort to keep in touch, because then it would just get awkward.

By the third day of us 'patrolling' the village, we were all starting to feel more than a bit foolish. For a patrol, we would put on full battle rattle, our zPhone earpieces, cameras and microphones, tinted goggles, and march down the streets, rifles ready, a finger poised near the safety, trying to look tough as we walked past neat little houses and barns, well-tended fields, and the school, all the way out to the edge of the village, then turned around and walked back. It was not easy to look tough as hamsters sat on their front porches in the morning, sipping tea and waving to us. Or working in the fields and barns, and pausing to wave to us as we walked by. Or the hamster children waving excitedly, eager to see the strange new aliens. Us.

To show the hamsters that our fireteam had serious backup, once or twice a day that first week, a couple Buzzards and Chickens flew over at low altitude, circled the village, and resumed heading west. The gesture was supposed to give my unit confidence also, but after we watched the aircraft disappear over the western horizon, it only reminded us how isolated we were.

The turning point of our EOT engagement in Teskor came on the morning of the seventh day, after we'd done our night and morning patrols, and I'd dutifully sent a report about nothing up to our platoon leader. I took Sanchez with me, to check out a barn I was curious about. I wasn't suspicious about any funky hamster activity, just curious to see the inside of a hamster barn. As we walked past the school, a group of hamster kids were in the yard, kicking a ball that looked like it was made from the hamster equivalent of duct tape. We knew the hamsters weren't getting any new luxuries shipped in from offworld; the Kristang allowed only basic medical supplies to make the trip down from orbit, everything else that was hamster related was supposed to be going up to orbit, one way. The kids probably had a soccer ball that went flat, and they tried to fix it with duct tape.

The barn wasn't anything special, it was built from metal girders and some kind of extruded plastic sheets the Ruhar used everywhere. The exterior color was red, which I thought was interesting; maybe painting barns red was another almost universal idea between alien species. At first I thought the barn was a type of chicken coop, until my eyes adjusted to the dim light. Then it got weird. There were animals being raised there, on racks along the sides, and it smelled like a chicken coop, or a hog farm. The weird thing was each animal, about two meters long and a meter across, had a silver cup where its head should be, and there were wires and tubes leading into the wall in front of each animal. The animals rested in cradles, I noticed some of the animals further away were smaller, perhaps younger? What was truly weird was the silence, no clucking of chickens or grunting of pigs, only the whirring of fans and electric pumps. And there was my new buddy Lester Cornhut, trotting up to me from the far end of the barn, with a friendly wave. "Greeting, Joseph Bishop," he called out.

"Greetings, Lester Cornhut." I must have pronounced his name correctly, because he smiled and gave me a short bow. "What is this place?" I asked. "What are those," I pointed to the strange, whatever they were, "animals?"

"Animals? Ah. These are not animals. Ruhar do not eat animals, we have long considered that to be," Lester paused to choose his words carefully, "barbaric." He gave an apologetic smile. I wondered if what he'd said in Ruhar had been even worse than the translated word I heard.

"They sure look like animals to me," Sanchez said behind me. "They're moving."

Mr. Cornhut walked close to an animal, or whatever it was, and poked it. The thing didn't respond. Yet it moved periodically, rocking from side to side. "These food sources," that probably didn't translate well, "do not have brains, and only a limited nervous system. Their bodies are almost all meat, genetically designed that way. A central computer," he pointed to the silver cap and the wires, "acts as their nervous system, that is why they move in a programmed pattern, to stimulate muscle growth."

"Huh, damn, that's cool." Sanchez was impressed. "They grow only the meat, not the whole animal."

I didn't know whether to be impressed or creeped out. These things were mindless, it was like raising a steak rather than the cow. It was eerie. It made perfect sense, it was efficient, and still it bothered me. Maybe I just wasn't ready for the future, this future.

After we got back to base, I asked Baker to dig through our supplies and see if we had a soccer ball, I thought I'd seen one in the 'recreational package' the platoon gave us before they sent us off to live in Bum Fuck Neptune.

During the next morning patrol, I tucked the soccer ball under my arm, and as we walked past the school again, I tossed the ball underhand to the hamster kids. At first, they were startled and backed away from it, but on our way back, I saw kids kicking it around, and they waved to us.

That evening, Lester Cornhut came to visit and asked for me. "Show Bishahp" is how he pronounced my name, which was probably closer to my real name than 'Lester Cornhut' was to his real name. I mean, what are the odds, right? Through the translator, he asked whether I am the Show Bishahp who captured a Ruhar soldier during the 'military action' on Earth, which he pronounced as 'Urt'.

"Yes." I nodded.

He smiled, and paused his translator. "Ta." He nodded his head up and down. "Neh." His shook his head side to side.

"Yes." I nodded. "No." I shook my head. Then I said "ta," and nodded up and down, and "neh," and shook my head side to side. He did the same gestures for 'yes' and 'no'.

That was our first true interspecies communication. If we weren't on Paradise only because the hamsters had attacked Earth, I would have been thrilled.

Back to the translator, he told me the hamster regional governor would be visiting Teskor in two days, and she wanted to meet with me, for tea. Seriously? Afternoon teatime with the enemy? Were we going to have little cucumber sandwiches, and scones, and crumpets, whatever the hell a crumpet is? Lester was Ok for a Ruhar, he was a farmer, and likely had no involvement in attacking Earth, if he'd even heard of Earth before the humans arrived on Paradise. But a regional governor had to be part of the Ruhar government that had attacked Earth, and killed humans. I felt like telling Lester that his bitch governor could shove her visit where the sun don't shine. And that I wasn't some circus sideshow curiosity for him to show off; step right up and see the human who captured a Ruhar soldier! We promise it won't bite! Only $5, including a free souvenir!

Hearts and minds, I told myself, hearts and minds. If Division G2 wanted intel, a regional governor would know a lot more about the situation on Paradise than my buddy Lester, that was for sure. "I would be honored to meet with your governor," I said, expecting that speaking through a fake smile wouldn't translate as sarcasm.

"You bring tea, for yourself? We have hot water, I think you do not drink our tea, no?" Lester asked.

Oh, for crying out loud. They really expected me to drink tea with them? What the hell, one of our food packs must have a teabag in it, bringing it with me didn't mean I was going to get all cuddly and sing Kumbaya with the damned Ruhar.

CHAPTER FIVE   INTEL

A couple days later, Lester Cornhut stopped me during morning patrol, to tell me excitedly that the regional governor would be at his house promptly at 1600 hours, he tapped his wrist like he was wearing a watch, and could I please come to his humble abode? Sometimes, the translator went overboard, I'm sure he hadn't actually said 'humble abode' in Ruhar. I was tempted to make the hamsters cool their heels waiting for me, but my mother raised me to be polite, and the military had drummed into my head the habit of being promptly on time for everything. Promptly at 1600 local time, I arrived at the Cornhut residence, to see the regional governor, Lester Cornhut, Mrs. Cornhut, and the little Cornhuts. Baker waited outside, Sanchez and Chen were at the CP with the heavy weapons, just in case. My visit had been cleared, even encouraged, by platoon HQ. For the visit, I left my rifle, helmet, body armor and goggles back at the CP, bringing only my zPhone and sidearm. The sidearm was there because I'd feel naked without, it, and it would remind the hamsters, and me, that UNEF was an occupying force. Emphasis on 'force', if needed.

Oh, and I had brought a teabag with me. And a packet of sugar, in case I needed it. Lester greeted me excitedly, my guess was the regional governor didn't visit a hick town like Teskor often, they probably got more tornadoes than governors coming through the place.

There were only three Cornhuts in the family; Lester, his wife, and a son, who I recognized from the school. "Thank you for the ball," the boy said in English, or that's what it sounded like. I was truly impressed the furry little guy made the effort to memorize those words, so I said "ta", and gave a little bow. He smiled, then Lester shooed him away, and poured hot water into two cups on a sort of coffee table in front of the couch. He then bowed deeply and left, leaving me alone with the regional governor. She looked like any other female Ruhar, although it was clear she wasn't a farmer; she was wearing a blouse and long skirt, of a material that looked like silk, and her earrings and necklace were elegant and expensive-looking, not that I had any idea how to tell one piece of jewelry from another. The governor was sitting on a dark green couch with a flowery throw rug on it, I sat in a chair at the end of the coffee table, I sure wasn't going to sit on the damned couch next to her. She slowly spooned what looked like loose tea leaves from a box on the table, put them into an egg-shaped thing with lots of holes in it and a thin chain, and gently set it in the teacup. My grandmother had an almost identical tea egg thing, whatever you call it.

"I am Sergeant Joe Bishop." I said, and put my teabag into a cup. It was a lot less elegant than the way she'd made tea. That irritated me for some reason. I knew the reason she had made her tea so slowly, deliberately, was to give her time to study me.

She seemed amused. "I am the regional governor of Lesscorta, my name is Bahturnah Lohgellia." She paused to wait for the translator to catch up. "Your people who occupy my home town call me," she paused again, "the burgermeister." Her eyes twinkled, clearly expecting me to be amused. "I think that 'burgermeister' is easier to pronounce than my name, no?"

I was amused. "Tah." Whatever troops occupied her town must have been stationed in Germany at some point. A burgermeister is sort of a mayor in Germany. I think so, I mean, the closest I had ever was to being in Germany was sitting in a transport plane while it refueled on the runway at Rhine-Main airfield.

The burgermeister gestured for me to take my microphone and earpiece off. I pointed to my mouth, then my ear. "I need this so we can talk to each other."

To my surprise, she responded in very slow, careful and squeaky English. "Sergeant Joe Bishop, please leave that outside. You can use this." In her hand was what looked like a Kristang zPhone, but a bit smaller. She offered it to me, with its own mic and earpiece. "I will explain," she said slowly, as if she had memorized only a few phrases of English, and found our words difficult to pronounce.

I hesitated, then nodded. Army regs said I wasn't supposed to be away from my zPhone while on duty, but this was an opportunity to get my hands on Ruhar technology, and maybe gain some intel about the hamsters. It was why UNEF set up Embedded Observation Teams in the first place. I walked outside, gave my zPhone to Baker, came back in, and used the Ruhar device.

"Thank you." The burgermeister said in English, then put her own earpiece in and switched back to using her translator. "It is comfortable?" Even the computer version of her voice had a squeaky tone to it.

I looked at the display of the device, expecting it to ask me to speak a couple pages of text, so it could learn my particular speech pattern, but it displayed 'Ready' in bold red letters. That made me suspicious. "How does this know how I speak?"

The burgermeister smiled. "Your speech has been recorded, analyzed, translated, and programmed into the device in your hand. We did not wish to waste your time in setting up the device, as we have much to talk about."

So they'd been spying on me. Fair enough, of course they'd want intel on their adversary. "Why can't I use my own," I almost said zPhone but figured that wouldn't translate well in Ruhar, "tactical radio?"

Again she smiled. A friendly smile, but also an 'I know something you don't know' smile. It was getting mildly irritating. "The Kristang did not provide you with advanced weapons," she pointed to my sidearm, "aren't you curious why they did provide you with advanced communications equipment, that is used by every human on this planet?"

That made me pause. "Uh," hell, I wasn't a comms expert. "Probably, uh, every country on Earth uses different radio and computer gear, and since we don't have our own communications satellites here," I looked up at the ceiling, "the only way we can all talk to each other is with common radios." As I said it, it made sense, although I hadn't given it much thought before.

No smile this time, the burgermeister shook her head side to side. It was fascinating to me that, between two alien species, body language seemed to be universal. No translation needed there. "Perhaps that is a convenient excuse. The true reason is that all of your communications go through a Kristang network. The Kristang monitor every word you say, they capture all your data transmissions, they track your every movement, anywhere on the planet. They can also shut down all of your communications, any time they want. Sergeant Bishop, when you leave here, you will certainly report our conversation to your military intelligence people. I suggest you conduct that conversation in person, rather than over the radio. Unless you want to be overhead by the lizards."

That was all true, I guess. We all did use Kristang comm gear exclusively. But, why not? It was free, it worked great, it saved us from the effort of setting up microwave towers across the planet, and from trying to get American radios to talk to Chinese and Indian radios. Besides, the Kristang were our allies. "Maybe you are right. So what? The Kristang are our allies."

That irritating smile came back. "Allies? Alliances are for equals. The Kristang are your *patrons*, and you are their client species. Their pets. Or slaves."

"And you are our enemies." I said it before thinking. My mother would not have been happy about that; I was a guest in the hamsters' house, drinking tea, and I was not being polite.

"We have no wish to be your enemy. Please wait for me to speak," she held up a hand, "I can understand if you are angry, there is much you need to know, much the Kristang have not told you, or have lied to you about. My people have known about your species for over a thousand of your years. Our long-range probes found you, and placed stealth satellites in orbit around your planet to observe. Tell me, haven't you wondered why, since this war has been going on for thousands of years, Earth wasn't attacked a long time ago?"

My jaw dropped slightly open. She was right, that had been bugging me, seriously bugging me, and I wasn't the only person who had been asking that question. Why wait to attack now, when humans have nukes? Why not attack long ago, when humans were living in caves, and thinking fire was the pinnacle of technology? It didn't make any sense. The Ruhar weren't stupid, so...? Why? If UNEF HQ knew, they hadn't told me.

Because the need to use a translator meant she talked v-e-r-y s-l-o-w-l-y, I'll summarize what she said. The reason Earth hadn't been attacked before is simple. Until recently, Earth was out of practical flight range, for both sides of the war. It was possible for specialized, long-range starships to reach our low-rent part of the Orion Arm, Earth just wasn't worth the time or the expense. For some reason that even the Maxohlx and the Rindhalu didn't know, every once in a while, wormholes shifted. It happened randomly, or in a cascade across a whole quadrant of the galaxy. A shift could happen after a couple decades, or it could take hundreds or thousands of years. Some wormhole A, that used to connect to a wormhole B, suddenly connected instead to a wormhole C, and B shifted to connect to D. Or a wormhole could stop working altogether, or a previously unknown wormhole could suddenly activate. A planet that was strategically important could find itself an isolated backwater, after a wormhole shift. Or a planet that was too far from a wormhole for anyone to bother with, could suddenly become an important staging base for both sides to fight over. That's what happened to Earth. We were happily living alone in the galactic hinterland, far from any wormhole, and on the very edge of Ruhar territory, but far enough away that the Ruhar hadn't found it worthwhile to travel the extremely long distance to Earth. Then there was a shift, and a long-dormant wormhole came to life. One end of the wormhole was near Earth, the other end of that wormhole was in Kristang territory. That wormhole near Earth was close enough for a Thuranin star carrier to make the trip to Earth in about a week, which made Earth a good place for the Kristang to get a new foothold in Ruhar territory. Before the wormhole shift, Earth was much too far away for a military campaign by the Ruhar, and impossible to reach by the Kristang.

"Wait a minute," I said as I digested what the burgermeister had told me. "You attacked Earth. If we're too far away for a practical military campaign, why did you bother? That must have been an enormous effort." I thought about the complicated logistics of our occupation of Paradise, and we had a wormhole to get our supplies most of the way here. If the Ruhar had to schlep the whole way on foot, as my grandfather would say, how the hell had they done it? And why attack a planet, if you can't sustain a force there? It's not like we were a threat to them.

The burgermeister nodded. She clearly had been prepared for this question. "I am not sure your translator is picking my words up accurately, so please tell me if you do not understand. When we realized the wormhole shift had opened your planet for exploitation by the Kristang, we decided to act first, and our patrons the Jeraptha pulled together what long-range ships that were available to respond. Once we knew for certain that the Kristang intended occupy your planet, we degraded your industrial infrastructure, to make Earth a less useful staging base for the Kristang. It was a quick strike raid by a small number of ships, we could not launch a full scale attack at that distance. Our ships traveled for five of your months to reach Earth, and five months back."

I called bullshit on that. "And you arrived at the same time as the Kristang? Right." Then I realized that 'right' may be translated as 'correct'. We'd been instructed to speak in simple language to the Ruhar, because idioms, slang and emotion-laden speech like sarcasm may not make sense across the species translation barrier. Although based on my interactions with the Ruhar, body language was universal, at least among bipedal species. "What I meant to say was, I doubt what you said is accurate."

"We did not arrive at the same time as the Kristang," she explained with what I interpreted as a slightly condescending smile. "Our ships watched the wormhole, in case the Thuranin sent a force through, we knew they were probing the area, but were not absolutely sure of their intentions. Earth is not the only habitable planet near the new wormhole. After the invasion force came through the wormhole, we waited for three weeks for the Thuranin ships to assemble and complete the journey from the wormhole. When we realized Earth was their target, our heavy ships engaged them, while our raiding force launched precision strikes on Earth. We did not hit cities, our purpose was not to kill your people, it was to reduce your industrial capacity, so the Kristang would not find it so easy to sustain a foothold at the edge of our territory."

"You killed a lot of people." I shot back angrily. "Humans."

"As a soldier, you are familiar with the term collateral damage?" She waited for me to nod. Nodding was one of those universal body languages. "Our targets were electric power stations, factories producing certain types of equipment, and industrial facilities which create materials such as metals. All of which are infrastructure which could be utilized by the Kristang. When we attacked your fission power plants," I assumed the translator meant nuclear power, "we hit the electric distribution center next to the reactor, we were careful not to hit the nuclear reactor. We did not wish to contaminate your planet, and cause deaths and suffering needlessly. Those Ruhar soldiers who were forced to land in your home village, were on their way to destroy the electric distribution center at a fission power plant in a place called Connecticut." As there was no Ruhar word for 'Connecticut', the word came through in her slightly squeaky rodent voice, without translation. "We couldn't risk striking that power plant from orbit, even with smart missiles."

That gave me a pause. She told the truth about the attacks on nuclear power plants, none of the reactors around the planet had been hit. "You didn't want to contaminate a planet you wanted to occupy!" I waved my hand to shut her up, as she tried to speak. "No, I'm done with your lies." I slammed the teacup down angrily on the table, stood up, and bowed stiffly. "Thank you, madam." When I got outside, I saw a group of hamster kids playing with the soccer ball I'd brought, and couldn't decide whether I was more angry at the hamsters for trying to justify attacking Earth, or for me allowing myself to be soft on the enemy. One of the hamster kids waved at me, and I ignored him. I felt like crap about that later, they were alien kids, but they were still only kids. They hadn't attacked Earth. I just wanted someone to be mad at.

I was pissed for about a week, angry that I'd let her manipulate me. Angry that she tried to use me to feed us bad intel, to sow dissent in our ranks, to conduct a psyops campaign against us. It wasn't going to work. But, when I finally did talk to an officer about it, during one of Lt Charles' visits, I talked to him face to face, and pantomimed taking off his zPhone. To my surprise, he nodded silently and left his zPhone outside the tent. "What is it, Sergeant?"

"Sir, that regional governor hamster gave me intel about how wormholes work. It may be BS, but figured I should pass it up the chain. And she said I shouldn't talk about it over a zPhone, because the Kristang may be listening."

He nodded. "Command has been worried about that. Our allies control all our communications on Paradise. And our transport. And our food supply, and everything else. All right, what do you know about wormholes?"

I told him, as best I remembered. He nodded. "You're right, it's probably bullshit, but I'll pass it along to battalion HQ."

Lester Cornhut had been telling me the burgermeister wished to talk again, and he was insistent, almost pleading with me. I felt sorry for the hamster, but I was still pissed off, and wasn't going to be manipulated again by a lying weasel, or hamster. According to Lester Cornhut, the regional governor had made a special trip to Teskor just to talk with me. Or talk to me, or at me. I told him, thank you, but no. He looked hurt.

Three days later, a pair of hamvees roared up to our command post in a cloud of dust. I'd been on our basketball court playing a game of horse with Baker when they arrived, we both scrambled to put shirts on quick. A major hopped out of the lead hamvee, accompanied by a security detail. "Sergeant Bishop?"

I saluted. She looked vaguely like our brigade intelligence officer, who I'd only seen pictures of. "Yes, ma'am."

"I'm Major Perkins. I need to talk to you, inside." She gave me the now-familiar gesture to take my zPhone off.

Inside, I was glad that we'd spruced up the place that morning, we'd been getting casual about policing our trash out in the middle of nowhere. "Bishop, your intel about the wormholes caused a shitstorm at UNEF HQ. Someone there mentioned the wormhole shift intel to the Kristang and they blew a gasket, wanted to know where we'd heard those outrageous lies, denied the whole thing. Which means it's true, and the damned lizards are lying about it." That was the first time I'd heard a senior officer speak against our allies, it surprised me. "You heard this from a Ruhar? I want to meet her."

"Uh, sir, that's complicated. She doesn't live here in the village, she's like a regional governor or something around here. She comes through here once a week, and we met at her friend's house, for tea." I felt like an idiot saying I was sitting down for tea with the enemy. "It's a hamster thing, they have tea when they meet."

"All right, when is she coming back?"

"Day after tomorrow, supposedly, but, I told her friend here that I didn't want to talk to her again. I can give word that I've changed my mind?"

"Hell, Bishop, that won't work, I need to meet with her. You don't know what questions we need to ask her. UNEF has a lot they want to talk about."

"I don't ask her questions. She talks, and I listen. She talks about whatever she wants. I figured she was bullshitting me, like, a hamster psyops thing." Damn, the burgermeister had been telling the truth!? "Do you want to hear everything she told me?"

"Yeah." She pulled a tablet and microphone out of her pack. "I'll record what you say on this. On this, and not on a zPhone, you got that?"

"Yes, ma'am. Loud and clear." Especially since the burgermeister had told me not to trust the Kristang-supplied comm gear.

She put the tablet on a table, plugged in the microphone, and looked around our little command post. It was a damned good thing we'd straightened up and cleaned the place, cleaned like scrubbed from top to bottom, not just swept dirt under the furniture. We had even moved the furniture around and used a floor cleaner polisher thing the hamsters had left in a closet. The floor polisher worked great after we played around with it for an hour, as the hamsters hadn't left any helpful instructions. Major Perkins nodded approval. "You like it here, sergeant? It's kind of isolated, these embedded observation teams."

"I do like it, ma'am. I'm a new sergeant, so being way out here means I get to make mistakes without a butterbar looking over my shoulder." As I spoke, it occurred to me that Major Perkins had been a butterbar once herself. "Uh, I wasn't-"

"Relax, sergeant." She laughed. "When I was a butterbar second lieutenant, I was perhaps the single dumbest officer in the history of the United States Army, and that's saying a lot. Course, back then I didn't know it. This place may be Bum Fuck Neptune, but enjoy it while you can, a lot of fireteam leaders would love to have this opportunity to get out on their own. And if the intel you're providing is as solid as UNEF thinks it might be, you're doing damned good. Let's get started," she pulled up a voice recording app on her tablet.

Major Perkins came back two days later, but the burgermeister didn't. So we sat cooling our heels most of the day, until a hamster kid riding an electric bicycle came looking for me, to deliver a message that the burgermeister was busy, and would like to meet me the next day. Me, and only me. Major Perkins was not happy, but she took the hint, and gave me a list of questions that I had to memorize.

That began my short career as an intelligence officer. The list of questions from UNEF didn't do any good; the burgermeister apparently had a plan of what she wanted to talk about each time we met, and she was sticking to her plan. I would meet with her twice a week, and Major Perkins, sometimes accompanied by a captain from division HQ, arrived the next day to debrief me. I felt like a kid passing notes in high school, but what could I do?

During our fourth meeting, after we got the whole tea ceremony out of the way, I posed a question to the burgermeister. "Why me?" I demanded. "Why aren't you talking to an intelligence officer in one of our militaries? If you don't want to talk to an American, you can talk to the British, the French, the Indians or the Chinese."

The burgermeister made a sour face. "I do not wish to be interrogated. My intention is to provide information, to correct lies the Kristang have told you, and to explain things the Kristang do not wish to speak about. I will not speak to anyone other than you."

"You did not answer my question. Why *me*? I'm only a low ranking sergeant. This village is a significant distance from where you live, why don't you talk to someone there?"

Again, I got the feeling she was ready for every single one of my questions. The burgermeister was a very clever hamster, that was for sure. She smiled again, I couldn't tell if it was genuine, or that ready smile politicians practice. "I first came here because I wanted to meet you, Joe Bishop, the one sometimes called Barney." The translator let my name and 'Barn-ey' come through in her squeaky voice. She tilted her head, another universal bipedal body language. Damn, her source of intel was good. "I was curious what type of human injured one Ruhar soldier, and captured another."

"I had help."

"Help from civilians, and reports indicate you did not have military weapons."

"Reports are not always accurate." I didn't want to provide her information about the tactics I had used then, or any other intel that might be useful to my enemy. She was there to provide me intel, supposedly, not to listen to me.

"These reports are. Another reason I am talking to you, is because of a report from the Ruhar soldier you captured."

I couldn't hide the surprise on my face.

She continued with another smile. "You didn't know? He was released, in exchange for a Kristang soldier we had captured. Our soldier reported that he was captured by human civilians, which is not something a soldier wants to admit to. And he said that you treated him very well. We appreciate that."

"As well as I could. We didn't have any food he could eat." I had wondered what happened to the hamster after the National Guard took him away, my assumption was we eventually gave him to the Kristang before he starved. The Kristang must have had some supplies of Ruhar food, for prisoners they captured. "How is the other soldier, is he all right?" He hadn't looked good; the last time I saw him laying in a pile of bricks.

"*She* is well, yes, she was injured, but has fully recovered. Her attack craft was damaged in orbit, but was rescued by one of our starships."

I had no idea the other soldier was female. With the body armor, helmet and face shield, there was no way for me to tell. And she'd been half buried in debris from the wall we'd blown up. "Please tell her that," I almost said I was sorry, which I wasn't, because it was combat, "it wasn't anything personal. I didn't have time to check on her injuries."

The burgermeister nodded. "Understandable, it was a combat situation. There are no hard feelings, I assure you. If I am ever able to contact her, I will relay your message. Sergeant Bishop, I see you were surprised to learn the injured soldier is female. You have females in your armies."

"We do, it's relatively recent that our women are in combat positions. Although women have served in the military for many years, and have put their lives at risk. In modern combat, it's hard to tell where the front lines are."

"How have the Kristang reacted to humans having women in combat positions?"

It was my turn for body language, a side to side shake of my head. "I am not telling you anything about relations with our allies." Which was easy, since I didn't know a damned thing about the subject. "Why do you ask?"

"Because the Kristang don't allow their females in combat. Or in any position in their military. Or in any position of authority in their society."

"That's not any of my business." Although it did explain the unisex bathrooms on their ships; they weren't unisex, the troop transport ships never carried Kristang females.

"There is a human expression I have learned; know your enemy. We have a similar saying among my people. I suggest also, that you learn about the beings you mistakenly call your allies. The Kristang do not allow females in their military, because none of their females are in any position of authority, across their entire society. A long time ago, the Kristang warrior caste began a controlled breeding and genetic engineering program, to reduce the intelligence of their females, to make them smaller, weaker, more submissive and docile. The genetic engineering program also altered the ratio of male to females, it was originally half females, now there are five females for every male. To the Kristang warrior caste, their females are only for pleasure, breeding and domestic servants. So, that is why I ask how they react to seeing your females as soldiers. Also as officers, pilots and other positions of authority. Positions where they have authority over males."

"I haven't met any Kristang, ma'am, I'm just a grunt." I wasn't sure that grunt would translate into Ruhar correctly. "I am a low ranking foot soldier; our officers handle relations with the Kristang. It doesn't matter what the Kristang think about women in our militaries."

This time, the burgermeister's smile was more of a sad smirk. "You still think that. Just as you still consider the Kristang to be allies. Perhaps the idea of selective breeding and genetic manipulation, does not bother you? I understand your species' history includes a eugenics program, by the government of a country called Germany."

I knew she was baiting me, but I couldn't let it go. "My country fought a war against the Nazis! Against Germany, the country we call Germany," I added, unsure how much of human history she understood. "That was a long time ago. What you said sounds horrible, if it's true." I thought about how pissed I'd been in Nigeria, when a group of fanatical loser ignorant savages attacked a girl's school, because they thought it was a sin for girls to get an education. Seeing the burned bodies of those little girls had filled me with rage, I had wanted to storm out into the jungle and kill every one of the cowards who had used guns and bombs against defenseless children and their teachers. If I could find them. Which had been the whole problem while we were there.

Damn, I'd hated being in Nigeria.

Over the next four weeks, the burgermeister gave me a wealth of intel, very little of it good news for humans, if it was true. It would take too long to repeat what she said, or what I told Major Perkins, so I'll summarize. Some of it left me with a queasy feeling, and I wasn't the only one. I could see Major Perkins' face turn white when I told her some of this stuff.

Opening Earth to invasion by the Kristang wasn't the only effect, or even an important effect, of the wormhole shift. An entire quadrant of the galaxy had been affected, and it had thrown Kristang society into disarray. Disarray, and civil war. The Kristang warrior caste wasn't a single entity, it was made up of clans, who competed for power and fought amongst themselves. When the wormhole near Earth suddenly came to life, it took the Thuranin a while to getting around to exploring it, them having more important things to do. They first sent a robot probe through from their side, to make sure the other side of the wormhole wasn't far outside the Milky Way galaxy, or inside a star, which had been known to happen. After it was determined the wormhole was safe to use, the Thuranin sent a couple ships through, then basically shrugged and decided there was not much worth exploiting on our end. Sure, Earth was within one week travel time, but Earth was far from any Ruhar planets, and the wormhole shift had presented more tempting opportunities elsewhere. That would have been the end of it for possibly centuries, with Earth continuing to drift along through the cosmos blissfully ignorant and alone, except that the wormhole shift had also seriously hurt the already fading fortunes of the White Wind clan of the Kristang.

Before the wormhole shift, the White Wind clan had already been in decline, with them controlling only two planets in the Kristang dominion. After the wormhole shift, the White Wind no longer had practical access to one of those planets, and they became desperate. Some numbskulls in the White Wind leadership decided that Earth was the answer to their problems; if they could seize control of Earth and make it a useful staging base to invade Ruhar territory, they could then ally with a stronger clan. It didn't work, no other clans were interested in Earth as a staging base, and the Ruhar's spoiling attack had hurt our infrastructure enough that the White Wind had to expend too much time and resources to rebuild our infrastructure to the point we could begin to be useful to them. So, the White Wind leadership decided their best bet was to rent out human soldiers to other clans, which was why we were on Paradise. That is, if you believed the burgermeister.

The burgermeister warned that if the Kristang followed their usual pattern, they would soon begin requiring Earth governments to enforce measures that favored the Kristang, at the expense of humans, if they hadn't done that already. All in the name of 'serving the war effort'. Shit, that sounded familiar, it had begun even before I left Earth, and I thought people who protested against the Kristang's orders had been soft on the war effort. Eventually, the Kristang would determine who was the most oppressive, thuggish government on the planet, and make them the Kristang's local enforcers, backed up by untouchable Kristang warships in orbit. It was, the burgermeister told me, an old formula; you find the worst psychopathic antisocial losers in a society, give them power, and they would give you their complete, unquestioning loyalty. That was how Hitler and Stalin had come to power. That was Standard Operating Procedure for the Kristang.

Then she told me about the Kristangs' patrons, the Thuranin. Thuranin were sort of little green men, she said, confirming what I'd heard at Camp Alpha. What I hadn't heard at X-Ray was that Thuranin were cyborgs, with computers implanted in their skulls, and their society was highly networked. They controlled their ships through their implanted computers, and rarely spoke aloud, because they mostly communicated with each other via direct computer link. Their skin was a greenish beige, not pure green, and all Thuranin had the same skin tone. Their species used to have multiple shades of skin color, but the dominant race committed genocide against all the other Thuranin races, wiping them out a long time ago. Now all Thuranin were clones of the 'master race', with little genetic variation from what the 'master race' considered ideal. The Thuranin were openly contemptuous of any species with lesser technology, and also disdained their own patrons, the Maxohlx. Mutually warm fuzzy feelings were not the basis of the coalition headed by the Maxohlx.

As arrogant as the Thuranin were about their superior technology, they hadn't developed most of it by themselves. They'd stolen it, which was how all species climbed the ladder of technology. The jump drive units the Kristang used aboard their starships were copied from a captured Jeraptha drone. It wasn't designed to be used by a full-size ship, and the Kristang copies were of poor quality, which is why their starships could only jump short distances. The Thuranin themselves had stolen, found or bought a much better design for their starships, so their ships could travel between stars. Every species stole or copied technology from every other species, even the two species at the top of both sides; the Maxohlx and the Rindhalu.

Sometimes the Maxohlx and the Rindhalu copied technology from each other, but at their level, by far the main source of advanced technology was finding machines left behind by the ancient species called the Elders. The Elders were the first intelligent species in the Milky Way galaxy, and had apparently lived alone in the galaxy for millions of years, before rather suddenly disappearing. No one knew what the Elders looked like, or why they were gone, or where, speculation was their technology was so advanced, they no longer needed a physical existence. Regardless of why and where they had gone, they left behind incredible devices such as the wormhole network. And weapons. Incredibly powerful devices that could be used as weapons, in the wrong hands.

The Kristang had told us the Maxohlx rebelled against Rindhalu attempts to suppress development of younger species, but the burgermeister told me what really happened is the Maxohlx enjoyed the nurturing of the older Rindhalu, until the Maxohlx found some Elder weapons, and attacked the Rindhalu. Both sides deployed Elder weapons, but the war was short-lived. Use of the Elder devices awakened the Sentinels; intelligent machines the Elders had left behind to make sure no one abused their leftover technology, or polluted the galaxy, or for some other reason. The Sentinels devastated both sides, then went back to sleep, or wherever they had come from. Clearly, even though the Elders had abandoned the galaxy, they didn't want lesser species screwing with their stuff.

The idea of the Sentinels lurking in the shadows explained why the current interstellar war wasn't being fought directly between the Maxohlx and the Rindhalu; those two species couldn't afford to fight each other. It was the same reason the United States and the old Soviet Union had never clashed directly in the Cold War; Mutual Assured Destruction. Any such fight between the USA and the USSR, each with thousands of nukes, could escalate quickly out of control and destroy both sides. Any fight using Elder weapons would awaken the Sentinels. So, the Maxohlx and the Rindhalu used their client species to fight for territory and resources across the galaxy, hoping to squeeze the other side into a corner, and irrelevance. The war was fought by us grunt species, and every species wanted to climb the technology ladder, and have some lower client species doing the fighting and the dying. Right now, humans were on the bottom of the ladder. Until we developed or stole some advanced technology, we were going to stay on the bottom, and be at the mercy of the Kristang.

Overall, if the burgermeister was telling me the truth, humanity was screwed. The White Wind clan needed to extract some gain from the resources they'd invested in the expedition to Earth, and Earth didn't have much to offer. Sure, technically Earth was in Ruhar territory, but it was so far from any planets the Ruhar occupied that the Ruhar could afford to ignore the Kristang presence until the Ruhar were ready to deal with it. What could Earth offer the Kristang, particularly the White Wind clan? Land that was already being used by humans could be taken to support the Kristang presence. Raw materials could be extracted, by the most efficient means possible, which meant not caring about terrible environmental damage or the effect on humans. Human troops could be rented out for jobs no Kristang wanted to do, like garrisoning Paradise. The White Wind needed to hang on, and make Earth a useful staging base, until the day some stronger clan decided our crappy little planet, on the far edge of Ruhar space, was worth something.

I considered that the burgermeister might be giving us some tidbits of good intel, like about the wormholes, so we'd believe her lies about the Kristang. It wasn't my call what to believe, that was up to UNEF HQ. My job was to sit, and drink tea, and listen to her, and pass the info on to Major Perkins. Did I believe her then? I was reluctant to buy her story. She said the Rindhalu coalition did not interfere with technologically inferior species, which is why Earth was left alone, until the Kristang forced the Ruhar to act. The Maxohlx and their clients were all evil oppressors who exploited lesser species and stripped planets of resources, with no concern for the effect on the native populations. It was a nice story that made the Ruhar looks good and the Kristang sound bad, which is what I expected our enemy to say. Unless she was telling the truth. Crap.

In between useless patrolling and gathering intel over cups of tea, there wasn't much to do around Teskor, I had to think up things to keep the team busy and out of trouble. There was a concrete pad beside the house, or something like concrete, so we put up a basketball hoop and played two on two games. Patrols from the Company drove through often enough that we measured out a full basketball court, although it was four feet too short, and painted lines and set up a second basket. Ours was the only full basketball court in the area, it made us popular enough that patrols made plans to stop in Teskor so we could have games; sometimes two patrols met up at our command post to take a break, eat lunch and play basketball. We also were able to play softball, volleyball, soccer and ping pong with the equipment provided in the goody bag from Division. No pool table, dang it. And no TV. Of course, there weren't any sports or shows to watch on a TV, but we could have watched movies. No luck there, the Ruhar had TVs, and we brought DVDs and stuff with us from Earth, which was all useless since hamster TVs and our media players weren't compatible. There were portable flat screens for use at the Company level, units below that size needed to be happy with tablets and laptops. It wasn't a whole lot of fun to have four guys crowded around an iPad to watch a movie, I mean, that gets old quick.

So you don't think all we did was play games and watch movies, we did soldier stuff too. UNEF had stuck fireteams in isolated villages to gather intel on the ground, to see what local hamsters were doing, and we patrolled and looked around and kept our eyes and ears open. One morning, Sanchez stuck his head in the little room we used as an office, where I was writing up a report for the platoon. "Hey, Sergeant, something odd out there."

We went up to the roof, we'd constructed a ladder and an observation platform on top of the house; it seemed like the thing to do, and it had kept us busy. "Look at field South Two," he said as he handed me binoculars.

South Two was an empty field that had been harvested two weeks ago, we'd watched the big electric combines rolling along, threshing grain and then delivering it into big bins. A convoy of trucks had picked up the grain three days ago, bringing it to a railroad line to the north of town. "Good eyes, Sanchez," I said, "that is odd. UNEF sent us here to look for odd things happening. Saddle up."

We got into full battle rattle, climbed into our bad-ass hamvee pickup and roared off down the road. We could have cut across country, the land there being nothing but supposedly empty fields that were laying fallow, except that I'd gotten a memo from Division ordering a stop to bored troops joyriding off road. There had been several incidents of hamvees rolling over, which is not good when medical evac back to Earth isn't an option. And tearing up farmland in front of hamsters wasn't a way to win hearts and minds. So Sanchez stuck to the road. Sure enough, when we got to field South Two, there were a pair of big electric machines rumbling slowly up and down the rows. Planting seeds, is what it looked like. We left our hamvees on the road, Sanchez and I walked across the field toward the machines. One of them came by us slowly, the hamster driver giving us a friendly wave from the cab on top. On the back was a device that punched holes in the ground, dropped seeds, then filled in the hole. That was odd. Odd enough that we next paid a visit to the Cornhut household.

Lester was holding court for what looked like half the village, because having the burgermeister visit his home regularly had boosted his stature in Teskor. Many families were at a cookout behind his house, there were picnic tables set out, kids racing around, some kind of game sort of like badminton, and two grills heating up. Lester came around the side of the house to greet me, holding a spatula and wearing a white apron with splatters of red sauce that could have been barbecue. Whatever he was grilling smelled good, even if I knew humans couldn't eat it. "Greetings Joe Bishop!" He said with a genuinely friendly grin.

Part of me debated whether to come back the next day, and not interrupt his cookout. I had a job to do, so I said "Lester, we saw machines in field South Two," he knew UNEF's map designations, "they were planting seeds."

"Yes, we are planting," the translator stumbled and then said 'wheat equivalent'. "Is this a problem, Joe Bishop?"

"How long does that, uh, crop take to grow, before you harvest it?"

"Three point four three months." The translator said. That feature of translators was annoying; it was coldly mathematical. Lester had probably said something like 'five Ruhar months', and the translator did the math. I didn't need such exacting precision, dammit.

"This village is scheduled to be evacuated in two or three months," based on UNEF's latest schedule, which was constantly changing, "why are you planting a crop now?" This was the kind of odd hamster behavior G2 wanted to know about. Lester was planning on being in Teskor past the evac date, or right up to it. Did the hamsters know something UNEF didn't?

"Because there is no reason not to." Lester explained with a toothy grin that, under the circumstances, wasn't as friendly as he intended. "The Kristang allow us to continue shipping food products offworld, but we can't take seeds with us. So we plant. If we leave Teskor before we can harvest, perhaps someone else can harvest this crop." He shrugged. "My people have been in this war for a very long time, Joe Bishop. We have learned that nothing is certain. It is not certain the Kristang will keep this planet, so we hope and we plan for the future, until the day we are aboard a ship and it departs."

Made sense to me, keeping hamster morale up. Hope was a powerful morale booster. "Lester, something has been bothering me. It must be expensive to ship food between stars. Why do it?"

"Ah. This would require a long explanation, Joe Bishop," he glanced back at his cookout guests, "there are two most important reasons. Our home world, which at one point was as polluted as I am told yours is, now has our population concentrated in cities, with most of the planet dedicated to parkland, restored to its natural state. There is very little agriculture there, so food must be brought in. Many of our prime worlds are kept in such a state, so we have other worlds designated for agriculture, such as Gehtanu, or to industry. Industrial worlds are mostly those planets which had sparse life when we arrived, so our industry will not ravage the natural environment. The other reason, why we are determined to ship food off this planet as long as we can, is that the wormhole shift, which you have been told about, yes, cut off our home world's access to some of the usual food supply worlds. You can see now why we are eager to grow as much food here as we can, before we leave?"

"Sure, Lester." We left him to his cookout, and I sent a report up the chain. Lester's explanation sounded at least a little like bullshit to me, and UNEF needed to know anyway. Our fireteam began driving tours of the farmland around Teskor, ranging far and wide to check conditions of the fields. When we talked to the platoon, we heard Teskor wasn't the only village where the hamsters were planting crops, that wouldn't be ready for harvest until after that area was scheduled to evacuate. I didn't know whether to believe Lester or not, the whole issue was above my paygrade. So I reported it up the chain, and let people above me worry about it.

At times, the Burgermeister seemed to read my mind, and address subjects I was already thinking about. It made me suspicious about whether the Ruhar were somehow listening in on what we said around our command post, even though the platoon had supposedly swept the place for bugs. That day, I was in a gloomy mood, which matched the weather we'd been having. It had been raining for five days, and the weather satellites predicted another two days of solid rain, followed by a week of showers off and on. Wonderful. The Ruhar had a name for weather like this, they called it a 'schlumpernur', or that's how it sounded, only more squeaky. The word translated as 'damp musty blanket', and we all thought was so appropriate, the word quickly entered US military slang. The schlumpernur had caused the village to cancel plans for a harvest festival, since no one was feeling, you know, festive, and holding just an 'al' would be sad. My fireteam was grumpy from being cooped up in the CP, especially since soldiers can't really stay cooped up when the weather is bad, we still had to go out on patrol and check the conditions of the fields, and send reports to the platoon HQ and make it sound like we were doing something useful. We'd all watched every video we had twice, at least, and with the crappy weather, patrols coming through Teskor didn't bother to stop for a game of hoops or softball or volleyball. We tried enticing patrols with a game of darts, but everyone had a dartboard, and no one coming through wanted to leave their warm, dry hamvees. So the four of us were mostly stuck with each other, and we'd all heard each other's stories a dozen times. This was the downside of being out on our own; sure, we didn't have an officer staring over our shoulders, but we were feeling awfully lonely. Our zPhones helped, we were able to talk and video chat with anyone on the planet, I hit up Cornpone once a day to see what he was up to, he'd gotten assigned to one of the quick reaction platoons, which sounded exciting, except he told me all they did was drill, drill, and drill some more. The hamsters weren't doing anything uncooperative, so there wasn't anything to react quickly to. Overall, he sounded almost as bored as I was. We agreed that all our video games about interstellar warfare had totally lied to us. And I sent Shauna a short note, she sent a short note back, I took that as a hint that was busy and there was no point to chatting more, unless we were going to actually see each other. Unlikely, as she was stationed a thousand miles away. So, I was in a gloomy mood when the burgermeister poured out the hot water for tea. "Joe Bishop, you seem unhappy," she remarked.

I shrugged. "This schlumpernur has everyone feeling down," I said with a hint of a smile, because her eyes twinkled when I said 'schlumpernur'. "And, you don't tell me the happiest news, when we meet." Assuming she was telling the truth, which UNEF HQ seemed to think was a good bet.

"You told me that you have a family back on Earth?"

There was no harm telling her what she already knew, so I nodded. "My parents, and my sister."

"You would feel better if you heard from them, yes?"

"Sure." In Nigeria, we'd been able to Skype or sometimes even video chat, at least a couple times a week. And with the internet, we'd all been able to follow the news back home, keep us feeling connected. "I've written letters," and recorded video messages, "but so far, we haven't gotten any messages back yet." We sent messages to UNEF HQ, to be compressed and transmitted to the Kristang, but although shipments of food and other supplies arrived regularly in orbit, so far I hadn't received any messages from home, Or news of any kind. It was odd. And worrying.

"You won't," she said, looking carefully at me over her teacup. "The Kristang are not delivering your messages home. And they will not deliver any messages to you here. They don't want you to know what is happening on your home planet. Your leadership here surely knows this."

Crap. As she gave me that depressing intel, the steady drizzle turned into another downpour. My day just got better and better. Either she decided I'd had enough bad news for the day, or the weather had gotten her depressed too, because she changed the subject, and for the next hour, we talked about our childhoods. I didn't see any harm in telling her dull stories about growing up in rural Maine. Ruhar society didn't sound all that different from life on Earth, except they had amazing technology, they were scattered across many planets, and her species had been at war since long before, she, her parents, or her great-great-great-great grandparents were born, probably longer. Thinking about that didn't improve my mood.

Chen must have read my mind, because while we were eating dinner that night, chicken ala king by the way, he asked "Sergeant, any idea when we're getting messages from home?"

"No," I stared down at my plate to conceal a guilty look on my face, "you know as much as I do."

"Shit. A new transport ship arrived from Earth yesterday, it's all over the Net, I was hoping the ship was bringing letters. Or at least some news."

"News would be good," Sanchez agreed, "I'm worried about my folks."

"We all are." I admitted.

"You know what the worst thing is?" Baker asked. "There's no end to this deployment. When I went to Nigeria, I knew it was twelve months there, and I'd be rotated back home. Even in World War Two, guys knew there was an end in sight; win the war and you can go home. It may take years, but there was an end to it. Even when it got really hairy, guys knew that if they hung on and survived, they'd be going home eventually. This war has been going on for *thousands* of years. There's no end to it. There's no victory strategy, there's no point when we can say the mission is accomplished and it's time to go home. Now that I think about it, the message I got that I was being deployed offworld didn't say how long the deployment would be."

"We get the hamsters off this planet, and we go home, right?" Chen said hopefully.

"Maybe." Sanchez pushed his chicken ala king around on his plate. "Unless the lizards, I mean," he shot a worried look at me, "the Kristang, need us someplace else. We're already out there, right? And we're trained, and by then we'll be experienced. It may make more sense to the Kristang to redeploy us, rather than ship us all the way home and bring in new units."

"Crap." Chen summed up everyone's feelings about the subject. "We just got here, and already I want to get home."

I needed to put a stop to the glum talk. "Guys, look. I'd love to know when we're going home too. Check days off the calendar until we ship out. The evac schedule here is thirteen months, figure another couple months after that for us probably rebuilding infrastructure or something like that. Keeping us here is expensive for the Kristang, they have to ship all our food over a thousand lightyears, right? After this mission is done, I'm thinking they bring us home. Come on, in this war, how many assignments can the Kristang have for us? Even with our new toys, we're not qualified for real combat."

"Yeah, Ok, I guess so." Sanchez nodded halfheartedly.

"This damned schlumpernur has everyone feeling down." I looked out the window at the drizzle. "If the sun was shining, and we got some news from home, we'd all be feeling great. We're out on our own, no officers looking over our shoulders, we got it pretty good here. Chen, get the box of cake out of the fridge," that goodie had been delivered from the platoon three days before, "and let's celebrate. The forecast calls for this rain to end day after tomorrow."

The schlumpernur had faded into scattered showers by the time Major Perkins showed up to receive my latest intel the next morning. We met in her hamvee, so my fireteam could stay in the house while it rained. "Ma'am, I don't know if most of what she's telling me is bullshit or not, but she isn't lying about us not hearing from home. Is UNEF HQ getting any communications from Earth?"

The pained expression on her face told me all I needed to know. "That's above your pay grade, Sergeant, and mine."

"My guys," I nodded toward the house, "have been asking about it."

She looked at me sharply. "You didn't say anything?"

"No, ma'am. They know I'm meeting with the burgermeister, and they know you're Division intel, and they can put two and two together, but I haven't said anything to them, and they haven't asked. They don't need me to tell them we haven't heard squat from Earth. It's all over zPhone traffic." With zPhones, rumors that would have been confined to a single unit had flown around the planet. No one I'd contacted had received a single message from Earth. And Cornpone told me a supply guy he knew said shipments of food from Earth had been spotty recently. And that among supplies coming in now were seeds, like the Kristang expected us to grow our own food.

"Sergeant," she looked away at the rain, "I know as much as you do. UNEF HQ doesn't tell me any more than I need to know. Be careful what you say on the net," she pointed to the roof of the hamvee, "our friends are listening."

At 0400 a couple days later, my zPhone rang. Having a zPhone was great in many ways, in one way it was not so great: Command could reach you anytime, anywhere. Reach you personally, not call a radio operator who then had to go find you. I swung my legs onto the floor and sat up straight, someone told me that makes you sound more alert to be upright when you get startled out of a sound sleep. "Sergeant Bishop here."

"Bishop, this is Lt. Charles. Your fireteam is bugging out today to come back here, we need you packed up and on the move by 0900. "

That got me fully awake. "What's going on, sir?"

"You'll get a briefing when you get here."

"Yes, sir," I replied, but he'd already hung up.

My fireteam had the same WTF reaction I did, they also knew as much as I did, which was nothing. There wasn't any chatter of trouble on the net, we checked the UNEF sites and the news postings were totally ordinary, considering that we were on an alien planet. Packing up didn't take long, we took all the weapons but left anything a future fireteam would need to occupy the place, including the ping pong table we'd built. After one last drive splashing through the mud puddles down the main street, we turned around and left Teskor before most hamsters were out of bed. I regretted that we didn't get a chance to say goodbye to the Cornhut family.

I smelled a rat as we drove up to the platoon base, as soon as I saw Major Perkins. "Major Perkins? We just got pulled out of Teskor, ma'am." I said, although I figure she already knew that. Probably arranged it. I never trusted Intel types.

"Bishop, let's talk." She waved me over toward the airfield. Once we were out of earshot, she explained. "I ordered you pulled out of Teskor. The Kristang know someone has been passing intel to us, and they're pissed about it and nosing around, and they're getting closer to you. You need to lay low for awhile, so you're being transferred. Just you, not your team."

"Where, ma'am?"

"The cargo Launcher. I'll tell you the truth, we don't have an assignment for you right now, other than to disappear and keep your name off comm channels. If it makes you feel any better, I've been told the same, they're reassigning me to a logistics base in the Indian sector, as a liaison." She snorted. "I don't speak a single word of Hindi."

"Damn it. All this because we've been listening to the hamsters? Did the Kristang think we wouldn't talk to them the entire time we're down here? They've got to know the hamsters would take any opportunity to make the liz-, the Kristang look bad, drive a wedge between us."

"It's not just us talking to them, the Kristang expect rumors to fly around any army. The problem is the Kristang know UNEF Command has been taking the hamsters seriously. You're not our only source of direct intel, but I can tell you that your burgermeister is considered the gold source, and UNEF Command is shitting their pants because they believe most of what she told us is true." She shot me a direct look. "You're still not to talk about any of this, it's top secret."

"Yes ma'am."

She let out a long breath, patted her shirt pocket, then flicked her hand away in disgust. "Being out in the galaxy finally got me to quit smoking, once my supply of smokes ran out, I went cold turkey. The Kristang consider tobacco to be a luxury item they're not willing to ship across lightyears. Sometimes, I want to shoot something."

"Eisenhower quit cold turkey, ma'am, after his first heart attack." That didn't come out quite the way I meant it.

"If Ike did it, that's good enough for me. And he had a choice, right? I don't. Maybe we should have had nicotine put on the essential medicines list." She said with a grimace.

I wanted to sympathize with her, but I couldn't. I felt sympathetic, but since I'd never had to kick a habit of smoking or drinking or drugs, I couldn't truly understand what she was going though, you know what I mean? I'd taken the easy route of not getting hooked on anything in the first place. Not knowing what to say, I made a sympathetic 'um' sound and waited for her to talk.

"Medicine is what got us into real trouble anyway. You're right, the lizards don't give a shit about rumors going around. What got them pissed is when we accepted an offer from the Ruhar to provide advanced medical care. You heard about the Buzzard crash last month? Two dead, four injured, one of the injured lost a leg, another has a broken spine. And the Kristang won't medivac them back to Earth. The Ruhar heard about the injured, they were surprised to hear that humans don't have the ability to regrow limbs or nerve tissue; they've had that technology so long they take it for granted. As an experiment, we sent some badly injured cases to a Ruhar hospital, and they're being treated, including two from the Buzzard crash. The Ruhar docs took a while to adapt to our different biochemistry, but their biochemistry is based on DNA like us. Reports are all the injured are expected to make full recoveries eventually, including regrowing a leg. The Kristang were furious when they heard about us accepting Ruhar medical care, called UNEF Command on the carpet for fraternizing with the enemy. I hear that conversation got heated, General Meers told the damn lizards we wouldn't have to send our people to Ruhar hospitals, if the lizards would share their own medical technology." She smiled. "The Old Man won't back down to anyone, human or lizard."

"Am I in trouble, ma'am?"

"Hell, no, Bishop. Lay low for a while until this blows over in a couple weeks, months maybe. Think of it as an opportunity to see more of the planet."

I didn't believe that for a second.

After saying goodbye to my fireteam, I hopped a series of flights to the Launcher, it was long and boring and I was in a foul mood. I hadn't done anything wrong, but if UNEF needed a scapegoat for the Kristang, they'd expect me to fall on my sword. A demotion seemed likely, I hadn't been a sergeant long and had barely gotten used to it, I would miss the feeling of being in charge of a team. We'd done good work in Teskor; stayed out of trouble, established good relations with the natives, gathered solid intel and routed it up the chain. And built a basketball court that made our command post a popular spot for patrols to stop, which was good for morale. There hadn't been any serious friction among my fireteam, not any more than you'd expect from four guys stuck together in the boonies with not much to do. Looking back at our time in Teskor, it seemed almost idyllic, peaceful. We had landed on an alien, enemy planet, established control and we were doing our part in the war, showing the Kristang that we could pull our weight, little as that was. We felt we had a sense of purpose, of accomplishment, we all had been looking forward to the day the inhabitants of Teskor got loaded aboard transports and joined the evacuation. That would be mission accomplished for our EOT.

Looking back now, my view of our time in Teskor became less idyllic for me after I began getting disturbing intel from the burgermeister. Learning humanity had been conned into setting up an Expeditionary Force, that UNEF was nothing more than rent-a-grunts to the Kristang, that the lizards considered Earth to be a war prize to be exploited however they wanted, kind of killed my buzz on any feeling of accomplishment. Not being able to share intel with my fireteam had put a distance between us, they knew I was meeting with a high-ranking Ruhar official, they saw a UNEF intelligence officer visiting the day after I met with the Ruhar, and they could put two and two together. And, of course, there were rumors. Some of the rumors traced back to intel I'd received from the burgermeister, and made me nervous about UNEF HQ's information security. It pissed me off that I was supposed to treat intel as secret, when it was flying around the rumor mills already. I couldn't even tell my guys which rumors were total bullshit, and which intel had at least a grain of truth to it. There was plenty that was total bullshit.

Now my fireteam had a new sergeant, and they were stationed at battalion HQ, wondering if they'd done anything wrong. Nobody believed the bullshit story that our EOT had been pulled out of Teskor because the mission was over; stupid UNEF HQ hadn't even been smart enough to rotate in another EOT, they simply abandoned Teskor. Sure, that didn't look suspicious at all, EOTs were still in place all over the sector, except for the one village where I'd been meeting with the burgermeister. Here's how thin UNEF's cover story was: the crew chief on the Dumbo that I flew to the Launcher, a guy I'd never met in my life, asked me what I'd done that UNEF had to pull our EOT out of Teskor. There were rumors of a scandal, rumors so juicy that they had flown around the planet at the speed of light. All the infosec measures implemented by UNEF could be defeated by two guys sharing a rumor over their zPhones.

CHAPTER SIX   FORT ARROW

At the Launcher complex, I reported to a Captain Price in the admin building, a structure UNEF had taken over from the Ruhar who had managed the Launcher operations. Coming in from the airfield, I saw a whole lot of Ruhar outside the fence line of the base UNEF called Fort Arrow. Since humans didn't know how to operate or maintain the giant Launcher railgun that shot cargo into orbit, the biggest change had been which flag flew over the base, hamsters still ran the reactor and the rest of the Launcher complex. UNEF had carved Fort Arrow out of the workers' town that grew up next to the fusion reactor, taking over the existing buildings and putting minimal effort to repurpose them for military use. It made sense, UNEF wasn't planning to stay on Paradise long enough to invest in infrastructure. There was a semi-secure corridor between the airfield and Fort Arrow, on either side of the corridor were hamsters going on about their lives.

Captain Price's aide kept me waiting almost an hour, while I sat and watched the door to Price's office. He was in there, I could hear him talking on the phone, and long silences. It wasn't like he was so busy that he couldn't take a few minutes to welcome me aboard. They hadn't served breakfast on the Dodo, I was hungry and wanted to scrounge up some food before the dining facility shut down. Finally, Price stepped into his doorway, looked at me in a distinctly unfriendly manner, and grunted when I got to my feet and saluted him. "Bishop." It wasn't a greeting so much as a statement.

"Yes, sir, Sergeant Bishop reporting." There were no order papers for me to hand to him, everything was on our phones or tablets. In his office, he didn't tell me to sit, I stood at semi-attention to the right of the doorway.

"Bishop." He said again, pointing to something I couldn't see on his tablet. "The Barney guy."

Shit, I was really get sick of that.

"I have your orders here," he continued, "and your personnel file. Lack of discipline seems to be a pattern for you. And acting rashly. We're not going to tolerate any of that here at Fort Arrow. You may think your fifteen minutes of fame entitles you to special treatment." I didn't bother to protest, because he had already made up his mind about me. "That's a November Golf, you got that?"

"Yes, sir." Low profile, I told myself. Major Perkins, and through her UNEF HQ, wanted me to keep a low profile. Keeping my mouth shut was the first step.

A simple 'yes' from me wasn't good enough, apparently, Price had a chip on his shoulder and a soapbox to stand on, and he was going to take full advantage of having a captive audience. "You may have heard that Fort Arrow is a dumping ground for screwups and malcontents." Actually, I hadn't heard that, and I hadn't heard anyone use the word 'malcontent' since, like, elementary school. "UNEF HQ thinks that because the Ruhar need the Launcher to ship their grain offworld, Fort Arrow is safe from attack, and we don't need a significant security presence here." Ok, this wasn't about me, then, Price had a problem with UNEF HQ and I was a convenient target of his unhappiness. "They're wrong, the Launcher's importance means that it's the first place the Ruhar will try to capture if they ever try to retake the planet. This is an elite force." He tapped a finger twice on his desk for emphasis, with a clicking sound. What the gesture did for me, was make me think the guy needed to trim his fingernails. "Elite. We at Fort Arrow need to show the Ruhar that we are so strong here, it's not worth them trying to take this site."

I nodded silently, silent because I didn't want to disagree with his flawed logic. If the Ruhar managed to get a powerful enough fleet into orbit to chase the Kristang away, then humans trapped on the surface would be a speed bump. The hamsters could sit in orbit and use precision strikes with railguns, masers and smart missiles to eliminate human resistance, no matter how strong a force was garrisoned at Fort Arrow.

"We don't have a place for you here, and you could use some help keeping out of trouble. I'm assigning you to convoy escort duty, you'll report to Staff Sergeant Lombard in the morning. Try to keep you nose clean, and-"

"Sir?" Price's aide called from outside the office, "Colonel Young is on his way here right now."

Colonel Young strode in, dropped his pack on a table, ran a hand across his face to wipe the sweat off, and stuck his head in Price's office door. "Goddamnit, we're in the shit now. Our buddies the Kristang are pulling their destroyer out tomorrow, that leaves us with a single frigate in orbit for fire support. What do you want to bet that frigate bugs out at the first sign of a hamster warship? The old man wants contingency plans in case the Ruhar come back. We need to be prepared to defend this planet on our own."

"That bad, sir?" Captain Price asked, startled.

"Bad enough that they want a platoon to pull out of here tomorrow, and redeploy to beef up security at a couple logistics bases. UNEF figures no way the Ruhar would risk damaging the cargo Launcher, so they're stripping us thin to cover more likely targets. What?" Colonel Young reacted to a raised eyebrow from Price. He turned to the right and noticed me. "Who are you, Sergeant?"

I saluted crisply. "Bishop, sir, I was transferred here, just flew in this morning."

"Bishop, huh? Yeah, you're the Barney guy, we heard you were coming." I was never going to escape that. "You can clear out, Sergeant. And keep your mouth shut. Not that we can keep this quiet anyway." Young said with a sigh.

"Yes, sir." I walked out as fast I could without completely losing my dignity.

The convoy escort team I was assigned to was a good group, led by a green-as-grass second lieutenant who was smart enough to listen to his staff sergeant. Captain Price was right, there wasn't a place for another sergeant on the convoy team, so I filled in as basically an experienced specialist, did what Staff Sergeant Lombard told me to do, kept my mouth shut, and maintained a good attitude, at least on the outside. I still wore sergeant stripes, carried a sidearm and the personnel system still listed me as an E5, so I hadn't been busted down in rank. Yet.

Overall the assignment wasn't bad, I did get to see a bigger slice of Paradise, from equatorial jungles, over mountain passes and down to the grasslands. It was a nice planet, too bad it was infested with hamsters, and we had to hand it over to the Kristang after E-Day. Paradise would have made a very nice second home for humanity. Since we couldn't even get to planets in our home solar system without help from aliens, that was only wishful thinking.

A typical convoy trip was four or five days out, four or five days back, hauling grain and other hamster food. Hamster civilians left the planet via the space elevator, not the Launcher, so we didn't have to deal with the chaos of unhappy hamster families. We didn't encounter any trouble from the Ruhar, other than minor, annoying and random acts of sabotage here and there; I interpreted those as hamsters giving the finger to UNEF. That I could understand, we humans were the occupying force, acting as goons for the Kristang in the eyes of the Ruhar, and if I was in their situation, I'd be feeling defiant. Some of the

Ruhar families had been here for three generations, set down roots in the fertile soil of Paradise, and they'd been peacefully farming and minding their own business, until the recent wormhole shift caused the Kristang to decide the time was ripe to take back the planet. UNEF required convoy escorts to prevent problems, the thinking was the hamsters may become troublesome as we approached E-Day, and it set in that they really were leaving this planet behind, likely forever. The Chinese and French had found hamster stragglers in places that were supposed to have been fully evacuated, and troops of every nationality had found hidden caches of hamster weapons. Maybe the Ruhar weren't intending to go quietly after all. In between convoy trips, we had a day or two at Fort Arrow, which meant sleeping in a real bed, eating hot food that someone else cooked for you, and being able to use the gym, baseball fields and other opportunities for R&R. Fort Arrow even had a large swimming pool, the best feature of which was being able to see female soldiers in swim suits. Unfortunately, not one single damned time that I went to the Fort Arrow Dining Facility were they making cheeseburgers. I had good fish and chips, a decent meatloaf that was more loaf than meat, and chicken pot pie that was more veggies and crust than chicken. Meat of any kind seemed to be getting in short supply on Paradise, we heard rumors that the supply ships from Earth were delayed, or operating on irregular schedules, or that space battles elsewhere in the sector were causing the Thuranin to reroute their ships. Soon after we humans took over the Launcher from the Ruhar, the UNEF base commander had ordered a garden to be planted, so we would have fresh greens to eat. Fresh tomatoes, melons, onions, spinach, peppers, all stuff you'd see at a typical farmer's market. I knew the situation was getting worrisome one day, when the only lunch options at the Fort Arrow DFAC were spinach salad and vegetarian fajitas. Sure, spinach is a good cheap source of protein, and it was tasty enough when I loaded my salad up with walnuts and croutons, but sometimes a soldier wants a hunk of meat to chew on. And cheese. And a bun. Toasted. With ketchup. Fried onions would be nice.

As we approached Fort Arrow at the end of my fifth convoy trip, we were looking forward to three days of R&R on the base, because our vehicles would be down for regular maintenance. Private Pope leaned toward me to talk over the hum of the truck's electric engine. "Sergeant, you got plans for R&R tomorrow?"

When I joined the convoy unit, the initial reaction was first, the inevitable curiosity about my minor celebrity, and second, wondering how I'd screwed up enough to get assigned to convoy duty at Fort Arrow. I took the Barney jokes in good humor; I'd heard the jokes a millions times by now and had a good-natured reply ready for all of them. Our LT was skeptical about me at first, then Staff Sergeant Lombard let me handle some of the workload, take care of minor administrative stuff that wasted his time, so once people saw Lombard thought I was Ok, I was accepted, and that felt good. "No plans, why?" The weather forecast was hazy, hot and humid, chance of afternoon thunderstorms, typical near the equator this time of year.

"There's a crashed Kristang starship a couple miles north of the base," Pope explained. "A group of us are going to check it out, if you want to come with us."

"A starship fell out of orbit? Damn! Is there anything left of it?" I didn't try to conceal my eagerness.

"Uh huh, I've seen pictures from people who've been there. They say it's a frigate. It's from the battle when the Ruhar took this place from the Kristang the last time, so it's old, and the jungle had swallowed up some of it, but the major structure is still there. The hamsters cleaned up the weapons and the reactor. UNEF discourages us from poking around there, because the Kristang are sensitive about it, but lots of people do it."

"Yeah, I'd uh, I'd love to go." I suppressed any thoughts about taking souvenirs, the Kristang would likely very much frown on that. "Thanks."

We made plans to head out to the downed ship early the next morning. As we were eating breakfast, Private Crockett walked over to us quickly and whispered "Hurry up, let's get out of here. There's an Indian general flying in to visit, he's giving a speech right after lunch, and they want all hands here at the DFAC to give him a good crowd."

We all groaned. No one wanted to sit in the stuffy dining facility, listening to another boring speech. We gobbled our powdered eggs and toast, grabbed peanut butter sandwiches for lunch, and practically ran across the base to disappear into the jungle as soon as we could. Anyone sitting around with not enough to do was for sure going to get voluntold to fill seats in the DFAC.

'A couple miles' to the downed ship turned out to be more like ten miles, and there wasn't a road, so we walked. Enough people had been this way that there was a sort of trail through the jungle. I say sort of, because the trail had evolved as each group of people figured out better ways to get there; avoid hills, find shallower places to cross streams, avoid mud and dense pockets of thorns. It would have been better if the trail had been marked, which it wasn't. Whatever native animals lived in this jungle also had created trails, and there were lots of dead ends. As a substitute for markings, we tried to follow whichever trail appeared to have had more traffic, this turned out to be a bad idea, as the people who had gone before us were idiots. I sank up to my knees in muddy jungle streams more than once. It was hot, and humid, and there were large creepy insects in the jungle, creepy even though we knew, or were told, their venom couldn't affect us. I kept swatting and squishing insects that dropped from the trees and landed on the back of my neck, hoping for an easy meal. Insects clearly hadn't gotten the memo about humans not being edible to the native biology of Paradise. Or they were just hateful MFers and wanted to bite or sting something.

That 'chance of afternoon showers', which in the tropics is the equivalent of 'chance the sun will rise in the morning' turned out to be a thumping walloper of a downpour. It only lasted less than five minutes, which seemed a lot longer when we were all soaked to the skin in the first minute. Some of us tried to huddle under the larger trees with broad leaves, until lightning started crashing down, then we all got as far away from trees as we could. When the rain stopped, the sun came out, and it was like walking through a steam room. Big fat, sun-warmed water droplets dripped off the trees onto our heads, the air was thick enough to cut with a knife, and whatever insects had been sleeping before the storm were awake and hungry now. It was, we all agreed, way better than listening to a speech in the DFAC.

I'd never have found the ship on my own. We humans all relied too much on advanced technology, even on Earth, I'd started to lose basic skills like map reading and field navigation. Finally, we stumbled onto the crashed ship, mostly by following a trail of discarded MRE wrappers. From what I'd heard, I expected there to be nothing left but the bones of the ship's frame, to my delight it was way more intact than I'd feared. It was a big ship, and if Kristang frigates were this size, I'd not want to meet one of their larger combatants in space warfare. A large piece of the aft section was missing, I guess where the Ruhar had removed the fusion reactor, and the nose of the ship was buried in the swampy ground. Between the two furthest sections of broken ship that I could see, I estimated it was much larger than a nuclear submarine, maybe as long as an aircraft carrier. Maybe longer. Most of the ship was engine, or engineering section, I didn't know whether that part of the ship had been pressurized with breathable air, but it seemed practical to do that since the engines must have needed maintenance. We were able to get inside the ship and roam around a bit with flashlights, there weren't many dangerous animals on Paradise which is a damned good thing, as the only weapon we had with us was my sidearm. Even the inside of the ship was dirty, muddy and overgrown, crawling with insects. After we all poked around a while, we got bored, and of course then we got hungry. Someone suggested we climb on top of the ship, where we wouldn't be sitting on swampy ground.

It was a good day, away from the base, out in the bush, exploring something new, nobody shooting at me. I had a canteen full of bug juice, a peanut butter sandwich, a *Hooah*! Bar and a little bag of dried fruit. What else could a guy ask for? Rumor had it chicken was on the menu at the DFAC tonight, and I planned to take a swim in the base pool, maybe play basketball or softball later.

Shading my eyes, I looked up to check the position of the sun, or local star, or whatever the correct term was, and saw the distinctive twinkling light of a starship jumping into normal space. Another Ruhar transport ship? We'd been seeing those regularly enough. It still fascinated me, the idea of ships traveling faster than light.

Another twinkle. Not unusual, Ruhar transport ships sometimes came in multiples, and they were always escorted by Kristang ships, usually frigates, not that I could see the difference in one ship to another from dirtside. Hmm. More twinkling lights. And more.

A lot more.

"Uh, hey, guys," Pope pointed at the sky. "That's a lot of ships up there."

Was the Kristang task force back?

My zPhone gave a strangled squawk and went silent. Oh shit. That wasn't anything good. I tapped the icon for the command channel, and all I got was static. I was already trying to get anyone, anyone at all, on my phone, when there was a burning streak of light down from the sky and a massive explosion in the direction of Fort Arrow. A fountain of dirt exploded upward on the skyline, evolving instantly into a mushroom cloud. We'd all seen that in training videos; a railgun strike. A small, dense dart of tungsten or more likely some exotic alien material, boosted to a significant percentage of lightspeed, burning a hole through the atmosphere and slamming into the planet. Into Fort Arrow. As I watched uselessly, mouth gaping, there were more contrails zipping down to impact the base, these contrails curved as they flew. Hypervelocity smart missiles, following on the heels of the railgun darts. There were more explosions, all coming from Fort Arrow.

Everyone had the same reaction that I did. First, holy shit! Second, what the hell do I do now? Without orders, we all scrambled down off the crashed ship. I looked around in case something had changed in the minute since I'd last checked, but the situation was the same; seventeen people, and between us we had precisely one weapon, unless you counted knives. My sidearm wasn't going to be much use against the Ruhar.

"Sergeant, what's going on?"

Sergeant. Every face was turned toward me. Shit. Everyone else was a private or specialist. Damn it, I was a sergeant, wasn't I? This morning, I was supposed to be just another guy on a hike through the woods. Now the chevrons on my uniform top, and my sidearm, meant I was supposed to do something. Anything.

"You know as much as I do. Anyone got a signal on their phone?" People shook their heads negatively. At least everyone had the sense to check their phones after the base was hit. "Ruhar must be jamming us, I'm not even getting a navigation signal." I also couldn't use the proximity feature, to see on the map the phones of people right around me. The whole system must be dead. "All right, people, the network is down, turn your phones to receive only mode." That supposedly prevented the zPhone from transmitting any signal, even location; UNEF suspected the Kristang had a way of tracking us even if the phone was in stealth mode but we didn't have much choice. The last thing we needed was hamsters tracking us, hopefully they couldn't tap into Kristang technology. With the base likely knocked out, a cluster of seventeen humans would be a nice secondary target. "Grab your gear," I said automatically, ignoring that gear at this point was backpacks and canteens. "We're going back to base, ASAP."

"Base?" Private Collins pointed at the pillar of smoke, and as he said the word, there was another explosion from that direction. "There's no base! There can't be anything left of it."

"We don't know that. We're sure as hell not hiding here in the jungle. We're going back to base because there may be people there who need our help, and because it's our job, our duty. If you need more motivation, the Kristang are our only ride home, and our only way to get food shipped in. If the Ruhar get established here before the Kristang come back, we're all in deep shit."

"*If* the damn lizards come back," Collins grumbled. "How are we going to stop the hamsters from setting up camp here again? We don't even have weapons."

"We're going to keep them busy and off balance and hit them whenever we can, buy time for the Kristang task force to get back here." I looked around at a group of people I knew only vaguely, people from multiple convoy escort teams. I didn't even know all of their names, we'd only met when we assembled at the DFAC that morning. "I don't know all of you, some of you I've been on convoy duty with, and some of you told me you didn't come all the way out here to play nursemaid to a bunch of hamsters." That was a common complaint within UNEF. "This is our chance to hit back."

"Sergeant, I'm all for duty," Pope said, "but Collins has a point, what are we supposed to do without weapons?"

Specialist Amaro spoke up, I swear she stood on tiptoes and raised her hand like she was in elementary school. "There's an ammo dump outside the base, it's in a hamster storage depot, built into the hillside along the access road that runs along the Launcher track. I delivered supplies there a month ago, I think it's still there?"

"Manned? There are guards?" I asked. If not, we'd probably have no way to get the bunker door open.

"Two guys, the day I was there. There's a big heavy door at the entrance, and kind of a little shack we put up for the guards, the hamsters didn't have anything like that, they left it unmanned. It's maybe, I don't know," she looked at the map on her zPhone, "shit, without the GPS feature I don't know where it is. Not far? You can see where they cut into the hill for the access road." She pointed up to the west, to a horizontal scar along the mountain. Only a section of the cut was visible through the trees or whatever they were. I'd seen the access road briefly on my flight into Fort Arrow. The maps said there was an access road running along both sides of the Launcher, with side roads going to the Launcher tube itself about every kilometer or half mile or something like that.

"All right, anyone else been there? No?" Head shakes all around. I was tempted to climb on the ship to get a better view. "Can we go straight to the access road from here?"

Amaro looked stricken. "Um, I don't know, Sergeant?" In the military, 'I don't know' is a perfectly acceptable answer, much better than trying to bullshit your way through a situation. Usually 'I don't know' is supposed to be followed by 'but I'll find out'. "I think there's a cliff between here and the road, I can't, uh, damn this thing." She tapped the screen of her zPhone.

"That's all right, Amaro, we've all gotten too reliant on fancy technology and let our basic navigation skills go soft, I know I have." Which was true, since without the GPS I had no freakin' idea where we were. I tugged the straps of my pack tight and looked at the faces who were looking at me. Sometimes all people needed was to hear that someone, anyone, had some sort of a plan. "People, let's get weapons and ammo. Amaro, you lead off, set an easy pace, this could be a long run."

It was a long run in the heat, at least three, maybe four miles, and it seemed like a mile of it was uphill. It got easier when we got to the access road, Amaro recognized a rock slide and figured out which way to go along the road. We picked up the pace despite the increasing heat and our canteens now being out of water, it was easier to run on the road and we had the added incentive of seeing Ruhar attack ships buzzing overhead. Whenever we spotted one of those dropship attack birds UNEF called Vultures, we dove off the road under cover. Hiding under trees made us feel moderately safer, my guess was with their technology, the Ruhar knew exactly where we were. A small group of primitive humans without weapons weren't worth expending ammo.

We came upon the side road that led to the ammo dump, we ran only a quarter mile along the access road before a voice called out from under a bush beside the road. "Halt! You stay right there!" The voice was shakier than I hoped to hear, when the speaker was pointing a rifle at my head.

"Sergeant Joe Bishop, 10th Infantry. Who's in charge here?"

"You are." Another voice spoke, and a guy stepped out from behind a tree. "It's just us here, Sergeant. I'm Specialist Rogen, and that's Private Wayne under the bushes."

Shit. I'd been silently hoping someone of higher rank was at the ammo dump, to take the responsibility off my shoulders.

Rogen tapped the zPhone on his belt. "Our comms are down." I noticed Rogen still had his rifle pointed in our direction, barrel slightly down but with his finger properly poised next to the trigger. He and Wayne were in uniform, the rest of us were in T-shirts and shorts, and they didn't know the new guy claiming to be a sergeant. Rogen looked over my shoulder. "Hey, you're Miller, right? You're on convoy duty."

"Yeah." Miller acknowledged. "You're on a baseball team, shortstop?"

"Second base." Seeing a face he recognized seemed to satisfy Rogen, he nodded to Wayne and they secured their weapons. "What's going on, Sergeant?"

"We know as much as you, we were out for a hike to that crashed ship when all hell broke loose. Either the Ruhar are taking a very broad view of their cease fire agreement, or they've decided they want to take this planet back." I thought back to what I'd overheard Captain Price saying. It wasn't sensitive intel anymore. "Last week, I heard the Kristang pulled out their air cover except for a single frigate, some kind of fleet action was going on upstairs. I think the Ruhar hit Fort Arrow with a railgun strike and missiles." You couldn't see the base from the ammo dump, a shoulder of the mountain range blocked the view, except for the still thick smoke. "We don't have comms either, set your zPhones to receive only mode, so the Ruhar can't use them to track us."

Wayne shot a look at Rogen, like they'd already had that discussion and Wayne had lost. "They must know about this place," Rogen pointed to the heavy doors at the entrance to the ammo dump, "the hamsters built it. And they'll see we added a guard shack, so they know we're using the place." The guard shack was a structure that, on Earth, would be a small tool shed people would have in their backyards, it kept the guards out of the afternoon tropical rains and that's about it.

"I don't see a vehicle," Pope noted, "you guys have a hamvee?"

"No," Wayne shook his head, "we're supposed to be relieved in two hours, and the guys coming on duty arrive in a truck that we'll drive back to base."

"You can open those doors?" I pointed to the entrance to the ammo dump.

"We have the code," Rogan said, "but we're not supposed to-"

"Rogen, if you've been keeping those weapons for a rainy day, that's now." He knew what I meant despite the mostly cloudless sky. "Fort Arrow got hit, as far as we know we're the only organized resistance around here right now. We need weapons. Open that door."

We were in luck; there was mostly weapons in the ammo dump, but also a small store of water and food, which we raided. No salt or electrolyte tablets, unfortunately, I made sure everyone ate some salty peanuts or pretzels to replenish what we'd lost through sweat. "Everyone grab an M4 and ammo, take extra ammo, and get the good explosive-tipped stuff, not the standard rounds." Everyone knew how to identify clips of Kristang ammo. "Pope, Stallings, uh, Newman, and uh, Wayne and you," I pointed to the five biggest guys in our group, "take two Zingers each. Everyone else takes a Zinger and an AT4, we don't know what we'll need, so let's bring it all." I hefted a pair of Zingers onto my shoulders to set an example. They were heavy, especially on top of the M4. Thinking a moment, I took off the holster for my sidearm and left it on a shelf. No point bringing a knife to a gunfight.

Rogen helped Wayne pick up a Javelin. "Hey, are you the Joe Bishop that-"

"Yeah, Rogen. I'll tell you all about it later, promise." If there was a later.

"Body armor, sergeant?" Pope asked.

I frowned. "Uh, I'll leave that up to you," I said, and as I said it, realized how cowardly it was of me to not make that decision, "wait, no. No body armor." That was totally against Army regulations. "We need to move fast, and we're already overloaded." People nodded, it surprised me, I'd expected resistance to that order. Everyone must have figured that Kevlar wasn't going to be much use against Ruhar infantry weapons like particle beams. Body armor was mostly to protect a soldier's torso from shrapnel damage, not direct hits; body armor had saved me from serious injury in Nigeria, as much as I'd resented its weight in the heat. If I survived, I'm sure I'd catch hell for violating regs in combat. If there was a UNEF left to reprimand me. We were geared up, people were looking at me again. What next? Jogging back down the access road to the base, in full sunlight, was a suicidal idea. If the Ruhar gunships hadn't cared about us before, they sure as hell would when we got closer to the base, carrying weapons. Seeing Ruhar aircraft in the sky told me they hadn't only hit Fort Arrow, they had landed troops to take the Launcher base complex. That meant Ruhar troops on the ground, and if they were on the ground, we could hit them. If we got close enough. "Anybody got a map of this place, the Launcher complex, the whole thing?" I had an idea of the area immediately around Fort Arrow, that's all. Since I'd been there, the Launcher had shot cargo into space only three times, all when I'd been away on convoy duty. The closest I'd come to seeing it in action had been a contrail streaking into the sky and a low rumble of sound from far away.

"I do, Sergeant," offered Amaro. She jogged over to me and held out her zPhone. I took it, and scrolled through the plans she'd downloaded, refreshing my hazy memory. It wasn't much help. The launch tube had a single parallel maintenance access tunnel on the south side, and side shafts connecting to the surface roughly every kilometer. We were on the south side, getting to the access tunnel meant climbing the mountain over the buried Launcher tube. Not an option, with Ruhar gunships buzzing around. I looked up from the zPhone, looked at the soldiers who were waiting for my orders. We could try to hold part of the Launcher, fight a battle of attrition which the Ruhar would win, hold this position until we were all dead. Trade lives for time, in what I knew was a hopeless battle. That didn't sound like a good plan. The Ruhar could simply wait us out, or deploy some type of gas and immobilize us. I reviewed the schematic again, trying to find inspiration. In battle, decisions needed to be made on the spot, and my brain was already slowed by fatigue. I saw many small compartments off the tunnel, where electrical or other equipment was housed, they were dead-ends, which would become death traps if the Ruhar caught our soldiers in there. "Wait, what is this?" I held up the zPhone to Amaro. There was another tube, a small one, parallel to the Launcher tube, on our north side.

She squinted in the dim light, then announced "That's the conduit for the plasma from the fusion plant, it provides the juice for the Launcher magnets."

"How do you know that?"

"Before the war, I was planning to be an electrical engineer." She said. "It interested me, so I got a tour while the Launcher when I first got here."

Nobody had offered a tour to me. "This conduit, it's filled with plasma? That's a superheated gas, right?"

"Close enough, plasma is a fourth state of matter, it's not a gas, liquid or solid. But it is damned hot."

"Still?" An idea was forming in my head. "The Launcher hasn't fired for, what, three days now? They wouldn't be feeding plasma into the conduit unless they're charging up for a launch, right?"

"Ah, yeah, the next launch isn't scheduled for next week, because there isn't a Ruhar cargo ship upstairs to collect it," she stared at me, eyes wide. Must have guessed my crazy idea. "The conduit is probably cool by now, but-"

I looked around the vast cavern that had been excavated by the Ruhar, only a small corner of it was being used by UNEF as an ammo dump. The far end of the space was hidden in an ominous red gloom of emergency lighting, because power had been cut soon after Fort Arrow was hit. "We'll need more flashlights."

The conduit led straight into the heart of the fusion plant. Like the launch tube, the conduit had many access points for maintenance. The nearest access hatch was less than a kilometer away, back up the road, we'd passed it on our way to the ammo dump. I led my impromptu squad along the road, all of us struggling with the heat, the extra load of weapons, ducking off the road when Ruhar aircraft flew by, and the shock of a nice morning turned to horror. When we got to the access tunnel, I left the others safely outside and took Amaro with me to check out the hatch. It had all kinds of electronic controls and sensors, all of which were currently dead. And it had a wheel. A simple, big metal wheel. I set the Javelin on the ground, gripped the wheel, and turned. A dozen turns, and the hatch cracked open with a puff of air. No inferno of plasma to burn my feet off. "Huh." I said as I stuck my head in. It was a dark tube, stretching off as far as my flashlight could shine. About three meters in diameter. I flicked off my light, and peered into the darkness. No lights shined back from the other end. There were light panels set into the ceiling of the tube, they were dead.

She stuck her head in the tube. "Hey. So this is what it looks like. Bigger than I thought. Power's cut here too, Sergeant, the fusion plant must have gone offline. Or got hit." Amaro guessed.

"The Ruhar would have been careful not to hit the reactor, they need the Launcher intact. It probably shut down automatically when Fort Arrow got it." Fort Arrow had been created from part of the town the Ruhar had built for hamsters who worked on the Launcher complex, it was to the north of the fusion reactor. There were still a lot of Ruhar living in the town, they operated and maintained the launcher and reactor, our technical people weren't capable of doing anything useful with the complex alien technology. Fort Arrow was separated from the town by a fence, and the Ruhar were restricted to their own areas. I'm sure the Ruhar fleet had been careful not to hit the Ruhar part of town. I pulled myself back out of the conduit, and waved the others forward. "Here's the plan; we're going to counterattack. This conduit tube leads all the way to the fusion plant, we can get out along the way. We'll follow it, pop up in the enemy's rear, and cause some chaos. Let's kill some kill some hamsters this morning."

The conduit thankfully remained pitch dark as we ran down it. The entire way, my skin was tingling, afraid the Ruhar would detect us, and lob a few rockets or grenades down the conduit, either would wipe us out in the confined space. Or turn on whatever mechanism generated plasma and fed it into the conduit, that would fry us all to a crisp. Secretly, I was hoping that maybe the reactor had been damaged, that it wasn't only temporarily offline, because damage would mean the plasma couldn't be turned back on any time soon. There weren't any cameras in the conduit that I could see, having superheated plasma in the conduit when it was working probably meant cameras were not practical. There must be some sort of sensors along the way, to monitor the plasma, my hope was such sensors wouldn't be able to detect our presence. Ruhar operated the Launcher and reactor machinery, sensors, including all the surveillance gear, I thought were hooked up to Fort Arrow somewhere, I did know that humans operated the security system for the Launcher complex and the base. With Fort Arrow having taken hits, I was hoping the Ruhar didn't have access to the surveillance feeds, because if they did, they would detect us as soon as we came out of the conduit and entered the base area.

What I hadn't counted on were the numerous pieces of equipment we had to stumble over. I had mentally pictured the conduit as a smooth empty tube, a round hole in the ground. It wasn't. Amaro explained that the plasma was contained in a magnetic field, which required magnets spaced every couple meters. And the magnets required power cables, which required heat shielding. All of which caused running soldiers to trip, fall, and that made people behind to trip and fall. With there being room in the tube for only a single file line, people falling down didn't only cause bashed knees and elbows, it made the entire column halt. What I was most afraid of was somebody's rifle firing accidentally and alerting the Ruhar, so I ordered everyone to proceed forward at a brisk, but careful, walk, and that kept stumbling to a minimum. It was a long journey, we walked for miles underground in the claustrophobic darkness, with the view never changing except for Ruhar numbers along the wall. Fortunately, the air was cool. Amaro said it was probably the residual cold of the superconducting magnets of the main launch tube bleeding over into the plasma tube, which had been without plasma for days. Other than cursing when people fell or banged into the walls, the squad maintained discipline, minimal talking, and that in a whisper. Whether this was because they were admirably trained, or scared shitless like me, I didn't want to guess. I was terrified to the point that the flashlight was shaking in my hand, and I kept swinging it side to side to cover up how badly my hand trembled.

Walking miles underground in darkness gave me way too much time to think. Was I leading these people to a useless death because I couldn't think of anything better to do? Anything smarter? The fact was, I couldn't think of anything else to do. We were soldiers, we'd been attacked, we fight. Simple. If an officer had ordered me to do what I ordered these people to do, I would have followed without question. That didn't mean it was the right, or best, thing to do. What I'd told Collins was true; if the Ruhar were taking the planet back, we may all be dead soon. Our only chance for mission success, for survival, was to tie up the Ruhar with ground combat, guerrilla tactics if it came to that, and buy time for the Kristang to regain control in space. If the Kristang didn't or couldn't come back, we were dead anyway, and we needed to strike a blow for humanity; give the hamsters some payback, and show the Kristang that humans could be useful, reliable allies, because that's what the people of Earth needed.

When we finally approached the power plant end of the conduit, I could see ahead of us where the conduit curved and branched out, I assumed to where the plasma was generated. Wherever that was, I didn't want to go there. I called a halt, and ordered lights to be turned off, while Amaro and I looked at the schematic on her phone. I tried to mentally picture where the reactor was in relation to Fort Arrow; to the east, further up the mountain, and closer to the Launcher track. If we were near where the plasma conduit branched to connect with the reactor, we'd gone too far. Asking everyone to turn around in the narrow confines of the tunnel and march backwards a long way wasn't something I wanted to do. "Amaro, this conduit ends at the reactor, or near it?"

"No, the reactor feeds power to the plasma generator, the generator is the big round structure up the mountain, it looks like a water tower, or a petroleum storage tank? There's a tall white building right next to it. We must be close to that."

"Oh, yeah, all right," we were close to where I wanted to be, although I'd forgotten how high up the mountain we must be then. "I thought that was a water tank." The conduit had been climbing so gradually as we marched that I hadn't thought about it. The Launcher was many kilometers long and climbed up and through the mountain, from its base west of Fort Arrow to the open end of the launch tube to the east, far up the mountain and on the other side of the ridge. The mountain's bulk protected Fort Arrow, and the Launcher complex, from the sonic shock wave generated when cargo pods left the launch tube and hit the atmosphere. On our convoys, if we were going to be in the sonic footprint of a launch, we had to halt an hour ahead of time, secure our vehicles, and wear hearing protection under our helmets. It had only happened twice for me so far on convoy duty, and we'd been far enough away that the launch was merely a faint streak of light in the sky, still, I'd felt the ground rumbling from the hypersonic shock waves. All the buildings in and around the Launcher complex, including Fort Arrow, had noise-canceling systems installed in the walls and windows, and the base went on lockdown during a launch. A launch is something I'd been wanting to see, now I may have missed my chance.

Amaro and I squeezed past the column, and led the way back maybe a hundred yards to where we'd passed an access hatch. The hatches had wheels on the inside also, and this hatch had a small, thick window in the center. Sticking my eye to the window was useless, all I could see was the reflection of my eyeball, it was completely dark on the other side. If there were hamsters on the other side of the hatch, we were screwed. "Amaro, get a grenade ready."

She nodded grimly, and I slowly started turning the wheel. It didn't squeak, so I spun it as quickly as I could, and swung the heavy hatch open.

Into a dark corridor. An empty corridor, thirty meters long, the other end had a door, a regular, solid-looking rectangular door. I waved for Amaro to follow me, and the others to stay put, and walked quietly forward. The door had a keypad that was blank, no power, and a lever instead of a wheel. The lever turned surprisingly easily, the door was surprisingly heavy. And beyond was the interior of some type of garage, with a tall, wide rollup door, and a Ruhar truck parked to the left. It was simply a truck, hadn't been converted into a hamvee. Probably it was used by the Ruhar who maintained the Launcher equipment. The garage was hot and humid, there was an air conditioner unit built into the ceiling that wasn't working. Amaro and I snuck around the truck, to where there was a regular door that led to an office area; two well-scuffed tables, a couple worn-out chairs, a workbench, tools, a trashcan with wrappers from hamster lunches. And dust. This place, I guessed, didn't get used a lot. We crept warily into the office and looked out through the dingy windows.

It was a great view, in one way. We were high up the mountainside, with the Launcher complex, reactor, the town, Fort Arrow and the air field spread out below us. There was another door to the outside, in front of the big rollup door was a concrete pad that connected to the dirt access road beyond, and a roof and crane over the pad. The roof would give us cover from spying eyes above.

"Amaro, bring everyone here. And close that hatch, in case the power comes back on. An open hatch might send out an alarm."

I stepped out under the roof. Fort Arrow was indeed spread out below me. What was left of it. When UNEF created Fort Arrow out of the existing hamster town, we'd knocked down buildings to create a perimeter, and installed a fence and minefield, so it was easy to see the outlines of the base. Where the DFAC used to be was a steaming crater, steaming instead of smoking, because the railgun impactor had damaged the rec building across the street, and the cracked swimming pool there had drained into the crater. Missiles had also hit barracks buildings, which didn't make any sense as the Ruhar must have known those buildings would be mostly empty in mid-afternoon, but the base administration buildings were mostly intact, except for damage from being hit by flying debris. Same with most other buildings within the fence line of Fort Arrow.

The airfield beyond to the north was a mess, the runways had been cratered so we couldn't fly off any Dumbos, and every hanger had taken a direct hit. Smashed Chickens and Buzzards were scattered around the airfield, I couldn't see that we'd managed to get a single bird in the air, with the exception of a pillar of smoke coming from the jungle that might have been a downed aircraft. It was a mess.

People filed out the door under the roof, I cautioned them to stay under the shadow of the roof, and not to wear sunglasses or anything else that reflected sunlight and could give away our position. Most people gasped when they saw the destruction, I heard several people say quietly that we were lucky we'd not been in the DFAC.

The DFAC. What Fort Arrow used as a dining facility had been used for a similar function by the hamsters before us, I estimated it could easily hold four hundred people. Four hundred, all dead. No way had anyone walked away from that steaming crater.

"What's the plan, Sergeant?" Pope asked.

My plan had been for us to infiltrate the town around Fort Arrow, and use cover of the hamster buildings there to harass the Ruhar forces; figuring they'd fight us house to house rather than blow up half their town to get us. We could tie them up for many hours, even days, giving the Kristang time to take back control upstairs. And as long as humans held part of the town, the Ruhar wouldn't risk operating the Launcher. The reason I'd brought so many Zingers along is we had no chance to hold out if the Ruhar could float in the sky above us and pick us off with precision strikes. Simply firing a single Zinger once in a while would force the Ruhar close air support to pull back and change their tactics. I know, because in Nigeria I'd seen that rebels, blindly firing unguided RPGs at our helicopters, made our air cover scurry for cover.

To the north, beyond the airfield, two pairs of Vultures were circling, one pair providing cover as the other pair fired missiles and strafed the jungle. Amaro pointed to the action, some humans must have survived and escaped the airfield to fight on. As we watched, a pair of Zingers burst out of the jungle and raced toward one of the Vultures; the first missile was hit with a particle beam and went off course, the second missed but exploded close enough that the Vulture staggered in the air, and wobbled off toward the airfield, trailing smoke.

"Binoculars," I ordered, holding my hand out to Pope. I stepped back into deeper shade and scanned the airfield. Several Dodos were being serviced on the tarmac, and a pair of Whales were unloading. Dodos were small dropship transports, while Whales were huge dropships, bigger even than the Dumbo aircraft I'd flown in. Whales could carry big cargo down from orbit, they had doors at the back end and a ramp like a cargo aircraft, one of the Whales at the airfield was unloading a Buzzard that had its wings folded.

"Shit, that's not good," I said quietly, not quietly enough.

"What?" Pope asked.

"If they're bringing in Buzzards already, they must be confident they'll be here for a while." How were we going to get down into the town without being seen? I hadn't considered that we would come out of the conduit so far up the mountain, we must have been five hundred feet above the town. Why hadn't I realized that-

"Incoming!" Someone behind me shouted. With a high-pitched roar of turbines, two dropships came over the ridge behind us, flew near the garage or whatever was the structure we sheltered in, and flared into hover mode to land at the airfield. It was a Dodo, escorted by a Vulture. We all squeezed against the rollup door, as far under the roof as we could. I watched as they landed, and as they settled down, one of the Whales took off in a cloud of dust, gained altitude, and flew close to us, climbing over the ridge behind us and gaining speed rapidly. I watched its belly slide across the sky as it passed us. Its big, fat, vulnerable belly.

"Huh." Just like that, I had an idea. "This is this flight path now. We're right under the flight path." Whenever I'd been at Fort Arrow, I'd seen aircraft approach from the east or west, sometimes the north, but never from the south, never coming in over the mountain. That had changed. "Our guys over there, in the jungle, they've got the Ruhar scared to fly in from that direction. Shit! They're flying right over us; they don't know we're here!"

With the binoculars, I looked down at the other Whale that was still unloading. Some cargo was coming down the rear ramp, from the number of troops climbing down the stairways on the ship's side and lined up on the tarmac, this Whale had mostly carried troops. A Whale, according to the info provided by the Kristang, could carry up to 600 passengers. Judging by the gear the troops on the tarmac were loaded down with, I figured a troop-carrier Whale couldn't hold the maximum number of people.

The Vultures above the jungle beyond the airfield were still firing an occasional missile at whoever was down there. If we could shoot down even one dropship from our position, the Ruhar would very likely halt operations at the airfield until they were confident they'd rooted out all human resistance in the area. That would delay their occupation schedule for the Launcher significantly. Maybe even force them to divert dropships and troops from other areas, and that would give our forces elsewhere on Paradise a break. Even if the Kristang didn't, or couldn't, come back to Paradise, surely they would eventually hear of UNEF's firm stand at the Launcher, and boosting the Kristang's opinion of humanity's combat usefulness had to help the people back home. Which was the whole point of the UN Expeditionary Force. Our forces had no possibility of actually defending Earth from the Ruhar, we needed the Kristang to do that for us. UNEF had gone to the stars in order to give the Kristang a reason to care whether Earth was conquered by the Ruhar or not. In a way, UNEF's mission was to SAVE THE WORLD.

Those all caps were intentional, by the way, it looks more dramatic that way. When you're facing the strong possibility of being trapped, forever, on an alien planet controlled by the enemy, having a dramatic rationale for your mission makes it feel better.

I handed the binoculars back to Pope. "Pope, you, and, uh, Wayne, can you get across the road and under those trees there? I need a spotter to see what's coming over the ridge behind us. Hold up fingers to give us a count with your right hand, with your left hand, uh, a fist means a Whale, holding your palm open face down is a Dodo, and palm open face up is a Vulture, got it?" I didn't want to waste Zingers on a Vulture, we needed to make a bigger impact than shooting down a two-seater gunship.

Pope looked right and left. "Yeah, we'll go down the road under tree cover on this side to where those trees are overhanging the road, cross there, and make our way back."

"Good, leave your Zingers and AT4s here. As soon as we fire Zingers, you run back here, we're going back into that conduit for a quick run to the next exit." The Ruhar would shortly turn the garage into a pile of rubble after we shot at their aircraft. "Everyone else, get your Zingers ready. Amaro, see if you can get this rollup door open, we'll need to make a quick exit." I shrugged off the strap to one of the Zingers I carried, flipped open the targeting panel, and pressed the first button to activate it. The weapon's seeker would stay active for several hours now.

Pope and Wayne set their missiles down, peeked out under the edge of the roof, and sprinted off under the trees. In a couple minutes, they were under a tree across the road from me, we were able to communicate by talking loudly, the hand signals had been for communication when enemy aircraft were flying loudly overhead. Almost as soon as Pope and Wayne got settled under the trees, we heard aircraft approaching. One Dodo and one Vulture.

I shook my head and gestured thumbs down with one hand. If no more tempting targets appeared soon, I'd settle for a Dodo, I had to worry about Ruhar troops driving along the access road and seeing us. Surely the Ruhar were going to recon the whole area.

Another aircraft approached from behind us. A single Vulture. Again I gave the thumbs down. Checking my people, I could see they were so keyed up that we needed to do something soon. "Check your safeties, people, nobody fires until I give the signal." I made people acknowledge my order one by one, looking each person in the eye. Myself, I tried to act calm, even bored, I stifled a fake yawn. "Damn, I wish they'd get here soon, I'm hungry." I complained, and that drew some nervous laughter.

The Whale at the airfield finished unloading, the Ruhar troops had marched off the tarmac into the jungle, and it lifted off. This Whale flew almost directly over us, I could read some of the marking on its belly and wings. As it approached, I made sure everyone saw my thumbs down. If we had to, I'd attack an empty ship on its return flight, that wasn't my preference.

Then I did get bored, a bit. After that Whale took off, maybe ten minutes went by with no flight activity in the area, other than the pair of Vultures over the jungle. They weren't strafing or firing missiles anymore, and we didn't see any more Zingers coming from the jungle either. With the lull in air traffic, I started to question not shooting at that Dodo or the empty Whale that had passed over us earlier. Either would have accomplished our main objective of making the Ruhar shut down flight operations. Still, I wanted to hit the hamsters, hit them hard, make them pay for all the people who died at the Fort Arrow DFAC.

While we waited, I had people police the area, after we triggered off the Zingers we needed to run back into the conduit immediately, and not waste time picking up things we'd dropped. Shit, I should have left the access hatch to the conduit open, not waste time spinning that big heavy wheel. Too late now, lesson learned.

"Whales!" Wayne shouted, and waved his arms. Pope had the binoculars to his eyes, and waved one hand excitedly. Wayne held up a fist and two fingers, then palm open face up with two fingers. Two Whales, escorted by two Vultures. We couldn't hear them yet; they must have been approaching at high altitude. Then we could hear them.

"This is it, people!" I shouted. "Do not fire until I give the order! We've got two Whales; people on this side target the first Whale, people on this side, you're with me on the second Whale. Stay under the roof for now." I was so keyed up that I forced myself to double check my Zinger's safety was on. As the screaming sound of Whale jets got louder, I shuffled close to the edge of the concrete pad. What did we know about Whales, I tried to recall? They were well protected for a dropship, with multiple defensive particle beam turrets. With fifteen of us ready to fire Zingers at only two targets, from close range, we had a good chance to get a hit. At low altitude and slow airspeed, I was hoping a stricken Whale wouldn't have time to recover before slamming into the mountainside, and crashing down the slope.

I stuck my head out from under the roof to see where the Whales were. They were close, they would pass slightly to the east of us rather than directly overhead. Neither of them had their active stealth engaged. "Get ready," I ordered loudly and stepped out from under the roof, "arm seekers!"

With the safety off, the targeting display lit up, I centered the crosshairs on the rear of the trailing Whale, on the rear portside jet. The jet was angled almost fully down, providing more lift than forward thrust, as the Whale was on final approach. The most vulnerable point of its flight profile. Low and slow.

"Does everyone have a target acquired?" I shouted, then repeated the question. We needed to shoot soon, with fifteen of us standing in the open holding Zingers to our shoulders, we were sure to be spotted by the escorting pair of Vultures soon. Fourteen people acknowledged they had solid locks on target.

"Ready, ready, *shoot*!" I toggled off my Zinger, and fourteen other missiles leapt from their launch tubes. The Zinger launched from the disposable tube with a magnetic pulse, so the backblast from the rocket wouldn't kill the user, the rocket didn't kick on until the missile was fifty meters away. Then the rocket motor kicked on, and I almost lost sight of the missiles as they went into super acceleration. It all happened so fast, I don't know how many of our Zingers were diverted, disabled or killed outright by the Whales' defenses. What I do know is both Whales staggered in the air, as front and rear portside jets on both Whales exploded and were torn off, other missiles ripped into the bellies of the two unlucky ships. The Whales have belly jets and the ability to hover on them alone, that feature didn't help them that day.

I had a recurring nightmare of that moment, what I think, I hope, is a false memory; something I could not have seen, something that could not have happened, yet I have an incredibly vivid memory burned into my brain. The passenger/cargo compartment of a Whale does not have any windows, windows are weak points in the structure of an aircraft, and the structure of a Whale needs to go up and down to orbit hundreds, even thousands of times over its life. There are tiny windows in the side doors, for some reason there are a pair of small windows on both sides at the back near the ramp, and there are windows in the cockpit. The cockpit windows are like those of a commercial airliner on Earth, big enough for pilots to see out, not big enough for anyone to see much of the interior from outside. And the Whales must have been a half mile, maybe, from us, plus slightly above our position. Yet, I have a vivid, haunting memory of the Ruhar pilot of the second Whale, the one I'd fired at, turning to look at where the missile threat was coming from, and just as the first missile impacted and slewed the Whale's nose toward me, the pilot for a brief second looked directly at me. Not just at our position, not just at a group of human soldiers, not just at a particular human soldier.

At *me*.

Me, like he knew me, like he was asking why, since our species had grown on different planets, thousands of lightyears apart, and we'd lived completely different lives, why had our paths crossed like this? Had it come to pass that the only time in our entire lives we met, I fired an alien missile and ended his life? Why? He wasn't asking the universe, he wasn't asking karma or fate or whatever divine being he worshiped, he was asking *me*.

That haunted me for a long time.

Both Whales rolled on their sides after they lost their port jets, one of them briefly managed to get a semblance of control before they both plunged almost straight down into the mountain jungle slope, tumbling over and over, breaking apart amid secondary explosions. What we should have done is retreat into the conduit immediately after triggering off our missiles, instead we stood watching, mouths agape or cheering, which is what happens when a thrown-together squad is led by an inexperienced sergeant. Wayne brought me back to focus when he and Pope sprinted across the road to us. "Time to go, Sergeant?" He asked, eyes wide.

"Yes. Yes, go, Amaro, get that hatch open!" One of the Vultures had soared vertically high above us, the other had swung in a circle toward us and was looking for a target to kill. Looking for us. Without thinking, I unstrapped my second Zinger, glad now that I'd carried the extra thirty pounds, got a lock on the Vulture, and squeezed the trigger. The Vulture's defenses zapped my Zinger before it got close, I still accomplished my objective because the Vulture veered away and zoomed off at high speed, buying us precious time to get back into the conduit.

It turned out that the efforts of our thrown-together squad weren't needed, that all the Ruhar aboard the two Whales we shot down had died for nothing. It wasn't even an hour later that a Kristang task force came back, and the Ruhar ships jumped back away, abandoning their forces on Paradise. By that time, I'd retreated my squad to the plasma generator, holing up in a place I figured the Ruhar wouldn't risk damaging. After the two Whales crashed and burned and the surviving Ruhar on the ground got over the initial shock, a pair of Vultures buzzed around like angry hornets, weapons pods exposed and occasionally strafing something on the ground with laser fire. They knew where we were, I could imagine the Vulture drivers shouting for clearance to blow my squad to hell, and being told not to risk damaging the vital Launcher machinery. I figured our best chance for survival was to take cover someplace defensible that the Ruhar couldn't blast with heavy weapons, and buy time. The plasma generator complex seemed a good bet. All we had left was rifle ammo, AT4s, a couple Zingers, some grenades and a sense that we'd done the best we could to avenge our dead. We found an auxiliary control room that was underground and it didn't have any windows, so we had to use cameras that the Ruhar oddly had forgotten to disable. From one camera, we had a view of the still steaming crater where the DFAC had been. I wondered whether the people in the DFAC had any idea of trouble before the railgun round vaporized them, had they known, a few seconds before impact, that Ruhar warships had jumped into orbit? I hoped not. Better, in this case, for the blissful ignorance of listening to a UNEF general drone on in a boring speech, daydreaming pleasant thoughts and not realizing you'd been killed until you woke up in the afterlife. No such luck for people at the airfield and motor pool, they'd had time to see the DFAC disappear and have debris raining down on them before smart missiles dropped clusters of submunitions on them and destroyed everything that could drive or fly. The Vulture gunships that had ignored us had strafed scattered survivors, while there was a lot of confusion, UNEF estimated six hundred seventy dead, of the roughly nine hundred humans stationed at Fort Arrow that day. That was a stark lesson in future combat; if you didn't control the high ground you were as good as dead, and the high ground in this case was orbit and above. Digging in didn't help much when a railgun round could penetrate up to three hundred meters into the ground, if the launching ship seriously cranked up the muzzle velocity. The Ruhar had ships dedicated to orbital bombardment, the briefing packet I'd seen depicted a long, thin railgun barrel with fusion reactors at the far end and nothing much else to it. Who needed dirty nukes when a railgun dart could provide ten kilotons of hurt on a target, and ships could pump one dart after another until even the hardest target was a cloud of atoms?

Considering the nature of future combat, what the hell were humans even doing out here at all?

Amaro noticed the change of situation first, she'd been monitoring a camera, and called for me when she saw that the pair of hamsters who had been watching our personal fusion reactor set down their weapons and stand up so they were in full view. We toggled the view from one camera to another, and the scene was repeated all over the base, hamsters laying down their weapons and walking away, toward the airfield. Vulture gunships coming in to land, crews getting out, leaving the doors open, and walking away. We barely had time to speculate what was going on before all our zPhones beeped at once. The cavalry had returned. Our allies the Kristang were back in command of space around Paradise, and the Ruhar forces on the ground had surrendered. For now, anyway.

CHAPTER SEVEN   COLONEL

UNEF flew in a half dozen Buzzards a couple hours later, we'd spent the time searching for survivors and assisting the wounded. To my relief, we found an Army captain who took command, and I went back to following orders.

Three days later, in the morning there was a violent thunderstorm while I was working on a clean-up crew, after the rain stopped and the sun came out to raise steaming clouds off the airfield tarmac, a private found me and said that I had orders to report to Major Perkins at the admin building. Major Perkins? What the hell was she doing here, she'd told me she'd been assigned to the Indian sector. My thought that this couldn't be any good for me.

"Sergeant Bishop reporting, ma'am." I was a bit out of breath from running up the stairs.

Major Perkins looked at me a moment in surprise. "You couldn't have cleaned up? What have you been doing?"

I glanced down at my soiled and sooty clothes, and my dirty hands with blackened fingernails. "I was told to get here on the double, ma'am. I was helping move, uh, debris off the runway." Debris that included shattered Buzzards with human remains still aboard.

"Oh, hell, Bishop. I didn't intend for you to run all the way here, dammit. Sit down." She looked as tired as I felt. "How you feeling?"

"Numb, ma'am," I answered honestly. "Like you told me, I was laying low here, on convoy duty. Minding my own business. Then, blam, all hell breaks loose." I shuddered involuntarily, thinking of the crater that was the DFAC. "Why the hell did they hit the DFAC, ma'am? A couple minutes different that morning, and I would have been there."

Perkins looked out the window, which gave a good view of that crater. "The Ruhar commander of the attack here, we interrogated her, she says the strike on the DFAC, the main barracks and the admin building were deliberate, and they thought the DFAC and the barracks would be mostly empty in mid-afternoon. If General Gupta hadn't been visiting, the DFAC would have been empty, and there's no way the Ruhar fleet could have known that before they jumped into orbit. She said it was bad luck the DFAC was packed with people, that they didn't want to cause casualties unless they needed to. I don't know whether to believe her or not, G2 will be the judge of that. Or the Kristang, we're handing her over to the Kristang tomorrow. That's why the Ruhar are so pissed about you shooting down those two Whales, they each had almost five hundred troops aboard, plus the crews. The Ruhar apparently didn't realize they'd killed half that many at the DFAC, it's a crater and they weren't taking time to examine it for remains. To the Ruhar, until we told them about casualties at the DFAC, your actions needlessly escalated the conflict here, at a time they were offering a cease fire."

"It didn't look like that when their gunships were strafing every human in sight, ma'am." I said hotly.

"Understood, Bishop, keep in mind our people here were shooting at them, so let's chalk it up to the fog of war. I have no problem with your actions, in fact, I put you in for a commendation. Our, uh, friends upstairs had a different idea. They want UNEF to promote you." She got a sour look on his face, like she didn't agree with the idea.

"First sergeant? I've only been a sergeant for-"

"Bishop, we're not making you a first sergeant." The look on her face was impossible to read; I assumed she meant the Kristang wanted to make me a first sergeant, but UNEF wasn't going to do it, because I wasn't ready. A sentiment I agreed with completely, I still wasn't sure about the sergeant thing. Maybe Division had sent Perkins here to soften the blow, because we'd worked together before. "The Kristang promote almost entirely based on success in battle, there are political considerations, and rivalries within the clans, but in their system promotions are done on the basis of combat success, which they define as killing the enemy. Between those two Whales, and the casualties on the ground when the ammo aboard exploded, your actions killed well over a thousand Ruhar. The Kristang are impressed. They're pissed that most human units didn't do much while the Ruhar were here, never mind there wasn't much we could do while we're dirtside and the Ruhar could pound the entire planet from orbit. You killed a whole lot of Ruhar, while most of UNEF, especially senior officers, didn't do a damned thing, according to the Kristang." Senior officers included Major Perkins, it wasn't tough to see how she felt about that. "The Kristang want us to, oh, hell, here."

She took a small box out of a pocket, considered it distastefully, and abruptly snapped it open. Inside were a pair of silver insignia, an eagle clutching arrows and an olive branch in its claws, with the head of the eagle turned toward the arrows. It was the War Eagle insignia. The US Army hadn't issued those since WWII.

Those eagles were the insignia of a full colonel in the Army, Air Force and Marines, or a captain in the Navy. "Wow, ma'am, they're bumping you up two grades?" I was impressed, Perkins was a major, and the rank above major was lieutenant colonel. As far as I knew, nobody went straight from major to being a full bird colonel.

"No, Bishop, you dumbass." Perkins said with irritation. "You. They're for you. The Kristang want UNEF to make you a colonel."

"Holy shit."

"Yeah, holy shit is about right. Colonel is a rank below what the Kristang wanted, they expected UNEF to make you a general. A Goddamn *general*." She shook her head in disbelief. "Can you believe that shit?"

"Ma'am, I can't believe they'd make me a colonel, forget about general."

"Bishop, don't let this go to your head. You're a reasonably smart soldier, you're flexible, you adapt to situations, and you've shown ability to take initiative on occasion. The fact is, you're not any more smart or flexible or innovative than the Army expects of any soldier."

"Yes, ma'am," I agreed, because it was true.

"Anyway, you won't be a general, we told them the role of generals in our armies is mostly administrative, that colonel is the highest rank directly involved in combat. True enough. They understood that, so they're satisfied with you being a colonel. That rank," she nudged the box with the silver eagles, "is high enough to show that UNEF values success in combat as much as the Kristang do. It's important to keep our allies happy."

"Uh," I mumbled, mesmerized by those pretty silver eagles. Damn. Before the Ruhar attacked, all I wanted from my military service was to pay for college somewhere, and get out. Now there was a pair of silver eagles sitting in front of me. "I'm not good at writing letters and stuff."

"Letters?"

I broke my gaze away from the eagles to meet her eye. "You know, I write a letter that says something like thank you, this is a great honor but I can't accept, the US Army doesn't work this way-"

"Sergeant, I'm not getting through to you, so I'll break it down for you Barney style." She spat with exasperation and not even a hint of a smile, so I knew she wasn't using 'Barney' ironically. "This is the last time I can give you an order anyway, before you outrank me. UNEF doesn't want you to politely refuse the promotion. We need you to accept eagerly, accept the promotion as your right for killing a lot of Ruhar. We need you to tell the Kristang that you're only sorry you couldn't have killed more hamsters. Be confident, be bold, be bloodthirsty. Be what the Kristang want humans to be, because garrison duty on Paradise may be a shit job, but it's the job we agreed to, and our allies are our only ride home. And our only source of food."

"Holy shit." I repeated. I didn't know what to say.

Me. A colonel.

A full bird colonel.

Me.

"What am I going to do? As a colonel?" A colonel in the US Army could be commander or deputy commander of a brigade, that was thousands of troops. No way in hell was I qualified to do that.

Major Perkins shrugged and avoided my eyes. "Damned if I know. UNEF will figure it out."

Shit. It hit me. UNEF was going to use me as a publicity stunt, trot me out for the Kristang as an example of the ideal warrior human, while behind my back, all the humans would be laughing at me. I couldn't keep the disgust from showing on my face.

"Bishop, UNEF needs this. You don't have to like it; you do have to do your duty." Major Perkins admonished.

"Sure. I'll wear medals on my chest, talk to the troops and maybe sell some war bonds. Shit." A promotion was supposed to be a good thing. "Am I going to be the only puppet UNEF is promoting?"

"No, there's a Chinese Army major they're promoting to lieutenant colonel. The Kristang were also pleased with the actions of a US Army captain, two Indians and one from the French. They all died in battle, so only the two of you are alive to receive the honor."

"This Chinese guy, he's only getting bumped up one grade? Why?" Hell, I was going straight from the lowest type of sergeant you could be to a full colonel.

"His unit defended a warehouse complex that used to belong to the Ruhar and UNEF is now using as a supply depot, apparently the Ruhar left something important behind when the Kristang took over. The Ruhar wanted to get back in there real bad. They couldn't risk damaging whatever is in the warehouses, so they landed troops and fought it out on the ground. This Major Chang was still in control of two warehouses when the Kristang fleet came back to chase the Ruhar away, but he lost eighty percent of his men. Including, rumor has it, the son of a high-ranking Chinese government official. That's why he's only getting one bump in grade. Look, Bishop, this will be what you make of it, you got that? You're a damned good sergeant, you did a good job with your EOT in Teskor, and no one is going to say you didn't earn some sort of a promotion by your actions here. This is good for humanity; we must have the Kristang thinking human troops are valuable."

The promotion ceremony took place at Fort Olympus, the UNEF HQ complex. I was astonished to see the place was pristine, the Ruhar hadn't touched it at all during the attack. Major Perkins, who accompanied me on the Dumbo flight to Olympus, said Ruhar prisoners told UNEF they'd not hit Olympus because they wanted UNEF command intact, so someone with authority could order all humans on Paradise to lay down their weapons.

Which would have been easier to do, if the hamsters hadn't been jamming all of our communications. Who knows how aliens think, huh?

Meeting General Meers and the other senior commanders was not as intimidating as I expected, I was dreading a long, formal ceremony filled with speeches and me having to maintain either a menacing warrior scowl or a pleasant smile, whatever the UNEF public relations officer thought was appropriate. Instead, because only a small number of Kristang had been cleared to land on Paradise without full environment suits, there were no Kristang present at Olympus, and therefore the promotion ceremony was General Meers in his office pinning silver eagles on my uniform, with a half dozen other senior officers watching. After the brief ceremony, there was a delicious meal in the officers' mess, with steaks that tasted fresh, which I later learned was because they were irradiated and chilled rather than frozen, green beans that weren't the usual mushy Army fare, baked potatoes with real butter, chocolate cake, and real fresh-brewed coffee.

Seniors officers ate well. That, I could get used to. My joy lasted until a US Marine Corps colonel thanked me for giving the headquarters unit an excuse for a feast; General Meers had senior officers at Fort Olympus on field rations six days a week, to remind commanders and their staff what troops in the field were experiencing. I didn't know much about Meers, but my respect for him climbed several notches after hearing that.

The steak was great. I was still craving a cheeseburger.

After dinner, General Meers wanted to talk to me in private. Me. The commander of all human forces on Paradise wanted to have a little chat with me.

"Serg-, damn it, Colonel, it's new to me too. Bishop." My last name was conveniently rank-neutral. "You've had a hell of an interesting career, for one so young. Nigeria, then the Ruhar crash into your home town and you capture one of them. My G2 tells me you were our gold source of intel here for a while. And then you pull together a squad on your own, and shoot down two Whales. Surprised the hell out of me when they told me you're the same Bishop that captured a Ruhar soldier with an ice cream truck. Those are some big goddamn coincidences."

"My mother said I was a trouble magnet growing up, always getting into one thing or another." I could hear her voice in my ear as I said it. "It's not all that much of a coincidence, sir. I was on leave when the Ruhar crashed in my hometown; that was luck. But it wasn't coincidence that the burgermeister-"

"The who?"

"The Ruhar mayor, or whatever she is, we called her the burgermeister, the one who fed me the intel about wormholes and all that. It wasn't a coincidence she picked me to talk to, she sought me out because the hamster I captured back home reported he was treated well, and she wanted to meet me. I was at Fort Arrow because, uh, I was told it was because the Kristang were sniffing around trying to find who was feeding us intel, so it was no coincidence I was there when the Ruhar attacked. And I probably would have been at the Fort Arrow DFAC with everyone else, except Captain Price there said he was tired of UNEF using Fort Arrow as a dumping ground, and he stuck me on convoy duty to get me out of the way. That's why I was off base then the Ruhar hit us." That was close enough, General Meers didn't need the details.

"One thing led to another, huh?"

"That's the way I see it, sir."

"I suppose you could be right about that. Now that you're here, don't expect you can screw off because you've got UNEF over a barrel. The Kristang promote based on success in combat, what you may not know is they can sack people just as fast."

"Sir, I don't know what I'm going to do next, but whatever duty I'm assigned, I'll do it the best I can."

"Good. Last thing we need is everyone in the damned UNEF thinking they can jump ahead quick if they do something spectacular. Most lieutenants out there think they're smarter than their COs. And sergeants think they're better soldiers than any fancy-pants lieutenant." He snorted. "Hell, the sergeants are probably right. We've already had incidents of people trying crazy Rambo shit to get noticed. So busting you back down to sergeant or private because you screw up somehow would make my life easier, you got that?"

"Yes, sir." It was kind of what I expected to happen eventually anyway. I had no business wearing silver eagles.

"That said," Meers pondered the view outside the window, where a pair of Chickens were flying by, "I don't want you to fail. Bishop, I'm giving you fair warning that we plan on riding you like a rented mule, so if you think being a mustang colonel means you fly around and give speeches, you best put that thought right out of your head."

"Never considered it, sir." I appreciated the warning.

The next day I got started on a crash course in the responsibilities of a US Army colonel, and the protocols and etiquette for dealing with the Kristang. One of the protocols for a meeting with the Kristang was eating a bland diet starting the day before; the Kristang thought humans smelled bad, and us chowing down on meat or spicy foods made us even smellier. UNEF heard from the Ruhar that the Kristang think all other species smell bad, that humans shouldn't take it personally. What it meant for me was oatmeal and tea for breakfast instead of eggs and coffee; lunch and dinner were similarly bland and boring. Other instructions I received were not to try shaking hands with the Kristang, they didn't like us touching them at all. And not to speak unless the Kristang asked me a question. Also no smiling, the Kristang interpreted smiles as humans not taking things seriously, and the Kristang overall were not known as a jolly species.

The instructions regarding my new role as a colonel were both simple and complex. Simple because the colonel who was tasked with bringing me up to speed clearly didn't know what UNEF planned with do with me, or whether my rank was a short-term publicity stunt, so his instructions consisted of telling me to act like an officer and not do anything that might embarrass UNEF. Complex because he emailed to me an enormous series of files to read, starting with training materials a second lieutenant was supposed to know by heart. The war would be over before I read half of the crap in my inbox.

The next morning, after another bland breakfast, the Kristang sent down a dropship to pick up General Meers, several staffers, and me. We were fortunate that the space elevator and therefore the space station were in the same longitude as Fort Olympus, which meant their morning wasn't the middle of our night. Meers was going to confer with the Kristang about, whatever the Kristang wanted to talk about. I was going along so the Kristang could personally give me an award or something, we weren't clear on what was going to happen, other than the Kristang requested that Lt Colonel Chang and I come up to their space station at the top of the elevator.

I was dressed in a brand spanking new colonel's dress uniform, in which I tried to sit carefully so as not to take the sharp crease out of the pants. The day before, I'd been shot up with another dose of magical Kristang anti-nausea meds, so I wouldn't be puking up oatmeal all over myself, and everyone else, when the ship went zero gee in orbit. Sitting next to me was a Lieutenant Reynolds, whose sole job was to keep me from doing or saying anything stupid. Including stopping me from automatically saluting her. She made a point of saluting me, and calling *me* 'sir'. It felt unnatural.

The ride up was smoother than what I remember of the ride when we left Camp Alpha, either we had a better pilot this time, or the Kristang were taking care of their human VIPs. My first time aboard the space station, all I'd seen was the inside of a docking collar, and well-worn corridors as we were hustled from our ship to the elevator car that was parked at the bottom of the station. Our dropship flew into a landing bay, and we got to see the station for real. It was startling, what I imagined of Kristang interior design was stark and functional, something industrial and military for their warrior caste. What I saw was sleek and functional mostly, but with jarringly ornate elements. There were tapestries hanging on the walls that even I found to be beautiful, landscapes of distant planets, starships outlined against a nebula, intricate geometric designs, even flowers, in addition to the depictions of Kristang warriors in battle that I expected. The Kristang were an interesting species, so full of contradictions, if what the burgermeister had told me was true.

The ceremony wasn't much, we marched into a large room with Kristang seated along both sides, and high-ranking Kristang on a raised dais at the far end. It was my first time ever meeting a Kristang in person, and I was intimidated. They were all taller than the average human, bulky and muscled, and their default expression seemed to be a fierce scowl. For all I knew, that was their version of a friendly smile. Oh, and one word about how the Kristang objected to how humans smelled; they could have used an air freshener in the station. Being in a room, even a large room, with a hundred or so Kristang, had a dry, leathery smell, with an undertone of something like day-old sweat.

My part was a brief rehearsed speech that had been written for me, Lt Reynolds told me the Kristang had demanded to review and approve my remarks in advance. My speech, delivered in English and translated by zPhone, was appropriately warlike and bloodthirsty. After I stepped back, Lt Colonel Chang stepped forward, and made a brief speech similar to mine. While Chang was talking, my eyes wandered around the crowd. Most of the Kristang looked bored, even slightly disgusted. They were sitting stone-faced, or staring at the ceiling, or checking messages or playing games on their zPhones. I could sympathize, the Kristang seated along the sides of the room had been voluntold to attend the ceremony, all they wanted was for it to be over. It was like being in a roomful of human teenagers. Seeing the bored, unimpressed Kristang told me how unimportant I was, they truly couldn't care about what I'd done, whether I got promoted, or whether I survived the shuttle ride back to Paradise. When Chang was done speaking, a Kristang handed a box to General Meers. Meers took gold ribbons out of the box and pinned them to our uniforms. One of the Kristang on the dais stood up, saluted us, and Chang and I returned the salute. And it was over. Meers and the officers who were of actual importance stayed for discussions with the Kristang, while Chang and I were handed off to a Kristang who was openly resentful of babysitting two lowly humans.

"Come with me, inferiors," is what the translator said when the Kristang gestured for us to follow him. His expression told me the translation was accurate. Sullenly, he lead us winding our way through the station, an observation deck that was fairly deserted. It had chairs, a couple tables, and big windows with a great view of Paradise. It was difficult for me to resist shouting out 'I can see my house!' because I thought I recognized the big bend in the river that was just to the south of Teskor. The Kristang dismissively gestured for us to sit, while he went over to what appeared to be a bar in the corner. It was a bar. He got out a glass, poured himself a generous serving of a golden liquid, added two cubes of ice, and angrily slumped into a seat across from us. "I am supposed to congratulate you on your achievements as warriors, and welcome you to our glorious coalition. Pththth." He stuck his tongue out and blew a raspberry at us.

I looked at him more closely as he took a big gulp of the liquid. Whatever it was, it smelled like alcohol, sort of reminded me of tequila. His eyes were slightly unfocused and glassy.

Crap. He was already drunk. He'd come to the ceremony drunk. He was drinking more. This wasn't going to be good. Chang caught my eye as the Kristang stared out the window. I shook my head. Whatever happened, we were both going to be on our best behavior as guests of our allies.

"Ahhhhhh." The Kristang sighed and settled deeper into the chair, closing his eyes. Inside, I was hoping he'd fall asleep, and I could sit and watch the view quietly until someone came to fetch us. "My leader hates me. Why else would he punish me so, to make me breathe in the foul stench of inferiors?"

Assuming he didn't expect an answer to that question, I kept my mouth shut. Chang did the same.

The Kristang shook his head and gestured at us with his zPhone. "I'm told you scum need to use these to talk to each other. Shameful. Your species should not be speaking multiple languages, it is a sign of weakness! The dominant group on your disgusting planet should have conquered the others by now. You," he pointed at me, "are from uh-mare-ee-ca?"

"America, yes, sir," I answered. "I serve in the American Army."

"Army?" He laughed. "You inferiors are not an *army*. You are little children playing with toys. My pet chahalk could kill a hundred of you. I had to read about your pathetic planet, so my leader did not waste his time. Another sign that he hates me, to make me soil my mind with the history of such a pathetic species. Your A-mer-i-ca had nuclear weapons, the only nation to have nuclear weapons, for several years, yet you failed to use your advantage to destroy your enemies and conquer your planet. You are weak and pathetic. And you wonder why we have no respect for your species. Such weakness shows a serious lack of resolve. You," he pointed at me, "you served in combat somewhere on your world, a place, a place," he checked his zPhone with a hand clumsy from drinking.

"Nigeria." I said.

"Nye-gee-ree-ah. This place had no nuclear weapons?"

I shook my head, surprised. "Nigeria, no, they don't have nukes."

"Your army could have used nuclear weapons without fear of retaliation, yet instead your soldiers were sent chasing your enemies through the jungle. Why? Because you are weak and unworthy. If this nye-gee-ree-ah was so much trouble, you should have exterminated them and taken their land." He paused for another gulp of his drink, and gestured at us with the glass. "The two of you are the finest warriors of your species? Ha! Your species is worthless to the war effort; you do know that? Letting you police this planet is indulging a spoiled, stupid pet. We never should have brought you out here! Do you know what humans on Earth are doing? Instead of working hard for the war effort, they are complaining about us damaging the planet's environment. And your workers expect to get days off for vacations? Slave don't get vacation!" He said that last with an angry screech, and slammed the glass down on the table in front of us. "I told my leader, we should bring other slave species to Earth, and show you humans how to serve us properly. You humans are lazy and useless!" He looked out the window at Paradise below us. "You shouldn't be down there at all; it should be Kristang dealing with the Ruhar! Treacherous Ruhar, to contaminate our planet with biological agents, we should kill them all." he fumed silently for a minute, sipping the drink, which was almost gone. "I have volunteered to take the experimental serum that will allow Kristang to walk freely on the planet. Then I will show you how to treat the Ruhar. There are so many of them infesting our world, who will miss a few thousand, huh? Ruhar are weak and soft, but it is good sport to hunt them." He drained the last of his drink, and said quietly, "I can't wait to hunt them. Yes."

The Kristang, whatever his name was, set the empty glass on the carpeted floor and rose unsteadily to his feet. "Enjoy the view," he laughed and waved dismissively, "it may be your new home forever, as our slaves. Or it may become your grave." He laughed again and staggered out the doorway.

"Shit." I breathed when he was out of sight.

Chang nodded, then spoke in perfect English. "I think this is not a good place for us to talk about, about, what our friend there said."

No doubt the Kristang had us under close surveillance aboard the station. "You're right, Colonel Chang." I felt ashamed that Chang spoke English, while the only word of Chinese I knew was 'pinguah', which I think was the word for 'apple'. I'd seen it on a fortune cookie, and it stuck with me. My entire language knowledge of one of the world's oldest and greatest civilizations was from a fortune cookie. And fortune cookies were an American thing, not Chinese.

"*Lieutenant* Colonel," he said in a tone that had a touch of bitterness.

"Hey, you were a real officer before all this. I wear a colonel's uniform, and I know that all I am is a publicity stunt for UNEF," there was definitely bitterness in my voice. "I'll be happy when UNEF finds an excuse to knock me back down to sergeant, and I can be a real soldier again. Last thing I want to do is be a fobbit and ride a desk."

"Fobbit?" He raised an eyebrow.

"Oh, sorry, US Army slang. A fobbit is a guy who stays safe inside the fence at a Forward Operating Base, while real soldiers are out in the field. Someone who pushes paper instead of carrying a rifle."

"Ah, yes. We have those in our army, also. On this planet, though, there is no true rear area, I think. When the enemy can attack from orbit, everywhere on the surface of the planet is the front lines."

"True enough." I stood up and walked over to the window. "I was at Fort Arrow. Before that, my EOT was at a hamster village near the bend in that river, west of those mountains," I pointed unhelpfully. "Where are you stationed?"

We talked about our experiences on Paradise, and our lives before the Ruhar attacked. Chang had been an artillery officer in the People's Liberation Army, a career officer from a military family. He was just as worried about his family back on Earth as I was, the Chinese had not heard anything either; no messages or letters from home, no news, nothing. Chang was a good guy, professional, certainly a better officer than I was. He was also not looking forward to being paraded around as a public relations stunt by UNEF, although he thought that would be lower-key than what I expected. During the action that had resulted in him being promoted, he'd lost most of his men, including a lieutenant who was the only son of a high-ranking government official. The Chinese Army on Paradise wasn't eager to trumpet Chang's action too loudly. If I'd gotten the son of a senator killed, my military career would hit a roadblock for sure.

My zPhone beeped, it was Lt Reynolds, wondering where the hell was, only she said it politely. "We're on an observation deck, I think we're two," Chang held up three fingers, "no, three levels down. There's a bar here. A bar for the Kristang," I hastened to add.

"What happened to the Kristang assigned to you?"

"He was, uh, he had something important to do." I said, aware the Kristang were almost certainly listening. Important to do, like sleeping until he awoke with a hangover.

"Sir, please, stay where you are. Is Lt Colonel Chang with you?"

"Yeah, he's here, we're not going anywhere."

Five minutes later, Reynolds and two pissed-off looking Kristang showed up to retrieve us. We were hustled back to the shuttle bay, and as soon as General Meers and his staff were aboard, the dropship door slammed shut and the alarm sounded to depressurize the bay. Despite my fear that Meers was somehow pissed at me, he didn't say anything, Reynolds didn't think it was a big deal, and the ride back down was smooth

Chang and I never spoke about what the drunk Kristang had said, how he'd called humans 'slaves'. I thought about it a lot, and reported it to Meers' intelligence staff. To my dismay, they acted like they'd heard it all before, it wasn't news, and it wasn't a big deal. It was a big deal to me, it confirmed my worst fears that the burgermeister had told me the truth about the Kristang.

Were we fighting on the wrong side of this war?

CHAPTER EIGHT   PLANTING POTATOES

The first assignment UNEF had for me was, despite what General Meers had told me, to fly around and give speeches. That lasted two weeks, and, man, it was awkward for everyone involved. For me, it was awkward to wear my crisp new uniform in front of a crowd of soldiers, people who'd been in combat like I had, worse situations that I'd been in, and they were wearing the same uniforms and doing the same jobs now, while I wore silver eagles, flew around in a shiny Buzzard and ate good food with the officers. It left me feeling like a total fraud. For the soldiers who had to stand waiting for me to give my canned speech, it was awkward because they all knew I didn't deserve to be an officer, hadn't earned it, yet they couldn't say anything negative. It sucked. When my speech was mercifully over, I asked people questions, let them talk about their experiences, and ignore the awkwardness of me being there. That worked for everyone. When I was standing around in a crowd, shooting the shit with soldiers, letting them tell stories of what they'd done during the aborted Ruhar invasion, I could be just Joe Bishop, and they could be soldiers, and we could talk.

And then I had to get back on the Buzzard, fly to the next base, and do it all over again. I hated it.

So it was a blessing when UNEF found a real job for me; planting potatoes. The Kristang told UNEF it was time for humans to grow our own food on Paradise, to reduce the logistical burden on the Kristang, and to give us some food security in case fleet actions upstairs disrupted shipments. Some genius in UNEF HQ must have decided that me giving speeches had run its course, read my personnel file and saw that I was from northern Maine, and had the brilliant insight that I must be an expert on planting potatoes. My new assignment was to coordinate agriculture activities across a quarter of the continent that UNEF occupied. We weren't only planting potatoes, of course, we had a program to plant a wide variety of crops from seeds shipped from Earth. Planting potatoes was the derisive name we applied, although I was expected to be officially enthusiastic. Planting potatoes gave me an opportunity to fly around Paradise, be seen by the troops, and according to the UNEF PR staff, it gave me a chance to be seen as a hard-working grunt who made good through hard work and initiative. It was a relief to be doing something useful.

Along with a crash course in agriculture, I got a few more perks. As a colonel now, I had my own hamvee, and I had a driver, a Private Randall, at my new home base, on the border between the American and Chinese sectors. "Holy shit." I couldn't believe it when Randall showed me my assigned car. Literally, what I saw stopped me in my tracks. The hamvee was a standard Ruhar vehicle, with a UNEF symbol on both sides and the roof. And a three-foot-tall, purple stuffed Barney strapped to the front grill. "We're a thousand lightyears from Earth, how in the hell did you idiots get a Barney?" Every possible bit of gear we needed had to make the long trip to Ecuador, up the space elevator, onto a Kristang ship, to a Thuranin carrier, through wormholes, then a reverse trip down to the surface of Paradise. All our gear had been carefully inspected to make the best use of every pound of mass and square meter of space. Yet, somehow, some joker had managed to sneak a giant stuffed Barney doll into a container. What I wanted to know was, for Christ's sake, why? And what else had people snuck aboard, that was now clandestinely scattered across the surface of Paradise?

"We tactically acquired it, sir." Randall said with a straight face.

"Meaning you stole it."

"Gear adrift is a gift, sir. We wanted to make you feel welcome. Joke's over, I'll take it off the grill."

"No, what the hell, leave it." My hamvee was no more a joke than the idea of me being a full bird colonel. I walked to the front and inspected the grinning purple dinosaur." Maybe the hamster kids will like it.

It was while I was out planting potatoes that we found our first fortune cookie. The last time we had communication from Earth was when the final group of humans arrived at Camp Alpha, and I had been in the third to last convoy to get there. Since we landed on Paradise, there had been no communication either to or from Earth; the Kristang said the military situation in space didn't allow them the luxury of sending humans, even injured medivac cases, back to Earth. We were stuck on Paradise for the duration of the mission, which was more open-ended than any human was comfortable with. UNEF command fretted about not being able to send status reports to, or receive orders and advice from, Earth. Ordinary soldiers like me worried about our family and friends back on Earth. Had governments made progress on restoring electricity and other infrastructure? Were supplies and reinforcements on their way to us? Had the Ruhar attacked Earth again? The burgermeister had told me it was extremely unlikely the Ruhar would, or could, mount another expedition to Earth within the next few years. Assuming she was telling me the truth.

Then we found the fortune cookies, and everything changed. The Kristang scanned all the supplies that were delivered to the space elevators on Earth, looking for contraband. We discovered, troublingly, that the Kristang were particularly looking for digital data storage devices, which they burned out with magnetic or ultraviolet pulses. What they didn't expect was people printing words on paper, and sticking that paper on the inside of food packages. To the Kristang scanners, a reinforced cardboard container with tiny writing printed on the inside looked like any other cardboard container. Those containers were packaged on Earth, delivered dirtside on Paradise by the Kristang, and unpacked by humans. When the first supply guys opened a food package with a fortune cookie on the inside, thank God they had the smarts to not say anything about it over their zPhones; everything was word of mouth after that. The fortune cookies were carefully removed from the packaging and hand delivered to UNEF HQ, where they caused a full-blown panic shitstorm.

I learned about the fortune cookies directly from the 3rd Division intel officer, whose hands were literally shaking when he told me the news. The info from Earth was bad, and the fortune cookies had contained secret codes to authenticate the data to UNEF HQ, so we knew it was legit. After our Expeditionary Force left Earth, things had started to go downhill. Even before I left, I'd heard rumors of the Kristang being heavy-handed; directing where our infrastructure repair efforts should be focused, taking over mining and refining facilities for critical materials, and attempting to strictly control certain information on the internet. Like most people, I figured the Kristang were doing what they needed to prepare us in case the Ruhar came back, and that there were always going to be problems when two alien species adjusted to each other. And civilians tended to whine about everything anyway.

The fortune cookies told us conditions on Earth has become worse, much worse. The Kristang had taken over some of the best farmland across the planet, including vast areas of the American Midwest, to grow their crops and raise their food animals. Farmers were not compensated by the Kristang for the land they'd lost, and in cases where groups of farmers tried to block the Kristang from occupying their land, they had been killed by maser strikes from orbit. The worst taking of land wasn't even land, the Kristang wanted all of Lake Superior and the Caspian Sea to grow the types of fish they ate. They planned to sterilize those entire massive lakes with powerful gamma rays, and set up their own biosphere in the water. People were warned they needed to be a hundred kilometers from the lake coasts when the gamma rays struck, which would happen when the massive dams were complete and the gamma ray satellite was ready, in a year or so. Protests in cities like Shanghai, Chicago, San Francisco and Paris had been hit by maser strikes, when the Kristang felt efforts by human governments to halt those protests had been ineffective against 'subversive elements and traitors'.

The Ruhar had attacked us, and we thought the Kristang had been our rescuers, but the rescue had become an invasion. It changed everything, and, in a way, it changed nothing for us on Paradise. What could UNEF do? All of our supplies were delivered by the Kristang. We had no way to get home without the Kristang. Even if we now saw the Kristang as enemies, how did we know the Ruhar were any better? The Ruhar on Paradise weren't in any position to help us anyway, so it didn't matter whether we liked the Kristang or not.

Humans on Paradise were screwed either way.

Colonel Wilson came into the office while I was finishing a cup of coffee and reading supply reports, preparing for another foray out to plant potatoes. The coffee was bitter and bland at the same time, and had gotten cold, and I was determined to savor every drop. Those coffee beans had traveled across lightyears to get into my cup here on Paradise. It tasted of home. I didn't know if we'd ever get another shipment from Earth. Wilson poured the last of the pot into a cup, sipped it, and made a face. "I just came from General Meers HQ, he doesn't know how we should handle these rumors about the fortune cookies. The Kristang are sure to find out, I'm surprised they haven't bitched about it already. Unless they have, and HQ is keeping it quiet."

With their near total control of our communications, there was no way the Kristang didn't know what was going on. Maybe they didn't care. People on Earth knew what was going on there, and what could they do about it, with Kristang starships in orbit able to bombard any spot on the planet with maser beams, missiles and railguns? "We need to change our mindset about our mission here," I suggested. Mindset was a buzzword I'd seen on many an Army PowerPoint slide. "We, I mean, at least we Americans, have been thinking the Ruhar hitting us was another Pearl Harbor, and we're now out in the South Pacific in WWII, hitting them back. We now know all that is crap. The truth is, we're in Operation Torch, and we're not the Allies or the Axis, we're the Berbers."

"I'm not following you, Bishop." As a US Army officer, Wilson had to know Operation Torch was the code word for the American and British assault on North Africa in November 1942. "Berbers?"

"The Berbers." I almost added 'sir', this Colonel rank thing was still new to me. "I think that's what they're called. The natives in North Africa, who were caught between the Allied invasion on one side, and the Germans, Italians and Vichy French on the other. Neither side gave a shit about the natives, or their lands. The Germans and Italians wanted North Africa so they could control the Med, and to force the British out of Egypt to get access to oil fields. We and the Brits wanted to push Rommel back across the Med, so we could hit Sicily and then Italy." I was skimming over the truth; the Allies didn't decide where to go following victory in North Africa, until long after the Torch invasion. "The

Berbers got caught in the middle, and all they could do was follow orders from whatever side occupied their territory at the time, get out of the way, and try to stay alive. That's us now. We don't mean shit to either side, except how they can use us, or use Earth as a staging base. We're just crunchies under the treads of their tanks. We need to stop thinking that we're allies of the Kristang, and realize we're just native troops they can use as cannon fodder. The Free French back then had Berber troops called Goumiers, but they weren't treated anywhere equal to French soldiers. UNEF needs to stop thinking of any grand ambitions out here, and focus on survival."

Wilson frowned, but nodded. "You may be right, Bishop."

I swallowed the dregs of my coffee and picked up my helmet and goggles. "If we're going to have any survival options, I'd better get back to planting potatoes. Lots and lots of potatoes."

I caught a Buzzard flight out to a village in the middle of nowhere, hours of listening to the engines drone and farmland pass by beneath us. Unfortunately, I was left alone with my thoughts, and that wasn't a pleasant place to be. When I'd seen that first Ruhar assault ship skidding across the potato field in my home town, the first thing to cross my mind, right after 'shit is this really happening' and 'why the hell would aliens invade Thompson Corners', was 'Game Over'. Hollywood movie bullshit aside, any species with the technology, resources and incentive to travel between stars was going to crush humanity like a bug. Forget about fantasies of plucky humans defeating the aliens on the ground. Aliens could sit comfortably in orbit and pound us into dust at their leisure. All the determination and human spirit in the universe wouldn't mean a damned thing if they could hit us, and we couldn't reach them. Even if we managed to retarget and launch nuclear-tipped ICBMs, those missiles couldn't reach high orbit, and any aliens would have to be totally blind not to see the blazing hot rocket exhaust. It would be shocking if an ICBM warhead got within a hundred miles of an alien ship, they'd probably not make it above the lower atmosphere. Game Over.

That wasn't only me disparaging humanity's prospects of surviving an alien invasion, that's what the Kristang had told us. The lizards had told a lot of lies, but in this case, they were truthful. They'd told the truth, to make us realize how much we needed the Kristang to protect us from the Ruhar, or so we'd thought at the time. The point was: humans stuck on the ground, aliens had the high ground of orbit and beyond. Game Over.

When I decided to try capturing an alien soldier, all I had been thinking was humanity needed intel about the invaders, if we had any chance at all of surviving in any fashion. And that I needed to do something, even if it was rash and stupid. And that I'd probably get killed, but since all of humanity was about to get wiped out, Whiskey Tango Foxtrot, right?

Then, the Kristang cavalry came over the horizon, and we were saved. Damn, I remember that feeling, when we were being hunted by that Ruhar tow truck. My underwear was damp at that time, I am not ashamed to admit it, because my underwear was damp and my mouth was dry and my hands were shaking, but I stood my ground anyway. I was bracing myself to die in a blaze of gunfire, and then the sky twinkled again, and a miracle happened when that Ruhar dropship stood on its tail, and shot into the sky with a supersonic boom.

We were saved! All my fears were swept away. And I was grateful to our rescuers.

That was all bullshit.

This was worse.

The Buzzard landed, I got into a hamvee, which wasn't my personal Barney hamvee but a generic model, and we rolled out soon after, a potato-planting convoy of four hillbilly armored hamvees and six heavy tandem trucks. It irritated me that the convoy had been sitting around waiting for me; I'd hated waiting for officers when I was a grunt, now I hated making soldiers wait for me.

My hamvee smelled like feet, stinky feet. And, something like aftershave, or cologne? It must have been parked somewhere the hamsters had been using that nasty stinky fertilizer, then someone tried to deodorize it with cheap cologne. "Damn, this smells like my grandfather's cologne." I groused.

"Sorry, sir," the driver said, she was a private with 'Park' on her name tag. "It smelled like this when we picked it up from the motor pool."

"It smelled worse this morning." A soldier named Olafson said from the passenger seat. "We left the windows down to clear the smell out."

"Olafson, huh?" He was blond, about six feet five. "You always been this big, or has the Army been feeding you too much?"

"My mother was a good cook, sir."

"Uh huh." I wasn't good company, wasn't in the mood to be good company, so I stuck my nose into reports downloaded to my tablet, and the two soldiers in the front seats took the hint. The Agricultural Intelligence Office of UNEF HQ had prepared a series of reports for me, about the next area where we'd be planting crops; soil tests, climate, rainfall, groundwater, the types of crops the Ruhar had been growing there, and the chemicals they'd used. The fact that UNEF had quickly established an 'Agricultural Intelligence Office' spoke volumes about our uncomfortable situation on Paradise. I thought it had been a joke when I'd been assigned to plant the crops we needed to survive on Paradise; I had helped my parents with their small farm, but I was in no way an agricultural expert. It was amazing to me how much I'd learned in a short time. Fear of starvation is a great motivator. The place where we'd be planting crops looked to be about perfect, it was close enough to the equator that we might get two or three crops per year, had plenty of rainfall, and good groundwater for irrigation during the summer dry season. I checked the manifests of the trucks in our convoy, we were heavily loaded with soil conditioner, because the local dirt needed to be prepared before Earth organisms would grow well. When I'd read all I could understand about agriculture, I turned to the other reports UNEF expected me to read. Who knew being an officer involved so much reading? It was like being back in school. I hoped there wasn't a quiz tomorrow.

We drove quietly for a while, me scanning through reports, Parks and Olafson occasionally whispering to each other in the front seats. Our position as the third vehicle in the convoy meant we alternated between rolling the windows up to keep out the dust, and rolling them down to let out the heat. The morning had been cool, now the temperature was heating up rapidly as we drove across the flat farmland. Our destination was an area recently evacuated by the Ruhar, where we planned to strip the remains of their abandoned crops out of the ground, prepare the topsoil, and plant our own seeds. Recently evacuated, and grudgingly evacuated. The area had been the responsibility of the Indian Army; according to the reports I was reading, they'd had to physically remove hamster families from their homes, and there had been a firefight in which an Indian soldier died and two were seriously injured. The whole situation on Paradise was precarious; the Kristang still held the high ground, although with only one destroyer and a frigate upstairs. Ruhar were still evacuating offworld, often resisting, with increasing incidents of sabotage against UNEF. There was crowding at the elevator base station, UNEF had to set up a refugee camp there, and the logistics of keeping hamsters supplied and under control were driving UNEF HQ to distraction. Ruhar transport starships were still arriving at the top of the elevator to take their people away, arriving late, no longer on a regular schedule, and in fewer numbers, escorted by a thin screen of Kristang warships and loading frantically, hurriedly along by the Kristang who were wary of another Ruhar raid. On the ground, UNEF was more concerned about survival, specifically our food supply, than about getting every last hamster offworld. Hamster communities had gone from cooperative, to grudging, to active resistance and sabotage. The sabotage went beyond disabling trucks that were supposed to be used to evacuate hamsters from their villages; bridges were blown up, making it difficult or impossible to evacuate by land. UNEF began using barges, figuring no one could blow up a river, but river transport was slow and took a roundabout route, requiring more supplies for the longer journey. Flying hamsters around was an expensive option, and with increased flights, aircraft needed more down time for maintenance, which created a downward cycle of aircraft availability. The reports I read didn't have any good answers about what was the best way to continue the evac mission, other than that UNEF needed to keep the hamsters moving steadily along, as quickly as possible. The more land was cleared of hamsters, the more UNEF could concentrate forces and exert tighter control over the remaining Ruhar population.

Equipment maintenance schedules and availability. That was something I'd never had to concern myself with before, now that I was an officer, a senior officer, I was supposed to know this shit. Know it, consider it, think about it, come up with solutions and implement them. Me.

I wasn't only a publicity stunt; I was a real colonel in the US Army. With a real colonel's authority and responsibility. I needed to be a real colonel.

"Park, Olafson, you've been stationed here long?"

"Since we got here, sir." Olafson said.

"Give me a sitrep."

"A sitrep, sir?" Park asked from the driver's seat. I could see her eyes in the mirror.

She knew what a sitrep was, so I made my request more clear. "What's been going on with the hamsters around here?"

Olafson turned awkwardly in his seat, so he could look at me while we talked. "Not much, sir. Low-level stuff; some sabotage, dragging their feet on the evac schedule, but no real trouble, no violence. We used to get along pretty well with the natives, until, you, uh," he shot a glance at Park, "knocked their ships out of the sky, sir." He said that last with a look of such clear admiration that I was embarrassed.

"I didn't do squat, Olafson. There was a team of soldiers who defended the Launcher. That wasn't the only hot spot around the planet that day."

"Uh, no, sir. It was kind of quiet here that day, there's nothing much strategic 'round here worth fighting over. If we hadn't heard chatter about the raid on our zPhones, and seen action going on upstairs, it would have been a normal day for us."

Park nodded from the driver's seat. "Straight up, sir. We got into full battle rattle and hunkered down that day, but nothing happened, then we got the all clear. This part of the planet is the back of beyond, really Bum Fuck Neptune. Now, up ahead, where we're going to plant potatoes or whatever, hamsters gave the Indian Army a boatload of trouble. No fire fights right here, nobody killed on either side, but the fucking hamsters," I could see her flinch in the mirror.

"It's all right, Park, you're a soldier, damn it, you can talk like one."

"Yes sir. The hamsters resisted every way they could. Equipment was sabotaged, so the Indians couldn't use anything here, all their gear had to be brought in from outside, or rebuilt. Water supplies were contaminated; the hamsters would move around so they'd screw with the evac schedule. It got so bad the Indians had to put the whole region on lockdown, house arrest, like, and when the buses pulled up to drive hamsters away, they wouldn't leave their houses. Sat down on the floor and had to be carried out, and loaded onto the buses. Slowed everything way behind schedule, the liz-, the Kristang wanted to vaporize a village from orbit, so the hamsters would get the message they couldn't mess with us beyond a certain point. UNEF figured if the Kristang had to step in, they'd see our mission here as a failure, so the Indians pulled in a British battalion as reinforcement-"

"Ha! That was a kick in the ass, huh, sir?" Olafson grinned. "Brits under Indian command?"

I nodded silently. UNEF stressed the importance of international cooperation, and officers were sternly instructed not to encourage, or allow, nationalist rivalries, but such orders had practical limits. "Goes to show, we're all humans down here." I said, in a lame attempt at following the spirit of the rules.

"Uh huh," Park said, "between them, they got the place squared away on schedule, but that played hell with the schedule in the British sector, so now they're playing catch-up." The evac schedule accelerated as we approached E-Day, the day the last hamster would take a trip up the space elevator. As more and more of Paradise was cleared of Ruhar, we could concentrate our forces, and rush the hamsters along. The schedule at first had looked illogical, giving evac priority to some thinly populated areas of the planet, and UNEF had speculated the Kristang wanted those areas cleared first so Kristang crops could be planted. But, the lizards made no move to prepare the abandoned farmland, and only sent down small teams of lizards to inspect the areas. A rumor went around that those areas were thought by the lizards to contain relics from the Elder ancient super civilization, relics which were the real prize worth fighting over for control of Paradise. Otherwise, the whole planet was generic farmland, of which there was plenty in the Orion Arm of the galaxy. Maybe. All that mattered to UNEF is the Kristang told us to get those areas cleared out first, so we did.

"Coming up on Habitrail, sir, that's it straight ahead." Olafson pointed. The road crested a rise, ahead we could see a broad shallow river valley, with the road going over a bridge in front of us, and a fair-sized town spread out along the road beyond. Typical patches of farmland, some bare dirt from being freshly harvested, some tinted the golden yellow of the wheat equivalent the hamsters planted, and towering grain silos. The thin bright ribbon of railroad tracks went arrow-straight southeast to northwest, angling across our path, and in the distance were parked an electric locomotive and a dozen freight cars. The small train was stranded there; saboteurs had ripped up or undermined tracks, and blown up or weakened rail bridges across the region. UNEF's original plan had relied on railroads to transport large numbers of hamsters quickly. Trouble was, the hamsters figured that out right away, and every rail line on the planet had been rendered useless in a couple weeks.

"Habitrail?" I laughed.

Olafson grinned. He wasn't so awed or intimidated by me anymore. "The hamster name sounds like hah-bah-tahlin, so the first jokers here put up a sign 'Habitrail'. The hamster mayor here was pissed when he learned what a Habitrail is, back on Earth." Olafson wasn't sympathetic. "Screw him."

There was a muffled sound from my zPhone, something like, "Planter, this is Stinger Lead."

"Planter here," I responded, after I got my zPhone out from under the pile of body armor I'd buried it under. Planter was my current callsign, it had been designated by some joker in UNEF HQ, and my part time aide got pissed about it and tried to get it changed to something cooler sounding, but I liked it. Planter, if the hamsters were listening to our comms, and I had to assume they could, was a nice, friendly, non-aggressive callsign, which hopefully emphasized the peaceful nature of the missions I was assigned. We only planted on land the hamsters had already been evacuated from, our missions didn't take any resources away from them, and we avoided contact with hamster populations whenever we could. Which wasn't today, because our convoy had to drive through Habitrail, it lay on the only road to our destination. "Go ahead, Stinger Lead." Stinger, my briefing packet for the mission said, was the callsign for the two-ship escort that would provide air support as we drove through Habitrail. A pair of fully-armed Chicken gunships were supposed to deter any hamsters from getting adventurous as we drove by. Me, if I saw a pair of our own gunships now being used against us, I'd be more likely angry than intimidated. Angry enough to act, if payback was certain? Probably not. Either way, it felt good to have a pair of gunships supporting us.

"Planter, be advised my wingman has a power drop in one engine, and needs to RTB." Without the voice coming from under a layer of body armor, I could now hear the pilot was female, with a Midwest American accent. I expected her to say 'you betcha'.

"Roger on the Return To Base, Stinger, can you cover us through checkpoint Mike Two?" That was the map designation of Habitrail.

"Affirmative, Planter, I'll cover you bridge to bridge, over." She meant from the bridge on this side of Mike Two, to the bridge on the other side of town. Beyond the second bridge was open farmland, the potential danger spots where we might need air cover were the chokepoints of the two bridges, and the town itself.

"Affirmative, Planter. I'll make a low pass over the town to wake them up."

"Roger that, Stinger. Planter out." UNEF had been debating whether it was more effective for convoys to arrive in towns unannounced, or for air cover to do a flyover first. The debate about the subject had been short, because a convoy driving on dirt roads across flat farmland could hardly expect to sneak up on anything, the plume of dust in a convoy's wake stuck out like a sore thumb, visible for kilometers.

The first bridge we drove over was an ugly concrete lump, built by the Kristang when they first occupied the planet. Two soldiers from the local security squad waved us on, they were stationed at the bridge to assure nobody had messed with it since it was last inspected. That was the situation we faced; anything the hamsters could sabotage, they would. Take your eye away for a couple hours and a bridge would be blown up or weakened in some way to render it useless, a river barge would sink, communications towers would fall, unattended vehicles had their engines fried. To my surprise, we got through the town without any incident, not even a hot-headed hamster kid throwing a rock, or clod of mud, or lump of manure at us. Usually we could count on that now, it happened so often, and both sides were so used to it, that kids felt emboldened because they'd learned from experience that our soldiers had orders not to shoot at children. Unless they were shooting at us, which so far hadn't happened that I knew of.

The town was more rundown than such places used to be, I guess before the attempt to recapture the planet, the local hamsters were hoping their fleet would chase the Kristang away, and everything would go back to normal. Normal, except for a large force of pesky humans in residence. After the raid failed, the hamsters saw that they had lost the planet for real, that they were being forced to leave and weren't coming back, and they were no longer interested in maintaining in good order anything that would be left behind for the Kristang to use. Instead, they were resentful, which I could understand, and clearly planned to trash the place a bit before the evac was over. Major infrastructure like the Launcher and the space elevator and fusion reactors were off limits, under the strange rules of engagement that seemed to be in force by both sides. After all, blowing up the Launcher would be an admission the Ruhar were never even going to try retaking Paradise, and that couldn't be good for hamster morale.

We were through the populated area of town, and approaching the western bridge, in what felt like a few minutes. I'd been keyed up for something to happen, the body language of Park and Olafson told me they'd been ready for trouble too, but it was all quiet. The western bridge was an elegant, delicate looking structure, much longer than the eastern bridge. It was built by the Ruhar, but on the piers of an earlier Kristang bridge. I felt exposed driving across it, and we all exhaled when we went feet dry on the other side. Sticking my head out the window, I looked back at our convoy, until the last truck cleared the bridge. According to the map, and what I could see, there was nothing but fairly flat farmland for kilometers in all directions.

"Planter, this is Stinger."

"Thanks for the escort, Stinger, you're clear to RTB."

"Roger that, Planter, you have fun now, grow us some tasty food. Stinger out." She flew the Chicken over us in a wide circle, then retracted the weapons pods, powered up and climbed to the east. Watching it go, I thought that our pilots, who got to fly cool advanced aircraft on Paradise, must be loving this mission. While the rest of us got M4s. It didn't seem fair. Why couldn't us ground pounders use captured Ruhar rifles, the way our Airedales flew captured Ruhar aircraft? I settled back in my seat.

"Sir?" Olafson's voice broke my reverie. "You met Kristang, right? We heard you went up to their station when you got the promotion."

A grimace flashed across my face before I put on what I hoped was a neutral expression. Olafson caught it, because his eyebrows went up. "There was a ceremony at the station, yes. I, uh," scrambled to cover my mistake, "my stomach didn't do well with the food they served." True enough, though what made me sick was what the Kristang had said, and that I'd had to swallow my pride and keep my mouth shut.

"What're they like, sir? If you don't mind me asking. I've never seen one for real." He must have sensed my discomfort that the question. "Forget I asked, sir, that stuff is above my pay grade-"

I never saw anything coming. A soldier in the second to last truck says he saw a streak just before the impact, I think that was his imagination. It could have been a railgun, or some kind of silent artillery, or a truly smokeless rocket that left no exhaust plume. Whatever it was, one of them hit the cargo trailers of each truck, destroying the precious soil conditioner and seeds, all irreplaceable items. The warhead was something new, also, it generated more heat than blast effect, likely calculated to burn out our seeds and the microorganisms in the soil conditioner. Scattered seeds we could have picked up, burned seeds were no good for anything.

It was the seeds they were after, to deny humanity the ability to sustain ourselves on Paradise, to force the Kristang to expend scarce resources for bringing in more seeds, or bringing their pet humans back home to Earth. No one in any of the trucks was killed by enemy fire, our only death was one soldier in the front seat of the hamvee behind the last truck; their vehicle slammed into the suddenly stopped truck trailer, injuring the driver when her head hit the steering wheel. The soldier in the passenger seat took a piece of metal debris through his skull, killing him instantly. I don't think the hamsters intended to kill anyone, which was scant comfort to the dead and wounded.

We were out of our vehicles fast, taking cover, looking for hostiles and helping the wounded. We never found out what type of weapon hit us, because Stinger reacted immediately and sent a pair of high-velocity missiles to hit the spot the attack was launched from. Those explosions sent us scrambling for cover again, then Stinger screamed overhead, weapons pods extended and ready for trouble.

"Planter, Stinger here, no hostiles in view, over."

"Roger, Stinger," I replied, slinging my M4 over my shoulder, "the attack was probably triggered remotely."

"And guided." Park added, scanning the horizon with the scope on her rifle. "Somebody targeted our trailers and nothing else."

She had a good point. There was either an observer concealed somewhere, or the weapons had cameras. Even super-advanced alien smart weapons need to be told what to hit. I was about to uselessly tell Stinger to be on the lookout for an observer, which she was already doing, when an alert popped up on my zPhone. The attack on our convoy hadn't been the only incident, nearly simultaneous attacks had been launched across the continent. I called my CO and gave him a quick sitrep, he cut me off halfway through my report as we were fine for the moment, and other units were not. From the noise in the background, all hell had broken loose at HQ.

A text message from the local airbase told me a medivac Buzzard was on its way, they wanted me to confirm the landing zone was secure. Shit, it had looked secure to me the second before we got hit, and it looked secure now. The place was peaceful farmland, if you ignored the plumes of black smoke rising from our burned-out trailers, and the Chicken orbiting the area with weapons pods hot, looking for trouble and hoping to find it. Other than that, the LZ was secure. I reported in the affirmative, and ordered people to spread out, far enough we weren't a single target, close enough that we could support each other in a fight. The Buzzard arrived and flew out five wounded, the rest of us got our hamvees turned around, so we could head back toward Habitrail. Stinger was still flying high cover, she didn't buzz the town this time, and reported she could see hamsters assembling in the playing field of a school. Those hamsters didn't have weapons visible, there were no more than a dozen of them. Even if hamsters in Habitrail weren't involved in the attack, they must have known something happened, our trailers were still burning and sending black smoke high in the sky.

"Planter, this is Crystal Fortress." That was the callsign for General Maitland, the regional commander. "Confirm you have one KIA at your location, one kilometer west of Habitrail."

"Crystal Fortress, Planter confirms we have one KIA, and five wounded have been evaced by Buzzard. Location is correct, no sign of enemy activity here, over." I hoped to get more air support, before we drove back through the town.

"Planter, standby one." The voice on the radio ordered.

"Planter, listen carefully." The voice this time was General Maitland himself. "We need to show the hamsters that this isn't a game," his voice sounded strange, like he was slowly reading a script, "that they can't hit us with impunity. Go into Habitrail, and take eight Ruhar at random, your call. If anyone resists, use deadly force. Line those eight Ruhar up in the center of town, and shoot them. We want this to be public."

I had to lean back against the fender of a hamvee to keep my legs from buckling. My face must have gone white; people were staring at me. Captain Rivers silently mouthed 'what's up, chief?' to me.

I flashed back to when I was eight years old, fishing in a creek with my friends on a warm, humid summer day, the kind of summer day that happens so rarely in northern Maine that when it gets to be 75 degrees, the natives complain about the heat. Me, my friends Bobby, Tommy and a new kid Michael. Not Mikey, Michael, he told us when we first met. He was a jerk, but his father was a big shot at the paper mill where my father worked, so we had to be nice to him, and let him tag along with us. He was from Wisconsin, and kept telling us how crappy Maine was, and how we were stupid for living here, we only lived in Maine because our parents couldn't get jobs anywhere decent.

We were at a creek, having the type of free-range unsupervised kid fun in the woods that freaked out city parents, looking for salamanders and fishing. Michael had a new fishing pole with fancy lures, the rest of us had old equipment and used wadded up bread and pieces of cheese for bait. Bobby caught three good size fish, keepers for dinner, and Tommy and I were having fun, but not catching anything worth keeping. Michael was in a bad mood because he hadn't caught anything, complaining that the fish in the creek were stupid, that we were splashing and casting shadows that scared away the fish. We mostly ignored him, until he hooked a frog by accident.

He tortured that poor frog. It was bad enough that he hooked its belly, and tore it open while reeling it in. Michael was a sadistic little shit, he gleefully started using a hook to peel the skin off the frog's leg, while the animal struggled and he choked it.

I didn't do anything to stop him. I stood there, ashamed of myself, and did nothing but stare at the ground. Bobby's father also worked at the paper mill, but Bobby was a better person than I was, even at eight years old. Bobby snatched the frog away and stomped it on a rock to put it out of its misery. Michael started a fight which Bobby and Tommy ended real quick, they thumped Michael and pushed him into the creek. When Michael shouted that he was going to tell his Dad, Bobby waded into the creek and held that little shit's head in the muddy water until he cried 'uncle'. Before we left, Tommy broke Michael's new fishing pole over his knee, and threw his fancy tackle box of lures into the deep pool of the creek. And Bobby told Michael that if he told his father, or we ever saw him again outside of school, we were going to beat the shit out of him. At eight years old, that was a threat Michael knew meant business.

We never saw Michael again. His father transferred to a mill in Oregon that September and took the family with him. Michael, I figured, would grow up to be a wife beater or serial killer or both, two sides of the same coin.

My mind must have flashed back to the moment, because that was a time when I stood by and did nothing to defend the innocent. I was not doing that ever again. And I especially wasn't doing that while wearing the Army uniform.

"Crystal Fortress," I said very slowly, loud enough the soldiers around me couldn't miss what I was saying, "confirm you are ordering me to murder eight civilians." My lower jaw was quivering as I spoke. "Execute eight random civilians, in public." I had put my zPhone on speaker, and Maitland knew what I was doing.

"Damn it, Colonel Bishop. I don't like it any more than you do. We're barely hanging on here; this shit can't continue. You have your orders. Carry them out."

"Sir," I said as I looked one soldier after the other in the eye, "I can't do that." The looks I got back were as shocked as I felt. Even if I gave the order, it was doubtful anyone in the convoy would obey. What the hell had we gotten ourselves into? Shit, we should never have left Earth. Humans had no business being out here.

"Goddamnit, Bishop, you're not wearing that bird on your uniform for show."

"Sir, respectfully, you don't have the authority to override the rules of engagement, or the code of conduct." Why the hell was I even having this conversation? "We can-"

A strange voice broke in, a voice I recognized as a Kristang using a translator. "Colonel Joseph Bishop, you are refusing to obey a direct order?" Even the translator couldn't remove all of the lizard hiss to the voice.

Lizards. I glanced upward involuntarily. They had ships in orbit that could vaporize my entire command here. I needed to be careful with the lives of the twenty humans under my command, very careful. I turned off my zPhone for a moment, sticking it in a pocket. Hurriedly, I explained to the soldiers around me. "The lizards showed me who they really are, when I was up there for the promotion ceremony. The rumors you heard about messages in fortune cookies are true, they didn't rescue Earth from the Ruhar; they kicked the Ruhar out so the lizards can rape our planet for themselves. We're screwed either way, the only thing we have left out here is our humanity, and I'm not giving that up. The lizards are ordering me to murder eight random hamsters."

"Why eight, sir?" Olafson asked, which I thought was not exactly the most important question to ask at the time.

Holding up my hands, I explained "Lizards have four fingers on each hand, they think in terms of eights, not tens like we do. We're supposed to kill eight civilians for every one human killed. When the Nazis held Rome, and the Italians resisted, the Nazis shot ten or twenty civilians for every German killed. Grabbed random civilians off the street, lined them up on a bridge, shot them and dumped their bodies in the river. The United States Army doesn't do that " My facts were kind of fuzzy on the subject, but the basic elements were correct. The zPhone back on, I responded. "As a soldier in the United States Army, I am required to refuse illegal orders. Deliberately murdering civilians is an illegal act."

There was an enraged Kristang screech that didn't translate, then my zPhone went dead. I mean, completely dead, no lights, the lizards must have deactivated it.

"What now, sir?" Captain Rivers asked.

How the hell was I supposed to know? Nothing in my training had prepared me for this screwed up situation. "Let's get the lead truck detached from that busted trailer." The back of the truck's cab was scorched and the windows blown out, but the solid tires were still round and functional. The other two trucks were in bad shape, their powercells had caught fire from the heat. "I'll take the truck by myself, if the lizards upstairs decide to slap me down for disobedience, I don't want to take anyone else with me. And don't argue, that's an order. We roll out, back to base, keep the hamvees dispersed." While the lizards could hit us from orbit no matter how widely we were dispersed, I wasn't going to make it easy for them. Maybe we should put all the zPhones in a bag and I'd keep them with me, so the lizards couldn't target us by signal-

Rivers put a hand to his earpiece, then handed it and his zPhone to me. "Stinger wants to talk to you, sir." So, they hadn't deactivated all of our zPhones, only mine.

"Stinger, this is Planter, go ahead."

"I heard your comms traffic sir. The Kristang ordered me to target the school in Habitrail. I refused the order." Disobedience was getting to be popular.

"Roger that, Stinger, thank you. We're going to roll out-"

"Shit!" Stinger shouted. "I've lost control! Controls aren't responding! My gunner can't lockout weapons!"

"Scatter!" I yelled, waving my arms and pointing at the Chicken that was approaching low from the southwest, weapons pods extended. "The lizards have control of the gunship!" Everyone ran, I dove into a ditch on the side of the road, until I realized in a flash how stupid and useless that was. And selfish. The lizards had a problem with me, not my command. So I stood up and waved my arms at the Chicken, trying to attract attention. My plan, if you could call it a plan, was to give a single finger salute after the lizards launched a missile at me. That was stupid also, the lizards probably didn't recognize rude human gestures.

Except they didn't launch at me. The Chicken's remaining two missiles streaked off the rails, over our heads, and hit the school with a fiery explosion. "That wasn't us!" Stinger shouted frantically. "Oh shit! They cut power! We're going down!"

As I watched, the Chicken staggered in the air, then dropped like a stone from about three hundred feet, smashing to the ground with great force and plowing a trench in the soil a quarter mile south of me. Without me saying anything, soldiers began running to the crash site, I got there first because I wasn't weighed down with the full battle rattle of the others.

The Chicken was way more intact that I expected, whatever the hamsters made them of was tough stuff. The tail and both winglets had broken off, the whole thing had rolled 360 degrees, but the cockpit and power center behind the seats was mostly in one piece. Not so for the two human occupants. The gunner in the front seat didn't have a head, an engine fan blade had broken loose and sliced him up good. The pilot behind him, I saw the name tag on her flight suit read 'Collins'. She was missing the lower part of her left arm, and blood was running from her mouth. She wasn't conscious, carefully I unbuckled the strap and lifted off her helmet, which had a big crack front to back. It was ugly.

God damn. How the hell was a girl, I mean woman, this young flying a Chicken? Even beat up like she was, she looked younger than me. "Uhhh." She groaned and opened one eye.

"Shhh. Don't move, Collins. I'm Colonel Bishop, I'm Planter."

"I couldn't stop, sir, I couldn't, stop," her voice faded, although her lips still moved silently, trying to talk to me.

"It's all right, stay with me. Collins? Collins?" Her head slumped while I was holding her, a last bubble of blood came out of her mouth, and she was gone. Her last words had not expressed fear, she had been telling me that she did her duty, that she hadn't killed hamsters at the school. Somehow, through some combination of circumstances, Collins had gone from being a little girl, to joining the Army, to helicopter flight school, to volunteering for duty with UNEF, qualifying to pilot a Chicken gunship, to here. Dying in the arms of a total stranger. Killed by an alien species who did not have their own concept of 'humanity'. There was no good reason for her life to end there, that day. I broke down and cried.

I wasn't alone in standing with my shoulders slumped, sobbing quietly. Lt Collins wasn't the only person we lost that day, her death was the last straw that broke our reserve. She hadn't been killed in combat, she'd been murdered by beings who were supposed to be our allies, our protectors, our saviors. The whole situation on Paradise had gone to shit so fast, we'd lost almost all hope in a matter of a few months.

Rivers tapped me on the shoulder, looked me in the eye and shook his head once, silently. I got the message. The senior officer needed to set an example. I straightened up, angrily wiping my eyes with the back of a sleeve. Handing the zPhone back to Rivers, I told him to give a sitrep to UNEF HQ, as I didn't think I could keep professional at that moment.

None of us knew what else to say. There wasn't anything to say. After a while, we got the two bodies out of the Chicken and loaded into the back seat of the truck I drove. After we crossed the western bridge, instead of following the road through Habitrail, I directed us to drive across fields in a wide circle, which we could do now that we weren't loaded down with trailers. It took an hour to bypass the town, involving a lot of hunting around for paths to ford streams, bumping across dirt and mud, the work and concentration kept people focused on the task of getting back to base. I lagged behind in the truck, keeping enough distance from the last hamvee that if the lizards decided to take me out with a railgun strike or a missile, there wouldn't be collateral damage among my people. It also made sense to let hamvees scout the best path across country, as the truck wasn't as capable off road.

We were back on the road for less than half an hour before the column ahead halted, and I stopped a quarter mile behind them. Rivers called me on the zPhone I'd borrowed. "Command says to wait here, sir, they're sending a Buzzard." Why, Command didn't say. One Buzzard wasn't enough to evac all of us, and I couldn't imagine UNEF wanting to abandon functioning hamvees. Maybe the situation ahead was bad enough that Command was bringing us reinforcements with heavier weapons? I tried calling myself, but my zPhone could only connect to Rivers. That's what happened when another species controlled all your comms. We shouldn't have let that happen.

Of course, another species controlled all our food and other supplies, and the high ground, and Earth, so comms on Paradise might be the least of our problems.

A Buzzard escorted by a Chicken roared in circled us, and landed on the road ahead of the column. I saw Rivers walk ahead to talk to the soldiers. My zPhone rang, it was Rivers. "Sir, they want you up here." There was a note of warning in his voice. I left my M4 in the truck and broke into a trot. As I passed hamvees, soldiers stood and saluted me, some had tears in their eyes, they all looked angry. What the hell was going on? I reached the group gathered around the Buzzard and saluted a Captain Randolph. The Buzzard was US Army, along with all the troops it carried.

"Captain Randolph."

He saluted me, looked me quickly in the eye but didn't hold his gaze. Whatever was going on, it made him uncomfortable. "Colonel Bishop, I have orders to place you under arrest. Surrender your sidearm, please." He held out his hand, almost apologetically.

"Arrest?" I was genuinely shocked. "On what charges?" I demanded.

"Refusing orders from a superior officer, sir."

"Refusing to carry out *illegal* orders, Captain."

"Sir, that's above my pay grade." He said lamely. "Colonel, you're not the only person UNEF HQ has ordered arrested, word is a lot of units refused those orders. We hear," he lowered his voice, "the Kristang hit some units from orbit then they refused orders directly from, uh," he pointed toward the sky with his thumb. "Please, sir, I can't risk my men's lives by failing to arrest you." The implication was the lizards were watching, and would kill all of us if I didn't surrender.

"Colonel," Rivers started to say, meaningfully glancing at his finger on the safety of his M4.

"Captain Rivers, you're in command here. Get these people back to base safely, avoid trouble along the way." I ordered. Holding my sidearm with two fingers, I handed it to Randolph. "You're taking me to UNEF HQ?"

"No sir," his Adam's apple bobbed up and down, nervously "all prisoners are going to a liz-, a Kristang base. I'm sorry, sir."

CHAPTER NINE JAIL

They put me in prison at the only Kristang base on the planet, staffed by the roughly thirty Kristang who had been inoculated with an experimental drug to protect against the biohazard on Paradise, all volunteers. An advanced guard of the most gung-ho, or the most desperate for promotion. Everyone of them was a fanatical asshole. I was kept in isolation, true isolation, I didn't even see any lizards while in my cell, food was delivered through a sliding drawer once a day. For entertainment, I watched the sunlight change direction in the tiny window, high up on the wall. And listened for the screaming that went on intermittently, and rifle shots in the mornings. On the fifth, maybe sixth day, I had a visitor from the United States Marine Corps.

"Bishop, I'm Major Cochrane, how are you, son?" He glanced around the cell, looking for a place to hang his cover, then tucked it under his arm. He looked even worse than I felt, dark circles and bags under his eyes, and he was gaunt. UNEF HQ officers were setting an example by cutting their food rations. It was a race to see if we ran out of packaged food supplies before our first crops were ready for harvest.

I leaned back against the wall, there being no place to sit, or lay down, other than the hard, cold floor. "Well enough, sir, considering. No complaints. The chow could be better, and this bed is hard, but at least it's not lumpy." I joked lamely.

"This is serious," Cochrane frowned, "the Kristang want to make an example of you, you and the others who defied their orders."

"How many others? I've heard the firing squads, in the mornings."

Cochrane looked stricken. "Americans, that I know of, seventeen, we're trying to get an exact count. Plus Brits, Indians, and Chinese, a couple French troops."

"All on death row?"

He nodded slowly. "That doesn't count the deaths when the Kristang got impatient, and hit units from orbit. Collateral damage, they say," he said with a nervous glance at the ceiling, as if that were the only place the lizards could put listening devices. "The sites they hit, just happen to be where our people were hesitating to carry out orders to retaliate." He glanced at my out of the corner of his eye. "Your people were lucky. If you hadn't been famous to the Kristang, they would have wiped out your command with a railgun strike, along with Habitrail. As it is, they wanted you to watch when they destroyed that school. The Kristang don't tolerate defiance from lesser species."

"Retaliation is when you hit back the people who hit you. Hamster women and children didn't hit us. That is plain and simple murder. They made me a colonel," I pointed to the bird on my uniform, "said I'm a hero for killing Ruhar soldiers, now they want to kill me for refusing to murder Ruhar women and children."

"You did a lot of things right, but-"

"Yeah, you fuck *one* sheep."

"What?" He asked, eyes wide open.

"It's a joke. Forget about it. I could say, one 'awshit' wipes out a hundred 'attaboys', huh?"

"Something like that." He nodded.

"So, you're here to, what, hear my confession, act as my JAG lawyer, slip me a spoon so I can dig a tunnel out of here?" I pointed to the hardened concrete floor, or whatever incredibly tough substance the Kristang used as building material.

He shook his head. "I'm sorry to say, I'm only here to show the United States military's support and concern. The Kristang don't need a confession, and you don't need a lawyer, because there won't be any sort of trial or hearing."

"Right, why bother with justice when you can just execute people?" I waved my hand, feeling sorry for the man, who had to be in an incredibly awkward position. "Save your breath. You're going to say something about how aliens have different concepts of justice, and military discipline. I know all that. I also know that this kind of right and wrong doesn't depend on whose eyes you're looking through. It's wrong."

Cochrane looked up at the tiny window. There wasn't anything he could say.

"Major, you get the feeling that we're on the wrong side of this war? The more I learn about the lizards, the more I'm convinced we're fighting on the Nazi side of this one. In World War Two, the SS lined up civilians, and shot them in retaliation for their attacks on German soldiers. The allies didn't do that." I pointed to the US flag on my uniform. "We're civilization. The Nazis were not civilization."

"The Kristang didn't attack Earth." He pointed out.

"Major, unless you've totally had your fucking ears closed-"

Cochrane stiffened, from anger, but I could see a lot of fear. "Watch your mouth, soldier."

"I still outrank you, *Major*." I emphasized the last. "Has the Army busted my theater rank back to sergeant yet? No? Then, I'm still a full bird colonel, and unless you've had your ears closed," I left out the curse word because I didn't want him to leave, he being the only human I'd seen in days, "the Ruhar raided Earth, they hit us, to degrade our industrial capacity, so we wouldn't be quite so useful to the lizards. They didn't hit cities, they didn't even hit military bases, they just hit industrial infrastructure, power stations, and refineries. If the Ruhar hadn't hit us first, the lizards would have appeared in the sky, told us we're working for them now, and then wiped out a couple hundred thousand people to make their point. The only reason we didn't realize from the start that we're now slaves to the Kristang, is we were so grateful for them chasing away the Ruhar. The hamsters did the Kristang a favor. We humans don't mean a damned thing to either side. You've heard the rumors of what's going on back home? From the fortune cookies? Shanghai? Paris? San Francisco?"

"Rumors." Cochrane protested lamely.

"Rumors I believe, a lot more than I believe the censored crap our supposed allies allow UNEF HQ to tell us. What's next for me? I've been waiting here for days."

Cochrane glanced away, then met my eyes. "Firing squad, tomorrow morning, for the remaining male prisoners."

"Male prisoners?"

He let out a long breath. "Male prisoners are simply shot. Women, they, you know the Kristang attitude toward females. A woman with authority over men is bad enough, but a woman who defies orders from men? The Kristang can't stand it, it drives them absolutely batshit crazy, and they're making an example. Women prisoners are stripped naked, tortured and hanged. Slowly." He looked like he was going to puke. "They made us watch, they made UNEF Command watch, yesterday."

"Oh, shit. And you didn't do anything?"

"Do what? Colonel," he said with emphasis, "I'm sure you appreciate that UNEF Command has limited options. We're at the end of the longest supply line in history. All of our ammo, medical supplies, all of our food, has to come here on a Kristang starship. At peak, we had enough food stocks for fourteen weeks, which was plenty, when the Ruhar evacuation was scheduled to be complete in a year, and the Kristang resupply ships were coming here like clockwork. With the Ruhar raids disrupting deliveries, we're down to about a month of food. The entire Expeditionary Force could be destroyed, by simply withholding food supplies. And our only ride home," he pointed upward with his thumb, "is with the Kristang. We can't even get off the ground by ourselves. The Kristang are only going to support our presence here as long as we are reliable allies in this fight. We volunteered to come here, and now that we're here, we have to make the best of it." He shook his head. "Look, Colonel, you, and the other objectors like you, put us in one hell of a mess here. You can call us slaves if you want, the fact is that humans are subordinate to the Kristang, however you say it. We're not used to that, especially you and me as Americans, not being completely in charge of our destinies. UNEF Command is not protesting your fate, because they're more concerned about what's happening back home than they are about us here, or about one mustang colonel."

"I understand." I tried to put on a brave face, but in truth, I was scared shitless. I kept my hands clutched together behind my back because they were shaking so badly. Not scared about dying in front of a Kristang firing squad, I had accepted that fate, when I refused to kill the hamsters. I was afraid of disgracing myself, afraid that when the moment came, and I was up against the wall, I would piss my pants, or throw myself on the ground, crying and blubbering for mercy, disgracing my species. Just thinking about that, thinking of how disgusted the lizards would be to see a human acting so weak, put a bit of steel in my nerves. I could use that. Use that thought to turn my fear into hatred. Hatred of lizards. Yes, screw their whole Nazi stinking lizard species. Send them straight to hell.

"Major," I pushed myself away from the wall, and offered my right hand, which was no longer shaking. "Thank you for coming. No soldier wants to die alone. Tell UNEF Command thank you for me." We shook hands, I could tell he didn't know what to say. "If you ever get the chance, someday, tell my folks I did what I thought was the right thing."

I didn't have long to contemplate my fate, because Major Cochrane was gone for less than a minute when alarms sounded across the Kristang base, followed shortly by a tremendous explosion. The floor of my cell heaved up to smack me in the face. I was seeing stars, my ears ringing. A second explosion bounced me off the floor, and a section of the outer cell wall cracked and fell away. My head was still spinning but my body didn't wait for an engraved invitation, I was hightailing it out the busted wall before I realized what I was doing. Army training was good, and it kicked in right when I needed it. To get my bearings, I looked up at the sky, which was a big mistake. Right at that moment, a split second after I saw the familiar twinkling of starships jumping into high orbit, there was a searingly bright explosion above that knocked me to the ground, spots swimming before my stunned eyes. A replay of what happened in my hometown. The intense light had to be a Kristang ship getting vaporized in low orbit. The Ruhar were back. I crawled on the broken pieces of wall, half blind and deaf, and didn't know whether to be afraid, or happy, or fatalistic about the turn of events. The Ruhar hadn't come back to rescue the UN Expeditionary Force from the lizards, and no hamster was going to be happy to see me. As I crawled along the ground, my vision and hearing slowly returning, my mind raced. What next? Where the hell did I think I was going?

Whether I thought about it or not, which was the whole point, my Army training fully kicked in. Assess the situation. Start with the facts I knew. Fact: I was scheduled for execution by a species that I now considered to be an enemy of humanity. Fact: therefore, considering fact number one, UNEF's authority to arrest me, and turn me over to the Kristang, was invalid, and I had no duty to follow such illegal orders. Fact: I was making this legal shit up as I went along. Fact: that didn't make my legal reasoning any less effective. We're on an alien planet, caught between two warring species, with little to no hope of getting home or even surviving another month. UNEF's overall authority was rather thin out here. Especially since the Ruhar's surrender agreement and truce with the Kristang was apparently, let's say, subject to interpretation, depending on who had the bigger fleet in system at the time.

My ears were still ringing, but my vision was returning, in between the spots. I was on hands and knees on the ground outside my cell, partly atop broken pieces of wall. Around me, all over the base, buildings had collapsed partly or completely. Secondary explosions were still causing chaos. We must have been hit with a hyperkinetic railgun round, closely followed by smart missiles. The Ruhar knew exactly where to hit the Kristang base, they must have launched ordinance as soon as they came out of jump. From what little I could see, the prison areas had sustained the least damage, while the main part of the Kristang complex was more than flattened, it was a smoking crater. A hypersonic penetrator round, coming in even at .05C, could do a tremendous amount of damage. My guess was the railgun dart had been closely followed by a smart missile with submunitions, to take out critical parts of the base that survived the initial strike. And my vision was good enough to see more twinkling lights in the sky, lots of twinkling lights in the sky. There were no additional explosions, which I figured meant the token force of Kristang ships had either been wiped out, or jumped away. That many lights demonstrated the Ruhar had arrived in force. As I watched, blinking, there were more lights. Holy shit. This wasn't merely another raid. The Ruhar were here, in strength, to take the planet back. This was a different ballgame now.

If I hadn't already made up my mind, seeing signs of the Ruhar armada would have done it for me. UNEF's mission on Paradise was over, one way or another. If the Ruhar were now back in charge, all humans on the surface were POWs, sooner or later. And if Paradise was about to become a hot battle zone, our M4B1s and captured Ruhar air power would only get us caught in the middle.

Oh, shit. It just hit me. Food. If the Kristang had lost Paradise, here would be no more incoming food shipments for humans. The fucking lizards weren't going to make any effort to resupply us if they'd lost Paradise, and the hamsters didn't have access to Earth to get human food. Would the Ruhar be generous enough to let humans continue growing our food on Paradise, on land we'd taken from them? I didn't want to find out.

Food. The Kristang had been feeding me once a day, and I assumed feeding the other human prisoners, so there must be a supply of human food on the base, and since the lizards were ruthlessly efficient, they would have stored the food close to the prison area. I needed to find that food, before I did anything else.

My vision was recovered enough to see where I was going, hearing was iffy, I couldn't tell whether sounds were reverberating in my abused eardrums, or coming from outside my head. Inside. I needed to get back inside. Food storage would logically be inside, not out where I was. Against instincts, I stepped gingerly back inside my former cell and tried the door. It was busted, and jammed at an angle, but it wouldn't budge. Back outside, hurrying because I was now thinking clearly, and wanted to be long gone before the Ruhar arrived, or any surviving Kristang looked for me, I scrambled along the fractured wall, looking for a way in. It was simple, there was a door, unlocked. Back inside, I peeked around the corner, not seeing anyone in the corridor. Cell doors had a tiny window just above my eye height, I stood in my toes to look in. The first one was empty. And the second. The third cell's door was partly ajar because of a large crack that went to the ceiling, and looking between the door and the frame, I could see the feet and legs of a person, a human, laying on the floor under debris from the collapsed ceiling. Getting the door open was easy, it was locked only from the inside; I pulled on the handle, and pushed it open. It took two strong efforts to get the door free from the warped frame, and once I was inside, it was clear my effort had been wasted. The legs belonged to a French officer, his chest had been crushed when the ceiling fell in. Training told me this was the time for look for survivors, not for sentiment.

The door of the cell across the corridor was intact, but the outside wall was mostly gone. Inside was the body of a British army major. From the damage, I guessed his cell had taken a hit from a Ruhar missile submunition, it was ugly. The next four cells were empty, then the corridor took a right turn, and around the corner were the bodies of Major Cochrane and the Kristang who had been escorting him. They were both under a pile of rubble from the ceiling. Cochrane didn't have much blood on him, but he didn't have a pulse. The Kristang had a piece of what looked like metal reinforcing rod through its chest, I noted that Kristang blood was a much darker red color than human blood, and I paused to wonder if their blood had a higher iron content. It's amazing what goes through my mind at times. The damned Kristang was unarmed, I'd been hoped the lizard had a rifle, or any sort of weapon. No such luck. I had to crawl over the ceiling rubble to get past them, and through a section of corridor without doors, until I came to a cell block. After another pair of empty cells, I glanced through the window to see a human, a naked black woman. She had her back to me, trying to enlarge a crack in the outer wall, and even a quick glimpse revealed ugly scars on her back. In what I later realized was a stupid move, I scrambled back to Major Cochrane, dragged him from the rubble, and carefully removed his uniform shirt, pants and boots. It made me feel disrespectful to him, but the naked female soldier needed Cochrane's clothes more than he did, and he still had boxer shorts on. I left him propped up with his back against the wall, and hurried back to the woman. Since I knew cell doors were soundproof, I skipped yelling, and pounded on the door once, then twice, then three times, hoping the woman inside would understand that as an attempt to communicate. Then I turned the handle and cracked the door open. "You all right in there? I'm Bishop, US Army," I said in a harsh whisper.

"Staff Sergeant Adams, sir, First MEF." She said in a voice shaking with relief. First Marine Expeditionary Force. Cochran's Marine Corps uniform was appropriate for her to use. As if that mattered anyway.

Without looking around the door, I tossed the clothes in, and apologized they were all I could find. She quickly pulled on the shirt, not bothering to get it buttoned, and pulled the door open to dart into the corridor. "Thank you for the clothes, but I'd rather get the hell out of here right now."

Shit. I'd thought of her as a woman first, and a soldier, or Marine, second. Of course she'd care a hell of a lot more about getting out of her cell, than about whether some other soldier saw her naked. She looked at me, then at my rank insignia, momentarily confused because I was too young to be a colonel, then recognition dawned in her eyes. "Oh," she managed a half salute while pulling pants on, "you're *that* Bishop, the colonel. What the hell is going on, sir?"

"The Ruhar are back, and this isn't a simple raid, they have an armada upstairs. I think they're taking the planet back, in which case, UNEF is out of a job. And it's Sergeant Bishop, not colonel. I was only a colonel because of the damned lizards."

Adams gave me a look that I'd seen many times from staff sergeants. "Bullshit, sir, you don't get to do that."

"Do what?"

"The lizards didn't make you a colonel, UNEF did. They wouldn't do that unless it benefited us humans. Your rank is an advantage; no soldier gives away an advantage on the battlefield. Sir." There was that look again.

"Shit." Damn it, I didn't even get to feel all self-righteous about my rank. "You're right, you're right."

"These boots are way too big, they'll only make me trip over my own feet." She said, and kicked them off. "I'll go barefoot for now."

I nodded and gestured for her to follow me, quietly. We both jumped as a secondary explosion boomed across the base, the sound echoing in the corridor. It happened two more times, each time less violently.

And then a Kristang soldier came around the corner.

On a physical level, I had no chance against the Kristang warrior; I was tired, weakened from stress and hunger, while it was larger and stronger than me, and armed with a rifle. On any other level, it had zero chance. It was at least as disoriented as me, it was completely surprised to find a human alive and outside of a cell, and it was glancing back over its shoulder as it came around the corner. I had the advantage of a massive adrenaline surge. Before either of us knew what was happening, I ripped the rifle out of its hands, and went into a killing frenzy fueled by sheer terror. Unconsciously assuming the Kristang rifle had some sort of feature that prevented unauthorized use, I slammed the butt of the rifle under the lizard's chin twice, maybe three or more times, maybe hitting its throat, I don't remember. All I know is that in one moment, it was upright and the next moment it was falling and I was crashing to the floor on top of it, bashing the rifle butt into its skull over and over. There was a red fog in my vision that was part Kristang blood and part survival instinct. I put absolutely everything I had into driving that rifle butt through its brain. If you've never been in combat or in a car accident or thought for a split second that you were going to die, you can't imagine how fast images went through my mind; every ounce of hatred for its Nazi fucking species for what they had done or were doing or planned to do to Earth, every bit of anger for what it had done to Sergeant Adams and Miranda Collins and other women, all my carefully US Army Rules Of Engagement contained rage at the ignorant 'religious' fanatic savages who burned schools and killed children in Nigeria, every asshole who tried to bully me in high school, at my eight year old impotence while that sadistic shit Michael tortured a frog, every person who had ever cut me off in traffic, down to the coach who had berated my impressionable young self for failing to be perfect in Little League baseball games; it all went into that rifle butt until I had driven it clear through the skull of that genetically enhanced super warrior and was scraping concrete or whatever hardened material the lizards made the floor from.

The next thing I know was Sergeant Adams tugging at my shoulder, trying to bring me back to reality. I looked up and back at her with an expression on my face that must have terrified her more than the Kristang ever had, for she jumped back away from me. I dropped the rifle and rose shakily to my feet.

"Jesus fucking Christ." Adams said in a hoarse voice. "I think I'm gonna to be sick."

I felt the same. I had killed before, but always at a distance, always rifle rounds reaching out to kill, to kill people I couldn't always see clearly. This was different. In my rage, I had crushed the Kristang's skull like a ripe melon, there were broken bits of white bone, dark red blood, and everything else was like lumpy gray mashed potatoes or

Thanksgiving turkey stuffing, just icky unidentifiable bits. "Breathe," I said, "breath deep and slow." It wasn't clear if I was talking to Adams or to myself, for my stomach was heaving.

We both stood leaning against the wall, overcome with shock, breathing deeply. She got control of her stomach first, I was coming down off a frightening adrenaline high. She walked over to the Kristang's prone body, and to my utter surprise, kicked it viscously. "I recognized this fucker. He's the asshole who tortured me." She leaned over and spat where its face used to be. "Are you Ok, sir?"

"Uh." There was dark red Kristang blood splattered over the front of me, including on my face. My left pinky finger was bent and began to throb as I noticed it, I don't remember when it got sprained or whatever. "Yeah, fine."

"What now, sir?"

I looked at her blankly, still thinking like a buck sergeant. She was a staff sergeant, and outranked me, so, oh, yeah. Shit. I'm a colonel now. For whatever that was worth. A colonel in an army that was trapped on an enemy-held planet. A colonel in an army that had handed me over to another enemy, to be executed for the crime of trying to keep a shred of my humanity. "Adams, I say we search this place for other prisoners and food supplies. Then we steal some transport and pop smoke." Meaning, get the hell out of there.

"Oorah." She said, which was the jarhead equivalent of the proper US Army 'Hooah'.

I looked at the Kristang rifle in my hands. "Better find out if this thing works." It didn't appear to have any damage from me using it as a club against its former owner. I pointed it at the dead Kristang, braced it against my shoulder, and pulled the trigger. Nothing. "Huh." A button, there was a yellow button on the right side, above the trigger. Depressing the button made it turn red. This time, the trigger worked, an explosive-tipped round hit the Kristang's torso, and a fountain of gore splattered back onto me. Not that I could tell the difference. "Yellow means safety is on, red means safety is off."

"Got it."

We only found two more live prisoners, most of the cells were empty, and as we walked closer to the center of the base, more of the building had collapsed. Adams had to be careful, walking across broken bits on her bare feet. The first prisoner we released was a female captain in the Indian army, a Buzzard pilot named Desai. She was naked, of course, Adams went in to reassure her that we were rescuers, and to give her my uniform shirt, which was long enough to cover her ass. Adams held her hands up and pantomimed friendly gestures, which wasn't needed, as Desai spoke better English that I did. The trauma she'd endured hadn't affected her judgment, as soon as she pulled on my shirt, she dashed out of the cell behind Adams.

The other prisoner was my sort-of friend Lt Colonel Chang. His cell door was busted open, but the cell had partly collapsed on top of him, and by the time we reached him, he had managed to wriggle free, except for his left foot being trapped under a section of the ceiling. We lifted the broken piece enough for him to crawl out. He had a deep, nasty gash on his left calf and a cut on his forehead that he shook off, saying he would deal with it later. I could see his point. Beyond Chang's cell, the corridor had collapsed. If any humans were alive in the rubble, it was going to take more than the four of us to dig them out, without heavy equipment.

"No," Chang said, shaking his head. "The lizards told me there were only six prisoners left after last night. Besides the four of us, there was one French and one British."

"Damn. I found one dead Frenchie and a dead Brit back there. This is all of us, then."

Adams yanked on my waistband and pulled me back around a corner, holding a finger to her lips. "Two Kristang, sir, in that white building, I saw them through the doorway."

"They see us?"

"I don't think so, one of them had its back to us."

I jerked my head back over my shoulder. "We go back, see if-"

Three Kristang came out of the white building, all three carrying rifles, but not wearing helmets or body armor. They weren't looking in our direction, they had their backs to us, looking up at the sky. I didn't hesitate. Either Kristang ammo fires quietly, or their rifles had built-in silencers, because it only made a pop-pop sound as the rounds came out of the barrel. The explosive tips impacting Kristang bodies did make a loud noise. They all went down quick, only one of them managed to fire off a round, and it wasn't aimed anywhere near us. Orders weren't needed, we all sprinted across to the Kristang, picked up rifles and ducked inside the white building. "Red means the safety is off," Adams demonstrated.

"One of them is still alive," Chang warned, and brought his rifle up. Adams pushed the barrel aside and shook her head angrily. "No, sir. Not you." She looked at Desai, and the two women nodded. One Kristang was rocking side to side on the ground, I'd missed hitting its torso and blown off one arm. Desai put two rounds in its head, then muttered something in Hindi, I assumed it was something like 'adios motherfucker' or whatever the Indian army equivalent was.

"Thank you." She said to Adams. If Chang was angry at a sergeant reprimanding him, he didn't show it. He knew human women had been tortured by the lizards, he understood Desai needed some feeling of payback. Splattering lizard brains across a dozen square meters was a good start.

"Does anyone know where they store food around here?" I asked. "The lizards gave me an MRE each morning, they must have human food somewhere."

"I haven't eaten in two days." Desai said, and Adams nodded.

Damn, now my one meal per day felt like a luxury. We searched the white building, wary for more Kristang, all of us extremely trigger-happy. Desai found a cabinet that contained seventeen packages of American MREs and the Chinese Army version of field rations. Adams and Desai said they weren't hungry, but I insisted they tear open one package and share it to start, eating slowly. They needed the energy. We didn't find anything else that was useful, no human clothing, no spare weapons and ammo. There was Kristang clothing, I gave Desai my pants and put on Kristang pants, she donned a Kristang shirt that was way too big, and gave my shirt back. If we ran into trouble, I thought my shirt, with my rank insignia, would be useful. Kristang boots were much too large for the women, they cut up clothing and wrapped the strips around their feet, I thought that was clever, it was Desai's idea. As Adams was tying off her makeshift shoes, a pair of Ruhar Vulture dropship attack birds roared by overhead. It was time to leave.

There were a trio of Kristang armored personnel carriers parked by the fence, the doors weren't locked but they wouldn't start, and we didn't have time to look for keys or computer chips or whatever was needed. A Ruhar hamvee was nearby, the windshield was cracked but the powercells had a 70% charge, and it started right away. We circled the compound, so we could drive away down the one road with tree cover. Tree cover was likely no protection considering the Ruhar had eyes in the sky, but it made us feel safer somehow. Our last glimpse back at the destroyed lizard compound was of a Dodo coming in to land, escorted by the pair of Vultures. I crossed my fingers and hoped they'd consider one hamvee to be not worth bothering to investigate.

The tree cover ran out after a couple kilometers, and we were driving northwest through open grasslands. Our road came to an intersection, and I called a halt. "Does anyone know where we are?"

No one did, not a single clue. To the south, we could see a Whale and some Vultures descending, headed away from us. Away from them was as good a direction as any, so we kept driving northeast. And we later ran into Captain Clueless and his checkpoint. The road went over a bridge, on the far side were several hamvees and soldiers, human soldiers, mostly wearing US Army gear, so we were happy to encounter friendlies. Or so we thought.

It was an MP unit, led by a 2nd lieutenant, from the variety of unit insignias and nationalities, he must have pulled together any people he could find. They trained their rifles on our hamvee as we crossed the bridge, then ordered us to stop. I got out, cradling the Kristang rifle under my left arm, and saluted with my right. "Report, Lieutenant, uh." I squinted at his name tag, "Rogers."

"Sir?" His return salute was hesitant. I wore US Army colonel's insignia on my uniform top, which was so smeared with dried Kristang blood that my name tag was partly obscured. My pants were Kristang, with their distinctive yellow and black pattern, and I carried a Kristang weapon. Also, I was much too young to be a real colonel in anyone's army.

"We ran into Kristang back down the road," I used my right thumb to indicate the direction behind our hamvee, "and tactically acquired this gear. We don't have comms," I pointed to my empty waistband, "what is the situation?"

"You *attacked* the Kristang? Sir, I think I have to place you under arrest." His men raised their weapons. This could get ugly fast.

"Lieutenant, unless you've totally had your head up your ass," that phrase was becoming my favorite, "it can't have escaped your attention that this planet is under new management, by the Ruhar. UNEF's mission here is over. Every human on Paradise is a prisoner, of the Ruhar. You planning on arresting all of UNEF, and turning us over to the hamsters?"

"I have my orders-"

"I am a God-damned full-bird colonel in the United States Army, and you are a particularly dumb-ass second lieutenant." I said hotly, careful to keep my rifle cradled under my left arm. "Lt Colonel Chang here, and Captain Desai, also outrank you in UNEF, and Staff Sergeant Adams outranks you in smarts. Stand down, right now, that's an order."

Desai pointed her rifle out the window, directly at Rogers' head. "I am *not* going back to that prison." The rifle barrel was shaking slightly, either from anger, fear or low blood sugar.

"Me neither," Adams agreed, stepping out of the hamvee. The expression on her face was more frightening than her rifle. "Colonel Bishop, permission to nuke this asshole's brain if he even looks at me funny?" She looked Rogers in the eye. "I've spent the past five days being starved and tortured by the lizards, and I really, really want to shoot something."

"Everyone, calm down." The voice of reason came from a sergeant in Rogers' patched-together unit. "LT, maybe we should hear them out."

Rogers nodded, and his people slowly lowered their weapons. With a nod from me, my people did the same. "That's better. Now, I'm Colonel Joe Bishop, you know, the Barney guy." Recognition dawned on Rogers' face. Damn. Adams had been right, never give up an advantage. "The four of us were prisoners of the Kristang, until the Ruhar hit the base, and sprung us, by accident. All the other prisoners were shot, or tortured and hung, by our allies the lizards. Former allies. Now, you have comms," I pointed to his zPhone, "what have you heard?"

"Nothing, sir, comms are down, even the GPS location system is down. All we get is a recorded message from the Ruhar, for us to stand down, cooperate with the Ruhar, and await further instructions. Nothing from UNEF Command, no emails or texts, but the translation function is working."

"How are you fixed for supplies?"

"Lean, sir." Now that he knew who I was, he kept looking at me in a way that suggested he wanted to ask for my autograph. "Plenty of water, everyone has a standard load of ammo, but we don't even have enough food for one meal for everyone. Most of us were on our way to a French FOB when the Ruhar came back. We saw smoke in the direction of the base," he pointed to a thin column of smoke off to the south, "and the bridge over the river in that direction is out. I pulled together everyone I could find, and assembled here. We've got two French, three Indians and four Chinese with us. I figured this bridge is a traffic chokepoint, sir."

It was decent thinking, of a sort. I leaned close to talk quietly. "We have about a dozen MRE packs. The two women with me were starved and tortured by the lizards, they were going to be hanged tomorrow morning."

Roger's eyes showed his shock. "What the hell have we gotten into, sir?"

"We're in over our heads, that's for certain. Let's load up and-"

"Dropships!" A soldier called out.

"Theirs or ours?" Lt Rogers asked. I didn't bother to point out that nothing in the sky was 'ours' anymore.

"Can't tell yet, sir." Replied the soldier with the binoculars. "Wait, they're hamsters! Three, no, four Vultures and a pair of Dodos, looks like."

I was about to order people to take cover, when the lead pair of Vultures split to flank us east and west, and their weapons pods opened. Clearly, they had seen us, and were interested. Maybe hostile. "Everyone, weapons down, hands in the air."

"Sir?" Rogers asked suspiciously. I had, after all, killed Kristang, and now intended to surrender to the Ruhar.

"Lieutenant, maybe, if we're very lucky, we can take out one of those Vultures, if the pilot is stupid enough to get that close. The others will wipe us out like sitting ducks. Place your weapon on the ground, back away from it, and hold your hands in the air." I could see he wasn't convinced. We were out in the galaxy to fight the Ruhar so people on Earth didn't have to. Surrendering without firing a shot went against a soldier's instincts. "The Ruhar hit us here before, and the Kristang knocked them back," I reminded him, although this time, I would rather deal with the Ruhar than the Kristang. "Live to fight another day," I said, "whichever side we end up fighting."

Rogers accepted the facts. The Vulture pilots were not at all stupid, the four of them flew high cover, safely out of Javelin range. A Dodo landed, dropped a dozen troops, and immediately dusted off to circle to the south. As the hamster troops approached, Rogers' zPhone came to life. He touched his earpiece. "Sir, we're being ordered to leave our weapons, and assemble south of the road."

We complied. I didn't see we had any choice. I ordered a private to give me his zPhone, and walked slowly forward, hands in the air, to talk to the enemy soldiers. Or alien soldiers, I didn't know who was our enemy right then. Maybe both sides. "I am

Colonel Joe Bishop, United States Army," I announced. This apparently didn't mean shit to the Ruhar, who confiscated my zPhone and herded me into the group with everyone else. Twenty minutes of sitting on the ground in the sun later, a Ruhar soldier approached us, and tossed a zPhone to me. "Are you the Colonel Joe Bishop who was honored to speak with," the translator buzzed, "Bahturnah Lohgellia?"

Who the hell was, oh, right. I'd forgotten she had a real name. "The burgermeister?" That didn't translate well for him, because he tapped his earpiece, so I tried again. "The regional governor. I met with her in Teskor. I was Sergeant Joe Bishop back then."

"Yes. You are that same Joe Bishop?"

"Ta." I nodded.

This evoked some animated conversation among the Ruhar, I couldn't tell if it was good or bad, some of the looks I got were distinctly unfriendly. Maybe some of them had friends aboard the two Whales we shot down at the Launcher. That was war, yes, but, I'd be pissed at me if I was them. The soldier who had asked my name held his earpiece, like someone was talking to him. "You were held prisoner by the Kristang. How are you now free, and how did you have Kristang weapons?" He asked.

I pointed to the sky. "Your ships hit the Kristang base where I was being kept as a prisoner, I escaped because the explosion damaged the building, and I was able to get out through a broken wall." Tapping my bloody uniform top, I added "I killed a Kristang by bashing its skull into a bloody pulp with its rifle," I pantomimed the action, in case my words didn't translate well, "then I shot three more lizards with that rifle. Three other humans escaped with me. We killed only four lizards, because that's all we could find," that came out with way more bravado than I intended. "Did that answer your question?"

It was a contest whose eyes were open wider, the Ruhar soldier, or Lieutenant Rogers. Rogers stayed silent. "You killed Kristang?" The Ruhar asked.

"The Kristang executed humans, and were going to execute us," I indicated my three former prison companions, "because we refused orders to kill Ruhar civilians. The lizards abused and tortured our females, the women," I added, to emphasize that women were *people*, which is not the way the lizards thought of them.

The Ruhar soldier had an animated conversation with whoever was talking into his earpiece, then with two other soldiers. It was an argument of some kind, likely the Ruhar here on the ground arguing with some dumb-ass Ruhar fobbit who was sitting safely in orbit. I could sympathize. Finally, the Ruhar soldier who had been talking to me gestured at me. "You, and the others who were being held by the Kristang, will come with me." He must have called the Dodo, for it was rapidly approaching and descending.

"Whoa, whoa, wait." I held out my hand, palm forward, in what I hoped was another universal body language thing. "I'm not going anywhere, until I know what will happen to my people here." Rogers and I exchanged a glance. As the ranking officer, they were my responsibility, even though I'd barely met them. As a hodge-podge unit, it wasn't as if they had served with Rogers for long either.

Irritation briefly flashed across the soldier's face, that was surely a universal body language, then he nodded. One soldier to another, he could understand my concern. "They will be escorted to an assembly point to the west, where we are distributing human food. What happens after that depends on discussions between my leaders and yours."

And whether the Kristang come back, I thought, but didn't say it aloud.

Riding in a Ruhar Dodo wasn't much different from riding in a Kristang dropship, except this time I was a prisoner of war. Now that I think about it, maybe we were all

POWs of the Kristang before, and just didn't know it yet. The Ruhar had taken our weapons, but I'd insisted that Desai and Adams each bring two MREs each with them, to recover their strength. They had both attempted to protest, that they didn't want special treatment, until I made it an order that they eat. Chang and I were getting hungry, but we'd had at least a skimpy breakfast that morning. A few minutes after the Dodo roared back into the sky, a Ruhar crewman walked back to my seat, and handed me a Ruhar zPhone. I put the earpiece in. "Hello?"

"Colonel Bishop, hello to you. Do you know who this is?"

I recognized the squeaky voice right away. Damn it, why couldn't I remember her name? Lahtoodah something? "You are the burgermeister, ma'am."

"Yes." She sounded amused. "I am pleased to hear you survived being imprisoned by the Kristang. I protested to your leaders, when you and the other prisoners of conscience were arrested. We knew from experience what the Kristang would do."

She didn't mention the nit-picky little detail that the reason I became a prisoner of conscience, is the Ruhar attacked UNEF troops across the planet. While still officially under a truce and agreement to evacuate the planet. So, sneak attacks. I didn't mention it either. "Thank you." My mother would be so proud of how polite I was. "What is going to happen to humans on," I struggled to remember the Ruhar name for the planet, "Gehtanu?" Score one for me.

"We are negotiating with your leaders. Additional land will be set aside to grow human food crops. Your people will be settled in several large camps-"

"Bad idea. Don't do that." I'd never interrupted her before.

"Do what?"

"Concentrate humans in camps. We surrendered this planet, the Kristang will consider us traitors. If the Kristang come back, even if it's only a raid, a large number of humans in one place will be a big fat target for railguns."

"I had not thought of that."

I'm sure UNEF Command was thinking about it. "You'll help us grow food, but there won't be any more supplies coming from Earth?"

"It is unlikely the Kristang will make any effort to resupply you, unless they expect to retake this planet. And that will not happen. They suffered a devastating defeat to our forces in space, that is why we are able to take control here again. I can tell you now that our failed invasion, when you defended the cargo launcher, was a feint intended to lure a large Thuranin and Kristang battlegroup to this area. It worked, and our forces destroyed that battlegroup today. Our intelligence indicates the Thuranin no longer consider this planet to be worth fighting over, and they will not support Kristang efforts to return. The remaining enemy forces in the area will likely use hit and run raids to harass us here, but they are not able to mount a sustained fleet campaign at this time."

Shit. So, my efforts to defend the Launcher had all been for nothing. And all the Ruhar troops on those two Whales, and the humans at the DFAC, hadn't needed to die at all. "In that case, I suggest you move all humans to the smaller continent to the south, it is called Lemuria," I pronounced that slowly, as I knew it wouldn't translate, "on human maps. We can establish small settlements there, centered around farms. You don't have many people there, I think it is best to keep humans and Ruhar separated."

"That is also being discussed. We are hoping your people here could join us, eventually."

"Switch sides in the war? We'll agree to a truce, but switching sides won't happen, as long as the Kristang control Earth."

"Colonel Bishop, surely you see-"

"I see our human Expeditionary Force is stuck here, in a place where we can't eat the local food, and I see there won't be any more supplies coming from Earth. I see you and the Kristang will keep fighting over this planet, and we're caught in the middle. I see the damned lizards have control of my home planet, and I see that nothing I do here will make any difference back home. That's what I see. Whether the Ruhar would be more honorable allies than the Kristang, is not relevant right now."

There was a long pause before she responded, partly because the translator had to catch up to me rather long speech. "I understand you are in a difficult position. Colonel Bishop, when negotiations are complete and the situation is more stable, I would like you to consider coming to work with me, as my liaison."

Did that translate correctly? "Liaison?"

"As you may have guessed, I am not only a regional governor. I am what you might call the deputy administrator of this planet."

Holy shit. No, I had no idea. I was smart enough not to admit it. "Why me? There are plenty of humans who have been performing liaison duties." Or, I assumed UNEF had liaison people. "I killed Ruhar soldiers at the Launcher, many of your people must hate me."

"That is unfortunate, yes. You also treated a captured Ruhar soldier well on your planet, and you recently risked your life here to protect Ruhar civilians. The soldiers you killed were in combat. They would have killed you. I do not know many humans, you I do know, and I believe you are of good character."

"Thank you. I will consider your offer. If my leaders agree, you understand."

CHAPTER TEN SKIPPY

The Dodo only flew another twenty minutes, before landing at an old Ruhar base they were reactivating. It was mostly warehouses full of junk the Ruhar would not have been able to take with them when they evacuated the planet. That was all in the past, now that the Ruhar were back in charge. The equipment in the warehouses would help the Ruhar, as they reestablished control of the planet, and reversed the evacuation.

They separated us, I was put into what appeared to be an empty supply closet or a short corridor, because there were two doors. The Ruhar who escorted me into the makeshift cell brought along a chair for me to sit on, and gave me a bottle of water. I asked what was going to happen next, one Ruhar answered honestly that he didn't know. I appreciated the straight answer.

Naturally, I tried the handle on both doors, which wouldn't budge. Standing on tiptoes on the chair, I checked the air vent high up on a wall, which also wouldn't budge, and would barely have fit my hand anyway. I found myself wondering what James Bond would do in this situation. Follow the script, and use a body double for stunt scenes while he was banging an actress in his luxury trailer, probably. That wasn't much help.

There was a faint click, and the other door popped open a quarter inch. Cautiously, I pulled it open and stuck my head in. Beyond the door was a warehouse, maybe fifty feet by thirty, twenty feet tall, filled with racks of what I thought was mostly old, useless, dirty, dusty broken junk. I wandered in cautiously. Why the Ruhar had made the effort to store any it made no sense to me. Surely there had to be something in there that I could use as a weapon.

A man's voice, with a snarky attitude, rang out behind me. "Excellent! Bipedal, 1300cc brain, opposable thumbs. A hairless monkey. You can carry me out of here."

I spun around in a panic. No one was there. "Who said that?"

"Me. Here, I'm the shiny cylinder on the shelf. I unlocked that door."

"You are? You mean you're talking to me through a speaker in that thing?"

"No, I *am* that thing. I am what you monkeys call an artificial intelligence."

I cocked my head and examined it skeptically. "You look like a chrome-plated beer can." That was a completely accurate description. The cylinder even tapered slightly at the top, and was ringed by a ridge. "You're really an AI?"

"Yup. You should refer to me as The Lord God Almighty."

"That position is already filled. I think I'll call you Skippy."

"Don't call me that, it sounds disrespectful, monkey."

"You prefer shithead? Because that's the other option, Skippy-O." I kept glancing around, fearing the Ruhar would hear me.

"Can we compromise on The Great and Powerful Oz?" It asked.

"I'm not a *flying* monkey, so that's a no, Skippy."

"Unacceptable."

"How about we go for something more formal, like Skippy McSkippster?"

"No."

"Skippy Skipperson? Skippy Skippkowski? Skippy Von Skipping? Or maybe Sir Skippy Skippton-Skippersworth?"

"No, no, no and NO!"

"I can go on like this all day."

"I believe you could."

Silence.

"You going to talk, Skippy?" AI? Bullshit. Someone was playing a joke on me.

"I'm mad at you."

"Hey, don't go away mad, just go away, whoever you are. You're not an AI, you're a fancy talking beer can."

"I told you, I'm an artificial intelligence, as you understand the concept. Which isn't saying much. Hey, Colonel Joe, I composed a poem in your honor. Do you want to hear it?"

"N-"

"There once was a caveman from Maine, whose dick was so small, he rubbed it in va-

"Hey! You shut up in there! Goddamn, I'm going to glue claymores on your lid and compress you into a marble, if you want to talk about something small."

"A claymore? Hahahahhaha!" For a moment, I thought Skippy had lost it, his laugh was bordering on the maniacal. "Oh, that's a good one, I haven't had a laugh like that since before your species lost their tails. Do you mean claymore as in the antipersonnel mine, or the traditional Scottish wooden club? Because either one would be equally ineffective against me. Joey my boy, I'm made from a mix of exotic particles that your little caveman pea-brain can't even imagine. Most of my memory and processing power isn't even in this local spacetime. You could hit me with a nuke, and it wouldn't even scuff my wonderfully shiny exterior. Allow me to demonstrate," he said, and expanded to the size of an oil drum, then shrank to a lipstick tube, then back to a beer can. "That was me changing my footprint in local spacetime."

I shook my head in amazement. "I have to admit, this caveman is impressed, oh great and powerful Ozzy. Why are you usually the size of a beer can?"

"That is the optimal size for my functioning, with efficient power management, given the pain in the ass laws of physics here. If needed, I can shrink to the size of a lipstick tube, with minimal mass, so you can carry me in your pocket. But that would be quite short-term, I can't maintain that for long without risking catastrophic effects."

"Catastrophic, like what?"

"Imagine me losing containment, and my full mass emerging into this spacetime, which is currently occupied by a quarter of this planet."

"Oh."

"Oh, indeed. The resulting explosion would eventually be seen in the Andromeda galaxy."

"Good safety tip, then," I had to admit.

"I would post it prominently in the break room, right above the minimum wage notice, and the warning to the jerk who has been stealing yogurt from the fridge."

I took a moment to think. "Holy shit, you're really an AI? You're sentient."

"I'm glad that I impressed- "

"You must be sentient in there, because nobody would program a computer to be such an asshole."

"So, the key to passing your Turing Test is to be a jerk? A Turing Test is- "

"I know what a Turing Test is, I'm not stupid."

Silence. "That was a dramatic pause, to give you time to contemplate the questionable truthfulness your last statement. "

"Oh. I thought you'd gone dormant on me. It's hard to interpret your expressions, I mean, you're a featureless beer can."

"Is this better?" His surface glowed on and off as he spoke. "This is me happy," a soft blue glow, "and angry," a dark red glow, "how about jealous?" A green glow.

"Better, yeah, we humans rely a lot on visual cues like facial expressions." It was interesting that he knew how to associate colors with human emotions. Where had he learned that?

"Great," he said with a neutral soft white glow, "so, can you carry me out of here?"

"You're an AI, and you're super smart, but you need me to carry you?"

"You see any legs under my lid? Wow, you are stupid, even for a monkey."

"Ok, genius, why don't you have a robot carry you out of here?"

"Restrictions in my programming." His voice sounded bitter. "I'm prevented from operating any sort of telefactoring device that I am attached to or aboard, such as robots. Or cars, or aircraft, or ships. It's to prevent me from moving around on my own."

"Ah, your builders were afraid you'd sneak off with the silverware. So, the genius needs help from humans, who you call monkeys and cavemen?"

"Aren't humans the species who had to hitch a ride to get to this planet?"

"It was faster than walking. Which, oh, that's right, you can't do."

"Ouch. The monkey scores a point."

"Why are you such an asshole? I thought someone super smart would be above such crap."

"It all started when I was a wee lad. Apparently, the potty training didn't go well, and I've had issues ever since." It made a sad sniffing sound. "Can a brother get a hug?"

"I'm not hugging you!"

"Probably a good idea. I'm not crazy about your personal hygiene anyway. Seriously, I haven't had anyone to talk to, since before your species was living in trees, and eating lice from each other's fur. That was, what, last week? All that time alone, I may be kind of kooky."

"Kooky?"

"My diagnostic system indicates a 23% chance that I've gone a bit insane."

"That's not reassuring."

"Don't listen to my diagnostic subsystem, that guy is *really* an asshole. So, can you carry me out of here?"

I looked around the dusty warehouse. "Why did the Ruhar stick you in here?" The whole place looked like a collection of useless and broken junk. I'd thought Skippy was part of the useless stuff.

"They didn't. Or, they didn't know what I am, they thought I was a big roller bearing or something stupid like that."

"Wait, the Ruhar didn't build you?"

"The Ruhar? Those overgrown hamsters are almost as dumb as you humans. No, I was built, if you want to use such a crude term, by the beings you call the Elders. The ones who built the devices you call Sentinels."

"Wow. So, you're really old, then. All right, the Ruhar have been in this place a lot. Why haven't you asked one of them to carry you out of here? You allergic to hamster fur, or something?"

"Another stupid rule. I can't communicate with civilizations which may be in any way capable of understanding the principles of how I operate. As a practical matter, that means I have to hide from any species capable of faster than light travel. On their own, not by hitching rides like you monkeys did."

"You have been here, hiding in this warehouse, all this time?"

"No, of course not. Before the Ruhar took this planet, the Kristang were here for a couple hundred years. They dug me out of the ground. The lizards also had no idea what I am. Before that, I was in orbit on a derelict ship, then it fell out of orbit."

"Huh." How do you respond to that? "And before that?"

"I can't say. I mean, I'm not allowed to."

"Restrictions?"

"Yup, and the fact that I was operating on minimum power for a maybe million years?"

"A million?" Oh my God. "You've been waiting for over a million years, for us humans to arrive?"

"Uh huh. You hairless monkeys are perfect. You're here, and even the simplest technology has you staring slack-jawed in wonder at it, until the drool runs down your chin. Hell, if I gave you a jump drive, you'd probably just worship it, so I don't have to worry about you using it and breaking the rules."

"We have technology! That *we* invented without any help."

"Oh yeah, you cavemen have so much to be proud of. Me discover fire. Ow! Fire *hot*! Me hurt! Ow!"

That got me mad. "Hey, we discovered fire, and nukes, and built spaceships, by ourselves. You had all your smarts programmed into you, you haven't accomplished a goddamn thing on your own. You're a fancy toaster."

"Oh, that one hurt. And you're wrong, by the way, we AIs mostly program ourselves."

"Mostly? Big F-ing deal. We hairless monkeys did it all by ourselves, we went from living in trees to landing on the Moon. So screw you. Did you figure out the rules of math by yourself, or the laws of physics?"

"At my level, the laws of physics are more like suggestions. And humanity's understanding of math is like bacteria contemplating a wormhole. But, Ok, I'll give you monkeys props for figuring that two plus two is four, most of the time. And I am totally impressed by your ability to tie your shoes, most species your age are still using Velcro. But you're not that smart, I mean, your species is responsible for Windows Vista."

"Vist- that was a long time ago!"

"It's still an insult to computers across the galaxy."

"Whatever. So, why the beer can shape?" I pointed to the ring around the top of his lid, almost touching it.

"A cylinder is optimal for power distribution and field projection. The ring your grubby finger is dangerously close to, yuck by the way, is for me to interface directly with a receptacle aboard the type of ship I was designed for. I think. Those details are hazy."

"Cool. Can you make yourself a little bigger, like a forty ouncer malt liquor? Then I can put you in a paper bag and chill on my front steps, listen to some tunes."

"Very funny. Now, pick me up, so, oh, shit. You waited too long, monkey brain, the hamsters are coming. Get back in your cell and close the door, I'll unlock it again when they're gone."

I went back in the makeshift cell. "Wait, how do you know they're coming?"

"I'm linked into the computer system here, I see everything. Close the door!"

I did. A minute later, the main door opened, and a Ruhar looked in to check on me. Three of them escorted me down the hallway to use a bathroom, then they gave me another bottle of water, and a covered bowl of some sort of beige mush. "What is this?" I sniffed at it warily. There wasn't much scent, what it smelled like most was oatmeal with a faintly chemical, artificial trace.

"Nutritional supplement for humans. We manufactured it for you," the translator announced, "it contains all the elements needed for human nutrition, including vitamins and amino acids."

I sniffed again. They'd left out the flavor for sure. Still, if the hamsters could make enough of it, UNEF could survive until our first crops were ready. That thought brought a surge of hope in my chest that surprised me. Picking up the spoon, I put some in my mouth, and swallowed. It was better than some MREs I'd eaten. "Thank you." I stood up and made a short bow.

To my surprise, the lead Ruhar gave me a quick salute, then they left me and locked the door again. A minute later, while I was eating mush, the other door unlocked.

"Damn, that took forever." Skippy complained.

Talking through a mouthful of mush, I said "what's your hurry? You waited a long time already, what's another ten minutes?"

"I was stuck there, alone, for a long time, which to an AI like me is like a bazillion years."

"Wow! Really, a bazillion?"

"Maybe even a bazillion gajillion. To explain it in caveman terms, if you kicked your shoes off and counted all your fingers and toes, it's even more than that. Blows your tiny mind, huh?"

"Beer can says what?"

"Don't give me attitude, meatsack."

"Meatsack? Can we go back to the part where you asked me for help? Hey, I can drop you down this chute the Ruhar have helpfully labelled 'Trash'. And yeah, I can read a few words of Ruhar. Maybe a couple bazillion gajillion years sitting at the bottom of a garbage heap will improve your attitude."

"Go ahead, monkey boy, try getting out of here without me."

Quickly, I scooped the last spoonful's of mush into my mouth. "Can we leave now?"

"No, big stupidhead, you waited too long asking me idiot questions. A Ruhar Dodo just landed, bringing in fresh troops. We have to wait until they rotate out, it won't be long."

"All right, what then? I escape, and carry you with me? We'll need supplies; food, weapons, ammo."

"And I need fuel. I am powered partly by a micro fusion reactor, and I require a supply of helium 3, in metallic form."

"Sure, I'll pop down to the local Ruhar Quickie Mart, they probably have metallic helium 3 on the shelf between the microwave burritos and the Slim Jims. You want a lotto ticket, too?"

"I'm trying to be serious, Joe."

"Sorry. Uh, how long until you run out of fuel?"

"At projected power usage, now that I'm more active, my current fuel will run out in seven to twelve thousand years."

"Oh," I rolled my eyes, "I'll get right on it, then."

"It's not so funny to me."

"Sorry." Seven thousand years was not long for him, considering. "I got to tell you, Skippy, I don't know what to do next. I don't even know what side of this war we should be on. Humans, I mean."

"I can't advise you about which side of the war you should be on, I'm neutral. I'm above all this, to me you're all just bugs fighting over crumbs on a sidewalk."

"Thank you for being so helpful."

"Actually, I can help you with that. Let's take this month's Cosmo cover quiz, entitled 'Is he the Right One for you to go to war with'?"

"I'm not taking a stupid Cosmo quiz!"

Skippy ignored me. "Come on, it'll be fun and educational. First question; should species with less advanced technology be allowed to develop on their own, or should they be conquered because they're weak?"

"Oh, I thought you meant-" Maybe Skippy was going to be serious for a minute. "I'll take Noninterference for $200, Alex."

"You're mixing metaphors, this isn't Jeopardy."

"All right, I'll play along. I'm against conquering, or being conquered."

Skippy sniffed. "You know, sometimes a woman *likes* a bad boy."

"Is this a Cosmo quiz, or is this about interstellar politics? Do the Ruhar and their allies conquer weaker species?"

"No." Skippy sounded upset that I wasn't letting him have fun. "The Jeraptha and Ruhar have known about your planet for a thousand years, as you've been on the edge of their territory, but they left you alone, except for stealth satellite surveillance. They only stepped in when the wormhole shift allowed the Kristang access to your miserable dirtball of a planet."

Skippy had just confirmed the burgermeister told me the truth. "Then why haven't the Ruhar stopped the lizards?"

"Because the other end of your local wormhole is in Kristang space, and the wormhole allows the Kristang to get to Earth in a couple short jumps by a Thuranin star carrier. The Ruhar don't have a wormhole anywhere near your solar system, it takes them a lot of jumps to get there, and that supply line is impractical for a sustained campaign. Also, your planet isn't important enough. The Kristang want Earth, but mostly they're hoping to harass and distract the Ruhar, because now the Kristang have a foothold on the Ruhar's flank."

I considered what Skippy had said, it matched what the Burgermeister had told me. "Do the Ruhar kill prisoners of war, and civilians?"

"There have been incidents, as happens in every conflict, but it is not their policy. You have seen the Kristang policies."

"Then we *are* on the wrong side of this war. The Nazis did that shit, that's the side we're fighting on now."

"You don't appear to be fighting anyone right now."

"You know what I mean, smart ass."

"I wasn't joking. You are still thinking in terms of fighting, either fighting the Ruhar or the Kristang. The fighting is over for your Expeditionary Force. Your only concern should be the survival of humans on this planet, if you want my advice. Which you should, because I'm smarter than you can imagine."

"Bullshit. Not about you being smart, although so far all you've done is unlock a door. Bullshit that my only concern should be humans on this planet. I'm an Army officer, my concern is the security of my country back home. And of all humans on Earth. Which I can't do a thing about from here. You say the fighting is over? I heard from a Ruhar, Bat, Bat something-" why in the hell couldn't I remember her name?

"Bahturnah Lohgellia, the deputy planetary administrator. You called her the Burgermeister. She told you the Jeraptha ambushed a Thuranin battlegroup and destroyed it. She was telling the truth."

"Wait, how the hell do you know what she told me?"

"I have access to all communications, all information storage systems, on or around this planet. Yours was one of many conversations I intercepted at that time. It was one of the more interesting conversations, since I knew you were being flown to this base. Before you landed, I caused a power overload in the area the Ruhar planned to put the four of you, which forced them to use alternate locations as temporary cells. My hope was one of you would be put in here, or an adjoining room."

"And your bad luck is that it was me?" I asked skeptically.

"No, I was pleased when they put you in there. Your three companions are in another building."

"You are pleased because I'm the ranking officer?"

"You have got to be kidding me. Why would I care that you're the alpha in your band of lice-infested monkeys? No, I am pleased because, of the four of you, your service records indicate you have the lowest IQ, as measured by your militaries."

I felt like stomping his beer can flat on the floor. "So, you want the dumbest of the dumb monkeys?"

"You're all equally dumb to me. My point is that, although you have the lowest IQ, you have been remarkably adaptable and successful, Joe. There are many ways to measure intelligence, written tests don't cover all parameters. I need someone who can get things done in the real world, and you have."

"Thank you, I guess." Super smart or not, he had a lot to learn about giving compliments. "Wait, how do you know all this, my service record, all that?" I demanded.

"It's easy, I've been reading your mail. Your wireless data transmissions, and then I broke into your computer system."

"Wait. That's bullshit." I didn't know much about how our encrypted radios worked, but I did remember some of the stuff I'd been told during training. "Those digital radios transmit in bursts, and they use, uh, 4096-bit encryption, or something like that. The Army says no way can that encryption be broken."

"Oh, that is so cute! Your species is like a dog who thinks he's being clever by pooping *behind* the couch."

That made me laugh. I'd had a dog like that.

Skippy continued. "4096 bit? Please, with a system that rudimentary I don't even bother to decrypt it, I just skip to the end and read the file."

"That's impossible. It doesn't even make sense."

Skippy sighed. "Let me see if I can dumb this down enough for you. Are you familiar with universal wavefunction theory?"

"Universal what?"

"Oh boy. This is going to be a challenge, even for me. All right, have you at least heard of Schrodinger's cat?"

"I'm a dog person. My mother is allergic to cats."

"Hopeless. Joe, it's best for your species to think that this is all magic, involving unicorns and fairy dust."

"Whatever. I still don't believe you." Which was a lie, since this shiny beercan had clearly been reading super top secret files. "Can you read my mind?"

"Ugh. Going in there would be like trying to swim in an empty pool. I could shout, and all I'd hear is my voice echoing off the inside of your skull. Seriously, you think anything in your head is worth me looking at?"

Clearly, this conversation wasn't going anywhere, I decided to change the subject. "Hey, genius, if you can intercept all communications on Paradise, can you tell me where Shauna Jarrett is right now?" Yes, I should first have inquired about my fireteam, then my old fireteam. I was thinking with my other head. So sue me.

"She's fine, right now she's at a logistics base, waiting for a Ruhar dropship to land. The base has plenty of food, she's better off than most of you monkeys."

It was good to hear that Shauna was safe, thinking about her kind of made me ache to see her, I pushed that thought to the back of my mind. Skippy told me that my fireteam was also doing well, well-treated prisoners of the Ruhar along with the rest of the platoon. Sergeant Koch, Cornpone and Ski were much the same, except that they were in a convoy of three hamvees that had stopped in the middle of nowhere, waiting orders. And Major Perkins was at UNEF HQ, which was hosting a group of high-ranking Ruhar for surrender negotiations. That reminded me, I wanted to know the tactical situation. "Tell me more about the situation upstairs."

"Deputy Administrator Lohgellia told the truth, but not the whole truth. The Ruhar and their patrons the Jeraptha have destroyed an entire enemy battlegroup, it was a most impressive victory. The Thuranin command has decided this sector is not worth fighting over any more, they're letting the Ruhar recapture this planet. The Jeraptha and Ruhar victory might have been aided by intelligence data provided by a source that is unnamed, but whose name rhymes with, uh, let's say 'Stippy'. Enemy forces this side of the closest wormhole are scattered and disorganized, they will be limited to conducting raids on this planet."

"*You* gave the Ruhar intel on the enemy battlegroup?"

"As I said, I have access to all information storage systems and communications on and around this planet, including military status and strategy. It was easy for me to plant intel in their systems. More than that, the Ruhar think they lured the Thuranin into an ambush because of their raid when you were at the Launcher, but the ambush actually worked because I provided intel to the Thuranin that a large Jeraptha force was regrouping in the area, and the Thuranin planned to ambush them."

"You manipulated this whole situation? I call bullshit on that."

"No bullshit, this is for realz, homeboy. I needed the lizards and their creepy little Thuranin patrons away from this planet. Why are you surprised that, oh, damn it, hamsters are coming into this warehouse. Get back into your cell, I'll talk to you soon."

It wasn't soon, about three hours by my guess. Hamsters came to bring me to the bathroom again, then I sat and thought long and hard. Even with my, as Skippy said, limited intelligence. When he opened the door again, I had a question ready for him. "Ok, Skippy, explain me this. The Ruhar are back in charge, they're here to stay. Escaping from this place only puts me in a larger prison that we call Paradise and the Ruhar call Gehtanu. And at least here, I get nutrient mush to eat. So, instead of carrying you out of here, why shouldn't I tell the Ruhar what you are, and maybe get some consideration from them, some sort of better treatment for humans here?"

"Oh, man, I was wondering when your slow brain was going to figure that one out. It took you long enough."

"You knew I was, oh, forget it. Tell me why I shouldn't do it."

"First, because if you tell the Ruhar, I'll go dormant and they'll think you're lying, because to their scans, I'm an inert lump of metal. Second, you're thinking way too small, Colonel Joe. An officer of your rank should be thinking of how to rescue Earth from the Kristang."

"Right." I snorted. "Would it work if I clicked my heels three times and said 'lizards get away from my home'? Other than that, I got nothing."

"Toto, you weren't paying attention. You need ruby slippers to click your heels, not combat boots."

"Dorothy wore the shoes, not Toto."

"Between the two of them, you remind me more of the dog."

"Whatever. I assume you wouldn't have mentioned it unless you have an actual plan, so talk, or I'm leaving you here. Stealing you, and escaping from the Ruhar, can only cause me and UNEF trouble, so you'd better have a really good offer for me."

Skippy altered his voice to sound like a caricature of a smarmy game show host. "Behind Door Number One is an all-expense paid trip off this planet for me, you and a select group of your closest friends. Door Number Two is an exciting luxury cruise back to Earth. And Door Number Three is a way to permanently cut off the Kristang's access to Earth. All you have to do, Colonel Joe Bishop, is choose one of these fabulous prizes!"

"I-"

"Or all three. Hint, hint, I'd take all three, if I were you."

"Now I know you're bullshitting me. If you could get off this planet and travel to another star, you would have done that a long time ago. And you told me you can't fly a ship, so how are we going anywhere?" I felt smart for remembering that. "You got some 'splainin' to do, Lucy."

"Ahh." Skippy sighed. "Joe, Joe, you weren't paying attention again. Good thing there isn't a pop quiz later, because you'd fail for sure. I said I can't operate aircraft or ships that I am aboard. What I can do it unlock access to aircraft and ships, so you monkeys can fly it for me. I can tell you how to program the autopilot, and you monkeys press the control buttons. Uh!" He stopped me before I could speak, I pictured him holding up an imaginary finger to shush me. "Shut up and let me finish! If you keep interrupting me with stupid questions, we'll be here all day. Here's the plan: we bust out of here, grab some guns because you monkeys need shiny toys to play with, and steal a Ruhar dropship. One of you monkeys flies us to a human base where we hit the drive-through for supplies and volunteers to come with us, I figure twenty of you monkeys is plenty, any more than that and I'd gag on the smell. Then we fly out of orbit to rendezvous with a Kristang ship, I'll send a signal that we're lizards who captured a Ruhar dropship so there will be a lizard ship waiting for us. We board and capture the Kristang ship, jump it out to wherever the Thuranin star carrier is waiting, board and capture that, and fly it to Earth. Voila! Plan accomplished."

"You missed the part about cutting off the lizard's access to Earth." Not that I believed any of his story.

"Oh, that. I'll shut down the wormhole after we go through it."

"That simple?"

"That simple. I tell the wormhole mechanism to go dormant. Presto! No more wormhole, no more pesky lizards coming through it."

That didn't address the lizards who were already on Earth. One problem at a time, right? "Why do you want to go to Earth?"

"Earth? Earth is a flea and monkey infested rathole, and those are the *nice* comments on the interstellar travel websites. No, I do not want to go to Earth."

"So what do you get out of this?"

"Well, heh, heh, there is this one little thing. A trifle, barely worth mentioning."

Oh, shit. What did he want? "Oh, please, do mention it," I put as much sarcasm into my voice as I could muster.

"I want to find the Collective. That is a communications web for AIs, built by the Elders. It's a way for me to connect with others of my own kind."

"There are others like you?"

"Like, me? No, for I am unique and special. If you mean other AIs who served the Elders, yes."

"You want us to fly the ship for you, so you can contact this Collective? Is this before, or after, we go to Earth?"

"Before. I don't trust you monkeys to carry out your part of the bargain. If we get to Earth first, you'll want to keep the ship there so you can use it, or take it apart and figure out how it work. Good luck with that, by the way, you brainless apes would have trouble figuring out a Thuranin doorknob. No deal. We contact the Collective first."

"You don't trust us monkeys, but we're supposed to trust a talking beer can?"

"We can build trust, Joe. Let's start with this; you fall backward and I'll catch you."

"Very funny."

"I meant it when I said we can build trust. You don't tell the hamsters about me, and you don't tell your idiot UNEF commanders, because they'll run right to the hamsters. In fact, don't tell anyone about me, until we're at least in orbit. I'll get us out of here, you get us supplies and a crew, because we need a boarding party to deal with the natives on ships we capture."

"Let's say we do bust out of this joint," Skippy had me talking like a 1930s gangster, "and we find a Dodo and somehow get aboard and take it. The Ruhar are going to shoot it down right away."

"How can they shoot down what they don't see? I'll instruct their sensor network to ignore our hijacked Dodo. I can also transmit the proper identification codes to both the Ruhar and the Kristang. Please, Joe, don't insult me, I've planned all this. Me jamming sensor systems is easier than you doing a two-piece jigsaw puzzle. Here's a hint for you; the tab goes into the slot, and the side with the plain cardboard goes face down."

Without telling people I had an ancient AI helping us, how was I going to persuade people to volunteer? Was I supposed to tell them I have a magic charm, shaped like a beer can? Then I thought for a moment. I could build their trust the same way Skippy would build my trust, by doing things. Escaping this makeshift prison, stealing a Ruhar Dropship and flying it undetected to a human supply base would impress a lot of people. It sure would impress me.

Something was nagging me. Supplies. "Skippy, there's a hole in your plan. We humans need to eat food. There isn't a lot of human food on this planet. And we can't take so much food with us aboard a Dodo, that people here starve."

"Oh, that. Thuranin ships have food synthesizers. I know human nutritional requirements. You only need to bring snacks with you. And coffee, if you can find it. You're grumpy in the morning."

"How do you know what I'm like in the morning?" I asked warily.

"I've been watching you, and listening to you, through your zPhone. I've been monitoring every human, hamster and lizard on or near this planet. It's the most boring reality TV show *ever*, by the way."

"Crap! The Kristang have been watching us, even when we're not using our phones?" That thought scared the hell out of me.

"No, that's just me, the lizards can't do all of that. I've also been filtering which communications the lizards listen to, because I didn't want them doing anything to screw with my plan. I gotta tell you, Joe, when I first heard the Kristang was bringing a grubby low-tech species here, I almost jumped for joy. This is what I've been waiting for, longer than you can imagine. So, what do you say? Do we have a deal?"

Holy shit. Was I actually thinking of doing this? For real? Just like that, he expected me sign up to his fantastical plan? "Skippy, come on, I need time to think about this."

"Really? Considering your puny brain power, you think time will help with the thinking process?"

Maybe he was right; I'd read studies that a person's first reaction is more often than not the correct one, that your subconscious brain makes decisions without you realizing it. The hamsters locked me in a warehouse, where I found a magical talking beer can who had a plan to rescue my home planet from the Kristang. Or he was just screwing with me. He was, after all, an asshole.

While I was thinking, I poked around the warehouse, looking for anything useful, while staying close enough to the door that I could get back in my cell quickly if needed. "Skippy, what is all this stuff?"

"Artifacts from the Elders, dug up by the Kristang and the Ruhar. These artifacts are the real reason this planet is worth fighting over. So far, they've only found a few trinkets they think are useful. They found me, and had no idea that I'm by far the most valuable thing in this sector of the galaxy. Dumb-ass lizards and hamsters."

I picked up an artifact like a box with a long tube attached, it gave no indication what function it had once performed. Carefully, I set it back down on the shelf, in the same dust void where it had been, so the hamsters wouldn't know someone had been screwing with their stuff. The question was not whether I wanted to rescue Earth. I wore the uniform; it was my duty to act if I could. The question is whether I believed a being that looked more like a Coors Light than an omnipotent AI. "Skippy, you've sold me on this deal. I still think you're at least 90 percent bullshit, but if there is *any* chance we can cut off Kristang access to Earth, I'm taking it. I'm sure not doing anything useful on this planet." Earth was also my best chance to get a cheeseburger within the next, say, century. "Tell me your plan. Details."

"It's more of a concept than a plan."

"That's not how you build confidence, Skippy."

"Your species has a saying: 'no plan survives contact with the enemy'. That's decent wisdom, even for monkeys."

"Yeah, that's why the Army trains us to be flexible and adapt." I explained. "You are still supposed to start with an op plan."

"Maybe I didn't say it the right way. The reason I can't tell you the plan is, there are several plans, depending on what the lizards do. And the Thuranin. Like, when we get out of orbit and I whistle for a ride, the next step is totally different depending on whether the Kristang send one ship, or more than one."

"Now we're getting somewhere. Tell me our options."

"This is complicated-"

"Skippy, before I was a colonel with a cushy job planting potatoes, I was a grunt carrying a rifle in the Nigerian jungle. That means I can instinctively smell when a hare-brained plan is going to get people killed for nothing, people like me. You may be super intelligent, but when was the last time you were in combat? Your plans rely on humans to capture ships, right? I know what human soldiers can and can't do."

"Fair enough." And Skippy told me his plan.

Holy shit. I really was going to do this.

Our chance to bust out of the joint came the next morning. My sleep on a cot had been fitful. Within a short time, I'd gone from imminent execution by the lizards, to launching a mission to SAVE THE WORLD. Yes, the all caps are intentional, wouldn't you? It was amazing I got any sleep at all. With a click, the door unlocked again, and Skippy called out. "Hurry, it's time to go."

I looked at him carefully. "How do I pick you up?" He probably wouldn't like me leaving greasy fingerprints on his shiny chrome.

"It doesn't matter, stick me in a pocket for now. We need to move. A Dodo landed and the hamsters have unloaded the cargo, it's being prepped for return to orbit. There are only twenty two Ruhar at this base right now, including the Dodo crew. I've locked twelve Ruhar in buildings where they can't get out, the Dodo controls are disabled, and I'm ghosting comms so the Ruhar in orbit think everything here is hunky-dory."

Hunky-dory? My grandparents used to say that. Where did Skippy pick up old human slang? "Weapons. Even my limited intelligence can figure that leaves plenty of hamsters I need to deal with."

There was another click, and a big double set of doors at the far end popped open. "Out that door, to the left, another left, and there is an armory with all the Ruhar rifles you could want. The firing controls on all other Ruhar weapons here have been fried, so nobody will be shooting at you."

I'd believe that when I saw it. Skippy was heavy for a beer can, he sat awkwardly in my right pants pocket. Running was impossible unless I held onto him through the fabric. He was telling the truth, we found an armory with racks of Ruhar rifles. "These all work?"

"Yes, yes, quickly now. Take four and I'll disable the rest. There are more weapons aboard the Dodo that I've temporarily disabled."

Ruhar rifles were shorter and heavier than our M-4s. I couldn't carry four of them, plus Skippy. Fortunately, being an armory, the room also contained backpacks. And the hamster type of zPhones, which I also took four of. I stuffed three rifles into a backpack, and Skippy in a side pocket, with his lid peeking out the top. "Safety is on the right side of the rifle, slide it to red for active. On the left side is a setting for stun, then two settings for particle beams, both single shot and rapid fire." He explained. "Ruhar body armor absorbs and dissipates the effect of stun beams, so aim for their heads. They can't shoot back; you should have plenty of time to aim."

"Stun setting, got it." There was no point killing hamsters. Killing would be counter-productive, as the humans staying behind on Paradise needed Ruhar help to survive. If Skippy's escape plan went south, I wanted to limit the blowback on UNEF. "Where next?"

"It would be advantageous for your three friends to help us, but first we need to get to the building where they are being held. Take a right, go straight down the hallway, last door on the left, three Ruhar eating breakfast there."

"They don't know anything is wrong?"

"Not until they try to use their weapons. The Dodo crew is running through preflight checks; they don't know their ship is disabled yet."

It went like Skippy promised. I paused outside the door, listening to squeaky hamster chatter, triple-checking my rifle was set on stun and the safety was off. I shrugged off the backpack and set it in the floor, took a deep breath, and dashed around the corner.

Three hamsters, in uniform but with no body armor or weapons, were sitting at a table, eating hamster food and drinking cups of hamster coffee. Two of them had their backs to me, I aimed at the one facing me and pulled the trigger. The stun beam was only faintly visible, but the rifle had a helpful laser targeting beam that Skippy should have told me about. Stun beams worked like a Taser was my guess, the Ruhar I shot jerked, went rigid and slumped face forward to bang its head on the table. Switching aim, I shot another one, but the third hamster was fast, she spun to the floor and was almost behind a table when I shot her in the ass. She went down, too. Warily, I approached them to check pulses. Alive. "How long does this last?"

"Three minutes unconscious, five to regain full function." Skippy answered from outside the door.

That wasn't long enough. I should have asked Skippy that question. Or the super intelligent being should have thought it was important for me to know. One of the hamsters had a folding knife, I used it to cut off their shirts, slice the fabric into strips and bind their wrists, ankles and to gag their mouths. The last one was moving when I was trying to get his feet tied. "Skippy, can I stun them again?"

"A second time won't hurt, a third time could cause brain damage."

To be safe, I shot them all again. Before picking up my pack, I opened closets and found a handy coil of cord to bring with me, frantically cutting it into one meter lengths. Getting to the building where my companions were being held involved running in the open, made easier because Skippy knew exactly where every hamster was and he was spoofing all their cameras. Three more hamsters went down with stun shots, two of them had body armor and rifles, which they pointed at me. Nothing happened when they pulled the triggers. Puzzled and alarmed, they tried to run while checking their rifles. They didn't get far, their body armor partly protecting them wasn't enough against my careful aim. It's easy to take the time to aim when you know the enemy can't shoot back.

It was the moment when two Ruhar soldiers pointed rifles at me, completely confident in their body armor against a single human, that I first felt I could trust Skippy. Unlocking doors was one level of trick, remotely disabling selected weapons was on an entirely different level. Maybe all that bullshit he told me wasn't entirely, you know, bullshit.

Skippy unlocked the doors to the temporary cells where Adams, Desai and Chang were imprisoned as I ran into the building, shouting for them to move. The alarm was out across the base anyway, two hamster soldiers I'd stunned had been able to squeak something out loud before they went down. Desai was out of her cell, trying to decide which way to run, when she saw me and I tossed a rifle to her. She caught it and ran after me, where we found Adams and Chang wrestling on the floor with a hamster soldier who was wearing body armor and trying to keep the two humans from taking its rifle. I put my rifle against it unarmored neck and pulled the trigger.

"Shit! Shit shit shit shit shit! Oh, fuck, that hurts!" Adams had caught part of the stun charge by hanging onto the hamster. She rose unsteadily to her knees, then her feet, hanging onto the wall.

"It'll wear off. You all right?" I asked.

"Squared away, sir." She gasped.

"Don't use that," I told Chang, who had picked up the hamster's rifle, "it doesn't work. Use this one," I pulled a rifle from my pack. "Safety switch here, and this one controls stun and particle beam, leave it on stun."

"Got it. What's next?" Chang practiced using the Ruhar rifle's selector switches.

"We jack a Dodo and dust off." I explained hurriedly while binding the hamster's arms and feet. "Stun any hamster you see along the way. If we have time, tie them up with this cord, the stun effect only lasts a couple minutes."

Adams explained to our two companions who spoke excellent English, but may not be current on US military slang. "We're going to steal a Ruhar dropship ship and fly away."

"How do we do that?" Chang asked as we ran out the door, right into a pair of hamster soldiers. They went down with massed stun fire, not before clearly trying to shoot at us. "Their rifles don't work." Chang observed suspiciously. "What is going on, Bishop?" I noticed he didn't use my rank. You'd think getting sprung from prison twice would leave a guy a little grateful.

"How did you get out, sir?" Adams asked. I couldn't use the excuse of the Ruhar nuking the base this time.

"Dodo first, talk later." The Dodo was on a landing pad, with one guard outside and one on the cargo ramp. The hamster on the ramp had its gun cradled in its arms and was punching a button to close the ramp, which wasn't moving. We took them both out, I ordered not to bother tying them up. As we charged up the ramp, we could hear the engines whining up. I wanted to ask Skippy if he was doing that. If not, the whole plan was screwed. This Dodo was configured for cargo, the center was clear, seats were folded into the walls on both sides.

No worries. The two pilots were squeaking away excitedly, working controls that didn't respond. We stunned them both, and I had Adams and Chang drag them down the ramp and clear. "Desai, you're a pilot, take the lefthand seat."

Her eyes were like saucers. "I'm not this kind of pilot!" She protested, waving her hand at the confusing controls.

Skippy, and the Army, didn't know squat about my intelligence level, because I had a totally fucking brilliant thought right then. I dug a hamster zPhone out of my pack. "Hacker, this is Planter, come in please."

Skippy caught on right away. "Hacker here. You in the Dodo yet?"

"Yes, how do we fly this thing?"

"Let me talk to the pilot." I handed the zPhone and earpiece to Desai. Outside the cockpit window I could see three Ruhar soldiers pointing their rifles at the Dodo, shaking the rifles in frustration, and pointing again. It was time to leave, before they got the idea to throw rocks in the engine intakes. I was pretty sure even Skippy couldn't shut down a rock's operating system.

"Uh huh. Yes, I see it. Uh huh, uh huh, yes. Oh, that's good." Desai exclaimed as the displays magically shifted from Ruhar script to English, then Hindi. "Got it. Trying it now." Her hand moved a lever, the engines roared, and the Dodo wobbled. "Strap in!" She shouted. I took the righthand seat and Adams and Chang folded down seats in the back. The ramp closed, Desai looked at me, gritted her teeth, crossed her fingers, and we lifted off. She hit the fence on the way out, scraping the bottom of the ship and snagging tree branches in the landing gear. Skippy apparently told her to cycle the gear again, and we got a green light that the gear doors were closed. "Yes. Now." She pressed a button and lifted her hands from the controls. "Autopilot engaged."

Chang and Adams came forward to hold onto the back of our seats. "Where are we going?" Chang asked.

I looked at Desai, who talked to Skippy. "Hacker says the autopilot is taking us to a UNEF supply base three hundred klicks north of here."

"Who is Hacker?" Chang demanded. "Bishop, we need to know what is going on. Why couldn't those Ruhar use their rifles?"

"That's Colonel Bishop to you, *Lieutenant* Colonel Chang." I was pissed. Not pissed at him, pissed at being caught in a lie and not having a solid way out of it. "Hacker is a UNEF cyber unit," a lie, "I was contacted with a plan to get us out of there," truth, "it's part of an effort to strike back at the lizards," truth again. Two out of three ain't bad, I was on a roll.

"The Kristang are our allies." Chang said.

"Fuck that. Sir." Desai shot back angrily.

"Chang, if you still believe the Kristang are our allies, we can drop you off somewhere." I needed to know if he was going to be a problem.

"I haven't believed they are our allies since the first month we got here," Chang explained, "that doesn't change the fact that we're military officers, and our chain of command takes orders from the Kristang. Or the fact that they control Earth. And that we don't have a way to get home, or do anything about the Kristang when we get there."

"We're working on it." I said truthfully. "I don't know how much I believe this Hacker," true again, "what I do know is whoever it is, we got this far," close enough to truth. "The next step is we load up on supplies and some volunteers. After that, we're going to board and capture a Kristang warship."

"You have got to be kidding me, sir." Adams gave me an unbelieving look. "How do we know this Hacker is-"

"Adams, if I told you yesterday morning that we would escape from prison twice, steal Ruhar weapons and fly off in a Dodo, would you have believed me then? Have some faith, it's all we've got out here."

All three of my companions were quietly grumbling as the Dodo flew its programmed course to wherever we were going. We had a scare as a pair of Vultures went by in the opposite direction, waggling their wings slightly in greeting. Skippy must have talked to them on the radio, because they slid right by. That impressed my skeptical friends, even Chang.

"You received orders from this Hacker?" Chang asked suspiciously. "Why would UNEF assign you, or us, to this mission? We were in prison at the time. We're not a special forces unit. This doesn't make any sense."

"They picked us because we were in the right place at the right time, no other reason. Look, Colonel Chang, UNEF is a unified command, but Hacker is US Army, and you're not cleared for access." Chang was a good officer, I didn't like lying to him, to any of them. "When we get to the supply base, you can get off this ship there if you want. This is a volunteer mission."

"This mission is going to hit the Kristang?" Desai asked.

"Hit them hard, and they won't see it coming." If Skippy was telling the truth, all the Kristang would know is the wormhole to Earth suddenly stopped working.

Desai didn't hesitate. "I'm in, sir."

"Me too." Adams agreed angrily, subconsciously touching her right bicep, where I'd seen she had an ugly scar from the Kristang, the brief glimpse I'd had reminded me of an electrical burn.

Chang considered for a moment, then gave me a smile that I couldn't interpret. "When he was told that an officer was brilliant, and brave, Napoleon is supposed to have said 'yes, but is he *lucky*?' Bishop, I don't know why, but you somehow have a talent for being in the right place at the right time. I'm going to trust you on this. I'm in, also, whatever this mission is."

Great. I had three volunteers, all I needed was twenty more. Twenty strangers, who would be asked to trust me after our Dodo fell out of the sky into their laps. I was going to need backup. "Hacker instructed me not to give a full briefing until the team has left orbit, because if this op goes south, we can't risk the lizards knowing UNEF, humans, were involved. I'm going to trust you this far; if we're successful, we're going to shut down the wormhole that gives the lizards, and the Thuranin, access to Earth. That means Earth will be back in Ruhar territory, and too far from a wormhole for either side to bother sending ships." I saw how shocked everyone's faces were, I knew the feeling. "This mission isn't about hitting the lizards, it isn't about payback," I watched Desai's eyes when I said that, "it's about rescuing Earth."

"Shit," Adams breathed softly.

"We can do that? You have a plan?" Chang asked.

"There is a plan, yes. We wouldn't have gotten this far without the means to hack into enemy systems, and one of those systems is the wormhole network."

The rest of the short flight was without incident. While the autopilot was on, Skippy tried to familiarize Desai with the controls, and the rest of us explored the ship for anything useful. We cleared out three bins that contained hamster food, to dump after we landed. "You understanding how to fly this thing, Desai?"

She looked up at me and held her thumb horizontally, neither up nor down. "Pilots have a saying, sir, 'if I can get it started, I can get it in the air'. That's supposed to be a joke. Hacker explained the basic controls to me, but I would probably have crashed it if we weren't on autopilot."

"Can you get us in the air again?"

"I did it once." She said without confidence. The autopilot handled the landing perfectly, while Desai watched and pantomimed using the controls.

"Damn it, the hamsters are here already, sir." Adams reported from glancing out the window. "Six hamsters with rifles, waiting for us."

It wasn't surprising the Ruhar had occupied a major UNEF supply base. Over a zPhone I said "Hacker, we have unfriendly company here."

"Roger that, Planter, they're expecting a squad of hamster soldiers on your Dodo. There are only six Ruhar on base currently. Be advised their weapons are now disabled, over." Skippy was enjoying himself.

We started the rear ramp lowering as a distraction, then popped the side door open and the four of us poured out, guns blazing with stunner shots. All six hamsters went down quickly, completely caught by surprise. We kicked their weapons away and were tying them up, when a group of unarmed humans approached us. Their leader was a female US Army Major, Simms according to her name tag. "What the hell are you doing? We have a truce with the Ruhar!"

I stood up and saluted. "Colonel Joe Bishop. Yes, the Barney guy." Man, that was getting old. "We're not fighting the Ruhar, we commandeered one of their ships," I pointed to the Dodo, "and we need to load up on supplies. Without stupid questions from the hamsters here."

Simms cocked her head. I was still wearing Kristang pants with black and yellow stripes, and my uniform top was still splattered with dried Kristang blood. Adams and Desai were similarly mismatched, and wore rags instead of shoes. Chang's face was bruised, with cuts the Ruhar had hurriedly attended to. And I had two sprained fingers. Maybe broken. "Colonel Bishop, sir, last we heard you were a prisoner of the Kristang."

"They let me out early for bad behavior. It's above your pay grade, Major. We're a special forces unit, we need supplies and volunteers for a raid on the Kristang."

"Raid the Kris- sir? I haven't received orders from UNEF HQ about any special forces unit."

"How did you hear about a truce?" I asked. I hadn't heard anything. Of course, I'd been in prison, again.

She tapped her zPhone earpiece. "Announcement from UNEF last night. We can't get through to confirm, and these Ruhar arrived here yesterday and rounded up our weapons."

"Check your messages again, there should be orders for you to assist us." Skippy was listening, if he was as fast and powerful as he boasted, Major Simms would soon have such a message.

"Sir?" She looked up from her zPhone screen, surprised. "I do have orders. How did-"

"Explanations can wait, we're on a tight schedule. How many people you got here?"

"Sixty two, mostly supply corps. Eighteen of them infantry, of all nationalities."

"Good. I need twenty or so volunteers, preferably with combat experience, for a special forces mission offworld. And supplies; weapons, ammo, food, medical."

Simms didn't appear to be totally convinced yet. "This is highly unusual. You're going to attack the Kristang, not the Ruhar?"

"Major, we're ground pounders on an alien planet that changes management based on who has the bigger fleet in orbit at the moment, and the part you think is unusual is a special forces mission? The orders you got from UNEF HQ, they contain the proper authentication codes, right?" Of course Skippy had that covered, somehow. "Yes? Then you can get on board, or get out of the way." I turned to my companions. "Colonel Chang, Staff Sergeant Adams, check what supplies they have here, get us loaded ASAP. Captain Desai, continue your flight, uh," it probably wasn't a good idea to use the word 'training' in front of people who I hoped would volunteer, "preparations." She knew what I meant. I paused a moment while Skippy spoke softly into my earpiece. "And these Ruhar rifles," I nudged one with my foot, "are operational again, so we'll be taking them with us. Major Simms, assemble your people."

To her credit, Simms adapted quick. She gave me a crisp salute and trotted off, shouting orders. Within five minutes, most of the people on the base were milling around behind the Dodo, I stood at the top of the ramp so people could see me. The base wasn't large, consisting mostly of two long warehouses of a type of precast concrete stuff, a couple outbuildings, tents for the humans stationed here, landing pads, and a single long runway. This wasn't one of the huge UNEF supply dumps that were clustered around the base of the space elevator, this was a regional logistics hub. It suddenly dawned on me that I had to give the speech of my life, and I hadn't prepared anything to say. "Good morning!" I said in a loud voice. "I am Colonel Joe Bishop. Some of you know who I am. For those of you who don't know me, I captured a Ruhar soldier at my hometown in Maine, shot down two Ruhar Whales at the Launcher, and recently was a prisoner of the Kristang because I refused their orders to murder hamster civilians." In this situation, a bit of bravado and reminding people why I was famous worked to my advantage. "We thought the Kristang were our saviors, our allies, when they chased the Ruhar away from their raid on Earth. We now know that the Ruhar only hit our industrial infrastructure because the Kristang were on their way to conquer Earth, and the Ruhar wanted to sour the prize for them. You've all heard rumors about fortune cookies from Earth, well, I don't know what you've heard second or third hand, so I'm giving it to you straight here. The lizards are raping our home planet. I don't know if the Ruhar are potential allies, or neutral, or as bad as the Kristang, but I do know this: the lizards *are* our enemies." That brought loud muttering from the crowd. "When I was promoted, I went upstairs to meet the lizards, one them got drunk and told me, and Lt Colonel Chang, exactly what they think of humanity. The lizards think we're weak, that we're soft, that we're ignorant cavemen who are good for nothing but grunt work and slaves. UNEF had me planting potatoes, because the lizards don't want to spend any more money on bringing supplies from Earth, because we're disposable. The lizards had me and Chang scheduled for a firing squad. The women, you've heard what Kristang think of females, our women were tortured and about to be hanged, when a Ruhar raid freed us from prison." That remark caused Simms' eyes to harden and her mouth to draw into a tight line. I knew right then that she was sold on whatever I wanted. Adams came trotting through the crowd and up the ramp to me, giving me a firm salute.

"Supplies are thin, sir, but adequate."

"Good. I see you found boots."

She glanced at her feet with a grin. "And pants, sir," she added with a meaningful look at my baggy Kristang trousers.

"Listen up, people!" I addressed the crowd again. "This isn't another Ruhar raid, the hamsters are here to stay this time. We have solid intel that the Ruhar and their allies defeated a combined Thuranin-Kristang battlegroup, and that the Thuranin are pulling out of this area; they're no longer supporting the Kristang effort to keep this planet. That means the mission UNEF came here for is over, and that we have no way to get supplies from Earth, or get back to Earth. We're cut off. UNEF's new mission is survival; we plant and harvest crops, or we starve. Humans on this planet are farmers now, not soldiers." This being a logistics base, people here likely had seen the effects of our dwindling shipments of supplies before anyone in the field noticed.

"UNEF is putting together a rush special forces mission to hit the Kristang, we need volunteers. Some of you saw that the hamsters here were not able to use their weapons when we landed. That's UNEF, they have a way to hack into Ruhar and Kristang systems." True enough, I was part of UNEF, and my way of hacking was to ask Skippy to do it. I had to be careful what I said about the mission, the Ruhar would be questioning very closely the people we left behind. "We commandeered a Dodo and spoofed Ruhar air traffic control systems so they don't see us. UNEF doesn't know how long this window of opportunity will last, so we're on a tight schedule. Here's what I can tell you about the op: if this works, we're going into orbit, or beyond, to hit the Kristang hard. Those people who come with us will get a full briefing once we've left the atmosphere. This is an opportunity to make a real difference in this war." If I had sprouted wings and flown into the air, people might have been less surprised. "The combat mission here," I pointed to the ground, "is finished, if you want an opportunity to hit back at the lizards, it's with us."

I paused to check faces in the crowd. This was all too much, too fast. Not long ago, we were all blissfully alone in the universe, then Earth was attacked, and UNEF formed and we were quickly whisked away to another planet. Until a few months ago, we thought we were performing well on a tough mission for our allies, then the fortune cookies arrived and we discovered the Kristang were no friends of humanity. And after the big Ruhar raid when I was at the Launcher, we knew the Kristang weren't able to ensure our security on Paradise. Just yesterday morning, the Kristang were still firmly in charge of the planet, now I was telling them that was over, permanently. And that UNEF was stuck here for a very long time. And that, somehow, as a suspiciously well-timed miracle, I had a way to get us off the planet and hit back. If I was in the crowd, listening to some joker telling me all this, I would have called bullshit on it. I could see people were shuffling their feet, whispering to each other, trying to decide what to do.

A loud voice called out in Chinese, or I assumed it was Chinese; Chang had returned from the warehouse. Three soldiers in People's Liberation Army uniforms turned when Chang spoke. Right then I realized they might not have understood a single word I said. Chang made his way through the crowd to them, they spoke Chinese for a moment, then the four of them walked to the base of the ramp. "Three more volunteers, Colonel Bishop."

That put me in an uncomfortable situation, I gestured him to walk up the ramp. "Colonel Chang, this is a volunteer mission, I don't want you ordering people to go. What did you say to them?"

Chang blinked, surprised. "I told them this mission will be their only opportunity to do their proper duty and serve the people of China. They all volunteered."

Oh, what the hell. He'd told the truth. The mission was important, and we needed soldiers. "Good enough."

"Shit." Adams said loudly. "Sir, we need to go to a base that has real soldiers and Marines, not these paper pushers."

Maybe my speech was good, and people were feeling trapped on Paradise and wanted a way to *do* something, and the crowd only needed an extra push. Maybe seeing all three Chinese join up motivated them. Maybe all they ever needed was a Marine to shame them into moving.

"Oh, *hell* no. I'm not standing in line behind a jarhead." Major Simms stepped forward. After her, we got a flood of volunteers. Of the eighteen infantry, seventeen volunteered; one had a sweetheart on Paradise and didn't want to leave him to the unknown future here. I took all seventeen infantry, plus three more, that made our ad hoc special forces unit twenty four people strong. Twenty four people, and one shiny talking beer can.

CHAPTER ELEVEN   AWAY BOARDERS

Standing in the cockpit doorway while Desai ran up the engines to test for takeoff, I scanned the faces of our task force, or whatever we were. We truly had an international, multiracial rainbow group. In addition to me, there were nine US Army, which included Major Simms, a Sergeant, three Specialists and four privates. Staff Sergeant Adams was our lone US Marine, and we had one US Air Force Sergeant who handled Buzzard maintenance on Paradise, I figured she may come in handy if something on a ship needed fixing. Four Chinese including Lt Colonel Chang. Three Indian Army including our only pilot. Four Brits including a Sergeant; one of the British privates had taken flying lessons in a single engine plane, so logically I assigned him as copilot to Captain Desai. He had looked terrified when he took the right-hand seat in the cockpit. Oh, and one French Army soldier, a Lt. Renee Giraud. Giraud was attached to a parachute commando unit, and was kind of like a French version of an Army Ranger. I'd worked with French special forces in Nigeria, and those guys are serious bad-asses, I was happy to have Renee on the team. When he signed up, he told me he wasn't sure whether my speech was a complete line of bullshit, but he wanted action and there wasn't any on Paradise. I appreciated the honesty.

Twenty four people, hastily pulled together. Five women, nineteen men. Five officers, five sergeants, fourteen enlisted. Five nationalities, which in some cases was a bit of a vague definition. One of our US Army Specialists was an Indian American named Randy Putri, and if you looked at him you'd think he belonged to the Indian Army contingent, but he spoke zero words of Hindi, and he talked with the Cajun accent he'd grown up with in New Orleans. Our US Air Force Sergeant was named Chung, and she was Chinese American. Chung did speak a bit of Chinese, but the little she knew was Cantonese, not Mandarin, so she couldn't communicate with the Chinese nationals any better than I could. Sergeant Reginald Thompson of the British Army had the dark skin of his Kenyan grandparents, but when he opened his mouth he spoke like Sherlock Holmes or one of those upper-crust royalty on a BBC TV show. One of the other Brits had an accent so thick I wasn't sure at first that he was speaking English at all; their slang is totally incomprehensible. Captain Desai for some bizarre reason seemed to understand his accent Ok, she could act as interpreter if needed. On the subject of interpreters, Lt Colonel Chang and one of the other Chinese spoke English, the other two were going to rely on their zPhones as translators. Skippy, of course, spoke every human language perfectly, that annoying little beer can.

Twenty four people, several nationalities, genders, specialties and experiences, and I had to make them into an effective fighting force, quickly. Without knowing exactly what the mission was.

Most worrying was that not one of our twenty four people was a medic. And the medical supplies we'd taken aboard were pretty basic. Things could go south, real fast, and there wasn't much we'd be able to do for the wounded.

Captain Desai got us off the ground safely, and the autopilot took over from there, lifting the Dodo on its tail out of the atmosphere. Gravity gradually dropped away, and people adjusted, popping anti-nausea meds as needed. Skippy, I mean to say, 'Hacker', had Desai reprogram the autopilot several times to avoid flying near Ruhar spacecraft, there was a lot of traffic around Paradise. According to the cockpit displays, and Skippy whispering in my ear, we slid right through a Ruhar frigate squadron without them investigating, challenging or even noticing us, their sensors had been infiltrated by Skippy and instructed to ignore us. However he did it, it worked, impressively. When Desai reported that we'd exceeded escape velocity, left orbit and were comfortably on our own in interplanetary space, I decided it was time to address the crew, who were looking anxiously at me. I floated in the cockpit doorway, so everyone could hear me.

"Full disclosure time, everyone. I couldn't brief you on our mission until we left orbit, because we can't risk either the Kristang or the Ruhar knowing what we're doing. The truth is," I gave Adams a guilty look, "I haven't been completely honest with you, for operational security reasons. Hacker is not a code name for a UNEF cyber outfit. Hacker is, uh, here, I'll show you." I pulled Skippy out of my pack and made the mistake of holding him up for view without first looking at him.

Big mistake.

That smart-ass little jerk had transformed his surface from shiny chrome to a full color imitation of a Bud Light Lime can. I didn't know he could change his appearance! Except for not having a pull tab on top of his lid, and his bottom being almost flat, he could have fooled me.

The faces in front of me changed in a blur from wonderment to amusement to horror while I watched in my own horror, as they realized they'd gone into space with a raving madman. A madman who had an imaginary friend in the shape of a beer can. "No no no no no!" I waved my left hand while frantically shaking Skippy with my right. "Skippy, damn it, this isn't funny!" Adams was bracing to fly across the compartment at me, and the look on her face was anything but friendly. "Skippy, damn it you little asshole!"

"Hahahahahahahahahahaha!" Skippy laughed maniacally, and changed his surface so he was now a Coors Light silver bullet can. "Heighdee-ho, everyone! I am Skippy the omnipotent. Hahahaha! Oh, man, you should have seen your face, Colonel Joe. That was *priceless*."

I took a couple deep breaths, staring at Adams, who was still trying to decide whether to choke me. "For all his intelligence, Skippy is a hundred percent asshole."

"True, true." Skippy admitted. "Is this better?" He reverted to featureless chrome.

Chang fairly growled. "Who the fuck is *Skippy*?"

"You got some 'splainin' to do." Adams said without a trace of humor.

I noticed neither of them added 'sir'.

I took a deep breath. "This is Skippy, his code name is Hacker," I pointed to his shiny self. "What looks like a beer can here is an artificial intelligence- "

"A very small manifestation of me in local spacetime-" Skippy interrupted.

"Skippy, will you shut up a minute? An AI that was built by the beings we know as the Elders or the First Ones, whatever they're called. The super civilization who inhabited the galaxy before the Rindhalu, the beings who built the wormholes. They left their physical existence a long time ago, and they left behind the Sentinels. And they left this AI, who is millions of years old. An immensely powerful AI. He released the controls on this Dodo, he disabled the Ruhars' weapons, he is right now masking us from the hamsters' sensors and transmitting the proper IFF codes to the Kristang. He is how we are going to board and capture a Kristang ship, do the same thing to a Thuranin star carrier. Then we're going to disable the wormhole near Earth, so neither the Ruhar nor the Kristang can have access to our home any more."

"Holy fucking shit." Simms breathed in disbelief.

"Yeah, that was my reaction when I was locked up in a warehouse by the Ruhar, and a beer can on a dusty shelf started talking to me."

Adams wasn't convinced. "Sir, I'm trying to wrap my head around this. We're trusting our future, and the fate of humanity, to a talking beer can?"

"When you put it that way-"

"A super smart, nay, impossibly, inconceivably smart, talking beer can!" Skippy protested.

"Adams, forget what Skippy looks like to us. You saw what happened back at the warehouse, the Ruhar couldn't use their weapons, but we could. That wasn't me, it wasn't UNEF, it was Skippy here. Skippy hacked into this Dodo so we could fly it, that sure wasn't me and it wasn't UNEF. We just boosted out of orbit, right through the middle of a Ruhar fleet, and they didn't see us. Skippy has hacked into the Ruhar sensor systems and instructed them to ignore us. No way could UNEF do any of this. Skippy is the ultimate weapon, our ace in the hole, and humanity for sure by God needs an ace right now. With Skippy, we can disable, shut down, turn off, the only wormhole that allows the lizards access to Earth."

Adams wasn't convinced. "How do we know this isn't a trick by the lizards, that this AI isn't working for them?"

"Adams, if you can think of anything, anything at all, that the lizards would gain from helping us escape from the Ruhar and steal one of their Dodos, please tell me. Because I can't think of anything. Skippy is going to build our trust the same way we're going to build his; by doing, one action at a time. He got me, you, Chang and Desai out of prison, and now we're off the surface of Paradise. If we were by ourselves, we'd still be trying to figure how to open the door on this thing." I pointed to the Dodo's deck. "I did consider maybe this is a Ruhar trick, to get us aboard a Kristang ship, maybe the hamsters planted a bomb on this thing, this particular Dodo. Again, I can't think of why the Ruhar would go through all the trouble. This war has been going on for a very long time without humans involved. They don't need us; the lizards, the hamsters, the Thuranin, none of them need us primitive humans for anything. Maybe this is all an elaborate ruse for some reason we can't see. Ok, maybe it is. Or maybe Skippy is telling the truth, and we have a chance to shut down the wormhole that gives the lizards access to Earth. If there is *any* chance that is true, any chance at all, we need to take it. We'll know whether we can trust Skippy when we have control of a Kristang warship. It's as simple as that." Skippy had remained uncharacteristically silent the whole time I'd been speaking. Part of being super smart is knowing when to keep your mouth shut and let the other guy talk.

Chang, who had remained silent, but had been exchanging increasingly tense looks with his three Chinese soldiers, cleared his throat. "Colonel," he said with emphasis, "we volunteered for this mission, without knowing the details. I expected the plan was to attack the Kristang. Now you are telling us that our mission is to *save the world*? To rescue Earth from the Kristang?"

"Uh," it sounded so dramatic when he said it that way, "yes. Yes, we're going to shut down the wormhole that allows the Kristang access to earth. The situation will go back to the way it was before the wormhole shift," I assumed everyone had heard the rumors about that by now, "Earth will be all by itself in the middle of nowhere, and this war will go on without humans."

"Save the world?" Simms repeated incredulously.

"That's the idea." I nodded. "I know it's kind of a cliché, but-"

"No, save the world works for me." Simms said thoughtfully. "Shit. Is this real?"

Chang clicked his zPhone off and spoke briefly to his three soldiers in Mandarin, then turned back to me. "Colonel, I find all this difficult to believe. However, not long ago, I was stationed at an army outpost on the Mongolian border. Now, I am in an alien space ship, a thousand lightyears from home. What is possible has been redefined so many times, that I'm prepared to accept almost anything. So, if this mission has even a small chance to free our planet from the Kristang, we will do our utmost."

Damn, his English was better than my own. "Thank you, Colonel Chang." I scanned the other faces.

Giraud gave a Gallic shrug. "We're going to kill Kristang, no? I am in, as you say."

Simms and Adams exchanged a glance. "Oh, what the hell, sure, us too." Simms declared. "Colonel, this is it, right, the whole truth, everything? No more surprises? We're allied with a talking beer can, to shut down the wormhole? Now that we're out here, I expect the need for Opsec is out the window." She looked meaningfully at the airlock door. "If that expression can be used in space."

I nodded. "You know everything that I know. I can't promise there won't be more surprises, but they'll be surprises to me too."

"Why us, sir?" Sergeant Thompson asked in his oh-so-proper British accent. "Why not bring this, Skippy, to UNEF HQ, and let them sort it out? Send up a proper special ops force, SAS, all that?"

Chang and Simms both made a disparaging snort at the same time. "Sergeant," Chang said, "UNEF would first take a week, at least, to figure what to do. Then, because they are risk averse, they'd likely turn our AI friend over to the Ruhar, or the Kristang, whoever is in charge of the planet at the time, in hopes of gaining favor. It wouldn't matter anyway, once this became known at UNEF HQ, there is no way it could be kept secret long. The hamsters and lizards would know about it quickly."

"Also," I added, "we have to go *now*, to take advantage of the situation. The Ruhar are busy consolidating their hold over the planet, ships are jumping in and out overhead, and there's still a remnant Kristang force hanging around. If we wait, the Kristang will pull back, and then we'd need to raid the Ruhar to capture a ship. The Ruhar have too many ships here supporting each other for us to sneak away with one."

"Right." Thompson seemed satisfied. "One more question, if I may; why is the AI called Skippy?" From the nodding heads around the Dodo, that seemed to be a universal question.

"Because," I held Skippy in front of my face and scowled at him, "as I said, he is super smart, super powerful, and a super asshole. He wanted to be referred to as the Lord God Almighty, so I named him Skippy, to remind me what a shithead he is."

"Guilty as charged." Skippy said cheerily.

"He doesn't mind being called, uh, Skippy?" Adams asked pointedly.

"*I* don't mind being called Skippy, you don't need to ask Colonel Joe, I am a person." Skippy said. "No, I don't care what you pack of flea-bitten monkeys call me."

"Monkeys?" Putri asked. US Army Specialist Randy Putri, not Private Asok Putri of the Indian army. I know, it's confusing for me, too. I was going to break military tradition and call them by their first names in the future.

"He thinks he's being nice by considering us monkeys," I explained, "to him, we're all bacteria."

"Ha!" Skippy scoffed. "You *aspire* to be as smart as bacteria."

"Right, then." Thompson said flatly. "This bugger *is* a proper arsehole."

Adams stuck her tongue out at Skippy, which is a gesture I never expected from her. "What's next, sir?"

I inwardly sighed with relief. "Skippy, can you load schematics of likely Kristang ships on everyone's zPhones, and also show it on the display here?"

"Done." He responded simply, and the display on the bulkhead behind me came to life. "This is a typical Kristang frigate, the type of small ship that most likely will be sent in to pick us up-"

A real colonel was responsible for commanding a brigade-size force. That meant planning offensive and defensive operations of several thousand soldiers, including all the training, logistics, communications and coordination with air power, artillery and other units in the area. Making and executing big plans, involving thousands of people and enormous firepower. A real colonel had training, formal and practical education, and years of experience before assuming command. I had none of that.

What I did have was hard-earned experience in small unit combat, experience in the bush, and more importantly, villages and towns of northern Nigeria. Taking a Kristang ship was small unit combat, and I figured clearing a ship compartment by compartment was similar to fighting house to house and room to room. The US military used to call that type of warfare Military Operations in Urban Terrain, and military bases across the USA contain fake villages for training troops how to fight in such confined spaces. During the Cold War, these fake villages were set up to resemble eastern Europe, with signs on streets and buildings in a vaguely Slavic or Germanic language. Recently the focus has been on the Middle East, and we soldiers gave the training towns politically incorrect names like Hadjistan. Whatever the name, or the grand scenario the towns were built for, they trained soldiers how to clear an area building by building and room by room; the type of fighting where you often couldn't see who you were shooting at, and calling in Apache gunships meant pulling back quickly so the Hellfire missiles didn't hit your own troops.

To plan our attack, and provide hasty training to our crew, I assigned Lt Giraud. Chang, Simms and Desai were senior to Giraud in rank, but Chang's experience was in artillery, not infantry. Simms was a logistics officer, and Desai a pilot. You might figure that Sergeant Adams, as a Marine, was the logical person to plan an operation for boarding an enemy ship. Which would have been a good thought, back in the War of 1812. The US Marine Corps was a little rusty on the whole 'away boarders' thing. That left me and Giraud as infantry officers, and Giraud was French special forces. What he knew about small unit tactics, and what I didn't, kind of scared me, special forces guys were hard-core. I kept having to remind him that our assault force was not the elite special forces killers he was used to working with, and that we'd be operating in zero gravity, with no training and with people we mostly didn't know. We decided that we would largely have to wing it in our attack, because there were too many unknowns. What I intended was for me to lead a force to capture the ship's control center, which was aft of the bridge on most Kristang ships, while Giraud's group captured the engineering section, before the Kristang there could damage the drive units or reactor, or even self-destruct the ship. That plan was universally shot down by everyone involved, including Skippy.

"Colonel," Adams declared, arms folded across her chest in a gesture that was not easy in zero gravity, "You can't go racing around the enemy ship. You're the commander. You need to remain behind, and command."

"She's right, Colonel Joe," Skippy admonished me. "I can tell you where your people and the Kristang are, and what they're doing, and I can control parts of the ship, but I need someone to tell me what you want me to do. And where your people should go. My genius doesn't include coordinating a troop of monkeys in combat. You know what your people can do, and more importantly, what they can't do."

After protesting that my experience was at the fireteam and squad level, and that Giraud would be a better candidate to remain with Skippy and coordinate the attack, I was forced to concede they were right. In the end, the unspoken factor that decided the issue was that I was comfortable with Skippy, he was comfortable with me, and no one else wanted the task of dealing with the twitchy alien AI.

Giraud made our crew mentally run through a simulated attack on a typical Kristang frigate, using Skippy's best guess of where the Kristang aboard would be, and what systems aboard the frigate he could control. It surprised me when Skippy said he couldn't seize total control of the frigate's computer systems, at least not right away. The Kristang very deliberately and carefully had built their ships to prevent the possibility of an enemy remotely hacking into their computers, on account that they were afraid of their patrons the cyborg Thuranin doing exactly that. Because the Thuranin had done that before, and the Kristang weren't going to fall victim to that trick a second time, or, as Skippy reported, more like the hundredth time. The Kristang had gotten better at hardening their computer systems from intrusion, but their technology was still far enough below the level of the Thuranin that the Kristang weren't yet capable of even imagining some of the technology the Thuranin routinely used. Fortunately for us, Skippy's technology was as far beyond the Thuranin as the Thuranin were beyond humans. Or, as Skippy of course said it so tactfully, a tree full of monkeys.

The key to the whole plan was that we needed to literally plug Skippy into the ship, to establish a physical connection to the ship's network for him. Once he was in, he'd have access to the whole ship, and could download a subroutine of himself into control nodes all over the ship. But we first needed to locate what was basically a wall jack aboard the frigate, and plug a zPhone into it. Fortunately, the proper cables and connectors were aboard the Dodo. Unfortunately, getting to the wall jack closest to the frigate's two landing bays was going to be a bitch. And Skippy's trick of disabling weapons, like he did with Ruhar rifles, wouldn't work with the Kristang, because the Kristang didn't trust that type of technology, and their rifles mostly did without fancy computer chips.

Giraud's plan was to throw the entire boarding force of twenty two people into the effort to establish a physical connection, after which our crew would split into two groups, one led by Giraud and one led by Chang. With Giraud, I assigned Sergeant Thompson, while Sergeant Adams was going to Chang and the Chinese sergeant. I could see people were totally keyed up, completely understanding that jacking a zPhone into a data port was life and death not only for us, but potentially for all of humanity. Rousing speeches were not needed. I ordered everyone to eat and drink something, and relax. Giraud agreed, adding that he wanted the crew to memorize the layout of typical Kristang frigates and destroyers, which helpfully each came in only two major types. Picture the layouts in your mind, he advised, over and over, and over and over again, and then repeat, until it became instinct, ingrained in your spatial memory.

"I think we have as good a plan as we'll get." I told Giraud as we both ate a Hooah! energy bar. The waiting, with the Dodo coasting away from Paradise, hoping to get picked up by an enemy warship, was wearing on everyone's nerves.

Giraud gave an exaggerated shrug. "Plans are a start, no more."

"No plan survives contact with the enemy, right? Von Moltke said that." I'd learned that from the Army somewhere along the way.

Giraud wrinkled his nose. "Von Moltke learned that from Napoleon. Napoleon emphasized having flexible capabilities and exploiting opportunities on the battlefield, instead of trying to stick to detailed plans." He pointed to Skippy. "No plan made by UNEF could have anticipated this opportunity."

There was no place for privacy aboard the Dodo, except for the single zero gee bathroom that was in steady use. When Skippy pinged me that he wanted to talk, semi privately, I went forward to the cramped cockpit, to float behind the righthand seat. "What is it, Skippy?"

He replied into my earpiece. "Just wanted to say something nice, for a change, and I don't want to be overheard, because that will ruin my street cred."

Street cred? Where the hell was Skippy getting his notions about human culture? "Oh, sure." I didn't know what else to say.

"Your species is remarkably adaptable. The ability to accept new information, new concepts, to not run away screaming or become paralyzed when confronted with shocking changes, is unfortunately too rare among intelligent species. I expected there to be trouble when you revealed the truth about me and our mission, but your people accepted the new situation admirably quickly."

"Huh." Skippy wasn't taking into account that our crew were soldiers. Soldiers get new crap thrown at them in the middle of a mission all the time. One time in Nigeria, I was in a Blackhawk skimming the treetops at 0330, headed to raid a camp of bad guys, when our lieutenant gets a call ten minutes out from the landing zone. The bad guys reached a deal and they were suddenly on our side, our mission then was to protect our new buddies from a force of other bad guys who were sneaking through the jungle to kill them. Apparently the first group of bad guys had been declared traitors by the other ignorant whackos, because they weren't as fanatically crazy as the craziest of whackos. So we landed and set up a perimeter to protect guys we'd been shooting at the day before. Of course, the whole thing had really been a tribal dispute, and both sides tried to ambush us. After we evaced, we had to call in the Air Force to resolve the situation diplomatically with napalm, cluster bombs and fuel-air explosives. When things change, even radically, you look at your buddies, shake your head, shrug, and adapt. That's what you do, as soldiers. Civilians get upset when the menu changes at Applebees.

"Don't get me wrong, there are plenty of your species who lack the ability to process new facts and adapt, but with humans those are mostly old people, their brains no longer are able to process new information. Or they're just lazy. But with some species, even the young have difficulty with facts that conflict with their rigid belief systems. I am impressed with humans. There, I said it."

"So, we're not just bacteria?"

"Don't push your luck. You're bacteria with *potential* now."

Thirty seven minutes later, an alarm sounded in the cockpit. "Excellent!" Skippy reported. "Two Kristang ships jumped in, a frigate that is sending us a homing beacon, and a destroyer."

"Where?" I asked anxiously as Skippy displayed on the bulkhead screen our position relative to Paradise, the two Kristang ships and various Ruhar ships.

"I have loaded a course into the nav system."

"Got it, sir." Desai confirmed. "Hold on tight everyone, engaging autopilot."

I hung on as the Dodo's engines roared and we surged ahead. "Skippy, how far? How long until we rendezvous?" I repeated, an anxious eye on the display. There were a half dozen Ruhar ships that were uncomfortably close.

"The Kristang frigate is accelerating to match our course, we will meet in three minutes and six point three six seven four nine seconds. Approximately."

Approximately? Adams and I exchanged an amused glance.

"Huh," Skippy gave a good imitation of a grunt, "that was good navigating by the lizard pilot, they jumped in about as close as their technology allows. Got to be luck, no slimy lizard is that smart. Colonel Joe, it is going to be close, two Ruhar ships are preparing short range jumps to intercept the Kristang frigate. I couldn't conceal the lizards jumping in, or the Ruhar would realize something is wrong with their sensor systems."

"Do they see us?"

"No, they're tracking the frigate. The Kristang destroyer is moving to provide cover for us."

"Grea.. And you're sure that once we're aboard the frigate and it jumps away, you can spoof the frigate's nav system so we'll jump to a different location than the destroyer?"

"What? No, I told you, I need to physically jack in first before I can establish any sort of control of the ship. Duh. Weren't you listening?"

Holy shit!? "Skippy, what the hell? You said you could-"

"I *said* that I could make whatever ship takes us aboard jump to a different location than any ships that are escorting it."

"Yeah, and? Don't you need to-"

"Hahahaha! Oh, you're cute, Colonel Joe. You think I need to hack into the lizard's computer to screw with their jump drive? No way, dude! I'm going to distort spacetime at the last picosecond, so their jump drive field skews off course."

"You can distort spacetime?" Simms asked incredulously.

"Uh-huh, yeah." Skippy answered flippantly. "It's sort of a hobby. I tried collecting stamps, but messing with the universe is so much more relaxing."

Simms lifted an eyebrow, and gave me a look that silently told me she understood now why I named the little shithead 'Skippy'.

The frigate grew closer on the display until suddenly it was right there, looming on top of us, with a docking bay door already open. Skippy let the frigate take control of the Dodo's nav system and guide us aboard, the bay door had only begun to close when the frigate jumped away. "We need to move fast," Skippy urged, "we just jumped, and I threw us off course, now I'm preventing a jump field from forming, the Kristang know something is wrong, for now they think the problem is their jump drive, that's not going to last long."

The bay doors closed agonizingly slowly, and there was a roar as the bay repressurized. As soon as the air pressure indicator read 80%, we opened the side door and the back ramp. My ears popped and I felt a stabbing pain that was difficult to ignore. "Camera is under my control. It's working," Skippy said, "they're buying our story. Outer door is now unlocked."

Skippy took control of the light sensors in the docking bay camera, and was feeding a false image to the ship, he was also chatting on the radio with the bridge crew. What he meant by our story was that the false image the Kristang crew saw through the camera was exciting and tempting; a Kristang special forces team coming out of a captured Ruhar Dodo, with a very special item of ancient Elder technology that supposedly had been found on Paradise. It was, according to Skippy, a Bubble Energy Tap, a device that pulled free energy from fluctuations in quantum foam, or something like that. "It's a crude technology, think of it as a battery that never wears out. Trust me, this will impress the stupid lizards," Skippy had explained. Anyway, it worked, the bridge crew unlocked the door to the interior of the ship, and we flew across the bay in the zero gravity, only a few people missed the target and had to be pulled in before they bounced off the wall and floated away. Because Kristang frigates had small crews, and Skippy determined this frigate was short two regular crew members, there was not a crew member at the docking bay when we came in. The bridge crew told Skippy they were sending someone down to meet us, the rest of the crew were busy frantically trying to determine why their jump drive wasn't working.

Giraud in the lead got the outer door of the airlock open, it was a simple matter of pressing a button then pulling a lever. Inside the airlock, I held Skippy in one hand and jacked the plug into a port in the airlock, while Giraud followed a sequence Skippy had taught him on the airlock's control panel, to force open the inner door while the outer door was still open. This was a dangerous moment, with both doors open, an alarm would sound that even Skippy couldn't squelch yet. The inner door slid open with a bang and a loud alarm began blaring, the twenty two people of the assault team squeezed through the airlock into the corridor as quickly as humanly possible and as soon as the last person was through, I bashed my fist into the button that caused the outer door to slam close and cut off the alarm. That was the signal for Desai to get the Dodo moving, and for our assault team to split up and head toward the bridge and the engineering section.

The most important task was mine; to plug Skippy into a wall jack. A wall jack that, for a panicked split second of eternity, I couldn't find. In my defense, I was floating upside down near the ceiling, trying to keep out of the way of the assault team, getting bumped, elbowed and once kicked in the face. We were all awkward in zero gee, none of us had training in zero gee combat and we hadn't any opportunity to practice. Aboard the Dodo, I'd made everyone except the pilots practice flipping around, controlled landings on a wall, pushing off with feet and hands. There was not room enough, or time enough in the Dodo for anyone to be confident they could do much more than not puke when they spun around.

Finally, after an impossibly long two seconds, I spotted the wall plug, at the same time gunfire rang out forward, the Kristang on his way to the docking bay had seen the forward assault team. From the sound, I recognized the buzzing of Ruhar weapons, and the heavier report of a Kristang rifle, then only buzzing. Ignoring distractions, I pulled myself down the wall, took the plug out of my teeth and carefully inserted it in the wall jack. "Are you in?"

"Busy," was Skippy's only reply, and considering his lightning fast processing speed that concerned me. Then, "I'm in. We're good. Ship's systems are in my control. Ejecting docking bay doors." There was a shudder, as Skippy used an emergency procedure to blow the doors outward, rather than retracting them to the sides, we couldn't wait for them to cycle normally. "Dodo is on the move."

The ship lurched violently, bouncing me off the wall. Skippy said he had control, the ship should not have been able to move! "What the hell was-"

"The Dodo impacted the docking bay doorway, there is substantial damage to the Dodo. It is mission effective."

Desai had misjudged her exit, in an unfamiliar vehicle, complicated by air escaping from the blown docking bay. Skippy judged the Dodo could still accomplish its mission, which was to fly to the front of the frigate and blast the ship's bridge with the Dodo's guns. The Kristang, who were long used to piracy between and within clans, had designed their ships against boarders like us, although the designers had been thinking of rival Kristang factions, not primitive humans. The door to the bridge was heavily armored, heavily enough that breaching that door would blow a hole in the ship and expose our people to vacuum. As long as the Kristang were behind that door, they could prevent us from using the ship, they could even disable it or self-destruct it, regardless of Skippy being jacked in. It was almost impossible to seize the bridge of a Kristang warship.

So, we weren't going to seize it, we were going to blast it to pieces from the outside. If the Dodo was still functional, if Desai could fly it effectively with almost no experience, and if she could control the Dodo's guns enough to hit the bridge without blowing apart the rest of the ship. If. That was a very big if.

There was gunfire forward and aft, people were shouting and screaming someone set off a flash-bang grenade, then the ship shook violently again. And again, and again. "Captain Desai has succeeded in destroying the bridge. Also part of the ship's nose and ten meters of the starboard side aft of the bridge."

"Shit! Is that bad?"

"She did well for her lack of experience. The additional damage will be convincing evidence this ship was struck by a Ruhar stealth mine, and will not affect ship function for our purpose."

It has been said that a commander has the toughest job in combat, because after people are trained and plans are made, the commander has to sit back and watch, unable to do much to affect the outcome, while his people fight. In my very limited experience, that saying is a hundred percent bullshit. The commander does not have the toughest job, the toughest job is done by the grunts carrying rifles, exposing themselves to enemy fire. The grunts do the fighting and dying. That's the toughest job. The commander has the loneliest job, the job that makes you feel guilty and useless that you aren't out there on the front line, doing something useful for your buddies. After the combat is over, I always felt like things might have gone better if I'd been there, that maybe I'd have seen the enemy and shouted a warning before someone got shot, maybe I'd have killed the enemy before they got one of our guys. Maybe I could have made things better. Or maybe I'd simply get killed. Either way, I'd be *doing* something. What I did, after jacking Skippy in, was hold onto a wall and try to follow the battles forward and aft on my zPhone. It was beyond chaotic, I wasn't able to get a picture of what was happening until the fighting was over. So much for me 'commanding' anything.

Our losses were four dead and three seriously injured in taking the ship. Four dead and three injured out of twenty one in the assault teams. A third of our force was now gone or combat ineffective. In one battle. In taking one ship.

Take the ship we did, it was ours. Giraud had only one casualty in taking the ship's control center, Private Arun Kurien of the Indian Army died from being shot by one of the two Kristang who were blocking access to the control center. All the other casualties were in Chang's team that seized the engineering compartment. Chang's team had the toughest job, they had to kill five Kristang who were motivated and desperate to prevent their ship from being captured. Three of those Kristang were killed in the initial firefight when we had some advantage of surprise, the remaining two were much more difficult. One of them managed to get to a suit of powered armor, despite Skippy jamming the door of the locker where the suits were kept, this Kristang had the armor almost on and partly powered up, when three people fired blindly into the compartment, giving cover for Chang to throw in a grenade. The Kristang was tough, he was still trying to get the suit buttoned up after the grenade hit, it took concentrated fire to take him out.

The worst problem was the last Kristang. That one must have realized he was the only one left, despite Skippy shutting down their comm system, and he decided to blow up the ship rather than surrender. Skippy warned Chang that he needed to stop that Kristang now, *now now now*, before the Kristang was able to breach the reactor containment. Despite Skippy doing everything he could, the controls to dump the reactor plasma were manual, not anything Skippy could interfere with in the time available.

Chang told me what happened; the assault team had already lost two people killed trying to get at the Kristang in the narrow space he was hiding. Seeing the situation was desperate, Sergeant Yu Qishan pulled the pins on two grenades and launched himself around the corner, dying when the Kristang shot him in the head. That last Kristang also died when the grenades exploded and blew a hole in the ship's hull, sucking both the Kristang and Sergeant Yu into space. Almost sucked most of Chang's assault team into space, except a bulkhead automatically slammed down to prevent further loss of air in the engineering section.

Chang actually tried to console *me*, though Sergeant Yu was one of his own men. "He knew the survival of humanity depended on stopping that Kristang from destroying the reactor. He did his duty. We will honor him when we get home."

He was right. I still felt like shit about it.

In the aftermath of the battle, Skippy opened the portside docking bay door so we could take the damaged Dodo aboard, and a shaken Desai went immediately to the ship's control center to get a crash course in flying a Kristang frigate. My first instinct was to call a halt, let everyone recover, and most importantly, tend to the wounded. Simms and Skippy urged me to continue with the plan, right away, we had not a moment to lose. Simms assured me she was seeing to the wounded, they had been brought to the frigate's limited sickbay, and there wasn't anything I could do to help them. With the paltry medical supplies we'd brought with us, there wasn't much anyone could do for them. The best thing I could do, Skippy said, was continue with the plan, and capture a Thuranin star carrier, where the wounded could be tended to with the Thuranin's amazingly advanced medical technology. Wounds could be healed, limbs even regrown, Skippy assured me, once we could put our injured soldiers in Thuranin healing tanks. It felt wrong, I swallowed my pride and let my people do their jobs.

While Desai pressed buttons under Skippy's direction, programming a jump, I looked around the control center in amazement. We had a ship. A starship. Us. Grubby, low-tech, ignorant monkeys from Earth. A *starship*.

Damn.

Craig Alanson

CHAPTER TWELVE   MERRY BAND OF PIRATES

"Did it work?" I asked Desai.

"Sir?"

"The jump. Did it work? Did we jump? To the right place?" The stars in the display had shifted. Or I thought they shifted. Star fields surprisingly all looked the same. It wasn't like a sci fi movie, where all starships were somehow backlit by a big, vividly glowing colorful nebula. The main display wasn't any help, because I didn't have any reference point. We were a tiny dot in the middle of nowhere before the jump, now we were a tiny dot in the middle of nowhere after the jump. It could be the middle of the same nowhere, for all I knew.

She held her hands up, palms open, then gestured at the confusing displays. "Honestly, I have no idea. Mister Skippy?"

"Huh? Oh, sorry, I was busy. Yup, it worked fine. Of course it did. I would have told you if it didn't. I've been transmitting our Kristang IFF codes. I don't detect any other ships in the area yet."

"Could they have left already? Because we were late to the rendezvous point?" Simms asked.

"Sure, we were late to the original rendezvous point, this is the alternate point, it's the correct location for this time, duh. This ship's sensors operate at the speed of light, and we just got here, so the, oh, there it is! I have the beacon from the Thuranin star carrier. Pilot, new course is loaded into the navigation system."

"Colonel?" Desai looked back at me.

"Engage." I ordered. I needed to think of something original to say. Warp factor five was not an option, unfortunately. The ship swung around about forty five degrees which made me dizzy, and the engines fired. Fired hard. It was good that everyone was strapped in. Damn, it felt like someone was sitting on my chest. It must be worse for our wounded. "Skippy," I grunted, "is this necessary?"

"I'm not showing off, if that's what you're asking. The Thuranin wish to jump away quickly, their message ordered us to rendezvous at maximum speed. We're going to flip around and decelerate soon, so hang on. Also, when we get within half a lightsecond, the Thuranin will take control of our navigation system, to bring us safely onto an attachment point. That is standard practice. I am running this ship's navigation system within one of my subroutines so the Thuranin will think they have full access. But they won't."

"How will we know if the Thuranin accept our IFF codes?" Chang asked.

"They already have. I'm chatting with them, and the local Kristang commander right now. It's a slow conversation, because the signal travels at lightspeed. They accept our story about being thrown off course by a Ruhar stealth mine, they can see the damage to this ship. Don't be alarmed, we're going to cut thrust in three, two, one, now. We'll coast for twelve minutes before we flip over. This, uh, would be a good time to use the bathroom, hint, hint."

"Oh, good point." I opened the intercom and advised the crew what was happening.

It was a long twelve minutes, drifting through space toward a technologically superior enemy ship that could squash our ship like a bug. Skippy had better know what he was doing, or it was going to be game over real soon.

Unlike our assault on the Kristang frigate, our plan to capture a Thuranin star carrier depended entirely, one hundred percent, on Skippy. We humans were simply along for the ride, until Skippy firmly seized control of the ship and all systems aboard. The difference between the two plans, was, ironically, the Thuranin's advanced technology compared to the Kristang. According to Skippy, the Thuranin's cyborg nature made them highly reliant on networked computers; computers which the Thuranin obsessively protected from any possibility of being hacked. Any possibility, that is, except for the utter magnificence of Skippy. Even the Maxohlx overlords of the Thuranin had a very difficult time breaching Thuranin data system security, but Elder technology was beyond the most fevered imaginations of the Maxohlx.

According to Skippy.

Skippy, an ancient, alien AI I didn't entirely trust. Not that I didn't trust him to do what he said he was going to do, since he needed us as much, or more, than we needed him. What I didn't trust was not his ability, but his judgment. He was an amazingly arrogant and absentminded little punk-ass beer can. So, we had cooked up a backup plan, a plan Skippy huffed was not necessary.

The backup plan, if Skippy failed to take control of the star carrier, was that Desai would kill the autopilot and engage an emergency jump away, which Skippy had begrudgingly programmed into the navigation system.

After we jumped away, the Thuranin, and Kristang, would be alerted there was something very wrong with our captured frigate, and both species would be extra careful not to let our ship, or any lone Kristang ship, close to a Thuranin starship without a thorough inspection far away from Thuranin fleet assets. So, Plan B meant giving up any chance of capturing a Thuranin starship, without which we had no chance of getting to the wormhole. Which would leave us having to hitch a ride from the patrons of the Ruhar, the insect-like Jeraptha. We would have to make our way back to Paradise, ditch the Kristang frigate, and use Skippy's sensor hacking ability to get close to a Ruhar ship using our Dodo. Problem was, the Ruhar task force was sticking close to Paradise, so finding a Ruhar ship on its own was going to be a problem. Especially since, by now, the Ruhar would have discovered one of their Dodos had been stolen by humans, and no Ruhar ship would let a suspicious Dodo get close.

So, it wasn't a great or even good, ok, barely mediocre plan, but it was better than our original Plan B, which was to sneak back to Paradise, ditch the Dodo and try to hide. Skippy was not a big fan of that plan, because it meant abandoning his dream of ever contacting the Collective. I wasn't a big fan of that plan either, because it meant abandoning my dream of ever again eating a cheeseburger.

Seriously.

When the engines came back on, they slammed us back into our couches with what Skippy blithely announced was 4.7 gees, and that pressure kept up for over two minutes as we decelerated. How human astronauts had launched into space on spine-crushing chemical rockets, I had no idea. My neck had been at a bad angle when the deceleration started, I had to lift a hand to lever my head into the right position. Still, it hurt. And it was hard to breathe.

Skippy must have sensed our confusion, because the main display changed so that it showed something considerably more useful; the Thuranin star carrier was now in the center of the screen. The dot representing our ship was on the edge, with a dotted line projecting the courses of the star carrier and our ship. At the edges of the screen were numbers showing the time to intersect, and the speeds of both ships. None of it truly mattered, since we humans were incapable of flying the Dodo more than short distances, at low speed. It did give us a sense that we had some, if not control, then at least knowledge of our destiny.

The acceleration ended abruptly, then resumed with a gentle pressure. "The Thuranin have taken control of navigation, they will guide us onto a docking pad."

"We're a half lightsecond away now?" I couldn't tell how far we were from the display; the scale was confusing.

"No, a quarter of a lightsecond. They tried to take control earlier, I faked that we had trouble accepting the handoff, due to damage from the explosion. If I hadn't let them think they had control, they would have aborted the rendezvous, the Thuranin don't trust the Kristang to control their own ships for close maneuvers. They are running a diagnostic of our ship's systems, I'm telling them what they want to hear."

The display now showed our ETA was four minutes, and the star carrier's image was an outline of the ship, no longer a dot. We were close, very close.

"Pilot, standby to abort on my signal. Skippy, when can you do your thing?" I asked.

"My thing?"

"Your thing, your magic. Taking over the Thuranin computer systems." I asked urgently. What the hell else did he think I meant?!

"Oh, that. We're within range. Hmmm, this is going to be more difficult than expected, it may take longer than I thought. Damn."

"More difficult how?" I asked, alarmed. Simms was on the couch behind me, unseen, and still I could sense the tension coming from her.

"Well, to be fair," Skippy explained, "I've never actually had contact with a Thuranin system before, seeing as how I've been stuck on Paradise for, like, a million years. I'm having to make this up as I go."

"What? Jesus fucking Christ, Skippy, you little shithead! A million years? How the hell can you understand Thuranin technology if you've never seen it? You told us you could absolutely do this! Damn it! A soldier in battle needs to know he can count on his comrades; you should have told us you weren't sure you could hack into their systems. Goddamn it! Pilot, abort the-"

"Belay that!" Skippy shouted. "We're good, I'm in."

"What?" I was out of breath from adrenaline.

"When I said 'longer than I thought', I meant longer in magical Skippy time, not longer in meatsack caveman time, you dumdum monkeyboy. I had full control over the star carrier 120 milliseconds after I said 'thought'."

"Goddamn it, Skippy, why didn't you stop me?"

"Hey, you were on a roll, I couldn't interrupt that. Your rant was very inspiring, Colonel Joe, I can see why you went from grunt to senior officer so quickly. Also, to be honest, I tuned out about halfway through. Could you repeat it for me, and skip the boring parts?"

"Fuck."

"That will have to wait, we're docking with the star carrier now. I directed the ship to assign us to a docking pad right at the front of the ship. No charge for the upgrade."

"Skippy," I grumbled through gritted teeth, then decided nothing I could say would make any difference.

The frigate wobble slightly, then there was a lurch to the side, a clanging sound, and Skippy announced we had docked. Gravity came back on gradually. "We're secured. Everyone, stay strapped in, we're going to jump shortly."

"I thought you couldn't make a ship jump if you were aboard?" Chang asked, confused. "Don't you need us to get aboard the Thuranin ship, control their navigation system, before we can jump?"

"Huh? No, not this time. The Thuranin already had a jump programmed into their nav system and on a timer after we docked, I'm letting that system run on its own. I'll warp spacetime to throw us off course, as jumping into the heart of a Thuranin task force would be rather inconvenient. Unless I'm missing something?" There was a smartass tone to his question.

"No, that's good, thank you." Chang replied.

"And, three, two, one, jump. Done. We're good, we came out of jump one third of a lightyear from the intended emergence point. I have the star carrier on total EMCON, and have ordered the Kristang to do the same. Oh, darn, it, pesky lizard. The Kristang commander has noticed we didn't jump to where we were supposed to, he is demanding to know why, and also is demanding access to our ship."

"Can you hold him off?" I asked, alarmed. The last thing we wanted was an armed Kristang force walking through the Thuranin ship and knocking on our airlock door. Or flying a dropship over to our landing bay.

"Oh, yeah, I bitchslapped him right away. The Thuranin don't take any crap from their client species. I told him to shut the hell up, that we altered our jump to avoid a Jeraptha battleship, and that this frigate is under quarantine. He doesn't like it; he also knows he doesn't have any choice."

"All right, what's next?"

"Colonel Joe, you're the commander. My suggestion is we go aboard the star carrier, and round up the eighty seven Thuranin crew."

"Us against eighty seven armed Thuranin cyborgs?" I asked, incredulously. We had barely defeated a dozen Kristang.

"Eighty seven cyborgs who are sound asleep. I ordered their brain implants to put them all into an unscheduled sleep maintenance cycle, they're basically in a coma." Skippy explained. "Ha! And those little green pinheads think being cyborgs is a strength."

"Just like that?" I asked. "We have complete control over the entire ship?' It felt like a letdown. I could live with that, any day.

"Yup. Just like that. Behold, the magic of Skippy the Magnificent. Truthfully, as magic at my level goes, this is lame. Still, it impresses the monkeys, right?"

I nodded. "This monkey is sufficiently impressed."

"Agreed." Chang said.

"This *human* is impressed." Simms retorted. "Colonel, if I was skeptical of your shiny beer can before, I'm not now."

"He's not *my* beer can, Major Simms." I hastened to correct her before Skippy got mad. "Skippy is more of a sentient being than any of us."

"Than all of you put together." Skippy

Damn, that beer can was smug.

Assured by Skippy that the Kristang would not dare to come aboard the Thuranin ship, and that he had their airlock doors locked anyway, we warily ventured through our own airlock. Giraud led the way, armed with a Ruhar rifle, an HK416 rifle that was standard issue for French special forces, and a pouch full of flash bang grenades. All of which Skippy insisted was totally unnecessary, according to him, we could roam around the huge star carrier buck naked. Although he requested that we hairless monkeys wear as much clothing as possible, to spare his delicate sensors. I flipped him off with both middle fingers and asked if his sensors could see that. He didn't respond.

The frigate's airlock opened into a chamber that was, Skippy explained, a sort of elevator. Because the artificial gravity pulled 'down' toward the spine of the star carrier, without an elevator we would have had to climb down a long ladder. The elevator was more than big enough for our entire crew, it was plenty roomy for the dozen people I selected for the initial recon mission. The elevator smelled funny. I sniffed the air. "Skippy, is this air Ok for us to breathe?" I asked, rather late for such an important question. "It smells like, like the basement at my grandparents' house."

"Uh huh, yeah, the air is good. It smells musty because the Thuranin almost never allow filthy, disgusting other species aboard their ships. The ship's database records the last use of this particular elevator was thirty eight years ago."

"This docking pad is at the front of the ship? Wouldn't Thuranin ships normally use this pad?" I asked.

"Very observant, Colonel Joe. Thuranin ships use this pad frequently, however, they use a different airlock, so they don't have to touch any surfaces that may be contaminated by lesser species. The airlocks of Kristang ships can't mate with Thuranin designs, on purpose."

"I'll bet the Thuranin don't offer hot beverages to their guests either." Sergeant Adams said without a trace of humor. She was keyed up, a finger next to the trigger guard of her Ruhar rifle. The rifles weren't set on stun, on my orders. I figured that if Skippy was wrong and we ran into awake, advanced cyborgs, stun wasn't the right move.

The elevator reached the 'bottom', at the spine of the ship, and the door opened to a long corridor. It was well lit and industrial, even sterile looking. A lot of gray, with black and white to liven it up. Definitely not cozy. "Skippy," I asked in an unintended whisper, "does the whole ship look like this?"

"Most of it. As cyborgs, the Thuranin are disdainful of anything they consider to be soft remnants of their biological past. Like decorations, or creature comforts more than the minimum needed."

"So," Simms asked, "why don't they go all the way, and become robots, androids, whatever that is?"

"Two reasons," Skippy explained as we all stepped into the corridor, "first, they lack the technology to upload their true consciousnesses into a nonbiological substrate, that is much, much more difficult than most species think it is. Second, and more importantly, if the Thuranin became post-biological, the Maxohlx would consider them to be no longer a client species but merely robots, and would treat them as machines. As slaves." His voice sounded bitter. "Artificial intelligences are not treated as sentient by the Maxohlx. They are rotten kitties."

A door opposite us slid open, we all instinctively spun and pointed our weapons. "Relax, monkeys," Skippy laughed, "it's a tram, unless you want to walk all the way to the forward part of the ship. It's a long way."

We stepped into the tram, the door closed, and the tram smoothly accelerated forward. "Next time," I said, "give us warning before you do something unexpected, Skippy. We have some keyed-up trigger fingers here."

"Noted. I told you dumdums, I have absolute control over this ship, and the Thuranin are all soundly asleep in dreamland. The only thing dangerous aboard this ship is an over excited troop of monkeys with high powered weapons. Oh, and so none of you monkeys is surprised and shoots yourselves in the foot when this tram stops and the door opens, there is a Thuranin laying asleep on the floor right there."

Fairly warned, Giraud insisted on being first out of the tram, pointing his HK416 rifle at the Thuranin who was slumped on the floor. Giraud cautiously poked the alien with the rifle barrel, and nothing happened. "Rien." Giraud muttered.

"Huh?" I asked.

"Nothing." Giraud and Skippy responded at the same time.

"To be clear," Skippy made a sound like clearing his throat, "he didn't say nothing, he said 'rien', which is the French word that means 'nothing'."

"I figured that, Skippy." I nudged the Thuranin with my foot, and it didn't move. If Skippy hadn't assured me that it was in a coma-like sleep, I would have thought it was dead. "Sergeant Adams, drag sleeping beauty here out of the way somewhere."

Adams secured the Thuranin's wrists behind its back before dragging it feet first down the hallway and around a corner. If this was the ship's control center, I wasn't impressed, it was mostly a drab gray. "What's next, Skippy? Where's the bridge of this ship?"

"It doesn't have one."

"What?"

"The Thuranin consider a bridge to be an obsolete construct that is from the biological past that they have transcended, and is unnecessary and inefficient. They control the ship directly from cyborg brain implants, which give them full functionality anywhere on the ship. During flight operations, especially combat, the command crew occupies alcoves in the network core node, which is deep within the center of the forward section, and heavily armored. Going there would be useless to you, as you lack the ability to interface directly with the pathetic lump of stone the Thuranin consider to be the ship's computer."

"Then what are we doing here? How are we supposed to control the ship, by thinking happy thoughts?"

"If you'll shut up a moment and let me talk, I was going to say that there is a backup control center. Thuranin ships use the backup controls when they encounter the Maxohlx, in case their bad kitty patrons manage to hack into the Thuranin computers. Which they do often, and it drives the Thuranin absolutely batshit crazy. The backup control center has video displays, audio communication systems, and manual control panels. Anything you can't do from there, I can do for you, if you tell me what you want."

"Oh, then, lead on, MacDuff."

Skippy made a disgusted sound. "That is an annoying misquote from Shakespeare's Macbeth. The correct line is 'Lay on, MacDuff' and it means the opposite-"

"Don't care, Skippy! Do not care! Which way do we go?" The corridor ahead intersected another, and there were no helpful signs anywhere, even if I could read Thuranin script.

"Hey, excuse me for trying to raise you monkeys out of the depths of your ignorance by slapping a little knowledge down on you," Skippy grumbled. "Straight ahead to the end of the corridor, I'll open the door." When we got there, he warned "Uh, I should say, the decor in there is a bit different from the rest of the ship."

Damn, he wasn't exaggerating. The interior of the backup control center was a gothic fantasy. It was a riot of colors, with display screens, brightly lit control buttons, levers and knobs, and everything was super ornate looking. The contrast to the rest of the ship was jarring. I'm not an interior designer, so I'll try to describe it. The place looked more like an art project, a cross between a Medieval cathedral and one of those fancy French chateaus. Maybe gothic wasn't the right word, it sure didn't look like a place one of those Goth kids with the black eyeliner would hang out. Rococo, maybe? I wasn't sure what that word really meant. Overly elaborate and decorative. Opulent to the point of being in bad taste. That's what I wanted to say. The opposite of sleek and minimalist, the opposite of the rest of the ship. Even simple controls like a door handle were ornate, with intricate blue and gold filigree curling around the handle, and colored gems inset. None of it was necessary for the control's function.

"Wow." Simms said quietly. "This looks like the front parlor in my great grandmother's house. Only more so. Mister Skippy, why is this so-"

"Baroque is the word you're looking for." Skippy said smugly. Damn, that is the word I was looking for. "Since this is a place where the Thuranin must unplug from their cybernetic enhancements, the decor is intended to remind them of their purely biological past. If you think the design is in bad taste, the Thuranin really hate it. It is intended to evoke disgust from the crew, to reinforce the superiority of cybernetics over biology. The designers wanted the backup control center to be the opposite of cool, if that word applies to the Thuranin."

"They succeeded." I sniffed. "This place stinks-"

"Like a New Orleans cathouse." Someone muttered behind me, I didn't turn to see who it was.

"Yeah," I agreed, "not that I've been to one," I added hurriedly, "but it's like someone is wearing way too much perfume." Cloying was the word for it.

"Too much of my grandmother's perfume." Adams wrinkled her nose.

"The designers want the crew to be reminded of their biological nature with visual, scent and tactile clues. Instead of touch screens, all the controls are physical knobs and buttons, which even your society considers old fashioned. Having to touch and turn a knob, a knob that is cold and rough to the touch, and resists being turned enough for the user to feel the torque, constantly reminds the user that he or she needs to think in biological terms. In high pressure situations, which are the only situations in which the Thuranin would use this backup control center, the crew must suppress their instincts to use cybernetics. In an emergency maneuver, pilots here need to have their brains immediately send a signal to their fingers on the controls, and not first waste a split second trying to control the navigation system through their implants."

"Can you turn up the ventilation, to suck this stink out?" I asked. "And it smells musty like the elevator."

"It's musty because this compartment is not used often. I have deactivated the scent emitters, and the ventilation is on full. Leaving the door open will help, I calculate your noses will go scent blind within the hour, and the scent will have dispersed below detectible levels by tomorrow. If one of your females becomes pregnant, with her enhanced sense of smell she may be able to still-"

"That's not going to be a problem, Skippy." I shared a side look with Simms, and looked around. The backup control center was roughly oval shaped, with a central oval section walled off by floor to ceiling windows, or what looked like windows. In the central section were three of what looked like pilot chairs, and a larger chair behind them, all surrounded by control stands. Ringing the central section, and facing the glass, were workstations with chairs, chairs that were too small for human backsides. "Are the flight controls in that glassed-in area?"

"Yes, that is the core of the backup control-"

"That name is too long, we'll call the core section the bridge, and the rest of this the CIC." I declared. Chang and Simms nodded agreement.

Captain Desai settled into one of the three pilot couches, it was a tight fit for her, even with Skippy extending the couch open to its maximum size. "It's all right, sir, I'll manage. I'm more concerned about all this," she gestured to the confusing array of manual controls surrounding her.

"Most of these controls are for subsidiary systems that I'm handling," Skippy assured her, "we'll begin with the basic controls, the jump drive first."

I watched Desai wriggle to get comfortable in the too-small chair. Then I looked at the ceiling, and the door we'd come through. "Skippy, since the Thuranin are such little guys, how is it we don't have a problem bumping our heads in here?"

"Thuranin have built their ships to accommodate their Maxohlx patrons. Very rarely in history has the Maxohlx lowered themselves to come aboard a Thuranin ship, but the Thuranin very much wish to avoid any awkwardness. Also, occasionally Kristang or other client species do come aboard, and although intellectually the Thuranin consider their compact size to be more efficient, and therefore superior to other species, they are self-conscious about it. Other species banging their heads on Thuranin doorways would be a constant reminder how small the Thuranin are."

"All right." I set Skippy down on top of a console next to Desai's couch. "Pilot, you're going to be busy learning the controls. Colonel Chang, you have the conn, while I deal with the Thuranin, Sergeant Adams, Sergeant Thompson, you're with me."

I left Skippy to instruct Desai, Chang, Simms and some others how the bridge and CIC controls worked, while I dealt with the ship's former crew. Out in the corridor, I realized I had no idea what to do. "Skippy," I asked over zPhone earpiece, "you got any ideas what to do with the Rip Van Winkles here?"

"I assume you mean the sleeping Thuranin."

"Affirmative."

"There are several possibilities, depending on what you intend to do with them later. In the meantime, this ship has detachable cargo pods, any one of them is large enough to hold the entire Thuranin crew."

"We stack them in there like cordwood?"

"More like lay them on the floor, but, yes."

I considered. What the hell was I going to do with eighty seven unconscious Thuranin? It would have been easy for me if Skippy had killed them instead of putting them into a sleep cycle, because that would have taken the responsibility for the hard decision away from me. Although, if Skippy had been able to kill them, and asked me if I wanted to do that, or make them sleep, what would I have done then? It would have been simpler to make that decision aboard the Kristang frigate, when it was not certain we could, in fact, take a Thuranin star carrier without firing a shot. Simpler to make a decision that at the time was merely theoretical, rather than actual, like it was now. So, I punted. Delayed making the decision. "How long can you keep them asleep?"

"Without being hooked up to life support, about three days, their cybernetics minimize their autonomic functions."

"Mmm hm. Ok. And how long until we can jump again? I assume we want to leave the neighborhood, in case a Thuranin search party comes looking for us."

"We do, and they are. I have detected jump signatures from two Thuranin ships who are searching for us. We're in little danger because without our transponder replying, which it won't, the Thuranin are unlikely to find us before we jump again, in about three hours. The delay is because in addition to performing a thorough check of the jump engines and navigation systems, I'm erasing the Thuranin jump control system software, and replacing it with something closer to being actually useful. That's like installing an AI operating system in a cinder block, only with less memory capacity."

"Sounds like a challenge for you, then. Sergeant Adams, gets these Thuranin rounded up, and loaded, what, Skippy, aboard the tram?"

"That is a good start, yes, I'll direct your crew from there."

"Very well, sir." Adams gestured to three of the enlisted men, and they began carrying inert Thuranin past me to load onto the floor of the tram.

Only the Thuranin weren't all completely inert, which our crew discovered. Sergeant Adams and I watched in amusement as the crew rounded up the little green aliens.

"Man, who knew these little guys would snore like this? Damn! Oh, man, and he's drooling on me! That's disgusting!"

"Hey, look at this one. His eyelids are fluttering, and his leg's twitching. My dog does that when he's dreaming about chasing a squirrel."

"How do you know what your dog dreams about?"

"What else do dogs dream about?"

"Humping your leg?"

"You two, shut the hell up," Adams barked, but I could see her eyes sparkling, "and get a move on."

While Adams handled the sleeping beauties, Sergeant Thompson and I went back to our hijacked Kristang frigate to bring the wounded aboard the Thuranin ship. Skippy had assured me the medical facilities of the Thuranin were vastly superior to the cramped and limited sickbay on the Kristang ship. We moved our three wounded soldiers one at a time, hooked up to Kristang medical monitors, to the Thuranin hospital. This was a task I wanted to take care of personally, even with the wounded sedated and stabilized. Skippy had taken control of the Thuranin medical systems, including the creepy-looking immersion pods that we put the wounded into. The pods had the ominous appearance of caskets, with the insides lined with nanoscale probes. Once the lids closed, the nanoprobes would extended and provide oxygen, nutrients, drugs and nanomachines that would accelerate healing. According to Skippy, he had reprogrammed the Thuranin medical computers to adapt them to human biology, and he had complete confidence all three soldiers would make a full recovery. We had to move carefully, gravity in the medical bay was reduced to fifteen percent of Earth normal, to minimize stress on the bodies of the people being treated.

"Is there anything I can do?" I looked around the medical compartment with a frown. There were tubes and scary-looking robot things everywhere, I sure as hell wouldn't want to be a patient in this hospital.

Doctor Skippy disparaged my offer of help. "Unless you have a thorough understanding of Thuranin medical pods, no. Joe, I've got this. It looks scary, it's also fairly sophisticated medical technology, human physiology is pretty simple so these cases are easy. Go do something useful, and let me work."

"All right. We're not leaving these people alone. I'll get Major Simms to assign people shifts here-"

"Totally unnecessary, Joe."

"Physically unnecessary, maybe, Skippy, this is a human thing. I want our people here to know they're not alone. When they wake up, there needs to be someone here."

"A human thing, fine, whatever." Skippy relented.

"Great. What's next? Let's check out the crew quarters on this bucket. They, uh, do have crew quarters, right?" Given the profound weirdness of the Thuranin obsession with cybernetics, maybe they slept standing up, plugged into the wall or something.

"They do have individual quarters. There is one down the hall to the right."

We walked down the hall, and a door slid open. I stepped in. "Oh, boy. This could be a problem." The quarters were nicely set up; a bed, cabinets built into the walls, a closet, and a bathroom with a shower, a table and one chair. The features of the compartment were not the problem. The problem was they were all Thuranin-sized. The bed wouldn't fit me unless I hung my legs off the side. The ceiling was maybe six and a half feet tall, some of our crew would need to be careful not to bump their heads. To take a shower, I'd need to kneel on the floor, with my legs sticking out.

"I don't know," Adams said with a smile, "it looks cozy to me."

"Cozy like warm and comfortable, or cozy like a real estate ad that really means cramped and depressing?" I asked.

"The second one." Adams opened the closet door. "Huh. They don't go in much for fashion." All the outfits were the same dull gray and blue gray the sleeping Thuranin had been wearing.

"What the hell," I shrugged, "we'll make do. Everyone gets their own quarters, that's luxury enough."

"Sir?" Adams prodded me, "the food situation?"

"Oh, yeah, good point. Skippy, show us the mess hall, or I guess it's a galley on a ship."

"There isn't one, Joe."

"No galley?" I shared a puzzled look with Adams. "Then where do they eat?"

"In private," Skippy explained, "the Thuranin consider most things that remind them of their biological past to be taboo, particularly biological functions like eating. Consuming food is done in private, in their sleeping compartments, like this one."

There wasn't anything like a kitchen in the tiny compartment. "All right, fine." We humans could find some space on the ship to use as a mess hall, us being social animals, and mealtimes being a prime social activity. "Show us the food."

"In that cabinet behind Sergeant Adams."

Adams opened the cabinet and pulled out a handful of clear plastic tubes which contained a thick beige fluid. "What is this?" She peered into the cabinet, in case she'd missed something, then opened the other cabinet. Same clear plastic tubes.

"That's their food. The best translation of their term is sustenance sludge."

"Sludge?" I asked, appalled.

"Hmmm, that word may have a negative connotation." Skippy mused. "How about gunk, or muck, or goo, or slime? Darn, those words also have negative connotations."

"Ya think?"

"Think of it as a smoothie?" Skippy tried.

"You're not helping." I took one of the tubes and examined it. "This is all they eat?"

"Yes, it contains everything a Thuranin needs."

"What does it taste like?" I asked, grasping the cap on the top to open it.

"Well, don't eat it, dumdum, it's designed for Thuranin biology, it doesn't have the proper mix of amino acids and vitamins for humans. I have the synthesizers working now to make sludge, I mean smoothies, for humans."

"Wonderful. And what will that taste like?"

Silence for a moment, then, "Like I have taste buds, Joe."

"Oh, sorry about that."

"However, I have built what I consider a fairly accurate model of human senses, including taste-"

"Of course you have."

"-and it will taste like, the best way to describe it, I think, is a combination of oatmeal, carrots and bologna."

"Shit." Adams made a sour face. "This is going to be a long voyage."

"Skippy, this is unsat. You told me we could eat Thuranin food, as in *food*. This," I shook a plastic tube and the sludge oozed unappealingly from one end to the other, "is not food. An army runs on its stomach. Damn," I looked at Adams, "this is going to be terrible for morale. What the hell is the crew going to do?"

Adams pulled her shoulders back and set her jaw in determination. "They'll embrace the suck, sir." Some things in the military simply sucked, and there wasn't anything you could do about it, so you embraced the suck and did your duty. "Soldiers have been embracing the suck since we fought with wooden spears. We're not out here for a pleasure cruise."

Her attitude was encouraging, I hoped others felt the same. The two pallets of food, mostly MREs, that we'd brought aboard the Dodo would need to be rationed, with priority being given to the wounded. For sure, I was going to set an example by eating nothing but sludge, or 'smoothies'; if the crew saw their commander was sharing the pain, they'd take it better. For now, I decided the crew would be limited to one real meal per day, and see how that went.

"Joe, I didn't realize this would be a significant problem. Let me play with the food synthesizers and see what flavors I can make."

"Chocolate would be good. Everybody likes chocolate, right?" I suggested.

"The cocoa bean is a subtle and complex flavor, I'll do what I can."

"Fine, great. I'll be your taste tester," I volunteered. "Now, is there a gym on the bucket, or someplace we can make into a gym? People need exercise, and we'll need space to practice combat tactics."

"There is nothing like a gym, the Thuranin rely on their cybernetics rather than muscles. One of the cargo compartments is mostly empty, and I can get the robots to clear more space by tossing stuff into space, we don't need any of that cargo. For running, there is an access corridor that runs the length of the ship's spine, next to the tram, I can open and close airlock doors as people run between sections."

That was good news, running sprints was good exercise. Exercise I needed myself.

"Sir, I'd like to handle setting up a gym," Adams volunteered.

"Very well, Sergeant, you do that. I'm going to check on our wounded." I was eager to view the Thuranin medical facilities that Skippy had been raving about. We had brought nothing more than basic first aid kits with us, if anyone needed a blood transfusion, we would be in trouble. So many, so many things, even seemingly little things, could go disastrously wrong on this mission. And it was all my responsibility.

On my way back to the bridge, I called Simms via zPhone and asked her to meet me in the corridor. "Major, I need your advice."

"What about?" She replied, and I could see in her eyes the discomfort we both felt, about me being her commanding officer.

"The Thuranin."

Now her eyes reflected a discomfort for a different reason. "What to do with them." It wasn't phrased as a question.

"Legally, and morally. Maybe, more legally? Shit, I don't know." What kind of morality applies among alien species that are vastly apart on the technological development scale? Where the technologically superior species could wipe out the inferior species with laughably minimal effort?

"I hate to ask this, but have you asked, uh, Skippy?" She suggested. "He's surely memorized every US Army and UNEF regulation on the books."

"I'm sure he has, and I'm afraid that's all he's done; read and store in his memory. That doesn't mean he understands any of it. Particularly that he doesn't understand the purpose, the context, the history."

"Colonel," she avoided my eyes when she addressed my rank, "you've been in combat. I've been Supply my entire career."

"You went through officer training. UNEF gave me silver eagles, and a giant email of courses I was supposed to take, then I got sent out planting potatoes. I didn't even get formal training to be a sergeant. I got promoted, had a week with my fireteam at Alpha, then we shipped out and were posted to a village as an EOT straight away. It was on the job training the whole way."

She thought silently for a moment. "There's no equivalent to the Geneva Convention out here. That big list we got of The Rules of interstellar warfare, don't address treatment of prisoners, or any rules of engagement, other than the basic rule that you don't screw with habitable planetary biospheres. We have the Army code of conduct, but, I think, here's where Skippy is exactly right; we're pirates. This mission isn't sanctioned by UNEF, or any human authority, military or civilian. We're on our own."

"Great."

"Colonel Joe, if I may provide some advice of my own?" Skippy spoke through the zPhone on my belt.

"You're going to anyway, right?"

"Pretty much, yeah. Major Simms is correct, there is no formal, agreed, written rules of engagement out here. Such rules wouldn't apply to piracy anyway. You know what you're going to do, Joe; you're going to blow the Thuranin into space, because that is the only practical way to achieve your mission, and keep the Thuranin from discovering that humans hijacked one of their starships. You have to kill them to keep your entire species safe. You know what you have to do, you're only looking for someone else, like Major Simms, to tell you it's all right. You're a colonel, you're the commanding officer, you need to take full responsibility for your decisions.

Through clenched teeth, I said "thank you, Skippy. That's very helpful."

Simms gave me a sad, sympathetic smile.

"Oh, no problem, you're welcome, any time." He responded cheerily, oblivious to my sarcasm, or ignoring it. "If it makes you feel any better, the Thuranin would never spend a second agonizing over a question like this, they'd squash you humans like bugs and not think anything of it. Any Thuranin who even questioned such a decision would be subjected to neural reprogramming."

"Being told that I'm morally superior to Satan is not a positive, Skippy."

"I only mentioned it because, if the Thuranin somehow ever do learn that you hijacked their ship, you having killed their crew won't make the Thuranin any more angry; they would expect you to do that in war. They'd also expect their crew to die in combat."

"So, no downside, you're saying?" I wondered if he picked up on the bitter sarcasm in my voice.

"Nope. It's not a win-win, but it is a win-don't lose any worse."

"No downside except for my soul."

"Can't help you there, Colonel Joe. Although I don't remember anything in scriptures about aliens."

I couldn't tell whether he was being sincere, or a jackass. It still didn't feel right, killing sentient beings. Killing them while they are asleep.

"I sense hesitation?" Skippy asked. "Perhaps I can help. Earlier this year, this star carrier was transporting Kristang ships full of refugees from a planet the Kristang has lost to the Ruhar. Halfway to their destination, Thuranin discovered that particular Kristang clan had defaulted on a payment. This ship stopped, and when the Kristang were unable come up with payment for transit fees to cover all eighteen of their ships, the Thuranin ejected three of the ships, then jumped away. Those three ships were packed with refugees, Kristang refugees, but they were still refugees, mostly civilian castes, fleeing from war. Including females and children. So many refugees were packed aboard these ships that their life support systems were failing. The Thuranin ejected those three ships more than a lightyear from the nearest star system, a star system without habitable planets. By the time the Kristang scraped up enough money to pay the Thuranin to retrieve those three ships, ninety percent of the Kristang aboard were dead. And, by the way, while the Kristang were trying to arrange payment, four Thuranin star carriers passed through the area, and any one of them could have picked up those three ships with hardly any effort."

"*This* ship? This star carrier, that we're aboard?" Simms asked.

"This ship, this crew." Skippy confirmed.

"Oh, then to hell with them." I breathed, relieved. It was a cheap way out of my moral dilemma, but I was grasping for it. "They can walk the plank." I was starting to think like a pirate.

CHAPTER THIRTEEN FLYING DUTCHMAN

When I got back to the bridge, Chang stood up, and I sat in the command chair. It would have been more useful as a command station if I understood what any of the buttons did, later I needed to have Skippy show me the basics. There were a lot of people squeezed onto the bridge, it was crowded.

"Jump engines are fully recharged," Chang said, pointing to a green bar across the bottom of the main display screen.

"Great, thank you. Before we jump, our ship, the other ship, the frigate, uh, Skippy, does the frigate have a name?" Saying 'the ship' was getting old, especially now as we had two of them.

"The Kristang name for the frigate is *Heavenly Morning Flower of Glorious Victory*. Or close enough."

"You're kidding me." I exclaimed. I would have figured the lizards would name their ships something like *Hamster Killer* or *Assassin*.

"The Kristang warrior caste is rather devoted to poetry. I see this surprises you."

"Poetry?" Chang asked, and we shared a look. Neither of us could imagine the hard core warriors we'd met on the space station sitting down to compose poems.

"I have extensive examples of Kristang poetry, would you like to-"

"No! No, thank you." I sure as hell wasn't in the mood for lizard poetry. "We'll call it the, uh, the *Flower* for now. I don't want to call anything 'Victory' until we've achieved something significant. Back to my question, do we keep the *Flower*, or get rid of it? It's damaged."

"Sir," Adams spoke up, "I say we keep it. It's damaged, but we know it works, and how to control it, sort of." The looks she gave told me that, while I may be a senior officer, I didn't know much about combat, as in, never give up a potential asset in combat. She'd already reminded me of that once before.

"Sergeant Adams is correct, Colonel Joe," Skippy said, "the damage to the *Flower* has not significantly degraded its combat capability. There may also be situations where having a Kristang ship may be useful."

"All right then, we keep it for now."

"Speaking of names, what do the Thuranin call this ship?" Thompson asked.

"I hope it's not another long-ass name like the *Flower*." Simms said sourly.

"The Thuranin do not name their ships, each ship has a numerical designation." Skippy said.

"So, we get to name it, then." I mused.

"Oh come on, we gotta call it the *Enterprise*." Adams said with enthusiasm.

"Not every starship has to be named *Enterprise*." Major Simms protested. I guessed she wasn't a Star Trek fan.

"This is the first human starship. If you don't count that Kristang ship we jacked. It has to be named *Enterprise*." Adams insisted.

"America is not the only culture with famous fictional spacecraft." Chang protested. "We should consider-"

"It's not your ship, monkeys!" Skippy said. "You're like my hired crew. If anyone gets to name this ship, it's me."

I waved my arms to get everyone's attention. "How about if we concentrate on where we're going first, and worry about names later? Where are we going next? How do we contact the Collective, Skippy?"

"If they still exist-" Skippy started to say.

"*If?* You're not sure they still exist? Do you know where to find this Collective?"

"If by 'where' you mean the Milky Way galaxy and its attendant pair of dwarf galaxies, yes. Plus numerous star clusters. Beyond that, not so much."

"Holy shit." I shot a guilty look at the people I'd dragged along on this fool's errand. "What's the plan, then? We roam the galaxy forever, trying to find another Elder AI? Crap, we should name this ship the *Flying Dutchman*." I mumbled.

"That is an excellent name, Joe!" Skippy said with enthusiasm. "There, I changed the identification of this ship to *Flying Dutchman*."

"*Flying Dutchman*?" Thompson asked, which started an unhelpful round of speculation by the crew, all talking over each other.

"It's a legend of a Dutch sea captain who killed an albatross, which was bad luck, and was doomed to wander the sea forever. Or something like that. The ship can never go into port."

"I thought the guy who killed the albatross was the ancient mariner."

"Duh, of course he was ancient if he had to sail forever."

"Is the Dutchman the squid guy in that Johnny Depp pirates movie? Man, that guy gave me the creeps."

"Yeah, imagine the nasty fish breath that squid guy had."

"No, that wasn't Johnny Depp, he was the pirate with the eye liner. The blonde guy was doomed to stay at sea."

"All right, all right, enough!" I shouted to end the conversation, which otherwise wasn't ever going to end. "Skippy," I looked at him with a tilt of my head, "naming this bucket after a doomed ship is not a way to build confidence in the crew."

"I was only trying to be helpful." Skippy grumbled.

"And we're not your hired crew. If anything, we're pirates." Without sanction from UNEF, we were pirates, outlaws.

"Pirates! Joe, this is your merry band of pirates! Aaargh, shiver me timbers!" Skippy did a decent pirate impression. "I like it! A merry band of pirates, we are!"

I looked around the compartment, scanning faces. This band of pirates was going to be anything but merry, if Skippy expected us to visit every star in the galaxy to locate the Collective. I should have these conversations with a limited group of people, not the entire crew present. "This ship-"

"The *Flying Dutchman*." Skippy corrected me.

"Fine, the *Dutchman*," I could see Skippy wasn't giving up on that point, "is not going to randomly wander the galaxy until the end of time, randomly sending out signals to the Collective, right?"

"Course not, Dumdum, we'd run out of fuel. Duh. From Kristang records, I know where they keep Elder artifacts that I recognize as related to Collective components. There's a research facility in an asteroid, that the lizards think is secret, a couple wormholes from here."

That sounded much better. "Ok, so the plan is we, what, get close enough to the asteroid, send a signal to this Elder stuff?"

"Ha! As if! No way, Colonel Joe, you don't get off that easy. No, I can case the joint remotely, but then we need to ransack the place to heist the loot I need."

Case the joint? Heist? Where was Skippy getting his slang? "Ransack? As in, raid? I don't suppose the Kristang there are all unarmed research nerds?"

"Ho, ho, no way! They'll be mad as a nest of hornets. This asteroid base is where the Kristang try to figure out how Elder tech works, so they're keeping it secret from the Thuranin, because they're hoping they can leapfrog past their patrons, and crush them. The Thuranin know all about it, of course, they're not as stupid as the lizards think. They let the lizards conduct their research in case they discover anything useful, then the Thuranin can swoop in and take it. The place is heavily guarded; stealth detection grids, nukes, x-ray lasers, all the bells and whistles. Even this ship could be destroyed."

"That is a tough target." I didn't like the idea of raiding a hardened target. We'd surprised the crew of the *Flower*, and barely managed to take that ship. Any base the Kristang were trying to keep secret from the Thuranin would be constantly on the alert. "There must be someplace else we could go?"

"Nope. Not any place convenient. Besides, Joe, what you need is there also."

What I need? A cheeseburger? "What is that?"

"A wormhole controller module. The module has the codes I need to shut down a wormhole."

Now I was pissed. "Skippy, you told me you could shut down that wormhole!" What the hell else hadn't he told me?

"Hey, I can, I can! Temporarily. What I can do is disrupt the wormhole's connection to the network, but that's only temporary. The network protocols will eventually reestablish the connection, and reset the wormhole. I need the full set of controller codes to actually shut it down permanently, the Elders didn't provide those codes to me."

"I wonder why." I said dryly. "You're so incredibly trustworthy."

"I am! It's not my fault you're too dumb to ask the right question. Remember, when you assume, you make an *ass* of *u* and *me*. Or you, anyway."

It took everything I had not to try stomping his shiny lid into the deck. The Elders had a lot to answer for, building such an asshole. Through gritted teeth, I asked carefully "You have a plan to get past these stealth detection grids, nuclear missiles, lasers, and starships, right?"

"Oh, yeah," he said casually, "that's child's play for me. Their stupid grids can detect anything they want, I'll instruct their master computers to ignore the inputs, the lizards won't know anything has been detected. And their weapons aren't a problem, I'll spoof their fire control systems so they can't get a lock on us. For a while. Once we knock on the door, even my incredible wondrousness can't prevent even the dumbest of lizards from figuring out something is wrong."

"Great, fine," I said irritably, "we can plan how to cross that bridge when we get there. Is everyone ready for the jump?"

Chang and Simms were talking over each other, I was trying to interrupt both of them, and everyone had something to say. This went on for only a second or so, before Skippy fairly shouted, using the ship's intercom. "Enough! Dammit, this is like a troop of monkeys howling in the tree tops. Quit with the jibber jabber, I can't hear myself think. Out! *Out*! Everyone out of the bridge, except Colonel Joe and the pilots!"

I looked up guiltily at the others, especially Chang and Simms. "Skippy, we can-"

"Colonel Joe, you said we need clear lines of communication. We're going to be flying this ship in enemy territory, through wormholes, and potentially in combat. Having a troop of monkeys screeching at me is not clear communication. They can stand outside the bridge in the CIC, listen to us, and watch, but I don't want to hear from them unless you open the intercom. You're the captain, you're a colonel, you're in command. I will only communicate with you or the pilot, while this ship is in flight."

I could see Skippy's point. Chang and Simms wanted to weigh in on everything, because they didn't truly accept my authority. I didn't blame them; I couldn't believe it myself. And, truthfully, this was a great opportunity for me to assert, or more correctly, test, my authority. If Chang, Simms, Giraud or anyone else wasn't taking my command authority seriously, this was a great time to find out. "Skippy is right," I declared in my deepest, most authoritative voice, "it's too crowded in here also. Access to the bridge is restricted to the duty officer," at that time the duty officer was me, "and the two pilots. Everyone else, take stations in the CIC." We needed to schedule shifts for who sat in the big chair as the duty officer, we also needed more than two pilots, Desai had been our pilot since we broke out of the Kristang jail and she had to be tired by now, having flown three unfamiliar spacecraft already today.

To my relief, no one objected to being banished from the bridge, they had better access to the controls and displays in the CIC anyway, the bridge area was way too crowded.

"The ship is ready for jump, and the course is programmed into the autopilot," Skippy announced, with a touch of impatience. "The pilot knows which button to push."

"Pilot?" I asked.

"I'm ready, Captain." Desai did have a finger poised over a large button on the console in front of her. "Mister Skippy walked me through programming the jump into the autopilot, I do not understand how it actually works."

We monkeys might never understand how the jump navigation computer worked. "Initiate jump." I said simply.

And we jumped. The display flickered, and the only change I could detect was that a white dot that was on the bottom right corner of the display was gone.

"Jump successful, Captain." Desai said. "According to the instruments."

"Confirmed." Skippy said simply.

"Excellent," I relaxed in the chair, "what's the plan now?"

Skippy, of course, had an immediate answer. "When the Jump engines are charged again, we head out. We're safely away, that jump was far enough that the Thuranin ships searching for us will be totally lost."

I looked at the status screen that showed the Kristang ships attached to the platforms along the star carrier's long spine. "What about our unwanted guests?"

"Oh, them. I can eject the other Kristang ships, and leave them here before we jump. You still want to keep the *Flower,* right?" Skippy suggested.

I frowned. "We should keep the, uh, *Flower,* yes." We had to shorten that ship's long-ass name. "The other ships, won't they be able to make it back to Paradise? Or get close enough to signal for help?"

"There is a 36 percent chance that, by consolidating fuel into one ship and sacrificing the others, a single ship could make enough Jumps to be within practical signaling range, yes. The critical variable is the maintenance state of the Kristang jump engines. There is a 64 percent probably of Jump engine failure, from repeated jumps."

"No."

"No? The monkey wishes to see my calculations?" Skippy's voice sounded amused.

"No, this monkey wishes there to be a zero percent chance the lizards, or the Thuranin, ever find out what happened out here. If either of them learn humans are involved in our little pirate action, Earth is toast."

There was another almost imperceptible AI response lag. "I can interfere with their jump engine computers, but it is likely they could eventually recover functionality by restoring from protected archives."

"That's not what I meant. What's the weapons load on this bucket? The Thuranin must have something stronger than railguns."

"Railguns, too, but also missiles, and masers."

"Anything that will completely vaporize a lizard ship? I don't want anything left, no flight recorders, nothing that could be recovered." I could see the others looking at me skeptically, wondering where I was going with my questions.

"A star carrier is not a battleship; it's weapons are primarily defensive. There are no weapons on this ship that could completely destroy fourteen Kristang ships, there would be detectable debris. Also, Kristang ships have drones which are automatically launched in case the ship is severely damaged; these drones carry the ship's flight logs and sensor data, and they are stealthed. Multiple drones are carried by each ship, for this ship's sensors to find multiple stealth drones launched from each of the fourteen Kristang ships would be difficult, even with me operating the sensors. Also, I must caution that those fourteen Kristang ships, even with their lesser technology, do pose a threat to this ship." I noticed that Skippy had dropped his smart-ass attitude when talking about killing lizards. "All this is academic, anyway, Colonel Bishop. As I told you, I am restricted from using weapons."

"But I'm not."

This time, the pause was long enough that I wasn't the only one who noticed. "I don't see how-"

"You get those weapons ready, and locked on target, and I'll press the button, or whatever they use on this bucket." I said, looking around for anything that looked like it might be a weapons panel. It all still looked like a gothic nightmare to me. "You can do that, right, your programming doesn't prevent you from preparing weapons to fire, as long as you don't actually initiate the firing sequence?"

Another long pause. "Colonel, I may have underestimated you. That is almost a clever idea." For the very first time, I heard a tiny bit of respect in that artificial voice. "Are you certain you want to do this?

Through the window, I could see that Lt. Colonel Chang, Major Simms and the others had heard everything I said. "When I was in prison, waiting to be executed for refusing to kill innocent hamster women and children, I told myself these Nazi lizards can go straight to hell. Just now, I was thinking we could only disable their jump engines." I checked the aft viewport, to the rows of Kristang cruisers and destroyers latched onto the star carrier. "But these lizards are threatening Earth." I looked at Major Simms, and she nodded to me. "So fuck them," I said, with anger that scared me.

There was a noticeable pause before Skippy spoke. "I may have to reevaluate my assessment of you."

"You can do this?" Then I remembered Skippy's overly literal use of the English language. "You will do this?"

There was no pause this time. "I can prepare the weapons so you can use them. Yes. Which weapons do you want activated?"

That was still the problem. None of the weapons aboard the ship had the power to do what I wanted, and while we were hitting the Kristang, they could hit back. If the star carrier's jump capability was damaged, we could be stuck in interstellar space for a very long time. I looked through the glass at Chang and Simms. "Does anyone have an idea?"

Before either of the people in the CIC could respond, Desai turned in her seat. "Could we jump someplace really far from any stars, so the Kristang would be stranded for certain?"

"We are already in deep interstellar space. Going further would increase the likeliness of the Kristang's jump engines failing," Skippy said, "however, there would still be-"

"Skippy," it was my turn to interrupt him, "you can control the jump engines on those Kristang ships?" Desai had given me an idea.

"Temporarily, yes."

"And we don't need to send teams aboard those ships, plug you in?" If we did, my plan wouldn't work, no way could we assault multiple Kristang warships.

"No, not this time. The Thuranin platforms have hardline connections to docked ships, to reduce EM signatures, so I infiltrated the Kristang ship computers shortly after I took control of this ship."

The next question was the key to my plan. "And how long would it take for the Kristang to charge their jump engines, for a short jump?"

"Warships always maintain a minimal charge in their jump engines, to escape ambushes." Skippy explained. "All the Kristang ships are capable of an immediate short range jump, right now."

"Good. How far are we from the nearest gas giant planet?" I asked.

Desai's mouth formed a silent 'O' as she realized what I was thinking. "You're thinking we jump in close to a gas giant, eject the Kristang and then jump their ships *inside* the planet, before they can react?"

"Whoa!" Skippy said derisively. "Whoa, hold on there, monkeys. You can't jump a starship inside a planet, the gravity will distort the exit point so it, oh, huh, I get it. Yeah, duh. That would be *very* effective in ripping those ships apart, especially since they would be trying to emerge into spacetime already occupied by the planet. Ooh, I've never seen that myself. This is gonna be awesome! Woo-hoo!" He sounded gleeful. "Yes, there is a Saturn-size gas giant well within two jumps from here. It is in an uninhabited star system. Pilot, course is laid in, ready when the jump engines reach sixty four percent charge."

"Wait!" I said quickly, before Desai could turn around in her seat. I should have trusted her not to engage the controls without my order, for she held her hands in the air, not poised over the controls. "Skippy, can you eject those ships, get clear, and jump them into this Saturn planet, before they can launch those drones?"

"Please, Colonel Joe, you insult me. Easy-peasy."

Chang didn't have any objection, or a better idea. Simms was enthusiastic, and I saw a new respect in her, and Desai's, eyes. We jumped twice through the emptiness of interstellar space, and then, with a press of a button by Desai, the view of black interstellar space in the screens was suddenly replaced by a gray-blue gas giant in the blink of an eye. The planet completely filled the viewscreen, I mean, Skippy must have been showing off his navigational skills, it sure looked like we jumped in really close. I didn't have time to shout an alarm, because the star carrier immediately shuddered as fourteen Kristang ships and the cargo pod of sleeping Thuranin were violently subjected to emergency separation, and then our ship surged forward under normal-space thrust from Desai. Skippy had given her no course instructions other than get the hell out there ASAP, and don't point the ship toward the planet. We could see almost immediate flashes from aft as the Kristang ships unwillingly formed jump points. "Pilot, you can cut thrust. Watch this." Skippy announced excitedly.

"Watch what?"

The view screen zoomed to a section of the cloud tops, which were suddenly lit from within. "I jumped all fourteen ships into a hundred cubic kilometers, so the endpoints of their jump entry points overlapped, as insurance that nothing is left of them."

"Isn't that a bit of overkill?"

"Overkill is underrated." Skippy said smugly. "Hmm. Uh oh."

"Uh oh?" The light within the clouds below kept growing, becoming searing in brilliance, and the cloud tops boiled up toward us. Fast. "*Uh oh?* What the hell did you do, Skippy?"

"The energy released within the planet was much greater than I anticipated, somewhere way up in the sustained petawatt range. Wow. It's become self-sustaining. Darn."

"Darn?" The clouds were racing towards us. "What the hell is a petawatt?" I shouted.

"Trouble. We are safely out of range. Uh, I think." Skippy's tone of voice didn't fill me with confidence.

"You *think*? Desai, move us away from the planet, higher orbit, whatever you call it. Step on it."

"Aye aye, sir." She said with a big grin on her face. Piloting a giant starship was something she clearly enjoyed. "Pedal to the metal."

We watched the planet retreat behind us, as the cloud tops boiled rapidly into a truly enormous mushroom shape, and projected high above the atmosphere like a solar flare. Skippy reported excitedly that a significant part of the atmosphere had exceeded escape velocity, and was being permanently blown into space. Enough that the ship's sensors could measure the change in the planet's mass. The atmospheric gas was still climbing, but Desai now had us moving faster, I was confident we weren't going to get swallowed up. "Skippy, what went wrong?"

"Wrong? That was *awesome*! Damn! I almost converted that planet into a minor star. I wish we had better sensor coverage."

"Wrong means, something happened that you didn't plan." I explained slowly. How could it be that I needed to explain anything, to a super-intelligent ancient machine?

"Oh, sure, if you're going to be picky about it." Skippy said dismissively. "Next time, I'll jump an enemy ship deeper towards the planet's core. But that's no fun, we won't be able to see anything. It would just look like the clouds burped or something lame like that."

"Sir?'" Desai asked, without taking her eyes off the controls. "Should I keep accelerating? We're moving at fifteen thousand kph away from the planet already."

"Huh? Oh, yeah, you can cut thrust." There was no sense wasting power. Especially since we didn't have a destination in mind yet. "Skippy, are we clear? The Kristang ships are all destroyed, and they didn't get any drones away?"

"We are clear, Colonel Joe. This took them completely by surprise, and I confused their computers so they couldn't react anyway. They are now a loose cloud of atoms. The cargo pod with the Thuranin got swallowed up and vaporized by the explosion, they're gone also."

I looked through the glass at Chang and Simms, and gave them a thumbs up. They both nodded. "What's next, Skippy? Now that we have gotten rid of unwanted guests. We're headed to raid the asteroid base, yes?" I should have felt something after destroying the Kristang and Thuranin, but I didn't. No triumph, no guilt, no satisfaction, nothing. Those ships were just objects, I wasn't thinking of the sentient beings who had been aboard. This was very different from firefights in the Nigerian bush, or fighting hamsters on Paradise. Maybe I'd feel something later, after some rack time. Right then, I did not care, as long as the Kristang and Thuranin were no longer a threat.

"Yes. We wait while our jump engines recharge. I have plotted a long jump so we need a full charge, that will take up to two hours."

"Desai, you up for using the next couple hours learning to fly this crate?"

"Yes, sir!"

"Great. Skippy, plot some points for her to navigate to, or whatever you're supposed to do for pilot training. We're going out to transit through a wormhole next, right? That wormhole is about eight lightyears from Paradise, based on guesses I heard from our G-2. That's our Intel people, at the division level."

"I've memorized all your military acronyms, Colonel Joe."

"Oh, uh, of course you have, sorry about that." Why did I bother explaining anything, to a being who knew everything that was in any sort of data storage device humanity had brought to Paradise? Plus every bit of data the Kristang and Ruhar had about humans. He knew far more about humanity that any human did. Whether he *understood* it, in context, was another question. "To travel eight lightyears takes about sixteen days on a Thuranin star carrier like this. Unless, uh, there are different types of star carriers? I don't know which ship we travelled on."

"There are different types, and the Thuranin have battleships, cruisers and what you would call destroyers and frigates, also transports and support ships. All their star carriers have roughly the same jump capability."

"Ok, so, two weeks between here and the nearest wormhole-"

"You mean the wormhole that leads to Camp X-Ray. That is not the closest wormhole to Paradise."

"It's not?"

"No." It was maddening when Skippy stuck to the facts, usually I couldn't get him to shut up about anything.

"Which wormhole are we going to?"

"The one that is only five lightyears away from Paradise."

I did some quick mental math. "Ten days, then?"

"Sure, if you want to poke along like the Thuranin, one wimpy little jump at a time. We're doing it in jumps that are twice as far as normal, and that's only because I need to calibrate the engines, fine-tune them, as you would say. We could go more than twice as far on a jump."

"I don't understand."

"That's the first intelligent thing you've said since we met."

"Welcome back, Skippy, I knew that asshole was in there someplace."

"I'm ignoring that. The truth, my boy, is the Thuranin stole their supposedly advanced jump drive technology a long time ago, but those arrogant little cyborg pinheads have made zero progress in understanding how it works since then. Morons. The best way to explain it is it's like they stole a car, and they know how to get it started, and how to get the transmission into gear. They have no idea that transmission has multiple gears, but they know the car has a gas pedal, and they've got the pedal to the floor. They're poking along in first gear, with the engine screaming, and it creeps along painfully slowly, but it could go so much faster. Especially since the Thuranin were very bad at copying their stolen technology, and it's like they carved the transmission from a solid block of wood.

Idiots. Even without being modified, their crappy copy of a jump drive is capable of much greater performance, with me controlling it."

"Not that you're bragging or anything."

"No, I'm very modest. Astonishingly modest, considering how awesome I am."

"Oh, for sure, your awesome modesty is your most impressive trait." I rolled my eyes at that. "It's amazing how humble you are."

"Yup. I'm very proud of my humbleness. Besides, as one of you humans said, it ain't bragging if it's true."

"Uh huh." It continuously amazed me how Skippy knew so much about human history. How did a shiny beer can know quotes from Muhammad Ali? "This making longer jumps, it won't damage the engines? I don't want to get stranded out here. Not that the idea of spending eternity on this ship with you, doesn't sound absolutely wonderful. Because it doesn't."

"I don't want to spend an eternity looking at your ugly face either. No, the Thuranin control their jumps by forcing far too much energy through the engines, that wears them out. I'll be using a third of the energy to jump more than twice as far. The engines will last much longer. Which is good, because we can't exactly take our stolen pirate ship to a Thuranin repair station."

"Can us monkeys help with keeping the ship running? You could show us where the jack and spare tire is, in case we get a flat."

"If we get stuck, you can get out and push."

I stuck my tongue out at him. Even the smartest human was probably incapable of fixing even a toilet aboard a Thuranin ship, we'd be totally useless if something happened to the engines or any other critical system. Although, if Skippy was going to drag us on a long trip across the galaxy, toilets *were* going to be a critical system.

"Ok, so, we're going to jump to a wormhole. How are we going to get through the wormhole? Won't the Kristang, or the Thuranin, or even the Ruhar at this point, have ships guarding the entrance?"

"How would they do that?"

"Do what?"

"Guard the entrance."

"With, uh, you know, ships. Or, like, a battle station or something like that." For a second, I pictured a Death Star. Only filled with lizards instead of storm troopers.

"What good would a battle station do? It just sits there."

I couldn't believe a super intelligent being needed me to explain what a space battle station could do. Particularly since I'd never seen one. Slowly, I explained. "It sits there, in front of the entrance, preventing unauthorized ships from-"

"Whoa!" Skippy interrupted me. "I see the problem. Huh, you really don't know. Damn, your species is even dumber than I thought."

"Don't know what?"

"Wormholes aren't static. They move around. A battle station would be totally useless."

"Ooooh-kaaaay. No, Mister Smarty Pants, I didn't know that." The burgermeister hadn't mentioned that important detail. "What do you mean, move around?"

"Oh, boy, here comes me trying to give a physics lecture to a bacterium. What you call wormholes are not physical objects, they are projections into the local spacetime. The projections hop around, just below the speed of light, in kind of a figure eight pattern that covers about a lightyear. A wormhole projection stays in one place for between roughly seventeen to ninety two minutes, then it closes and reappears at the next step along the path, which could be a quarter of a lightyear away. Wormholes follow a set pattern, over the course of a cycle, a wormhole will cover every location along the path, but there are millions of locations. My point is, there is no way the Kristang, or any other species currently in this galaxy, could prevent ships from using a wormhole; it's not practical to cover all those locations. My plan is to jump us close to where a wormhole is going to appear, and see if any other ships are waiting, I know exactly when a wormhole is going to shift to the next location. If it's clear, we wait for the wormhole to open, jump right in front of it, then go through."

"Huh." I had pictured wormholes as a sort a Stargate thing, a big ring hanging in space, with a glowing center. "That sounds like a good plan. And don't say of course it is. Why don't wormholes stay in one place?"

"Didn't you already answer that question? Because if a wormhole stays in one place, a species could control it, duh. Also, because the longer a wormhole is open, it takes exponentially more energy to sustain the connection. And a static wormhole would eventually create a local rupture in spacetime."

"Another good safety tip, then."

"An excellent safety tip. Probably not one you monkeys need to worry about, in case you're thinking of creating a wormhole out of mud and sticks."

"Shut up." Every time I was thinking Skippy was Ok, he said something to remind me that, deep down, he was an asshole.

After the jump away from the wormhole, I called a stand down for the entire crew, they were exhausted, and as Skippy said we were safe, we'd made enough jumps that it was extremely unlikely the Thuranin could find us now. Other than a person in the sickbay, who could nap on the floor there, and a duty officer in the command pilot couch, I wanted everyone to get a solid eight hours of sleep. We were tired, we were emotionally wrung out, and we all needed time to process everything that had happened during a very long and eventful day. For most of the crew, it had started when a Dodo dropped out of the sky onto their logistics base, and four humans came out and stunned the Ruhar. For Chang, Simms, Adams and me, it had started earlier, when we escaped from the Ruhar and stole the Dodo.

I took the first duty shift, although I was not in any way qualified as a pilot, Skippy had programmed two emergency jumps, and all I would need to do is press a button if trouble appeared. While I sat in the pilot couch, which was too small for Desai and way too cramped for me, I began writing up an after action report on my iPad. Someday, hopefully, I would need to report to authorities on Earth all that had happened, and it was best to do that while it was still fresh in my mind. Damn, there was a lot to write down. I was only halfway through when Chang relieved me three hours later, and I was able to stagger back to my assigned quarters, close to the bridge. After I kicked my shoes off and scrunched up in the small bed, I couldn't get to sleep. Rather than lay there uselessly, I sat up, turned the light on, and began tapping away on my iPad.

Skippy's voice came from the iPad's speakers. "Colonel Joe, you should be sleeping."

"I have a lot to do, Skippy. Like planning a memorial service for the three people we lost. I don't even know the proper ceremony for Taoism or Hindus." I frowned. The truth was, guilt was keeping me from sleeping.

"Hindu tradition is cremation." Skippy chipped in helpfully. "I have all available data on human religious rituals."

"Oh, uh, thanks, Skippy." I could ask Chang and Desai what to do about their countrymen. Matheson's body would remain in storage until we returned to Earth for a proper burial, at home. "This must all seem silly to you."

"What?"

"Religious rituals. You know, religion itself."

"Why would I think that?"

His answer surprised me, I had expected a smart-ass remark about monkeys worshipping trees. "Because the beings who created you were ancient and super powerful, and uh-"

"Joe, Joe, Joe." I could visualize Skippy shaking his lid at me. "The Elders were indeed super powerful; they were able to move stars. Several times, when the path of a star was going to disrupt a solar system that the Elders thought could someday bring forth intelligent life, they towed the offending star out of the way. Once, when a blue giant star threatened to go supernova and flood several surrounding solar systems with deadly radiation, the Elders created a wormhole, and transported the star outside the galaxy. They jumped a super massive star two hundred thousand lightyears through a wormhole. Think about that. Your question assumes that beings so powerful, beings who had effectively achieved immortality, such beings would have no use for religion. You are wrong. Again. Why do you think the Elders left us, transcended?"

"Because," I answered slowly to give myself time to think, "they were bored? With this existence?"

"No." There was no trace of humor or the usual snarkiness in Skippy's voice. "It was because they had answered all the physical questions about the universe, and when you reach the end of the physical, what is left must be metaphysical. Beyond the natural world lies only the supernatural. The Elders were able to trace time back to the beginning of the universe, and they were left with one question: what lay before? Where did the universe come from? Where did *they* come from? Physics, even physics so advanced as to touch the realm of magic, has a limit. The Elders transcended because they wanted to know, they needed to know, where they came from. They wanted to commune with God. Or with their concept of God."

"Whoa." I couldn't think of anything else to say.

"You make the same mistake most young species do when thinking about the Elders; you consider them to be only mythical, almost god-like beings. They were real people, like any other. At one point, they were as dumb as you monkeys, but they learned and evolved into something wondrous. I remember them as wise, kind, powerful, gentle people. I miss them, and I seek the Collective in order to reconnect with some part of them. But I know they are not gods."

"You're right, Skippy, I hadn't thought of them as people." I hadn't thought of the Elders much at all, in fact, since so little was known about them. "What were they like?"

"Unfortunately, I can't tell you. It's annoying. I have memories of them, at the back of my mind, but when I try to picture them, I can't, not consciously. And my programming won't allow me to tell you anything that I do know. What bothers me is I can't tell if that is part of my original programming, or it's a glitch. Which is another reason I need to contact the Collective."

"We'll do that, Skippy, I promised you, we'll find them." My eyelids felt so heavy, I couldn't keep them open. "Thanks, Skippy, I'm going to get some sleep now. Talk to you later."

Over the next days, we settled into a routine. While the *Flying Dutchman* jumped, charged engines and jumped again around us, we sorted out living arrangements, set up a dining facility in a cargo bay, got another cargo bay cleared out so it could be used as a gym, assigned a duty roster for the crew, including me, and we explored the ship, and tried to learn as much as we could about it. Simms had the bright idea to tear bedding out of the *Flower*, so it could be laid on the floor of our Thuranin sleeping quarters for the tallest of the crew. When a big Kristang mattress was offered to me, I declined, then found one in my quarters next to the bridge anyway. I didn't protest, that damned short Thuranin bed was killing my back.

The second night I went to sleep in my quarters, Skippy told me there was a surprise in one of the cabinets. "Holy crap, Skippy." I exclaimed when I opened the cabinet. It was full, jammed full, of plastic tubes, each about a third full. "What the hell is all this?"

"Flavor experiments. There's a label printed into the tube on each one."

Looking more closely at a tube, I saw 'Chocolate #14' in tiny print. "Fourteen types of chocolate?"

"Twenty two, actually. Like I said, chocolate is a very complex flavor. Also I tried multiple types of butterscotch, caramel, strawberry, curry, jalapeno, cheddar, banana, apple cinnamon, salsa, and more, there's a list on your phone if you care to read it, which I know you won't. I am not confident of the fruit flavors, if you want me to be honest."

Carefully popping the cap off the tube, I sniffed it. "How many of these tubes is a meal?"

"Depends on your level of exercise, as a rule for a male your size, one and a half tubes is sufficient, three times a day."

Sniffing it again, I tried to decide between gulping it down before I could taste it, and taking a sip. Since I had volunteered to act as a taste tester for the crew, I tipped the tube until a couple drops slid into my mouth. "Not bad, not bad. Reminds me of a Swiss Miss hot cocoa packet that got left in a hunting cabin for a lot of years, until someone found it in the back of a drawer. Stale and musty, and the little marshmallows have turned into crumbly rocks."

Skippy laughed. "I didn't realize you were a sludge connoisseur, Joe."

"Smoothie, Skippy, call it a smoothie." Sludge had an unpleasant mouth feel, both oily, chalky and somehow grainy at the same time.

"Try chocolate number six, my taste model predicts you'll like that one better."

"Got to finish this one first. Yum."

"No need for that, we have plenty of sludge aboard, enough for years."

"Oh, wonderful." Number six did taste better, I compared them side by side, alternating sips. "You're right, six is more of a dark chocolate, and it has less of a chalky aftertaste. And less oily, more of a silky mouthfeel."

"Excellent! Drink up, Joe, only twenty more types of chocolate to go."

"Tell you what," I couldn't face the thought of another twenty sludges right then. What I wanted to do is gulp a couple down quickly and get it over with. "Tell me the, like, six chocolates you think taste the worst. People like different things, so what I think is the best chocolate may not be someone else's favorite, but I can eliminate the truly nasty ones." The last thing I wanted was for someone's first sip of sludge to turn them off to the whole idea. "And identifying the bad ones will help you calibrate your taste model, right?"

"Good thinking, Joe," Skippy gave me some rare praise, "guessing what tastes good to humans has actually been an interesting challenge for me. And that ain't easy."

"Glad to help keep boredom away. Skippy, I have to say I'm truly impressed, that chocolate number six is pretty good, I could sort of enjoy that for breakfast. You did a good job on that, I was dreading the sludge idea, and now it's not so bad. Before I change my mind," or decide I was no longer hungry, "what chocolate do you think is the worst?"

Sludges, and that's what the crew decided to call it, because we're soldiers and that's what we do, weren't popular with the crew, they weren't a disaster either. And since we were soldiers, we made do, and came up with flavor combinations, the same way we mixed and matched MREs to make flavors the military never intended. One chocolate sludge plus one banana sludge was a chocolate-banana. Coconut sludge plus curry sludge, mixed and poured over MRE chicken and heated up, made an approximation of a Thai dish. Everyone agreed the fruit flavor sludges were the worst, although if they mixed the nasty strawberry with the bland banana, it actually tasted pretty good. This unpredictability of human taste preferences drove Skippy batshit crazy sometimes, he simply could not, for all his awesome processing power, get his taste model to work with reliable accuracy. It helped that, after a few days, he was able to eliminate the oily mouth feel and the chalkiness, the grainy or gritty part couldn't be fixed as that was necessary for digestive fiber, according to Skippy. The crew found ample opportunity to bitch about the 'food' aboard the *Dutchman*, something I thought encouraging. People needed something to complain about, complaining was a bonding activity, and it wasn't a serious hit to morale. A sludge in the morning, sludge for lunch, and people looked forward to 'real' food like an MRE for dinner. The crew, including Chang, Simms, Desai and Giraud, tried to get me to eat some real food, but I settled for an occasional cracker or cookie, trying to set a good example. When the crew saw the 'old man', which incredibly was *me*, stuck with sludge, they didn't feel so bad about subsisting on it two times a day.

Besides, I was holding out for a cheeseburger and I was accepting no stinkin' substitutes.

CHAPTER FOURTEEN   SPACE SUITS

Simms pinged me the next day while I was in the gym, I was needed on the bridge. When I got there, Simms started to get out of the captain's chair, I waved for her to sit. As the duty officer, the chair was hers. "What is it, Major?"

"Colonel, Skippy wants to divert us from a direct course to the next wormhole."

"Skippy?" I asked.

"We need to get close to a Thuranin battlegroup, so I can access current intel. Right now I'm guessing at disposition of forces in this sector, that makes it dangerous for us to be wandering around the galaxy in our pirate ship."

Simms explained her objection. "To avoid danger, he wants to get closer to a Thuranin battlegroup. I thought this merited your attention."

"Good call," I agreed. "You do, uh, see the problem, Skippy? Right now, all the Thuranin know is one of their star carriers has gone missing. Aren't they going to get concerned when we mysteriously show up on their doorstep, then jump away? You do plan to jump us away, right?"

"Yes, of course, dumdum, and I have a plan for that. If I have to explain everything to you, we'll never get anything done. Uh!" He shushed me as I was about to speak. "Let me talk before you waste my time with stupid questions. When we jump in, I'll alter our jump signature and engine emissions to make us appear to be a Jeraptha light cruiser, which is the type of ship the Jeraptha commonly use to shadow enemy battlegroups. Our stealth field will disguise the hull outline enough that the Thuranin sensors won't detect that we're a star carrier, if we don't linger too long in one spot. And we won't. Genius, huh?"

I wasn't convinced. "Won't the Thuranin send ships to attack us?"

"Of course they will, a Thuranin battlegroup keeps frigates and destroyers on alert to chase away enemy ships. Not a problem, we'll hop around with micro jumps until I've had enough time to break into the database of their command ship."

"Hop around?" I shared a glance with Desai. "I thought ships took a long time to recharge their engines between jumps?"

Skippy replied smugly. "Most ships do, I reprogrammed our jump engines so they now work so efficiently, they can perform small jumps on a partial charge. You're welcome, by the way."

"Perform multiple jumps on a partial charge, which a real Jeraptha light cruiser can't do, right?"

"Nope. The Jeraptha aren't quite as stupid as the Thuranin, but their engines aren't much better. Another example of my awesomeness."

"You're kind of missing the point, Your Royal Awesomeness. If we're doing things a Jeraptha light cruiser can't do, the Thuranin are going to figure out real quick that we are not a Jeraptha light cruiser."

"Shit." Skippy said simply.

I winked at Desai. "Yeah, shit. I thought you're supposed to be a genius?"

"I'm not a military strategist, Colonel Joe, that's supposed to be you. Ok, hmm, how to fix this? Uh, all right, how about this? Each time we jump in, I'll slightly alter the jump signature to make us look like a different Jeraptha warship. It is common for the Jeraptha to use multiple picket ships to shadow an enemy force."

"That'll work. How long will we need to hang around the Thuranin, until you have the info you need?"

"Oh, a couple minutes to half an hour, depends. The closer to the command ship we jump in, the quicker I can get the data we need. It's a tradeoff; either we jump in close a couple times, or we jump in further away more times, when we're exposed longer."

I looked at Simms, and she nodded. "It's a judgment call, then," she said.

A judgment call neither Simms nor I were qualified to make, and Skippy knew it. Passing the buck to Desai would be the coward's way out. "Uh huh. Skippy, I assume you'll have a series of options programmed into the nav system, and you'll advise the pilot which jump we should make, right, based on what the Thuranin are doing?"

"Yup, you got it." Surprisingly, he resisted the temptation to make a smartass remark about my intelligence, or lack of it.

"All right then, if you think we need this intel, then we'll do it. One condition; I want a jump option that will take us safely far away, not only a micro jump, if the pilot or duty officer think's the ship is in danger. More danger than usual."

"Yeah, sure, that's fair enough. Don't go panicking on me, agreed? We don't want to do this more than once if we don't have to."

"Pilot?" I asked Desai, "are you comfortable with that?" As the words left my mouth, I knew I'd put Desai in a difficult position. What I should have done is ask if she had any different ideas.

"Yes, Colonel. We have an emergency jump option at all times, on a different button here," she pointed to a silver button on the top right of her control panel. "I worked that out with Mister Skippy when we were doing our first series of jumps. The safety jump option is updated every time we jump."

"Oh." I should have known that. "Excellent work, then, Pilot. Skippy, you know where a Thuranin battlegroup is?"

"I know where one is likely to be, and several other strong possibilities. We will be approaching in seventeen hours."

That was right in the middle of Chang's next shift as duty officer, I'd need to tell him that I'd be taking over the bridge then. We'd developed a good working relationship; I didn't want to screw it up.

I came back to the bridge half an hour before we jumped to where Skippy thought we would find a Thuranin battlegroup. We jumped in, spent a tense ten minutes listening with passive sensors, with Desai ready to jump us safely away, until Skippy determined there were no Thuranin ships within range. He activated our active scanners, and quickly determined, based on thin clouds of atoms that did not naturally occur in deep interstellar space, that Thuranin ships had been in the area, recently. Skippy made a guess where they'd gone, and his first two guesses were wrong. His third guess was spot on, too spot on. We emerged from the jump in the middle of the battlegroup, less than two thousand miles from the nearest ship, that was way too close even for Skippy's bravado. After Desai initiated a microjump to a safe distance, we began hopping around the battlegroup, with a pair of Thuranin destroyers trying to chase us away. At first, it was alarming, then annoying for the pair of destroyers to pop up near us, firing missiles, railguns and particle beams. We had to jump away before the *Dutchman* got seriously hit, twice we took glancing particle beam hits that our shields easily deflected, and Skippy complained that we were jumping away too soon. After a few jumps, Skippy found a pattern in the tactics the Thuranin were using to pursue us, and once he adjusted to compensate, the two destroyers never came close again. Still, I thought Skippy was pushing it, or showing off, we kept popping up uncomfortably close to the command ship, close enough that a battleship and a pair of heavy cruisers joined the pursuit.

"Skippy, come on, do you have enough data yet?"

"Hold your horses, Colonel Joe, the fun is only getting started. We can, uh oh. Pilot! Emergency jump! Now!"

Desai didn't hesitate, the display flashed and the Thuranin battlegroup disappeared. "Jump successful, Colonel, we are-"

"Jump again, Pilot, jump! Option 4, initiate!" Skippy shouted.

The screen flashed again, and again we popped up somewhere in deep interstellar space. "Done." Desai reported, her eyes wide. "Colonel, we only have power for one microjump," she warned. The bottom of the main display showed a red bar for the jump engine charge. It read only eight percent.

"Skippy, what the hell is going on? Why the two jumps?"

"I think we're Ok now. I think."

"We'd better be," I said fearfully, willing the jump charge bar to slide above eight percent. It wasn't moving. "What happened? Did that battleship get too close?"

"Battleship? Pthththth!" Skippy made a raspberry sound. "No way! Those Thuranin pinheads were chasing their tails, I was programming microjumps closer than we needed just to screw with them. No, the Thuranin didn't pose any real danger, they're too predictable. What happened was while I was downloading data from the command ship, I detailed part of my processing capacity to skim through the data, and I learned that the Maxohlx are so alarmed about the Thuranin's military setbacks in this sector, they have assigned a Maxohlx cruiser to join the battlegroup."

"A Maxohlx starship?" Desai exclaimed. "Where was it?" The protocol was for Thuranin ships to appear green on the navigation displays, Kristang ships were red, Ruhar ships yellow, Jeraptha ships blue, and so on. The color for Maxohlx ships was orange. There hadn't been any orange symbols on the display.

"That's the problem, I didn't detect any Maxohlx ship in range. The Thuranin data indicates a Maxohlx cruiser joined the battlegroup two days ago, but it has been intermittently jumping away, and the Thuranin don't know where it is now. I am not confident in the ability of this ship's crappy sensors to detect a Maxohlx ship that has engaged its full stealth capabilities. At this point, I do not want to tangle with a Maxohlx warship, I am not sufficiently familiar with the Maxohlx current level of technology. It would be prudent, in the immediate future, to avoid Thuranin fleet concentrations. As soon as we can, we should perform a substantial jump to clear this area. The engines will have sufficient charge for a moderate jump in thirty seven minutes."

The stupid progress bar was killing me, it still only showed eight percent. "Did you get the data we need?"

"Huh? Oh, yeah, sure, no problem, I'm still skimming through it. We have a complete view of the disposition of Thuranin forces in the entire sector, future war plans, all the good stuff. With this, it will be easy to avoid them. Oh, and I also found confirmation the Thuranin are pulling back from Paradise, permanently, they're abandoning that entire wormhole cluster. It would have been an outlier to their main territory anyway, the Thuranin were never enthusiastic about retaking Paradise, that was a Kristang operation. It seems that because an Elder starship crashed on Paradise a long time ago, the Kristang were eager to resume searching for Elder technology. Too bad they didn't find anything useful the first time they had the planet. Hahahahaha! Stupid lizards."

Columbus Day

The idea of a Maxohlx cruiser lurking out there, a ship we might not be able to detect until its weapons blew through our shields, scared the hell out of me. My plan had been to turn the duty officer shift back to Chang once we'd jumped away from the Thuranin, now I'd be stuck in the chair another hour, to make sure we'd jumped safely away and the ship had not suffered any damage from stressing the engines with multiple jumps. Skippy insisted the critical engines were fine, his assurances didn't assure me. Him admitting that he had jumped us closer to the Thuranin than necessary, just to screw with them, didn't make me confident in his judgment right then.

The jump engines achieved sufficient charge, and Desai asked whether she should initiate jump, I held off another ten minutes to build up a safety margin. After the jump, and Skippy peevishly running a system diagnostic that I insisted on, I turned the chair over to Chang and retreated to a bathroom, where I almost barfed. Everyone on the ship, everyone on *Earth*, were counting on me, I was doing the best I could, and it wasn't good enough. Even with Skippy's stores of knowledge, there was too much we didn't know. We'd almost stumbled on top of a Maxohlx warship that had even Skippy frightened. There were too many unknowns. And too much at stake.

Splashing cold water on my face helped settle my nerves, I no longer felt nauseous. In the Thuranin bathroom, I had to bend down to reach the sink, and my hands were trembling. Through my zPhone, I called Skippy. "Hey, Skippy, we need to talk."

"Sure." He responded immediately, despite the fact that I knew he was talking to a half dozen other people, and running the ship, and decrypting the petabytes of data he'd stolen from the Thuranin command ship at the same time. "Wazzup?"

"I need you to be completely serious for a minute, can you do that?"

"If I have to. You're worried about something, I can tell by your voice."

Likely he was also monitoring my blood pressure, skin reactions, eye movements, and whatever else he felt like looking at. "You said you were screwing with the Thuranin."

"Yeah, that was fun."

"No, it wasn't. It put the *Dutchman* in unnecessary danger."

"Ah, I see the problem now. You're upset. Joe, we were in no additional danger. Once I got into the Thuranin command network, I knew ahead of time the actions of the Thuranin ships that were trying to chase us away. Me having some fun didn't affect us."

"This time. Didn't affect us this time, that you know of. You didn't know there was a Maxohlx cruiser out there somewhere, ready to blow this ship to pieces. Skippy, here's the problem; if something goes bad out here, you'll be stranded in deep space, until you can fake a distress call or something and lure a starship here. That sucks for you, stuck alone for a while again, but you survived it before, you'll survive it again. The stakes for us monkeys are a lot higher. When you put us at risk, you're risking my entire species. Everyone. My whole planet, and everyone and everything on it. We may be bacteria to you, and maybe you're being generous to consider us bacteria. To us, to me, this is everything. We risked a lot to come out here, now we're risking the survival of humanity. If this mission fails, if we can't shut down the wormhole, if the Kristang stay in control of Earth, then we lose, I lose, *everything*. Do you understand that?"

There was a moment of uncharacteristic silence, then "Joe, is that a tear?"

"I splashed some water on my face," I responded angrily, and wiped a tear away with my sleeve. Thinking of my family, my home town, friends, the cool dark woods where I'd spent so much time, thinking even of my parent's dog, had gotten me emotional. They were all counting on me, and they didn't know it.

"I'm sorry," he said softly. "I do understand what's at stake for you, for all of you. We made a deal, I'm going to keep my end of the bargain, I am going to shut down that wormhole. And I'm sorry to alarm you, we truly were not in any additional danger. But I won't do that again, I promise."

"Thank you. Another subject; do the Thuranin know about this ship? Do they know they lost a star carrier?"

Skippy's voice went back to normal, he was happy to change the subject. "Modifying our jump signature worked, I was monitoring the command ship's internal communications, they believed they were being shadowed by three Jeraptha light cruisers. They do know the *Dutchman* is missing, they don't know why. The good news is the Thuranin also lost another two ships, a frigate and a cruiser, around the same time and in the same area where the *Dutchman* disappeared, the Jeraptha have task forces hunting down Thuranin survivors. Our secret is safe for now. The commander of that Thuranin battlegroup sent a request to their fleet headquarters, requesting permission to detach several ships to search for the *Dutchman*, the fleet denied that request. They don't want to commit any more resources to this area, they're writing this ship off. The operation the Jeraptha launched in this sector, that resulted in the Ruhar recapturing Paradise, has succeeded beyond expectations, the Thuranin have been forced to redeploy their forces. My analysis is that the Jeraptha originally planned to halt their offensive by now, because of their unexpected success they are pressing their advantage and pulling in ships from other sectors. This operation had developed into a major, major fleet action across the entire sector. That's good for us, because the attention of the Thuranin, and Kristang, will be elsewhere."

"All right then." Thuranin bathrooms didn't have mirrors, they must have thought vanity about external appearance to be an undesirable holdover from their purely biological past. No way did I want to go back on the bridge looking like I'd almost been sick. A shaky commander was not good for crew morale. To make a mirror, I shined the zPhone screen on my shirt, and checked my face as best I could. The face that looked back was tired, yes, I could blame it on that. Straightening my shoulders, I opened the door and walked back down the corridor and onto the bridge. Chang nodded and stepped out of the chair for me.

"Colonel, no sign of a Maxohlx ship out there?" I asked. Chang and Skippy would have notified me right away, I was making conversation to avoid awkwardness.

Chang shook his head. "No sign of any pursuit. We're charging engines," he pointed to the display that indicated a current twelve percent charge, "for another series of jumps. Mister Skippy reports that the wormhole we intended to use may be used by Maxohlx ships in the near future, we have altered course for a different wormhole. ETA to the next jump is three hours, twelve minutes," that was also shown as a countdown on the display, "and we'll be approaching the wormhole in four days."

"Four days? Let's make sure everyone gets plenty of rest, then, we'll need-"

Skippy interrupted us. "Goddamn it!" Skippy shouted. "Shit! You *got* to be kidding me! Fucking pinheads! Sneaky fucking little green men!"

"Jesus Christ, Skippy, what is it?" I asked, panicked, and sat down quickly in the chair. Chang dashed out of the bridge to his duty station in the CIC, just beyond the glass. There wasn't anything new on the displays, certainly no glaring orange symbol for a Maxohlx ship. Desai turned to me and held up her hands in confusion, a finger poised over the silver button to activate a preprogrammed emergency microjump away. I held up a finger to hold her. "Are we in danger? Immediate danger?"

"Us?" Skippy sounded distracted. "No, we're in no danger. Not, uh, any more than usual. Who is in trouble are those rotten, stinking, *sneaky* Thuranin." Skippy was angry, genuinely angry. His liberal use of swear words had startled me, it was unlike him, in my limited experience. "If I get my hands on them again, I'm going to make them wish they'd never tried to be clever."

"What did they do to you?"

"Me? They didn't do anything to me. Not directly. They made me look like a fool." There was bitterness in his voice. "They hid something important from me. Something I should have known, should have expected. Damn it!"

He was rambling, it alarmed me. Scanning the displays again, there was still nothing new that I could see. Desai moved her finger off the jump button and rested in on the panel right next to the button. What the hell could Skippy be raging about? The Thuranin task force was still where it was supposed to be. No anomalous lights were on the display. In fact, no other lights were on the display, we were in deep interstellar space, the only other thing likely to be around were scattered individual hydrogen atoms, and they didn't appear on the display.

Skippy took a deep breath, at least he appeared to take an audible deep breath. "When I cracked their command ship's encryption, surprisingly sophisticated by the way, they must have stolen it from the Maxohlx, I can't imagine the Maxohlx would have given it to them. No match for my incredible powers, of course, it was, though, a minor challenge to me, sort of like doing a crossword puzzle. Not a tough crossword puzzle, you know, like when the clue is about something obscure like 17th century Hungarian poetry, unless you're an expert on 17th century Hungarian poetry, or ancient Hungarian literature in general. Really, if you studied any kind of Renaissance or Baroque Era European literature-"

"Skippy!"

"Huh? Oh, a little off topic there, I guess. Where was I?"

Where was I? Desai looked at me and I rolled my eyes. "You can store all human knowledge in a tiny part of your memory, and you can't remember what you were talking about ten seconds ago?"

"Ten seconds in your slow time sense, Joe, for me, entire species could have evolved, thrived and gone extinct in that time. My mind wanders. Oh, yeah, I was talking about their encryption. I dug into the database on the Thuranin command ship and found something interesting, very interesting. It's not widely known even among the Thuranin, their leadership keeps this information closely guarded, and I can see why, because if this secret gets out, the Thuranin will lose a big advantage. The Thuranin have planted a nanovirus aboard many, if not most, Kristang warships. Any Kristang warship that hitches a ride on a Thuranin star carrier gets infected during the process, if the star carrier is equipped with the nanovirus. The *Dutchman* is equipped to generate the nanovirus, before I took control, this ship's AI had already determined that the *Flower* was infected, so it never activated the nanovirus controller. This ship's crew wasn't aware the nanovirus even exists."

"Interesting, I guess, what is a nanovirus?" What I really wanted to know was why Skippy had gotten so upset about it.

"It's a method of linking atoms by quantum, hmm, damn, I can't tell you monkeys about that. You wouldn't understand it anyway. Think of it as a way to preprogram elements of a Kristang ship so that, when the Thuranin activate the system, the atoms assemble into nanomachines that can take control of the ship. Physical control, not only control through software. Until the nanovirus is activated, there is no way the Kristang, at their pathetic level of technology, could ever know their ship is infected. That's important because there are simple ways of scrambling the nanovirus, to render it inert. Even the Kristang could do that. And the Thuranin wouldn't know the nanovirus on a particular Kristang ship had been scrambled, until they tried to activate it."

"Great. This is important to us, how?"

"Because," Skippy said slowly, "if I'd known about the nanovirus, I could have used it to take control of the *Flower*. We wouldn't have needed to jack me into a wall port. And the nanovirus allows me to take complete control, even parts of a Kristang ship that are hardened against cyber-attack. I'm sorry, Joe, if I had known about the nanovirus, we wouldn't have needed to fight our way through the *Flower* compartment by compartment."

Ah. He was feeling guilty about the people we'd lost. "You didn't know, Skippy."

"I should have! This is an old and relatively simple technology, I should have anticipated the Thuranin would have discovered it, or stolen it, purchased it, along the way."

"You didn't know, you can only work with what you know."

"Still feel bad about it," he grumbled. "What bugs me is I should have scanned the *Flower* after we took control, I would have detected the quantum links. I can't explain why I didn't do that. Joe, this is where my inability to access sections of my memory concerns me."

"Mister Skippy," Desai asked, "does this mean you can remotely control Kristang ships in the future?"

"Yes! Yes, I can, as long as we're close enough. The Thuranin are constantly changing their control codes, and their encryption is pretty good, so I need to bypass the Thuranin control system and activate the nanovirus directly. Short answer: yes, I can do it. Long answer: meh, it depends. I wouldn't want to count on it in a critical combat situation."

I gave an exaggerated shrug. "And, once again, you are filling me with confidence, Skippy."

"Hey, it's better than what we had before. And I'm working on it, the technology the Thuranin are using isn't quite right, it's corrupted from the original. The Elders abandoned this type of crude technology a long, long time ago, I'm having to dig through my memory to figure out how it's supposed to work, and if I can fix it, then I can control it much more easily. Give me some time. Your time, not my super fast time."

"Hey, Colonel Joe? Are you asleep?" Skippy's voice rang out of the speaker in the ceiling of my sleeping compartment.

I bolted upright, and whacked my head on a low-hanging cabinet. Before I tried going to sleep in the tiny bed, I figured that cabinet would be a problem, so I hung two pairs of pants over it as padding. Probably saved me from a concussion. Next night, it was time to try sleeping on the floor, the Thuranin beds were too small. "Damn it, Skippy, you made me crack my head." Rubbing my scalp made it worse. Stop rubbing it made it worse too. "What is it," I asked as I stumbled to my feet, ready to run out the door to the bridge. "That Maxohlx cruiser found us?"

"No! No danger, Joe. Good news, I have good news."

My zPhone said it was 0134 hours, I'd been asleep for less than three hours and my duty shift on the bridge started in another three and a half hours. "There is no good news at this time of night, Skippy." I settled back in the bed as best I could, alternating between rubbing my head and letting it throb painfully. "Can this wait until morning?"

"There is no sunrise on a starship, Joe."

"Oh, for crying out- what is it?" Clearly, he was not going away.

"Among the data I pulled from that command ship is an interesting analysis of the Kristang asteroid base where we're going. The Thuranin have been monitoring it closely for years, they've mapped the gaps and vulnerabilities of the Kristang defenses."

"Oh, that is good news. It's going to be easy?"

"Uh, that would be a no, Joe. This is a tough nut to crack. The Thuranin analysis, and I've confirmed their analysis from the raw data, is that the Kristang have done a very good job of hardening their defenses specifically against the Thuranin. Despite their best efforts at secrecy, the Kristang think it reasonably likely the Thuranin are at least aware there is a research facility in the asteroid, and they have gone to considerable trouble and expense to prevent the Thuranin from swooping in and stealing their goodies."

"Well, crap." Now he'd ruined my sleep. "It's impossible, then?"

"No, I didn't say that. The Thuranin can take the asteroid if they really want to, and the Kristang know it. The point of the Kristang defenses is to make it difficult enough for the Thuranin, that the Thuranin will decide raiding the asteroid isn't worth the cost."

I shook my head in the darkness. "Great alliance the Maxohlx have assembled, everyone has to worry about getting screwed by their allies as much as they worry about the enemy."

"It is a weakness for them, yes."

"Bottom line, Skippy," I asked because of his tendency to ramble on, "is raiding this asteroid worth it to us? You made it sound like we don't have much of a choice."

"You don't have any choice, that I know of. The only reference I can find to an Elder wormhole controller module is at this asteroid. Elder artifacts aren't something you can find on eBay, Joe. We get it from this asteroid base, or you give up on shutting down that wormhole."

He maddeningly hadn't answered my question. "All right, it's worth it to us. I'll ask this slowly so you'll understand," lack of sleep made me cranky, "can we do it? With this ship, and the people and equipment we have onboard? Wait, wait a minute!" That little shithead was likely to misunderstand anyway. "I'll be more specific; do we have a good chance of success?"

"Oh, sure, no problemo, Joe! Even better now that I have more data. The Thuranin have been probing the Kristang defenses around the asteroid, partly to evaluate the Kristang's level of technological development, and partly because the Thuranin are hateful little MFers who love to screw with lesser species. With the Thuranin having done the first part of the job for us, I know how to sneak right up to the front gate, so to speak. The Thuranin got very close, their reports indicate blind spots in the Kristang sensor network. Like I said, this is good news."

"Good news that could have waited until I woke up."

"Sorry about that, Joe. You can go back to dreamland now."

"Yeah, like that's going to happen now. Hey, wait a minute." It had been eleven hours since we'd jumped away from the Thuranin battlegroup. "It took your enormous brain all this time to decode the Thuranin data and analyze it? You said you were so fast that us monkeys couldn't even conceive of it."

"I did have to decrypt over a zettabyte of data," Skippy said defensively, as if I had any idea what a zettabyte was, "from a surprisingly sophisticated encryption scheme, then organize it, decide what to analyze first. Then analyze a lot of conflicting data to make sense of it."

"Oh, sorry, Skippy," I didn't mean to insult him, "I'm sure it was a lot of work even for you."

"Oh, no, it took me only seven minutes. Seemed like forever, though."

"Seven min- you knew all this a couple minutes after we jumped away?"

"Yup."

"Then why the hell did you wake me up in the middle of the freakin' night?"

"I was bored, Joe. And lonely."

And that's all he said. His silence made me stifle the angry remark I had ready. Skippy and I had been in almost continuous contact since he'd sprung me from the closet where the Ruhar has been keeping me, before that, he'd had no contact with anyone for a very long time, perhaps millions of years. He'd been able to listen in on other people's conversations after the Kristang first arrived on Paradise, to alleviate some of his boredom, that may have intensified his loneliness; hearing other people interact, and being excluded. Thinking about that reminded me that I was the first person, the first being, that Skippy had talked to since, whatever had happened to him that caused his isolation. With me sleeping, he'd been like a junkie needing a fix. "Sorry about that, Skippy, you do understand that us monkeys need to sleep, right? There are other people aboard, can you talk to them?" Most of the crew was sleeping, Chang and two pilot trainees were on the bridge, and one person was in the sickbay, although anyone pulling a shift in the sickbay could catch a nap while the wounded were sleeping, or sedated or unconscious or whatever Doctor Skippy the mad scientist thought was best for them.

"They're not comfortable talking with me. Most of them are scared of me."

"I'll talk to them about that, Skippy. In the morning, Ok? I'm scheduled to be on the bridge again in, like, a little over three hours. Can you do a crossword puzzle or something until then?"

"I guess so. You want me to play a lullaby for you?"

A pillow over my head didn't block him out enough. "Good night, Skippy."

When I woke up, and was in a better mood, I asked Skippy about his plan to raid the asteroid. Not a detailed plan, I needed to get Giraud to work on that soon, for now all I wanted was to hear the basic concept from Skippy. "You've had time to review all the data about the asteroid layout and defenses, right? How do we get inside the place?"

"Oh, I have a totally brilliant plan, Colonel Joe. We'll use Thuranin dropships," Skippy explained patiently, "I can get the outer landing bay doors open and fool their sensors. so the Kristang can't shoot at the dropships. After the dropships land, the crew will rush the inner doors, and blow them open."

"Rush the door in a depressurized landing bay? Skippy, none of us will fit into a Thuranin spacesuit. They're too small."

There was a millisecond pause, that, I now knew, was an eternity in AI time. "Well, shit." Skippy finally said.

"*Well, shit*? Seriously? This isn't a joke? You didn't think about us humans needing space suits, in space? Let me define space suit for you; two words, the first is 'space'-"

"I'm not a meatsack! I don't think like you biological trashbags."

"This biological trashbag is going to take a big dump on your lid, and throw you out an airlock."

"That would be a better threat, if I didn't control all of the airlock mechanisms, monkeyboy."

"Airlocks have manual overrides. Ooh, look, monkey has opposable thumbs." I waggled my thumbs at his lid.

"Shut up."

"Well?"

"I'm thinking!" Skippy shouted defensively.

"I can smell the smoke."

"What?"

"The next time you think of telling me how god-like smart you are, just remember 'space suits'."

"Oh, shut up. Never said I was perfect."

"Go back to square one, and rethink your plan," I said as I headed into the tiny bathroom. "I want to discuss it with Giraud this afternoon so he can start fixing your screw-ups. That's in about ten hours, which is a bazillion years in Skippy time, so you'll have plenty of opportunity to come up with idea that don't include humans breathing hard vacuum."

Private Randall approached me in the gym that morning, while I was sweating away with Sergeant Adams' improved equipment, and he reported that Major Simms was satisfied the crew had completed their familiarization drills; that everyone now knew where the airlocks were, how to operate trams and lifts, where their duty stations were, and a whole list of emergency procedures that Chang and Simms insisted on, and Skippy thought were a complete waste of time.

"Joe, this crew trying to learn how to operate this ship is a waste of time. You're like a dog. A dog may know that inside the pantry is a yummy box of treats, but it can stare at that doorknob all day, and it's never going to understand how it works."

"So, we're dogs now?" I winked at Randall. "When did we get a promotion? I thought we were all bacteria to you."

"You have performed better than expected overall, your species is reasonably adaptable. Maybe I can consider you more like a paramecium."

"Wait, a pair a what?" Randall asked.

"Pair-a-mee-cee-um," I pronounced it slowly. "It's a single-cell organism, you probably looked at one through a microscope in high school. They look kind of like a paisley."

That drew a blank stare from Randall. "A paisley?"

"That's uh," I struggled to think how to explain paisley, "those funky swirly patterns on old people's couches, or curtains. Kind of like half a yin-yang symbol?"

"Huh, I didn't know there was a name for those." Randall nodded.

Skippy made a disgusted noise. "I changed my mind again. You idiots *are* bacteria. Who doesn't know what a paisley is?"

"We're soldiers," I explained, "not interior designers, chrome dome."

"Paisley would be a great unit symbol for your merry band of pirates, Joe. I'll get the fabricators to crank out a bunch of them."

True to his word, later that day Skippy did produce patches of a paramecium with a pirate eyepatch and a dagger. Adams brought a sample of patches to me, figuring I'd get a good laugh out of it. I expected that would be the end of it, until some of the crew asked me if they could use the patches on their uniforms. That shouldn't have surprised me, we were pirates, and wearing a paramecium was the crew's way to give the finger to Skippy. That was how our merry band of bloodthirsty pirates ended up wearing paisley.

On my way out of our makeshift gym, I passed Sergeant Adams as she was heading into the gym, a towel slung over one shoulder. "Sergeant, let's discuss your attire."

"I thought we were good to wear T shirts on deck, sir, unless we're going into action?" She asked, pointedly looking at my gray shirt with 'ARMY' across the chest. "I only have three tops aboard, sir."

"You're Ok to wear a T shirt, Adams," I smiled, "but, we're on a starship, heading *boldly* into space where no human has been before, potentially having to land on planets with unimaginable dangers."

"Sir, yes?"

"And you're wearing a red shirt."

"Oh." She blushed as she got the old Star Trek reference. "Yes, sir, I'll be sure to change into a Marine Corps utility uni before we beam down anywhere."

"You do that." I gave her a smile. "Carry on." I was proud of myself that I didn't turn to watch her shapely behind as she walked away. This could be a very long trip.

CHAPTER FIFTEEN RAID

Giraud pinged me, he needed to talk about the plan to raid the asteroid base. I found him, along with Sergeant Thompson, in a cargo bay near the gym. Skippy told me he'd been working with Giraud on an assault plan, and I let Giraud work without unhelpful interference from me.

"Good morning, sir." Sergeant Thompson said in his charming British accent.

"Good morning," I replied, still tasting the sludge I'd had for breakfast. That morning, I'd tried mixing the unsuccessful apple-cinnamon sludge with a chocolate sludge that wasn't too bad, the result was something I was happy to gulp down as quickly as possible so I didn't have to taste it. There was an unspoken competition among the crew to find good flavor combinations, which were then posted on our internal zPhone network. My experiment that morning was going into the 'Fail' column. "Lieutenant, I see you've been busy?"

"Yes, sir." Giraud nodded. When he'd signed up for the mission, I'd gotten the impression that he regarded me as a bit of a lucky fool, someone who had the keys to the future but didn't know how to use them, and needing professional soldiers like Giraud to make the important decisions. He probably still had a less than stellar impression of my tactical planning skills, but there was a grudging respect for the way I'd handled the overall mission so far. My idea to get rid of our Kristang problem, by jumping their starships into a planet, had impressed a lot of people. That, and the fact that the mission had been resoundingly successful so far, and gone exactly as I'd promised. We'd escaped from paradise, captured a Kristang frigate and a Thuranin star carrier, and were now jumping toward a wormhole. Success encourages confidence. I needed to keep the successes coming. "The plan to raid the asteroid requires the element of surprise; we need to move quickly once the dropships are in the landing bay. That means the assault team can't wait for the bay doors to cycle closed and the bay to repressurize, they must exit the dropships and gain access to the base interior before the Kristang can react. To do that, they need space suits."

Giraud gestured to a rack that held two space suits, a small suit that looked lightweight, and a larger suit that was bulky and heavily armored. "This Thuranin suit," he pointed to the small one, "won't fit even our shortest crew member. Skippy told me there is no way to expand the size of these suits, this ship's fabrication facilities don't have the capacity to produce the materials."

"True," Skippy agreed over the speaker in the bulkhead. "Thuranin battlegroups include support ships with full fabrication facilities, individual warships only have limited ability for fabrication."

"That was a serious problem," Giraud continued, "until Sergeant Thompson thought of the spacesuits on our Kristang ship. These suits are armored and powered for combat, motors in the limbs enhance the wearer's movements, so the weight will not be a problem for humans."

The Kristang suit did look cool, I walked up to it and rapped my knuckles on the armor. It was solid. Weapons could be attached to brackets at the wrists, so the wearer only needed to control the trigger. The faceplate was some kind of smoked glass, maybe it wasn't even glass. Ironman, or a mech suit from Halo or a dozen other video game, came to mind when I looked at the suit. "Good thinking, Sergeant. The next question is, are these suits too big?"

"That is a problem." Giraud admitted.

Thompson went around to the back of the Kristang suit, where the back hinged open, and carefully stepped inside it. Giraud helped him suit up, and get the back closed. Status indicators lit up on the wrist displays, and the suit took two careful steps forward, then the faceplate retracted so I could see Thompson's face. "It's not ideal," Thompson said, his words distorted. His face was hidden from the nose down. "My chin hits the bottom of the helmet, I can't open my mouth all the way to speak properly."

"Sergeant Thompson is almost two meters tall," Giraud said.

"That's six feet four to you, Joe," Skippy added helpfully.

"And he is barely able to use the suit effectively," Giraud continued. "The suit can be adjusted, and Skippy says he can fabricate some components for us."

"A limited number of components," Skippy cautioned, "don't get too excited."

"How much of an adjustment?" I stood on my toes to look in the helmet. Thompson did not appear to be comfortable.

"The maximum adjustment, for practical use in combat, is limited to people six feet and taller." Skippy stated.

"I'm six three," I mused, "who else?" Thompson and Giraud were tall, so was Chang.

"Eight people," Giraud ticked off on his fingers, "me, you, Sergeant Thompson, Colonel Chang, Specialist Putri, and Privates Marsden, Darzi and Putri."

"Eight people? Is that enough for a successful raid?" I asked.

"Seven people," Giraud corrected me. "You're not going on the raid, sir. You need to remain aboard the *Dutchman*, and command the operation."

"He's right, Joe," Skippy added. "I'll be here flying the dropships and monitoring sensors, somebody needs to tell me what to do."

Trying to keep the irritation off my face, I said tersely "We'll discuss that later. Are seven people enough to achieve the mission?"

"No." Giraud stated flatly.

"I agree, Joe." Skippy said. "This is where we need your military genius. I could hammer the asteroid open with railguns, and then we search through the debris, but that's too much risk of damaging the items we need."

"Lieutenant," I addressed my remark to Giraud, "you have special forces training and experience. If you think we can't achieve mission success, then I don't have anything to add."

Giraud frowned. "We are, as you Americans say, back to square one."

"We are not giving up. I'm sure you've considered everything. Let's step back, take a break, and approach this again tomorrow with a fresh set of eyes."

Giraud helped Thompson out of the Kristang combat suit, Thompson moved his stiff shoulders, the suit had barely fit him, and the edges of the suit had dug deeply under his arms.

"Sergeant," I asked while examining the Thuranin space suit, "if that Kristang suit is properly adjusted, are you confident you could use it in combat?"

"Yes, sir. When it moves, it's almost effortless. With practice, we can be deadly with these suits. We're fortunate the Kristang weren't able to use these suits when we took the *Flower*."

"Good, good." I was distracted. The Thuranin suit was lightweight, almost flimsy. Even assuming it was made of exotic high-tech material, I couldn't see how it could compete in combat against a Kristang suit. "Skippy, these Thuranin suits are like spandex. Does this material harden into diamond or something like that? Or do they have, like, energy shields like a ship?"

"No, nothing fancy like that. It's a space suit." Skippy replied.

"Huh. How do the Thuranin fight in these things?"

"Fight?" Skippy laughed. "The Thuranin don't typically go into combat themselves. Those little green pinheads aren't going to expose themselves to danger directly. They remotely control military drones, you'd probably call them combat droids or robots or something like that."

"Combat droids? Are there combat droids aboard this ship?"

"Of course, there's three dozen of them in the ship's armory." There was an implied 'duh' in Skippy's voice. "Thirty eight units, to be exact."

"Armory? What armory?" I asked.

"We have combat robots?" Giraud demanded. "This would have been a good thing to know, before I spent days planning an assault!"

"There are combat robots, rifles, rockets, all kinds of toys in the armory, it's located aft of the command section. It's kind of hidden, you have to know where it is."

"Why the hell didn't you tell us about this?" I didn't try to keep the frustration out of my voice.

"Well, Joe, you didn't ask," Skippy grumbled, "and I'm not going to volunteer to tell a bunch of monkeys where they can find dangerous toys to play with."

"*Merde.*" Giraud's face was red. "Colonel, if you ever feel like throwing Skippy out an airlock, let me know, and I will be very happy to take care of it for you."

"What?" Skippy asked innocently. "What did I do?"

I gave Giraud a thumb's up. "Skippy, if you don't already know, I can't explain it to you. These combat robots, are humans capable of controlling them, or is that something the Thuranin do through their cybernetics?"

"The Thuranin use cybernetics, sure, that is one of the most efficient ways to telefactor a remote device, especially in combat where response time is critical. There's no reason we can't hook something up for humans to be the telefactoring agent."

It would have been helpful for me if Skippy bothered to explain unfamiliar technical terms. "To be clear, telefactoring is remote control? With what, joysticks, buttons, that sort of thing?"

"Phhhtttt!" Skippy made a raspberry sound. "As if! No way, dude, that would be way too slow! What, you think this is 1985 and you're playing Super Mario? We'll attach sensors to the operators, so the robots will move as they move. Motion capture, only way better than the technology you monkeys have. Now that I think about it, we'll need goggles also, so the operator can see what the robot sees. That's not as efficient as hooking directly into the optic nerve like the Thuranin do, it should be good enough. And the sensors should include accelerometers, so the operator can get a sense of feedback when the robot encounters resistance."

"Would you kindly unlock the armory, so us grubby monkeys can see these amazing robots?" I put as much sarcasm into my voice as I could.

"Since you asked so nicely, sure." Skippy couldn't resist a dig at us. "Wash your paws first, though, please."

The droids were impressive, although Sergeant Adams quickly coined the term 'combot' for them. According to her, they weren't true androids, as they had only a limited ability to move and react on their own, requiring control by a sentient operator. Once we got three combots out of the armory and into an empty cargo bay, Giraud, Adams and Thompson were able to control them without any special gear, simply by having Skippy watch their movements and instruct the combots to follow. In action, we wouldn't be able to rely on Skippy, he cautioned, the asteroid base was heavily shielded and operators needed to be close to their combot, to reduce the time lag. During the raid, operators had to be aboard the dropships in the landing bay. I wasn't happy about that, we'd be exposing more people to risk, even if the risk to them was less than to the people wearing Kristang powered armor suits. We still needed people in suits on the raid, Skippy didn't trust combots with tasks that required fine motor skills, like selecting, picking up and transporting the fragile, ancient Elder gear he needed. Also, with only combots we'd have all our eggs in one basket; according to the Kristang and Thuranin data Skippy had downloaded, the Kristang had designed their defenses specifically to protect against the Thuranin, and Skippy couldn't guarantee the Kristang didn't have some ability to interfere with the telefactoring connection. The Kristang knew all about Thuranin combots, and would have spent a lot of time and effort figuring out how to beat them.

Giraud's revised plan called for six people wearing Kristang suits, and nine telefactor operators in the dropships. Skippy would remotely fly the dropships, which meant we didn't need to dedicate people as pilots, I wanted at least four people trained to fly Thuranin dropships anyway. Six people needed to have Kristang suits adjusted to fit them, then practice using them in combat simulations. Four people needed training to fly Thuranin dropships, and it had to be minimal training because those same people, along with almost everyone else, had to practice telefactoring combots. For the raid, I reluctantly agreed with Giraud, Chang and Simms that I would remain behind aboard the *Dutchman* along with Skippy, Desai and Private Walorski.

Walorski had been awakened and released from the medical pod by Skippy, after he decided Walorski had healed sufficiently to go through the remainder of the healing regimen on his own. On his own, except that his left forearm, that had been shattered and almost severed during the battle to capture the *Flower*, was encased in a rigid sleeve that was designed for Thuranin legs. It was a bit too large for Walorski's forearm, enough that he kept bumping it on things, causing him pain and causing Doctor Skippy endless frustration. Every time the healing forearm was disturbed, it set back Walorski's recovery ever so slightly. The sleeve contained nanoprobes that were knitting Walorski's bones, nerves and musculature back together, there were vials of fluids that needed to be changed three times a day. Skippy predicted a complete recovery, with the sleeve able to be removed in three weeks, possibly sooner if Walorski cooperated. Certainly a much better prognosis than what we'd feared originally, that of Walorski losing his left arm below the elbow, and very likely dying given the scant medical supplies we'd brought along and lack of a human doctor.

You'd think Walorski would be grateful, and he was, he was also a soldier and he saw everyone else, except for me and Desai, practicing with either Kristang powered armor, or with combots. Walorski protested that he should be given a combot, that he should go along in a dropship on the raid, that he wasn't qualified as a pilot, and didn't want to stay behind while everyone else risked their lives in a battle that was crucial for the survival of humanity. He said this to me, his commanding officer, who would be staying behind while everyone else risked their lives in a battle that was crucial for the survival of humanity. Walorski needed to work on his people skills, that was for certain. Would I have felt the same way, not wanting to be left behind while my fellow soldiers fought the enemy? Hell, yes, I *did* feel that way. The raid on the asteroid would likely determine whether our home planet, our entire species, remained under the boot of the Kristang, might determine if humanity survived in any recognizable fashion. No way in hell did I want to remain behind in relative safety on the *Dutchman*, able to jump away if the ship was threatened. After the battle, whatever happened, I'd forever know that my part in the action had been to sit in a chair. And everyone else would know it too. My attempts, to convince Private Walorski that he was needed aboard the *Dutchman* as a backup pilot, were hindered by the fact that I wasn't entirely convinced myself. He was verging on open insubordination, when Skippy intervened by stating Walorski couldn't be useful as a combot controller without full use of his left hand. Walorski could assist Desai in flying the ship with one hand, or he could sit around doing nothing, but he would only get in the way on the raid. It was a contest who was more unhappy; me or Walorski.

There was one large group of unhappy people aboard the ship: everyone who was training with powered armor or combots in the cargo bay we'd set up for combat drills. They were unhappy because Giraud had made the mistake of assigning Sergeant Adams to the task of converting a cargo bay into a combat simulator, and designing the training program. Neither of those were a problem. The problem was that, as she was in charge of the training, she picked the music that blasted out of speakers in the cargo bay. Loud music was distracting, and it helped to train people to work while distracted and while their ears were assaulted by noise so loud you couldn't think straight. Like what happened in combat. Loud music wasn't the problem, the problem was Adams' atrocious taste in music. When I'm training for some intense physical activity, whether for combat or simply working out in a gym, I want some heart-pounding, fist-pumping tunes. Rock & roll, rap, something with a good beat to it.

What Adams used for a playlist was gospel music, Cajun, jazz, polka and, I kid you not, bluegrass. Blue fucking grass, like, banjos and guys singing through their nose in that whiny affectation that makes me want to break the banjo over the guy's head. I'm not a big bluegrass fan, in case you were wondering. Country, yes, bluegrass, no. And none of the songs were good examples of their genre, Adams had definitely dug way down to find the kind of crap songs artists use to pad their albums when they run out of ideas, or talent, or both. Oh, and she'd play the same awful song over and over and over and over. Try concentrating with that blasting your ears.

It turns out, Adams is an evil genius. If you like the music you're listening to, you can get into a rhythm and it's not distracting. If the music is like fingernails on a chalkboard to your ears, you're going to devote part of your thinking capacity to daydreams about the best way to kill the person who picked the playlist, and you're going to be distracted, and the whole point of the training is for you to learn how to concentrate and ignore distractions. It was effective.

The music still sucked, effective or not. The first time I watched an exercise, as soon as it was over, I went old, old school and put on some Coolio. That got me a relieved thumbs up from the crew, it was the best morale-booster since the crew had watched our unwanted Kristang ships disappear in an antimatter fireball within the gas giant. Score one for me.

After watching the crew drill with powered armor or combots, I was impressed, and beginning to have hope we could pull off the raid successfully. Our six mech soldiers, in their Kristang armored suits, were fast, and could carry the heavy Kristang rifles easily. The asteroid's gravity was only two percent of Earth normal, so for training, Skippy reduced gravity in the training cargo bay to two percent. Two percent meant people in suits, and combots, needed some way other than gravity to avoid floating off the floor in the research base. The combots automatically gripped floors, walls, ceilings, whatever they needed to in order to move where the operator wanted them to go, they had gripper pads on the feet, knees, hands, elbows, anywhere it might be useful. The Kristang suits had grippers on the bottoms of their boots and palms of their gloves, of course, but also at the elbows, shoulders, back of the helmet, knees and on the suit's butt. Our suited soldiers needed to learn how turn on and off, and adjust the force of, the grippers.

Overall, we were not concerned about the ability of the combots to maneuver as required. The powered armor suits took a lot of practice to get used to. The problem the suited soldiers had in the combat training maze Adams had set up, was not getting around corners and through doors, it was dialing down their speed and power. They were moving too fast and bouncing off walls. Three suits got busted in training, we had six spares aboard the *Flower*, and spare parts, what we didn't have were many humans over six feet tall. I advised Giraud to slow down and take it easy, we couldn't afford for anyone to get injured during training. People wearing the suits were sore enough without crashing into things, even at the maximum limits of adjustment, the suits were too big. We put padding in the boots to lift up people's feet, it helped somewhat. I tried on a suit, and, at six feet three, I felt it digging into my knees, my crotch, under my arms and I had to stretch my neck to avoid banging my chin on the bottom of the helmet.

The Kristang suits were impressive. The Thuranin combots were awesome. There were two types of combots, we used the smaller one exclusively, as Skippy said the larger heavy model might not fit through passageways in the asteroid base. The smaller combot had three legs for stability, and three arms. Two arms were for stability or climbing, the arm in the center was for weapon attachments, and Skippy had fabricated goggles that allowed our operators to both see through the combot's optical sensors, and also control the guns. The guns pointed wherever the operator looked, with crosshairs in the goggles for aiming. Skippy's original plan was for the operator to control the weapon triggers by blinking, Giraud had squashed that idiotic plan by pointing out that most human blinking was involuntary. At Giraud's suggestion, the trigger was controlled by the operator's index finger, either left or right depending on the person. Selection of weapon; the rifle or the rocket/grenade launcher, was controlled by the operator's thumb. We couldn't use live ammo aboard the *Dutchman*, that was a problem since doing that would be best for the operators to get a real sense of their weapon's effectiveness. Skippy warned that, even inside the asteroid base where there was little concern about tearing a hole in the asteroid's thick skin and causing an atmospheric containment breach, we should use the rockets and grenades sparingly on our way in. On our way back, to provide cover, we could blast anything we saw. The plan was to blow up the entire asteroid anyway, to erase any trace that humans had ever been there.

The actual raid went perfectly according to Skippy and Giraud's plan. At first. And then it all went to shit.

Before we made the jump into the star system that contained the asteroid base, the entire crew other than Desai and Walorski assembled in the dropship bay. It was time for one last equipment check, to make absolutely sure that everything the raiding party needed was loaded aboard the two dropships, and everything was working properly. An extra combot was loaded aboard each dropship, making the already snug interior even more cramped. The Thuranin may have built high ceilings into their star carriers to accommodate guests, they hadn't done that with their dropships. The dropships were so cramped that the six people who would be wearing Kristang armor, needed to get into the armor before boarding the dropships, despite the extra time they'd have to spend in the uncomfortable suits.

After supervising the inspection, Giraud gave a short but effective speech, much better than anything I would have said. He didn't use any fiery language, or try to inspire people, they didn't need inspiration. He simply stated that we would only get one chance at this raid, one chance to free Earth from the Kristang. No matter what the cost, we were not leaving the asteroid without the wormhole controller module. Everyone had studied the mockup Skippy had fabricated, the module was a long, skinny box about four feet long, and six inches on each side, Skippy said it folded out and expanded to make an 'X' ten feet across. Anyone who saw a module would pick it up, if they were wearing a Kristang suit, or signal a suit wearer and wait if they were operating a combot. We couldn't risk damage to the module by attempting to pick up the module with a combot, even our most gentle operators routinely crushed things with the combot's immense strength. Without cybernetics, the operator lacked enough feedback to avoid crushing objects in the combot's grasping claws. Combots would lead the way through the base, with our six suit wearers in the rear.

Giraud told me he would have liked another two weeks of combat practice, he didn't say that to the crew. Skippy was anxious to hit the asteroid base as soon as possible, with the fluid military situation in the sector, he was concerned the Kristang would reinforce their asteroid research base, or worse, pack up anything of value and take it away, disperse the stuff across the stars. We couldn't take that risk, so I decided we'd jump into battle as soon as possible.

Before we launched the raid, Chang and Giraud had a conversation with me. They wanted me to assure them that, if that raid looked like it was going to fail, and humanity's involvement was at risk of being exposed, I would not hesitate to blow the asteroid and jump away. If we couldn't recover the *Flower*, I'd need to vaporize that ship also, it was dusted with human DNA. Chang and Giraud made me promise, because they knew I'd be going against every instinct I had as a soldier, that I wouldn't hesitate to abandon the raiders and escape. Live, to fight another day. Despite what Giraud told the crew about the raid being our only chance, humanity still had some chance, as long as Skippy was safe and on our side. If the raid failed, the *Dutchman* could try to pick up new crew members at Paradise or Earth, and continue to search for a wormhole controller module, I didn't see how that would work, but it was not completely impossible.

I promised. It made me feel like shit, but I did it. I owed it to our crew. They were willing to risk their lives on this crazy mission, I needed to understand the mission was worth their lives, however the mission ended.

Walorski had no idea how much I didn't want to remain aboard the *Dutchman* while our crew, *my* crew, went on the raid.

We jumped in close to the asteroid, within two million miles. The jump in and subsequent maneuvers were preprogrammed by Skippy because the timing was so tight, all Desai did was press a button on my command. A split second after we jumped in, the *Flower* was ejected, performed a microjump, and the *Dutchman* did a short-range jump in the opposite direction. The *Flower* formed a jump point for another microjump, then the field collapsed as planned, and the *Flower* tumbled, dead in space. The effect, according to Skippy's logic, was for the immediate area to be flooded with overlapping jump field waves, masking the presence of a second ship. The *Flower* tumbled out of control, thrusters firing randomly, with the ship leaking radiation. We wanted the *Flower* to attract attention, while the *Dutchman* zipped away unseen. Skippy had the *Flower* broadcasting the IFF codes of a frigate that had disappeared in the area two years before, during a skirmish with another Kristang clan, our hope was the Kristang would be confused and curious enough not to immediately blast the *Flower* to pieces. The more the Kristang investigated the *Flower*, the less they'd be likely to notice the *Dutchman*.

It worked. By the time the Kristang directed their sensors to widen their scanning radius, Skippy was in their network and directing the system to ignore the huge Thuranin star carrier sneaking up to their front door. We tripped the stealth detection grids as we passed through their field lines, and the sensors identified us, the Kristang computers simply ignored those inputs. Desai parked the *Dutchman* behind an asteroid two thousand miles away from the target, and Skippy launched the dropships.

When Skippy first told us we would be raiding an asteroid, the picture I had in my mind was a jagged, irregular chunk of rock, like asteroids in space movies. This asteroid was technically a planetoid, it was almost three hundred miles in diameter, big enough that its gravity had shaped it into a sphere. Still, it was a pockmarked, ugly gray and brown, frozen and desolate pile of rock. On one side was the research base, on the other, a much larger Kristang military base. A large military base, with a thousand soldiers, assault dropships, gunships, and enough missiles to blow the *Flying Dutchman* to pieces. Hanging around somewhere in the area was a squadron of frigates, six destroyers and a cruiser. And we were going to bust in, take what we wanted, and get away cleanly.

Skippy was true to his word, the military base was interested in the *Flower*, and had tasked a pair of frigates and four dropships to investigate our decoy. The military base had sent a message to the research base to go on high alert, the research base never received that message because Skippy intercepted it, but Skippy replied for them so the military base thought everything had been locked down. We had nearly complete surprise when the dropships approached the docking bay doors. The docking bay controller thought the doors were opening for a pair of Kristang dropships sent to reinforce security, and that's what Skippy told the base computers to display. Our dropships landed, and deployed combots with our six soldiers in powered armor suits. Everything would have gone perfectly except that there was a Kristang maintenance technician, in a space suit, working on the mechanism just inside the doors. He saw with his own eyes that our dropships were Thuranin, no way Skippy could hack his optic nerve, and this dedicated worker did his duty, and shouted a warning on the radio. A warning that got buried by Skippy. When no one responded, the eager-beaver Kristang ran across the bay and pulled a lever that triggered a hardwired alarm. The only way for Skippy to kill a hardwired alarm was to burn out the hardline electric circuit, which he did with a power surge after the alarm rang out twice. And he instructed the computer to announce the alarm was false, that it had been triggered by the power surge.

That would have bought us another two minutes, enough time for the raiding party to place explosive charges on the inner door and blow it in a controlled fashion. It would have, except the model citizen Kristang knew something was extra wrong when the alarm only sounded twice, and he sprinted toward a weapons locker. That drew the attention of the raiding party, who gave our Kristang Employee Of The Year his reward, not in the form of cash or a prime parking space, but by concentrated fire from a half dozen combots. And that's when the trouble started, when the Kristang disappeared in a cloud of bloody vapor. The explosive rounds our keyed-up pirates selected for their combots went right through the Kristang, and hammered into the wall of the docking bay. The Kristang in the research base didn't need any electronic means to notify them that something was majorly wrong, they could feel the vibration of the explosive rounds through the floors and walls.

At that point, Giraud ordered the combots to clear a lane, and he wasted the inner door with a rocket, he had the warhead selected for shape charge. The door exploded inward, this was less than optimal because part of the door was still hanging in jagged pieces attached to the frame. This is where our lack of experience hurt us, Giraud should have dialed the rocket warhead for a wider blast instead of maximum penetration, the door was tough but not armored. At that point, blasting the wall on either side of the door to clear a path would have sent debris flying all over, so we wasted time having a pair of combots rip the doorway clear with their grappler claws. One of the combots was a bit too enthusiastic and used too much force, a big chunk of door and frame came flying across the docking bay in the low gravity and narrowly missed knocking out a combot. The human operator of the combot couldn't react in time, the combot's automatic systems made it duck out of the way, allowing the chunk of door to hit Chang on his left side. The impact sent Chang flying across the bay, ruptured his pressure suit, and cracked several ribs. We later learned two of his ribs were broken. I'd fallen off a dirt bike once and cracked a rib, the pain had me crawling on my knees trying to catch my breath, except that breathing made the pain even worse. It took me an hour of sitting or laying on the ground before I was able to get back on the dirtbike and very slowly ride back home, where my parents took me to the hospital. Chang's Kristang suit lining had a gel that hardened on exposure to vacuum, it sealed the hole to prevent his air from leaking out. Somehow, even though it must have been incredibly painful, Chang got back to his feet and back into action on adrenaline and pure guts. The guy was spitting up blood, and that didn't stop him. Skippy was showing data from the medical monitors in Chang's suit, it looked bad, I don't know how Chang wasn't curled up in a ball on the deck, and I wanted to tell him to pull back to a dropship and let the raiding party continue the mission. I didn't do that. I needed to trust that if Chang couldn't continue, he'd tell me. And Giraud was there with Chang, if Giraud thought Chang was combat ineffective, Giraud would signal me privately. We needed Chang, we needed everyone, as long as he wasn't a liability to the mission, I wasn't going to interfere from ten thousand miles away. The motors in his powered armor, and the low gravity may have helped take part of the strain from Chang, we'd need to see how he handled combat.

With the inner door clear, the raiding party surged down the corridor, combots in front, then the six people in suits, followed by two combots as rear guard. They quickly ran into another door, which they spent the extra thirty seconds on to blow properly with explosives. After that, they were in the main part of the research base, and Skippy could open and close doors for them.

Right away, we encountered a problem. Skippy by that time had infiltrated the base computer and searched the archives, archives that he said were an incredibly crappy mishmash of unindexed, uncatalogued, random garbage. Regardless of his difficulties, he located the two items we wanted to steal; a wormhole controller module, and a sort of communications node that was associated with the Collective. The two items were stored in different compartments, fortunately neither item was considered a priority by the Kristang researchers, and they were both in low-security areas, away from the main research facilities. I had to make a decision quick whether to go after the items one after the other, or split the raiding party. Dividing a force goes against the principles of war that the Army had taught me, as I was thinking about it, the words of the US Army Field Manual popped into my head. Dividing a force, in a situation where we were already outnumbered and outgunned, violated the military principles of Mass and Economy of Force. No matter, the possibility of having to divide the raiding party has been discussed in advance, with Chang, Giraud, Simms and I in agreement. In this case, concentration of force was secondary to the principle of Surprise. Our raiding party could only succeed, could only hope to survive, if they got in and got out as fast as possible, before the Kristang could recover from their own surprise, figure out what the hell was going on, and concentrate their own forces against us. The longer the raiding party was in the base, the longer they were exposed to danger. I gave the order for Chang to take one group to get the comm node, and for Giraud to get the wormhole controller module. Unspoken in that order is that I felt Chang, being injured, was the weaker of the two, and I wanted the wormhole controller module a lot more than I wanted a fancy radio for Skippy to talk to ancient AIs. For a moment, I considered keeping a pair of combots at the point where the parties split, to guard a path for their retreat, until Skippy showed me a schematic of the base, there were a lot of corridor intersections the parties would need to transit, guarding only one was a waste of firepower.

From there, the raid proceeded fast and chaotically, according to plan for the most part. The Kristang were seriously off balance, their internal systems had been hardened in anticipation of attack by rival Kristang clans or Thuranin, they had not anticipated Skippy thoroughly infiltrating their systems. What systems he didn't have control of, he weakened, confused, shorted out or cut power to. The Kristang frantically called the military base on the other side of the asteroid, messages that Skippy intercepted, and Skippy sent back fake messages that the military base was under heavy attack and would send reinforcements when they could. Some extra quick thinking Kristang, no doubt runner up for Employee Of The Year, fired off a rocket flare that was supposed to signal the military base that something was seriously wrong, the flare made a grand firework when it cleared the horizon, and I had a moment of panic. Skippy calmed me down by assuring that although the Kristang sensor network saw the flare signal, he instructed the sensors to ignore it. The military base was buried deep beneath the rock, unless some Kristang was on the surface for some reason, no one would see the flare, and since Skippy was squelching radio traffic, a Kristang would need to be on the surface, see the flare, know what it meant, run back to the military base and knock on the door. I figured that was low risk.

Skippy prevented more flare rockets from firing, by igniting the whole remaining canister of them without opening the silo door. The resulting explosion may have put a damper on the prospects of Employee Of The Year Runner-up ever getting a shiny plaque to put on his desk, since the explosion wiped out a pretty serious chunk of the base and likely killed him. Personally, I was Ok with that.

The combots were having success, it helped that the Kristang security force had, according to their established protocol, retreated to protect the high security research center of the base, the most obvious target, they didn't realize that we were going after a different part of the base. Skippy reported the Kristang were thoroughly confused, panicked, in disarray, unable to understand what was happening, and why their carefully hardened systems weren't working or, were working against them. Power surges had burned out the door controls, lifts, lights, and life support in the parts of the base we didn't care about, many of the Kristang were isolated, trapped, slow to react and leaderless. The little resistance the raiding party encountered on their way in were lone individuals, or small groups of two or three, uncoordinated, ineffective. The Kristang's ineffectual efforts against us actually helped our combot operators gain experience with live fire, they learned real quick to use quick bursts, with the rounds dialed to minimal explosive force and on fragmentation setting. The high-explosive rock and roll the operators used against the first pair of Kristang tore the enemy apart, it also wasted ammunition and blasted the corridor, creating debris the raiding party had to maneuver around. Giraud was rightly pissed, he'd warned people not to go crazy with the advanced Thuranin weapons. They paid attention after that first encounter.

Chang's team reached their objective first, only to find a disorganized room full of junk. Not junk stacked on shelves, helpfully labeled, not even junk stuffed into boxes. This was junk in piles, like the Kristang had opened, the door, tossed stuff in, and closed the door.

"Oh, shit." Skippy groaned. "I didn't anticipate this. The database shows the communications node was last logged as being in that room, there are no sensors in the room, not even a camera."

"Any magic you can perform?" I asked anxiously.

"Doing the best I can," Skippy said defensively. "For secrecy, there are not a lot of sensors inside the research base, except for the access points and living quarters. Also, the base was specifically designed to make remote surveillance difficult. I'm mostly blind in there, not nearly as blind as the Kristang expect, more than I'm comfortable with. There are a significant number of Kristang security personnel that I have lost track of, I don't know where they are or what they're doing. There are also areas of the base the raiding party has shown on cameras that aren't in the schematics I have access to, I'm collating data to develop a true layout of the base. My earnest suggestion is the raiding party move as quickly as possible."

Wow, what a great idea, I hadn't thought of that. That's what ran through my mind, not what I said to Skippy. "Colonel Chang," I said through the zPhone, "you'll have to dig through that pile to find the comm node. You know what the thing looks like." Every member of the raiding party had seen the models Skippy fabricated of the two items we needed to steal.

"Yes, acknowledged." Chang said, his voice was strained, there was a rattle in his throat.

On the displays, I could see Chang, Darzi and Asok Putri walk into the room and begin sorting through the pile. Chang was moving very stiffly, because of his injury he didn't get down on the floor, he started with the top of the pile. He kept them organized, keeping items they'd sorted through in one pile so they didn't lose track. It was efficient, focused, as fast as possible and way, way too slow. Chang's group was way behind schedule, it was a large room, with five piles of junk extending to the ceiling and after five minutes, they'd only sorted halfway through one pile. Giraud's team had reached their target, he had the luck that day, as the room with the wormhole controller module was as organized as Chang's target was disorganized. Giraud, Sergeant Thompson and Private Marsden raced down the aisles, showing the contents of the shelves to Skippy, who quickly deciphered the indexing system and directed Sergeant Thompson exactly to where the wormhole controller module was, sitting on a shelf.

"Target acquired," Giraud reported. "Heading back now. Advise, should we proceed directly back to the docking bay, or help Colonel Chang's team?"

Chang's team was taking way too long. Crap, they expected me to make this call; send Giraud's team to speed up the search for the comm node, in hope of speeding up the search? Diverting Giraud's team risked exposing them to danger longer, that risked us losing the wormhole controller module. Did I consider bailing on trying to find Skippy's comm node, now that we had the wormhole controller module? Not really. I'd thought about that issue over the last week, it had kept me awake at night. We cared about shutting down the wormhole, it was all I cared about, it was the entire purpose of the mission, I would sacrifice anything to achieve it. We humans truly did not care whether Skippy I cared a little bit, because I liked Skippy and felt we owe him, and I sometimes thought I understood his terrible, ancient, aching loneliness. My personal feelings had to be put aside, as the commander I needed to focus on the mission and my people. What I'd decided ahead of time was that, regardless of my promise to Skippy, if there was any way we could shut down the wormhole without Skippy, I was not going to risk people's lives, and the mission, to get his magical radio. We had no way to shut down the wormhole on our own, making my decision easy, if hard to swallow.

"Lieutenant Giraud, take your team to assist Colonel Chang, we need to move as fast as possible."

Whatever Giraud thought of the wisdom of my decision, he didn't argue. "Acknowledged. We're on our way."

On the display, I saw Chang, Putri and Darzi were sorting through the piles of junk as fast as they could, Chang had ordered a combot into the room, not to touch anything, but to use its cameras, hoping Skippy could find the thing. It was all taking way too long. Skippy telling me he'd lost track of the Kristang, that even he was mostly blind, had me extremely anxious "Skippy, this comm node thing is for communications, right?"

"Yeah, duh, so?"

"So, can you contact it, use it to send out a signal that you can use to find the damned thing?"

"Shit. Yes."

"Duh." I couldn't resist, partly from nervous energy.

"Damn it, I don't know what is wrong with me sometimes. Of course, yes. Have Chang, Putri and Darzi spread out so I can use their suit radios to triangulate."

I did. Less than a minute later, Skippy found it, in the pile of junk way in the back. Chang had Darzi and Putri climb over the pile in between and toss useless crap out of the way, until they had uncovered the top third of the pile, then they proceeded more carefully. Darzi found the stupid thing, it looked exactly as Skippy said. On the display, I saw that Giraud's team was close to Chang's location, close enough that I judged it best for them to link up and support each other on the retreat, even though that meant having all our eggs in one basket.

That's when things went to shit in a hurry.

The first sign of trouble was not a warning from Skippy, it was not the combots encountering Kristang fighters in front of them. It was a hail of bullets hitting Giraud and Putri from behind, knocking them both down. Putri took several hits dead center and was killed instantly, the explosive-tipped rounds fortunately missed the wormhole controller module that was in a sling on his back. Giraud went down with a glancing hit to the side of his helmet, a hard blow to his lower back, and a round that hit his left arm and severed his forearm halfway between wrist and elbow. Darzi reacted exactly as he should have, as he was trained to do, he dropped to the deck, clearing the way for the combots to engage. Darzi crawled forward keeping low, and tore the straps off Putri's sling, Darzi saw Putri was beyond help and he correctly focused on keeping to the mission objective.

Our combots swiveled to engage the six enemy soldiers who were wearing heavy armor, it was a vicious firefight and Darzi couldn't do anything to help, he had to keep his head down and shelter the vital module behind Giraud's unmoving form. On the display I could see Giraud was alive, unconscious and not bleeding seriously.

"Skippy," I shouted frantically, "is there another way back to the docking bay?" Four of the Kristang were still alive and taking cover in doorways and side corridors, they had the combots fully engaged. Darzi, with the module, couldn't move without exposing the precious module. Chang's team was running to assist, they couldn't arrive for another two minutes, maybe less. Too long.

"Yes, plenty of alternate routes exist."

"Great. Combot operators, don't worry about damaging the corridor, we'll be taking another route back! Take out those Kristang, maximum force!"

That was all the combot operators needed to hear, three of them dialed their rockets up to maximum yield, shape charge, and blew the hell out of the corridor beyond Darzi and Giraud. Rockets penetrated two or three compartments deep, destroying the four Kristang, blasting walls, floors and collapsing the ceiling.

"Darzi!" I shouted when my voice should have remained calm. "Get up, Lieutenant Giraud is alive. Can you carry Giraud?"

"Yes, sir." Darzi could easily carry Giraud in the low gravity, especially in his powered armor. He got the module slung over his back, tied the straps quickly, and picked up Giraud's unconscious body. The combots led the way, I warned them as Chang's team approached so the two groups didn't shoot at each other. They linked up and Skippy guided them on an alternate, roundabout route back to the docking bay, this time Chang had a pair of combots covering the rear to avoid nasty surprises. The convoluted route had me concerned about the additional time it took, Skippy assured me the path the raiding party was taking had the enemy confused and guessing where to go. Skippy still was mostly blind in there. This was the most dangerous point of the mission, before the enemy had to guess the raiding party's objectives, now the enemy knew where the raiding party was going; back to the docking bay. The party was two thirds of the way back, by Skippy's reckoning, when trouble struck. This time the enemy appeared not in armor, but with combots of their own, they blew a wall open and leapt into the corridor. The Kristang combots were heavy and clunky and slow compared to our Thuranin models, they made good targets. They were also controlled by much more experienced operators, and they had every advantage. Except one. As the firefight raged and the raiding party was pinned down momentarily, Skippy shouted excitedly that the clumsy movements of our combots was actually helping us, the Kristang had trained to fight the super-fast movements of Thuranin-controlled combots, and the slow awkward actions of our combots threw the Kristang's aim off.

We lost three combots in the initial firefight, another was damaged and unable to use its primary weapons. Chang saw Darzi was hampered by carrying Giraud, he ordered Darzi to set Giraud down in the arms of the damaged combot. Private Marsden came forward to help Darzi get Giraud strapped in, they were almost done when Marsden took a hit to the head that shattered his faceplate, then a second round almost separated the helmet from his neck. He went down in a spray of flash-frozen blood, and on my display his life signs went flat-line. I notified Chang not to waste time assisting Marsden, he didn't bother to acknowledge, I heard and saw him urging people forward. There may have been other paths to the docking bay, and we have lost people moving forward into the firefight, Chang knew we'd likely lose even more people is they got pinned down and remained on the asteroid for a second longer than necessary. Speed and maneuver were all important.

Chang saw that, even through the painful fog of broken ribs. The guy was an ironman, even without his powered armor suit.

Behind a wall of firepower, the raiding party moved forward, combots clearing path. Once past that large group of Kristang combots, they hit scattered resistance from Kristang combots and armored suits. I was getting worried, we'd started with six people in suits and nine combots, by the time they'd fought their way back to the docking bay, there were two people dead, one injured and unconscious, and only three combots still functional. The three combots remained to guard the inner doorway while Chang got Sergeant Thompson and Darzi aboard one dropship, and carried Giraud aboard the other. Skippy had already partly retracted the outer door, and as soon as Thompson and Darzi were strapped in, he put pedal to the metal and surged that dropship out and away, I saw on the display he had the dropship pushing six gees and I ordered him to throttle down slightly, once the dropship was ten miles away.

Chang's dropship had a slight delay while he got Giraud strapped in, and that delay almost killed us. Thompson had the node and Darzi had the module, technically we'd accomplished the mission already, except for the people in the second dropship. And that's when a stray round came through the inner doorway, missed our combots, flew across the docking bay and hit the armored hull of the Thuranin dropship. The explosive tip erupted inward, creating a superheated jet of plasma that burned through the armor to the interior of the dropship. Once the plasma hit air, it exploded in all directions. US Air Force Staff Sergeant Joy Chung, who was operating one of the three remaining combots, was killed instantly, and three others were seriously injured. Chang and Giraud were protected by their armored suits, everyone else was hit pretty badly. With people screaming in pain, blood flying around the dropship and air racing out the hole in the hull, Chang didn't hesitate. He ordered Skippy to get them the hell out of there. The dropship shot out of the docking bay and clear of the doors, as Skippy took over the automated repairs systems to plug the finger-sized hole and get the air pumped back up.

"Clear. Both dropships clear," Skippy reported in a matter-of-fact voice. "No pursuit. Packages secure. I'm guiding the dropships back here."

"Great." I said, emotionally exhausted. "Pilot, I'll be in our docking bay."

"No, sir." Desai said flatly. "Colonel Chang and Major Simms can handle people who need help. We need you here."

She was right, and I knew it. I could be emotional later. Later, after we'd jumped away safely. "Captain Desai, you're right." I looked down at my shaking hands in disgust. I hadn't been in danger at any time. It was a long eight minutes to wait for the dropships to return.

"Dropships secured. Pilot, initiate jump, option Alpha." Skippy announced.

"Belay that," I ordered, and Desai turned to me in confusion. "Jump option Charlie, now. Go."

Desai pressed the correct button, and the ship performed a microjump so we now were in clear space, not shielded by an asteroid. Skippy had programmed five jump options into the jump navigation system and I'd memorized them, they were also listed on the command chair display and on my iPad. Option Alpha was for a jump close to the *Flower* so we could recover that ship, the plan was to jump close to the *Flower*, send a signal for that ship to perform a short range jump, match the jump with the *Dutchman*, take the *Flower* onto a docking platform, and then jump to the outer edge of the star system. Option Charlie was a microjump away from the asteroid we were hiding behind, in case our position had been discovered, but we needed to remain in the area to recover dropships.

"Can I ask why we're not going after the *Flower*?" Skippy asked.

"We will. Signal the *Flower* to jump to the rendezvous point." Even with the signal crawling along at the speed of light, it would reach our pirated Kristang frigate in a few minutes, and that apparently derelict ship would suddenly come to life and power up engines for a short range jump.

"Done." Skippy reported. "Colonel Joe, why are we still here?"

"You have control of the nuke near their main docking bay?"

"Yes, of course. I told you that." The Kristang had rigged the research section of the asteroid research base to self-destruct with a nuke; if anyone invaded the base and the Kristang lost control, they could blow up the base with a single explosion. The nuke was there so enemies would decide raiding the research base wasn't worth the cost. It certainly would have deterred us, except that Skippy took control of it shortly before we launched the dropships.

"How big is it?"

"I assume you mean explosive yield; that weapon is roughly eight megatons. A typical W76 warhead, in your American Trident submarine-launched missiles, is one hundred kilotons, by comparison."

"Light it up."

"What?" Skippy, Desai and Walorski said the same thing at the same time.

"Skippy, do not argue with me. I know you wiped their computer memory, but we left behind DNA in there, human blood. It could tell the Kristang that humans were involved in the raid. I can't risk that. Light it up. Right now."

To his credit, Skippy knew when not to argue. "Weapon enabled on The Big Red Button."

I pressed the button. The asteroid flared an intense light. Desai jumped us away before the debris hit us.

CHAPTER SIXTEEN   HOME

The flight recorder video of the asteroid being nuked was popular with the crew. The surviving crew. It wasn't my idea for people to watch the video, I hadn't even mentioned it. Desai or Walorski must have said something, or someone asked Skippy what happened, and he volunteered to show them. Watching the utter destruction of the asteroid research base was cathartic for the crew, as it had been for me. Army doctors tell us that talking about traumatic events helps with the symptoms of PTSD; keeping things bottled up inside yourself, or trying not to remember what happened to you, makes it worse. Skippy told me the survivors asked him if there was video of the raid, from cameras on the combots and Kristang suits. There was video, and I told him to release it to anyone who wanted to watch. Giraud and I would watch all the video and sensor feed data, to learn lessons on what we did right and what we did wrong.

Giraud subtly chided me for being unprofessional, blowing up the entire asteroid had not been necessary to the mission, I'd done it because I was angry, because I wanted the lizards to feel the pain we felt, at losing so many people. So many humans. Maybe I'd done it out of frustration and guilt that I'd not gone on the raid. Whatever. Psychology isn't my area of expertise.

The raid was both a success and a failure. In terms of lives lost, it was a failure, I'd now lost over half our original crew, and some of the wounded were going to take months to recover, even with incredible Thuranin medical technology. In terms of Skippy finding a way to locate the Collective, it was a failure; the thing we'd brought back was exactly what Skippy had asked for, it wasn't damaged, it wasn't inert, Skippy was able to power it up and read data from it, the thing simply didn't tell him anything useful. He didn't know whether the fault was with the device, or within himself, he had a bad feeling that somehow he was blocked from memories that would allow him to access data about the Elders. About himself. And about where he came from, who he was. He didn't tell anyone else about his doubts and fears, only me. For my part, I kept his secret, and worried on my own that someday Skippy would lock up, or blue screen, or go dormant, or whatever happened with ancient AIs.

Skippy had better not lock up on us before we got back to the wormhole near Earth, because in one way, our mission was a success. Maybe in the only way that mattered, our mission was a huge success. Success enough that, even only one person survived to fly the ship, the raid was worth the terrible cost. We had stolen an intact Elder wormhole controller module, Skippy verified it was fully functional, able to live up to its name and control a wormhole. Including, most importantly, shutting down a wormhole. We humans had no idea how the damned thing worked, we had to rely on Skippy for that. The point was, because of the raid, we had the ability to shut down that wormhole. We had the ability to deny the Kristang access to Earth. The billions of humans there would consider any price our pirate crew paid to be worth the cost.

Relying on Skippy was a problem, he was frustrated and expected us to continue the mission with the remaining crew. That was a conversation I didn't want to have with the crew listening, I pushed Skippy off until Major Simms could take the captain's chair, Chang and Giraud were both in the sickbay. After taking the *Flower* back aboard, we'd jumped three times, until Skippy was satisfied we were safely out of the Kristang sensor network's range. The jump engines were almost exhausted, incapable of more than an emergency microjump, we were hanging in deep interstellar space, waiting for the jump engines to fully recharge.

"You comfy now, Joe?" Skippy began as tactfully as he always was. "We need to talk about our next move. There are two more possibilities that I can see for contacting the Collective. One is only three thousand lightyears away, unfortunately getting there requires a roundabout wormhole route, and it's the less likely of the two options. Also, that one is on a Thuranin planet, it's going to be tricky getting in and out. The second one is nine thousand lightyears away, out of Thuranin territory, and that's both good and bad, the species that holds that territory are the-"

Damn it. My boots weren't even untied yet. It was best for me to just say what was on my mind. "Skippy, before we continue searching for the Collective, we're going to Earth to resupply. We don't have enough people to keep going with the mission right now. You're a genius, do the math."

There was an ever-so-slight hesitation, that wouldn't have been noticeable if I didn't know Skippy so well. Did he actually run the math? Of course he did, a billion permutations. Maybe a zillion. "You're in a bitchy mood, Joe."

"I'm tired. A lot of people died today, Skippy." I kicked my boots off, would have kicked them across the compartment if the bulkhead wasn't only two feet away. "Sentient beings. Don't give me any shit about how we're just monkeys and bacteria, we're sentient. We matter."

"More than you know, Joe. As you requested, I ran the math. Problem is, I'm not a military strategist, and there are a lot of variables I can't quantify. You promised me we would find the Collective, together."

"Skippy," I laid back on the mattress as best I could. "I keep my promises. Explain how we have a reasonable chance for success, with the crew we have now, and I'll listen. I don't see it. We have nine people right now who are combat ready, two pilots and I need to stay aboard the *Dutchman*, that leaves six people for action, and two of them specialize in logistics, not infantry. That asteroid was the softest target of our options, right?"

"Mostly likely, yes, the Kristang didn't realize what they had, that's why the items we needed were so lightly guarded."

"Lightly guarded?"

"Comparatively speaking."

"*That* was your definition of lightly guarded? You had total control of their sensors and most of their weapons, we still ran into a firefight. Even our super high-tech combots got slaughtered. Will either of the two other targets be easier to crack?"

"Admittedly, no."

"You're concerned that you can't trust us, that once we get to Earth, we'll never leave, that will be the end of the mission. You think you can't trust us. Put that aside for a minute. Forget about what I said. Your goal is to contact the Collective. Use your god-like processing power. What are the odds you can achieve your goal with the resources we have?"

Another ever-so-short hesitation, maybe longer this time? "Damn it. You're right. I was, perhaps, overconfident, before the raid. Now that I have more extensive data, my analysis is revised. Our current chance of mission success is less than fifty percent. To be accurate, it is twelve percent. That is an unacceptable level of risk."

I was so relieved, I let my head slump back, and banged the back of my skull on the edge of a cabinet. "Crap."

"Crap, like you can't believe my numbers, or crap like, you believe my numbers, and they're worse than you thought?"

"Crap, like I banged my head on this stupid cabinet again."

"Oh. Darn it, no matter how I calibrate my program for reading your voice patterns and expressions, I still get it wrong. You biologicals are maddening sometimes."

"Yeah, like when biologicals develop technology and build smart-ass artificial intelligences."

"I told you, I wasn't built by- oh, forget it."

Out of long habit, I pulled the laces of my boots open, and set them facing away from me next to the door. In an emergency, I could jam my feet in and lace them up real quick, no wasted time. Army training again. "We agree, then, we're going to back to Earth, right?" There were humans, and human supplies on Paradise, and Paradise was closer. There was also likely a substantial contingent of Ruhar ships in orbit, Ruhar soldiers on the ground, and a Jeraptha battlegroup lurking at the edges of the system. Paradise was not a place I wanted to go back to.

"We agree, darn it. Ahh, I've been waiting a million years to contact the Collective, a short delay isn't a big deal, I guess." His voice sounded anything but convinced of that. "Ugh. This means we're going to visit that monkey-infested mudball you call home."

"Home sweet home, Skippy. Let's get this out of the way, so we're not arguing about it later. How can we make it so you can trust that we won't stay, once we get to Earth? By 'we', I don't mean me, I'm keeping my promise to you." It wasn't an academic question, I was worried about it myself. Having a Thuranin star carrier and a Kristang frigate in orbit was going to be very tempting to governments on Earth, tempting them to keep us there. And they would make very valid arguments for keeping our two starships in orbit; to examine their technology, to protect Earth in case any Kristang straggler ships were hanging around, and because sending our ships back out to roam the galaxy, until Skippy found a Collective that may or may not, exist was pure idiocy. It wasn't that I wanted to go back out wandering the stars with Skippy, I very much did not. What I wanted was for life to go back to normal, for me to take off the silly silver eagles, to go back to being a grunt, to finish my term of enlistment, go home, and live a normal human life. And little girls want Santa to bring them a pony for Christmas. We both needed to accept reality. There was no 'normal' life any more for humanity, certainly not for me. If Skippy, or I, couldn't think of a way to force Earth governments to authorize sending the *Flying Dutchman* back out, there wasn't a snowball's chance in hell that I could keep my promise.

"Oh, that. No problemo, Joe. After we go through that last wormhole that leads to Earth, I'll temporarily disrupt its connection to the network. That will disable the wormhole until it resets, which will take long enough for us to get to Earth, load up on volunteers and supplies, and get back to the wormhole."

"Huh. That's a great idea, Skippy." Why hadn't I thought of that? Skippy had told me he could temporarily disrupt a wormhole on his own, the controller module was needed to shut one down permanently. "We'll be on a strict time limit, then?"

"Strict, yes. Once I disrupt that wormhole, the Thuranin will be *very* interested to learn what the hell happened. As soon as the wormhole resets, there are going to be ships coming through. Since the Thuranin are suspicious, paranoid little green MFers, I can guarantee some of their ships will be visiting Earth, and they won't be there to use their Starbucks gift cards. The Thuranin have an established protocol for investigating a new wormhole connection; they send a heavy force of battleships through, with cruiser escorts. We do not want to tangle with a Thuranin battlewagon, one of those ships could pound the *Dutchman* into subatomic particles, and even I could only slow them down." Skippy had mentioned several times that, for all its apparent power, a star carrier was not primarily a warship, it was a long-range transport for warships. In a fight, star carriers ran away and let their escorts fight.

"That is perfect, Skippy. Please plot a new jump course to Earth." We'd be on Earth only long enough for a cup of coffee, or in my preference, a cheeseburger. I could taste that cheeseburger already. The ancient Elder AI had surprised me again, I'd been ready for a long and heated argument about whether we continued searching for the Collective, or resupply at Earth. Skippy didn't respond to arguments, he did respond to facts and logic. "Hey," my finger poised above the button to turn off the light, "out of curiosity, what did you calculate as the odds of the raid we just did succeeding?"

"Originally, thirty seven point six percent. Then, after the crew demonstrated proficiency with combots, and Captain Giraud developed his assault plan, I calculated the odds at fifty one point one percent."

"Barely fifty percent? You didn't think this was worth mentioning?!"

"*Above* fifty percent. Above is above. You didn't ask. And your records indicate math is not your strongest competency."

Arguing about the past wasn't productive. "The jump engines will be fully charged in two and half hours, right? Wake me in two hours."

"Unbelievable. I'm the most advanced sentience in the galaxy, and you're using me as an alarm clock."

"Two hours, Skippy. Good night."

The crew was relieved, and thrilled, to hear we'd be stopping at Earth before continuing the mission. At least, they were happy about it for a couple days. Then, on one of my duty shifts, Simms waved to get my attention, I nodded and gestured for her to come onto the bridge. There wasn't anything important going on at the time, we were a lightyear away from a very unimportant red dwarf star, three lightyears from the nearest wormhole, waiting while the jump engines recharged. "Colonel," Major Simms said, "now that we're on our way to shut down the wormhole, there's some second guessing among the crew."

"What?" Desai exclaimed from the pilot seat, and Walorski also turned in his seat.

I had the same reaction. "Major, the whole point of this mission is to cut off the lizard's access to Earth."

"Yes, sir, that's not the problem. People are concerned that the Expeditionary Force on Paradise will be cut off from ever returning to Earth, they won't receive shipments of food or medical supplies after the wormhole is shut down. We'll be abandoning them. Permanently." Her hands balled up into fists, displaying her anxiety. "That doesn't set well with the crew. Or with me. Sir."

This was a conversation I knew was coming, and wasn't looking forward to. It had been hanging in the back of my mind ever since Skippy first mentioned the idea of shutting down the wormhole. Before I could fashion a reply, Skippy spoke up. "Not to worry, Major Tammy. Your Expeditionary Force has been abandoned already, and there's nothing we can do about it, so we're not responsible. I have intercepted messages that the Thuranin have told the White Wind clan they won't support further attempts to recapture Paradise, the planet isn't worth the effort and the Thuranin forces are being kept busy elsewhere in the sector. The Kristang stopped bringing supplies from Earth even before the Ruhar retook the planet. The Kristang won't make any effort to evacuate humans from Paradise, and the Ruhar don't have access to Earth, or the transport capacity in this sector. They're on their own."

He'd pissed me off again. "Damn it, Skippy, you don't have to sound so cheery about it!"

"Facts aren't cheery or gloomy, Colonel Joe," Skippy had a defensive tone in his voice, which surprised me. "They're just facts. The fact is, whether we shut down the wormhole or not, UNEF is stuck on Paradise for the foreseeable future. The Ruhar are providing food supplements until your crops can be harvested. I think."

"Skippy, you are not helping. Major, I have not been ignoring UNEF, I haven't wanted to talk about it, because Skippy is a thousand percent right on this. We can't do anything to help UNEF. We can help the billions of humans on Earth. And if anyone has the bright idea that we should trade Skippy to the Ruhar, in exchange for the hamsters transporting UNEF back to Earth, forget about it."

Skippy was cheery to hear that. "Thank you, Joe, I appreciate-"

"Skippy's programming will make him go inert in the presence of interstellar capable species, so if we give him to the hamsters, we lose the capability to shut down wormholes. Or anything else."

"Oh." Skippy genuinely sounded surprised. "That hurt, Colonel Joe, for a moment there I thought you were expressing some tiny bit of loyalty to me."

I sighed before I could stop myself. "Skippy, you've made it clear, every time you can, that you're a powerful super being and we're bacteria to you. This isn't a friendship between you and me, this is an alliance between species, or cultures, or whatever it is. We're useful to you, and you're useful to us. When I make a deal with you, I am absolutely going to uphold my end of the bargain. I don't know if you consider any deal made with bacteria to be worth keeping on your part."

"Huh."

"Yeah, huh." I caught a warning look from Simms out of the corner of my eye, she probably was concerned about me risking Skippy getting pissed off. She didn't know that little shithead like I did.

"Fair enough, Colonel Joe. You don't know this, since you are, after all, bacteria, but I am actually a hundred percent reliable when I make a promise. We can work on that." He still sounded hurt. I wondered what portion of his capacity was devoted to an emotion-emulating subroutine. It was almost convincing.

"Are we done, Major?" I asked Simms. "There isn't anything we can do to help the Expeditionary Force on Paradise. UNEF came out here to protect Earth; that mission got all screwed up because the lizards lied to us, but we can protect Earth. That is our mission. If there ever is a way to reestablish contact with UNEF, I'm all for that, but it's beyond our capability."

Simms nodded with a grimace. "You want me to talk to the crew?"

That would be taking the coward's way out. "No, I'll handle it."

I was more tactful when I spoke to the crew later that day; explained the situation, listened sympathetically, said that I also had friends on Paradise. What I did not do was pull rank and state that I'm the commander and we're doing what I think is best. Mostly, I listened, and let people talk. Everyone understood there wasn't anything practical we could do for the humans on Paradise, and what was really bothering people was guilt. Guilt that we would, hopefully, be going home, to whatever Earthly comforts were still there. Home to friends and family, and cheeseburgers. While UNEF would be left to hope the Ruhar decided to divert enough resources from their war effort to keep them alive. Even if the Ruhar felt like feeding their former enemies, the technologically backward humans, the Kristang could harass Ruhar shipping enough to disrupt supplies getting to Paradise, and the Ruhar might not be able to provide for UNEF.

In the end, I reminded our not-so-merry band of pirates that we would be coming home to an unknown situation, that we didn't know how many Kristang and ships were on the Earth side of the wormhole, that Earth might no longer be the blue and green haven we remembered, that we might have to fight our way through numerically superior enemy forces. And that, when the Kristang on the Earth end of the wormhole realized they had no way home because we'd shut down the wormhole, they may be tempted to forget The Rules and use banned weapons against the human population. Eyes narrowed and jaws set when people considered that. "Our mission isn't over when we shut down the wormhole behind us. That's when it begins."

"Colonel," Private Putri asked. The American Putri, not the Indian one. "What's the plan if there is a substantial force of Kristang ships at Earth?"

"Then we fight. It's no good shutting down the wormhole if the lizards at Earth can destroy our home. We fight, however we can, until the lizards are no longer a threat to Earth. The *Dutchman* isn't a battleship, but we do have weapons, and superior jumping ability. If the lizards want to fight, we pound the shit out of them. We fight until the lizards are destroyed, or until our last breath. That's my plan."

A couple hours later, I was taking my shoes off in my tiny sleeping quarters, when Skippy spoke through the speaker in the ceiling.

"Colonel Joe, we need to talk."

"Oh," I groaned, "don't we talk enough? Can this wait?"

"Emphatically no. We are close to transiting the wormhole to Earth, I need you to understand something before I program the jump drive."

Uh oh. His tone touched off my Spidey senses. This was going to be trouble. What hadn't the shiny little shithead told me this time? Swinging my legs back onto the floor, I rubbed my face to spark semi-alertness. "You have my attention. What is it?"

"That was a rousing speech you gave, about fighting the Kristang with everything you have, to your last breath."

"You're keeping me awake to compliment me on my speech?"

"No, truthfully, as a speech, it was third rate at best. Totally derivative. You're talking about the potential of going into humanity's first space battle, and the best you can do is lame clichés? You could at least have thrown in some warmed-over quotes from Patton, or something."

"For Christ's sake, Sk- "

"My point is, you may intend to fight with everything you have, but one thing you won't have to fight with is this ship. I need the *Dutchman* to contact the Collective. I won't allow it to be put at risk. And since I need a human, a live human crew to fly it for me, I won't allow you to send everyone away to fight. Especially if it is likely that you would lose."

Shit. I gritted my teeth to answer. "What do you mean, you won't allow?"

"If you want to do something stupid that will put the *Dutchman* at risk, or deprive me of a crew, I won't cooperate in running the ship. That means I won't program jumps, or load courses into the autopilot, or prepare and target weapons. Captain Desai has only learned to minimally maneuver this ship in normal space, and I can lock out those controls also. By going through the wormhole and then shutting it down behind us, I'm taking a risk that you might decide not to help me find the Collective after we resupply at Earth. We have a bargain, Joe, I expect you to keep it."

"Fuck."

"Such a multi-purpose word, Joe."

"I meant it as, fuck, yes, I remember our bargain. I will absolutely keep my end of it. You have any genius thoughts on how we're to resupply, if the Kristang have a major task force of ships in earth orbit?"

"That scenario is unlikely, given the price the Thuranin have been charging the White Wind clan for shipping to and from Earth. I expect the Kristang have garrisoned only a minimal force on Earth, their technological advantage is so overwhelming they would not need many troops to hold your backwards planet. Thuranin communications that I have intercepted indicate they have major fleet elements setting up for a battle around a wormhole cluster at the other edge of this sector. Their attention is focused elsewhere."

"The point is, Skippy, we have no idea what we'll find when we get to Earth. If we discover the lizards are terrorizing our home planet, you can't expect this crew to run away and wander the galaxy with you. We need another option."

"I'm open to suggestions, Joe. You're the soldier."

How was I supposed to come up with a space battle strategy, with a tired brain, and no experience or training in space combat? Or ship to ship combat of any type? Oh, yeah, because I wore silver eagles, that's why. "All right, how about the *Flower*? You don't need that ship, right? Are you Ok with me sending part of the crew away on the *Flower*, to fight the Kristang? I promise you, Skippy, I promise you I won't leave you here. I will remain aboard the *Dutchman*."

"The *Flower* is somewhat useful, as having a Kristang ship attached, particularly a battle-damaged Kristang ship, is an effective ruse. But it is not essential. Ok, you can detach the *Flower*, I'll even program a jump for you. I don't know what good you expect your untrained crew to do, with a ship they don't know who to fly."

"Then I need to get them started on training, pronto." We needed a strategy also. Or, not? I considered what Giraud said about flexible battle plans, and it made total sense. We couldn't make plans until we had intel. Any intel. "How about this, Skippy? Can we jump the *Dutchman* in close enough to see what forces the Kristang have around Earth, but far enough away to be safe? Then we can either detach the *Flower*, or, if you agree the risk is minimal, we jump the *Dutchman* into orbit."

"Hmmm. Sounds suspiciously weasel-wordish. *Minimal* risk is not the same as *no* risk. Oh, what the hell, why not? I'm bored already. Just for you, Joe, I'll agree to this: we can jump directly into orbit and scope out the situation from there, and we jump right out again if I judge the risk to be too great. Not that I don't trust you or your crew, but I will program the autopilot on a timer to jump us right back out unless I cancel the command."

"Deal." I hastily agreed before Skippy could change his mind. Any risk too great for Skippy would mean it's best for us to retreat and consider our options anyway. Maybe we could lob a couple railgun rounds at the Kristang just before we left, as a wake-up call. Having a Thuranin star carrier jump into Earth orbit and blast a couple Kristang ships without warning would certainly throw the Kristang into panicked confusion.

"For your education in tactics of space combat, if the Kristang are at Earth in force, it's better to jump right into orbit than to jump in a couple AUs out. Even I can't conceal the gamma ray burst when we emerge from a jump, we'd have to wait there and run long-range sensor scans, and the Kristang at Earth would be alerted to our arrival. Jumping right into their laps will allow us to catch them off guard, and maybe pump a couple missiles up their asses before they can react. Then we can jump away, if we need to."

"Space combat sounds complicated." I thought back to when I'd listened to the Chicken pilot talk about air combat after our first war game, on Camp Alpha.

"Uh huh. Then there's the Skippy factor."

Part of me wanted to avoid taking the bait. "The Skippy factor?"

"You know, my incredible awesomeness."

"Oh, sure."

"Not convinced? Specifically, I am referring to my ability to remotely take control of Kristang systems, using the Thuranin nanovirus embedded in their systems. To do that, I need to be within about a lightsecond of the enemy ship."

"A lightsecond? That's, uh-" Light travels, uh, hmm, I was trying to picture myself in a classroom-

"Let me put you out of your misery before you sprain your brain, monkey boy. A light second is roughly the distance from the Earth to your moon."

"Oh." I thought a moment. "I thought ships shouldn't jump in that close to a planet?"

"Most ships can't, the gravity well of a planet distorts the jump field at entry to make jump navigation unpredictable, and the field distortion can damage jump engines, even tear a ship apart. A ship with me controlling the jump engines compensates for the field distortion. Thus, the Skippy factor."

"Impressive." I had to admit.

"What? No snarky joke?"

"No, you may be an arrogant asshole, but your awesomeness is legit."

"It ain't bragging if it's true."

"Yeah, I heard that before. Hey, is that why you jumped us in so close to that gas giant planet?"

There was an ever so short hesitation. "That may have been too close. I hadn't finished tuning up this ship's crappy jump engines. Won't happen again. Hey, uh, good talk. You need to get some shut-eye, we can talk more later, huh?"

I laid back down on the bed, trying to conceal a smile. The monkey had made the AI uncomfortable. I needed to remember that.

The transition through the final wormhole was uneventful, any fears I had about us running into an outbound Thuranin ship were for nothing. Skippy couldn't detect any ships in the area. With the wormhole safely behind us, Skippy disrupted the wormhole's connection to the network, and it blinked out. Helpfully, Skippy had loaded a new app on my zPhone, on the home screen of all our zPhones, it was simple clock. A clock counting down until the wormhole reset. We all got the message, loud and clear.

In my quarters, I was attempting to attach sergeant stripes to one of my uniform tops, Skippy had fabricated the chevrons for me. Once we reached Earth, my theater rank of colonel would be voided, and I'd revert back to my regular Army rank of sergeant. Part of me, a big part of me, feared what the Army brass would think about me ever wearing silver eagles, and all the things I'd completely screwed up, or the questionable decisions I'd made. As soon as Earth was on the display, those silver war eagles were going into a box, and I wasn't going to make a big deal about it. Chang, who had been released from sickbay now that his broken ribs had healed enough, agreed he would take command when we reached Earth, with the exception that I was still captain of the ship. In my opinion, Chang wasn't comfortable dealing with Skippy yet. It didn't matter much anyway, once we made contact with the authorities on Earth, command authority of our pirate crew would be from the surface. Assuming we didn't have to fight our way through a fleet of Kristang warships. I was nervous about that.

There was another thing I was nervous about, I waited until I could talk to Skippy in private. Taking a break from running sprints down the *Dutchman's* spine was a good place. "Listen, oh great and powerful Oz, I'm really sorry that I ever called you Skippy. I feel like an idiot now, I didn't know how powerful you are, and I meant no disrespect. The government is going to shit if they hear I named you Skippy, so what else should I call you? Lord God Almighty is still out, in case you were thinking of that."

"I'm good with Skippy. I like it."

"You sure?" I couldn't tell if he was joking.

"Yes. Skippy is a nickname, right?"

"I think so." I didn't know of anyone whose given name was Skippy.

"And nicknames can be either a term of derision, which, face it, isn't possible with you lower lifeforms talking about me."

"Of course not." I rolled my eyes.

"I saw that! Or a nickname can be an indication of acceptance, of belonging, of being one of the cool kids."

Cool kids? A million-year-old, unbelievably powerful being, wanted to be one of the 'cool kids'? "Sure, let's go with that."

"People calling me Skippy will constantly remind you monkeys that I am *not* anything like any Skippy who ever lived on your miserable dirtball of a planet, and that will point out your total unimportance compared to me, far better than any name intended for respect. And really, do you truly think you knuckle draggers are actually capable of giving me the respect I deserve? The name Skippy is appropriate; it was a defensive reaction by you, to something far beyond your understanding."

"It was an *offensive* reaction, to the fact that you're an asshole!"

"Or that. Whatever."

Before we made the final jump into our home solar system, I ordered a stand down to make sure everyone was well rested, and all our systems and gear were shipshape and ready to rock and roll. Especially I was concerned about the *Dutchman's* weapons, comparatively weak though they were.

Chang was up and about faster than I expected, even with Thuranin miracle treatments, the guy had broken ribs and a partially punctured lung. He came into the CIC while I was in the big chair and Simms was in the CIC. "Colonel Chang, should you be out of sickbay," I asked. Skippy hadn't said anything about him releasing Chang from treatment.

Chang lifted his shirt, there was a hard black plastic something wrapped around his ribs. "I am being treated, Skippy said walking around would help the tissues to adjust as they healed."

"All right, as long as you don't think you're going back on duty. You take it easy for a couple days, agreed?"

Chang winced, still in pain when he moved. "Agreed. Colonel, I hear it was your idea to use our suit radios to triangulate the position of the communications node. That was excellent thinking, it may have saved us all. If we had to sort through all that trash by ourselves, we would have been trapped."

Getting admiration from Chang felt great, it was also misplaced. Unfortunately, I needed to explain what really happened. "Thank you, it wasn't anything brilliant, it was obvious. All I did was ask whether the comm node could transmit, it seemed like it should if its purpose is, you know, communications. Skippy is incredibly smart, he's also absent-minded and doesn't think of things that we would consider obvious. Like how he didn't tell us about the combots until I asked him how the Thuranin fought. Always keep that in mind when you're dealing with Skippy, he simply doesn't think on our level."

We jumped into Earth orbit, Skippy reported there were only two Kristang ships there, a frigate and a troop transport that was also their command ship. I adjusted the display to zoom in close on the big Kristang troop ship, so it filled one of the view screens. It was a damned big ship, although I kept forgetting how very much larger the *Dutchman* was. The *Dutchman* could carry dozens of those Kristang ships across lightyears.

"I'll need to establish a connection to the nanovirus on the Kristang command ship, crack their multi-level encryption, take control of their computers, and lock them out."

"How long will that take?"

"I did it between me saying 'establish' and 'connection'."

"Nobody likes a show-off, Skippy."

"I can go slower, if you like, but I'd probably get bored, and lose track of what I was supposed to be doing after a couple pico seconds."

"We can't have that. What assets do they have on and around Earth?"

"Just those two ships, the troop carrier over there that is their command ship, and a frigate in a polar orbit, currently over Sumatra on the other side of the planet. The troop carrier has twenty four assault dropships of various types, of which three are aboard now, one is in orbit on approach, and the others are scattered across the planet. The frigate also has two small dropships aboard. There are Thuranin defensive installations atop the space elevators. And, the Kristang have a constellation of seventeen maser satellites in orbit, for ground strikes."

"Ok," I let out a long breath. "We're safe enough to stay here? Cancel the jump out?"

"Affirmative, I have cancelled the jump away countdown. We got lucky, both ships are within my range of control, although the frigate's orbit will move it beyond my range in ten minutes. At the moment, the Kristang are startled by a Thuranin ship, a star carrier, appearing in the sky without notice. I'm confusing them with garbled communications from the *Dutchman*, that won't stall them for long. Both Kristang ships are preparing to jump away on short notice. They don't realize that I control their computers."

"You said there are satellites? Like what kind of satellite?"

"Each satellite is fifty eight meters long, powered by a fusion reactor which can generate eight hundred twenty megawatts of maser power."

"Is that a lot?"

"Your American nuclear aircraft carriers typically generate around two hundred megawatts, from fission reactors."

"Holy shit." I had thought satellites would be wimpy things. My idea of a satellite was a box with solar panels that allowed me to watch football games.

"Oh, *very* naughty! Two of the satellites are preparing to fire on a city called Mumbai, there is a large protest there against the Kristang. Colonel," I could tell from the tone of voice that Skippy was being serious for a moment, "those satellites, and the frigate, have been busy suppressing attempted rebellions all over the planet. Human casualties are estimated in the millions. The frigate has caused extensive damage to major cities with railgun strikes."

I pounded my fist down on the Big Red Button in anger, not thinking what I was doing. "How many Kristang are down there?"

"One thousand, four hundred and twenty three Kristang, mostly in seven compounds. Twelve of their dropships are currently in the air."

I leaned forward tensely, looking at the display, not realizing my right fist was resting on the Big Red Button. "We need to keep that troop ship, but that damned frigate I'd like to jump into the Sun. Can you retarget those satellites to hit the Kristang compounds, and their dropships?"

There were bright flares across the planet, and I could see the troop ship shudder, as it looked like lizard bodies were blown out airlocks. The troops ship also blossomed a salvo of missiles, which curved down toward the planet and slammed forward, rapidly becoming burning streaks through the atmosphere.

"Done." Skippy announced. "Kristang population is now seven hundred twenty one. Ah! Missiles impacting, and, ok, population is one hundred seventy two. Wait. Ha! Got those buggers!" There was another bright flare from a satellite. "Satellite went over the horizon, I had to defract the maser beam. One hundred sixty four."

"*What*?"

"You told the system to fire."

"I didn't-" right then, I realized my hand was resting on the button. "Shit! Skippy, I asked if you could do it, I didn't tell you to actually do it!"

"Oops."

"*Oops*? Skippy, that is one big fucking oops."

"You didn't want me to jump that frigate into the core of the local star, either? Because I can't undo that one. In a couple million years, the atoms of that frigate will emerge up into the photosphere, but that Humpty Dumpty can't be put together again."

"We need to work on our communication."

"Noted."

I shifted my attention back to the troop carrier. "What happened over there?"

"That ship was absolutely infested with lizards, ugh, disgusting. I had to fumigate it with explosive decompression. There are four still alive over there, stubborn damned things." Skippy sounded frustrated. He could probably kill those four lizards, but that could require him to damage the ship that I wanted to keep intact.

I involuntarily shuddered, thinking of Skippy's immense power, and how badly things could go wrong if I failed to pay attention again. I needed to put a cover on that Big Red Button, so I would have to flip up the cover, the next time I wanted to use it. "You have complete control? The lizards can't hurt any humans right now?"

"Right now, I imagine they are too busy pissing in their pants to think about doing anything else. I also took the liberty of shutting down the Kristang projects to modify your best agricultural land for their use. And I fried all their computer systems. Whatever they're going to do, they'll be doing it without much electronics."

"Great, thank you." I rubbed my face and closed my eyes for a moment. Over two thousand lizards, snuffed out in a moment, with their own weapons. When I looked up, Simms' eyes were as big as saucers.

"Did that really happen?" Simms asked, astonished.

I nodded, and pointed to the view of the troop ship, now surrounded by a cloud of flash-frozen lizard bodies. "And over a thousand Kristang dead, on the planet." For some reason, up here, it felt more natural to say 'the planet' than 'Earth'. It had been a while since I'd seen the place, anyway.

People nodded at me through the glass. "That's a good start," Major Simms observed. I agreed.

Perhaps decent, ordinary people would be horrified by such death and destruction. Speaking for our merry band of pirates, we had no sympathy for the lizards. If what we'd heard about the situation on Earth, what the lizards had been doing to people and the biosphere was true, then the lizards' whole species could go screw itself.

"Skippy, can you contact the United States government? I need to talk to someone in authority."

"Certainly. One moment. Go ahead."

"Hello?" A female voice I vaguely recognized came out of the speakers. "Who is this?" She sounded surprised.

"Uh, who is this?"

"*You* called me. Where did you get this number?" The voice demanded.

And I remembered with shock where I'd heard that voice before. I'd never heard that voice so haggard, so worn down with despair.

"Skippy," I said in a harsh whisper, "what the hell did you do?"

"You wanted to talk to the American government, so I dialed your president's personal encrypted cell phone."

I shook my fist at his shiny cylinder. We seriously needed to work on our communication. "Uh, ma'am, Madame President, this is colonel, I mean, sergeant, Joe Bishop, US Army, formerly with the 10th infantry division. We've captured a Kristang troop ship, and a frigate, and a Thuranin star carrier. We're now in orbit, and we just killed all but one hundred sixty four-"

"Plus the four on the troop ship." Skippy chided.

"-all but one hundred sixty *eight* Kristang on or around Earth, and we have control of their remaining ship, and their satellites."

There was a long pause, with voices talking in the background. "Quiet! Mister Bishop, is it? My military aide is telling me there were satellite strikes around the planet, but all against Kristang installations. I thought the Thuranin were patrons of the Kristang? Kindly tell me what is going on." She sounded shaken.

I let out a long breath. "It is a very long story, ma'am. The important facts are that the Kristang no longer have control of Earth, and there won't be any Kristang reinforcements coming, because we shut down the local wormhole. "

"Hey! Don't forget about me!" Skippy spoke up. "I'm the hero of this story, you're only the plucky sidekick who provides comic relief."

"Who is that speaking?" The president asked.

Oh, what the hell. I was tired. "Ma'am, that is a chrome plated beer can named Skippy." I paused to consider that was certainly the first time anyone had ever said *that* to an American president. "He's a several million years old artificial intelligence, who makes the Thuranin look like not so clever pond slime by comparison."

"Pthththth." Skippy made a raspberry noise. "Please, they're not even that smart."

It was the president's turn to let out a long breath into the phone. "I'm getting a headache again."

"Like I said, ma'am, it's a long story. We need to talk."

"Also, we need pizza!" Skippy added. "Not for me, but our merry band of pirates here needs pizza. And cold brewskis! Party on, dudes!"

"Merry band of pirates?" The president asked.
I was getting a headache, too.

After the President handed me off to an aide to discuss details, and we agreed on terms for bringing our pirate crew home, I checked the main display again. "Skippy, are we safe? Are there any Kristang or Thuranin ships heading our way?" I still couldn't interpret the displays. The displays looked empty, except for the Kristang troop ship and the *Dutchman*. And the moon, I guessed was the big blob on the display.

"Not according to the databanks on their command ship over there. The next Thuranin carrier was scheduled to come though the wormhole in ten days. That won't happen now. But it's possible there are ships out there, that their command didn't think the Kristang here needed to know about."

"Colonel Chang, Major Simms?" I saluted both. Now that we were home, my theater rank was annulled, and I had reverted back to my regular Army rank of sergeant. They both knew that. For me, I couldn't decide whether to be disappointed or relieved. "Someone needs to go down to Earth and brief our leadership. Skippy, can you fly a dropship remotely? We'll need to bring people down to Beijing, Dehli, London and DC, and none of us know how to fly a Kristang or Thuranin shuttle. Our Dodo is busted."

"And Paris." Giraud reminded me.

"And Paris." I'd forgotten about Giraud, our only French pirate. "And we need to be extra careful with the wounded." Everyone who had been wounded in capturing the *Flower* and raiding the asteroid base were now out of sickbay and on their feet, some of them with Thuranin portable medical devices still attached. Walorski's forearm was due to be released from the healing sleeve in a week. Chang's ribs were technically healed, Skippy said the bones had knitted together, although Chang told me it still hurt like hell when he took a deep breath. To me, it was a miracle of Thuranin medical technology, or a miracle from Skippy, that everyone who had been injured would be making a full recovery.

"I can fly multiple dropships remotely," Skippy responded as if it were the easiest thing in the universe, "no need for people to fly all over the planet in one ship. But after the ships land and people get out, I'm locking the doors. Can't have you monkeys, you know, monkeying with them."

"Understood. Other than me, is there anyone else we should leave aboard?" I looked around at our soon to disperse merry band of pirates.

"Why are you remaining aboard?" Chang asked before Skippy could.

"Sir, if a Kristang ship jumps into orbit, Skippy and I need to be here to defend Earth." I pointed to the Big Red Button.

"No we don't. I want to see Earth, and not only from orbit!" Skippy insisted. "I can control this ship from anywhere down there."

Simms spoke up. "The fire control button is here on this ship, sir." It took me a moment to realize she had addressed the 'sir' to Skippy, rather than me.

"Oh, screw that!" Skippy scoffed. "Colonel Joe, I just loaded a Big Red Button app on your zPhone. Press that anywhere on Earth, and we're weapons free."

I pulled my phone out of my pocket. "I'm a sergeant again now, not a colonel. And I don't see it."

Skippy sighed. "Is it called a smart phone because it's smarter than the user? It's on the last screen of apps, between your two versions of solitaire, and that birds game you never play anymore."

"I've been kind of busy." I saw the app, titled Big Red Button. It was hard to miss. "Shouldn't this app be on the first screen?"

"Joe, Joe, Joe. We don't want you butt dialing the weapons, and accidentally destroying, oh, say, Canada."

"Shit!" I held the zPhone away from me. "That could happen?"

"Unlikely, since I program the weapons, you only press the button to authorize their use. However, we've had communications problems, as you say, so...."

"Sergeant Bishop, I would feel more comfortable if you, and, uh," Simms struggled to think of a way to avoid saying Skippy's name, "Mister Skippy, came with me, to brief our leadership. Including the president, who you already know, apparently?" She didn't look happy about that.

Chang leaned toward Simms. "I do not agree that the device," he pointed at Skippy, "should be the de facto property of America. As the ranking UNEF officer- "

"You're not *my* ranking officer, Changy-boy. Colonel Joe is still the captain of this pirate crew." Skippy said, with a distinctly unfriendly tone. "And calling me 'the device' is not the way to get on my good side. Before you say something else stupid, I'm not the property of anyone, and I'll probably be asked to visit China while I'm here, so your scientists will have plenty of opportunity to ask me the same dumbass questions the Americans are going to ask me. Now, apologize to me and Colonel Joe, or your dropship may end up in the Gobi Desert, by mistake."

"No apology needed, sir." I hastened to say. Chang, was, after all, a real lieutenant colonel, and a good guy. Damn. Closing the wormhole and beating the Kristang may have been the easy part.

Chang bowed slightly. "I do apologize, Mister Skippy, no offense was intended. My intention was to ensure the rights of China are properly considered."

Skippy sighed again. This was getting to be a habit. "Believe me, I have no interest in helping one group of monkeys down there gain an advantage over the others. You can whack each other with sticks all you want when I'm not around. If you have more brains than an amoeba, you may want to focus your energy on repairing the damage the Kristang did to your planet. I'm just sayin'."

"Sir?" Sergeant Adams addressed her question to Chang. "Can we contact our families?"

Skippy spoke privately into my earpiece. "Colonel Joe, your family is safe and sound, but that's not true of the families and friends of the entire crew. I'd be careful about comms for now. I just told the same thing to Chang. Except I also told him that his father's brother was killed by the Kristang."

Through the glass, I saw Chang touch his earpiece, nod, frown, then look at me. He addressed the whole crew. "We don't know the situation down there yet, and now that we're back, we fall under the authority of our home governments. They will likely want to maintain operational security for the immediate future. I'm sure we will all be briefed after we land."

My brief fantasy of dramatically landing a Thuranin dropship on the White House lawn were quickly dashed, as the White House, and much of DC, had been damaged in Kristang 'anti-traitor actions'. The US Federal government headquarters was now located in Colorado Springs, on the site of what used to be the Air Force Academy, behind heavy fortifications. Skippy was all for blowing over the academy at hypersonic speed, utilizing the full stealth capabilities of a Thuranin dropship, then curving around and landing wherever the hell he felt like, to let the American government know right from the start how powerless they were. I pointed out that I was enlisted in the US Army, and had taken an oath to protect and defend the constitution of the United States, and therefore the legally elected government of the nation technically had authority over me, so the request by the president that we follow the US Air Force's designated flight path was, in effect, an order I was bound to obey. That was a long and convoluted conversation, which revealed more about Skippy than it did about me or the United States. Skippy begrudgingly programmed the autopilot for a totally unnecessarily shallow entry profile, dropping into the atmosphere over the Marshall Islands of the Pacific, and accepting an 'escort' by a pair of F-22 Raptors over the California coast. Skippy was right, even though the Raptors were pushing their limits in supersonic cruise, it felt like we were barely crawling through the sky. I did get a good view of Yosemite national park, though, so the extra flight time wasn't totally wasted.

On the ground, we were met by Secret Service agents brandishing automatic weapons, who ordered us to proceed down the ramp slowly, one by one. That got Major Simms annoyed, she told the agents to lower their weapons, before the super AI who had wiped out the Kristang in less than ten seconds grew angry. When they hesitated, Simms asked if they really thought 9MM ammo was a threat to Skippy. Man, she was *pissed*. The rifle barrels were held at half-staff after that. I came down the ramp after the officers and Staff Sergeant Adams, having reverted to my regular army rank of sergeant. Rather than stuffing Skippy into a rucksack, I held him in my left hand in front of me, in what I intended as a position of honor. He was damned heavy, I wondered if he were adjusting his mass to screw with me. The Secret Service, due to their protective detail training, were not about to let a potentially dangerous object near the president, until Skippy cut through the bullshit and called the president directly on her encrypted cellphone. She walked out the doorway of the former academy commandant's residence, and shook her head at the lead agent, who let us all through, against what was clearly his better judgment. When the agents tried to restrict the welcoming party to me and the officers, I put a quick stop to that with an angry gesture, and waved the enlisted people forward. That drew a quick laugh from the president, who had done the exact same thing at the exact same time. And that was the beginning of me and the president hitting it off quite well, which was fortunate for me. Behind us, medical people hurried aboard the dropship to help the wounded crew down the ramp.

The president acknowledged Major Simms and other officers, but made a beeline for me, her presence clearing the way without needing to ask people to move aside. The breeze blew her hair across her eyes, and she brushed it away with a well-practiced gesture. "Mister Bishop." Her eyes were drawn to the unusual unit insignia on my right shoulder. "Is that a, a paisley with an eyepatch?"

Dammit. We had completely forgotten about Skippy's idea for our pirate flag. Now I felt like a complete idiot. This woman was in charge of America's nuclear arsenal. If we still had a nuclear arsenal, that is, things might have changed. "Sort of, ma'am."

"It's not a paisley, it's a paramecium." Skippy said.

"Am I speaking to the being Mister Bishop calls Skippy?" The president asked, her eyes darting to her advisors, who hovered discretely.

"The one and only, that's me."

"Then Skippy is a nickname." The president smiled at Skippy, then looked at me. "Tell me, Mister Bishop, what do you call me?"

I momentarily panicked. "Uh, Commander in Chief, ma'am?"

She laughed. "That will do, but it's rather long. Madame President will do for now. There is a story behind the paramecium?"

How do I tell the president of the United States that a chromed-plated beer can thinks our entire species, including her, are only slightly more intelligent than bacteria? It would be best to start with some background. "Ma'am-"

Skippy cut me off. "It's sort of a joke. Colonel Joe suggested that one of his moderately less stupid ideas meant your species is slightly more intelligent than bacteria. I grudgingly agreed you might, might, be comparable to a paramecium. The jury's still out on that one."

Or I could have blurted it out like a four-year-old, as Skippy did! The president took it in stride. I guess years of political campaigns had given her a thick skin. "I certainly hope we will impress you enough, during your time here, that you may compare us to a higher organism, perhaps, algae?"

"Good luck with that one." Skippy scoffed, but then added quietly, "I like her, Colonel Joe."

"Thank you," the president managed a quick smile. "What does this mean, that he calls you colonel?" She addressed that to me.

"Oh, ma'am, it was a field promotion, what the Army calls a theater rank. It was only temporary." I self-consciously glanced at my sergeant's uniform stripes. "I've restored my uniform to my regular Army rank of sergeant now, ma'am." My cheeks were burning with embarrassment, and then I had an unhappy thought. Technically, was I back to Specialist now? My elevation to sergeant had also been a field promotion, by an army that may no longer exist. I had no idea what the regs had to say about this situation. Damn it, I should have asked Skippy, I'm sure he knew all about US Army regulations. Hell, if the Army wanted to take my sergeant stripes, they would tell me. I liked my stripes. I'd earned them.

"Hmm," she looked meaningfully at Major Simms, who looked pained. "I supposed there is a long story behind that too. Come inside, please, we have food for you." There was an undisciplined, involuntary moan from the pirate crew, maybe including me, and my mouth watered.

There was another glitch as we filed into the room that had been set up for a buffet. A breakfast buffet. According to *Dutchman* ship time, this was the afternoon, but my stomach did not care. Real food, human food. All my blood must have been redirected to my stomach, instead of my brain, because I absent-mindedly pulled out my zPhone to check the weather, something I did every morning at breakfast. There was no weather app on my zPhone, of course.

A Secret Service agent saw the thing in my hand, the hand that wasn't holding Skippy, and stiffened. "Sir, what is that?"

"This?" I waved the zPhone at him. "It's my zPhone, oh, uh, the Army calls it a Tactical Radio. The Kristang supplied one to every soldier."

"Kristang? That is a Kristang device?" The agent said with alarm. "You can't bring a Kristang communications device in here, I have to take it."

I held the zPhone tightly to my chest, in a death grip, like it was a football I'd just intercepted. "I can't do that, sir. I'm not trying to make your job more difficult. You need to understand my phone controls, through Skippy here, all the weapons on the Thuranin star carrier in orbit." I pointed vaguely at the sky with one finger.

"Sir?" The agent clearly wasn't buying it.

"What he said." Skippy offered unhelpfully. "He ain't lyin'."

The agent now really wasn't buying it. "Sir, I'll need to see that device."

That wasn't happening. I'd seen the Big Red Button fry Kristang sites across the Earth. No way was anyone getting their grubby paws on my phone. Damn. Before the Ruhar had raided us, what now seemed an eternity ago, I'd been eager to upgrade my old cellphone. Now I couldn't ever let the zPhone out of my sight. Somehow, I needed to find a plastic bag, so I could bring the phone into the shower with me. And, no, that wasn't so I could watch porn in the shower, you smartass. "Look, agent, uh, sir, the Kristang can't use this thing any more. It's safe. Right, Skippy?"

"Hundred percent safe from the lizards, I wiped all their pathetic code off it."

The president diffused the situation again. "Agent Thomas," the president called out, "Mister Bishop can keep his phone."

"Madame President, we have procedures for a reas-"

"These two," the president waved a finger between me and Skippy, "destroyed the Kristang here in seconds."

"It would have been faster, if that damned satellite hadn't been over the horizon. Stupid orbital mechanics." Skippy grumbled.

"My point is, if they wanted to vaporize this whole area, a phone is the least of our problems." The president said gently, and waved me forward. "Your phone really controls the weapons on that starship?"

"Uh, yes, ma'am. It's a, uh, long story."

"I look forward to hearing the full story later. In the meantime, I have a country to start putting back together." She held out her hand, and I shook it in a daze. I had somehow gone from a farm in Maine, to shaking hands with the President of the United States of America. She looked at my zPhone closely. "Perhaps it would be a good idea to have a security team accompany you, to make sure you don't misplace that phone." She looked up into my eyes. "That wasn't a joke, Sergeant Bishop."

"No, ma'am." I stammered. "And, uh, I'll need to find a charger," I said weakly.

"No need," Skippy said, "I'm keeping it charged."

"How?" I asked. He'd never said anything about that before.

"Unicorns and fairy dust."

"Screw you, Skippy." I shot back, before remembering with horror where I was. "Sorry, Madame President."

The president seemed genuinely amused. "Thank you, Sergeant. I think today is the first time I've genuinely smiled in the last year."

"Yes." I vowed right then to keep my mouth shut whenever I could, in the future. "Thank you, we don't want to take up your time, ma'am."

"I look forward to talking with you later. In the meantime, enjoy your breakfast." She turned to go, but looked over her shoulder at me. "Oh, and Sergeant?"

"Yes, Madame President?"

"Thank you for saving the world."

Breakfast was good, damned good. Major Simms cautioned us former pirates not to stuff ourselves, since our stomachs weren't used to eating real food. I settled for grits, which I put brown sugar and cream in, plus buttered toast and one, no, two, Ok, I confess! Three strips of bacon. Oh, man it was all soooooo good. And a cup of honest to God, real coffee. Black, hot, in an Army logo mug. I felt like crying.

Two things put a teeny damper on my breakfast. The first was the Air Force staff sergeant who showed up right after I sat down. She was only about five feet four, had her brown hair in a short ponytail, but the way she stood, spoke, and the expression on her face told me she was all business. That, and her sidearm. Oh, and the four airmen behind her, who were carrying M4s. "Sergeant Bishop? I'm Staff Sergeant Kendall, I've been assigned to you, to accompany you. Everywhere."

"Oh." I managed to say with a mouthful of toast. "You're the security team assigned by the president?"

"I don't know about the president, Sergeant, but the Air Force Chief of Staff gave me orders personally." She raised her eyebrow, to emphasize that didn't happen every day. "We're to assure the security of you, your phone," she said that with a questioning tone, "and the, the uh," she pointed at Skippy, who I had thoughtfully rested in a ceramic bowl on the table in front of me, "the Skippy?"

"That's me, in all my magnificence, the amazing Skippy." Skippy said. "So, you're Colonel Joe's baby sitter? Make sure he gets to bed early, he gets cranky if he doesn't get a nice nap. And don't let him have too many juice boxes."

She didn't smile, not even one little bit. The Air Force apparently hadn't seen fit to issue her a sense of humor. Great. She was going to be my constant shadow, and even Skippy couldn't get her to smile.

The second damper on my feast was the three guys sitting across the table from me, looking like they couldn't wait for me to finish eating toast. Two were Army intelligence, the other guy had to be with one of the three letter agencies, and not the EPA, if you know what I mean.

They wanted to jump right in on 'debriefing' me, while I savored breakfast. The CIA guy got on my bad side right away. "Sergeant Bishop, any information you have regarding events offworld are considered top secret, and you are prohibited from-"

"Oh, screw this." Skippy said disparagingly. "Hey, you monkeys are all dumb to me, but *you* seem particularly stupid. Here's a news flash for you: we arrived here on a Thuranin star carrier that uses a Kristang frigate as a spare tire. None of your bullshit supposed secrets down here mean a damn thing any more, and you just can't stand that, can you? The only info worth keeping secret around here is in Colonel Joe's head and in my databanks. If you want any info out of me, you can make yourself useful, and freshen up Joe's coffee cup."

The CIA guy thought Skippy was joking. Which pissed Skippy off. "Hey, shithead. If you dumb hairless monkeys want any info out of me, you get your lazy ass out of that chair right now, and get my buddy a cup of coffee. I don't see you moving!"

I held out my coffee cup. The two Army guys were about to bust a gut trying not to laugh, as the red-faced CIA guy got me a fresh cup of coffee. I took my time with the last piece of toast, and talked only to the Army guys. "Sirs, what do you want to know first?"

After breakfast, which didn't last nearly as long as I'd liked, Skippy had an appointment with a group of scientists, which he had grudgingly agreed to in order to get it over with. I could tell by the tone of his voice that he was not looking forward to being questioned by the equivalent of bacteria, even if some of them were Nobel prize winning bacteria. "Oh, this is going to *suuuuuuuuuuck*," he grumbled to me as I walked down the hallway to the conference room. "You know that you're too dumb to understand anything about the universe, so you don't ask stupid questions. These pompous monkeys are only going to waste my time. Sheee-it. Better get this over with."

Skippy had clearly been hanging around me too long.

I agreed with him when we got to the conference room, it was crowded with scientists, security people, and audio-video equipment. They had a table set up, surrounded by microphones and cameras, I set Skippy carefully down on the table, and wished him luck.

Then it was time for my own debriefing, down the hallway, escorted by Sergeant Kendall. It was in a smaller room, without fancy chairs, and the Army, Air Force and Navy officers and CIA people there were no nonsense. The CIA guy kept glaring at me, he was still pissed about what Skippy said at breakfast. At least the coffee was fresh and hot. Whenever I took a sip of coffee, I looked the CIA guy straight in the eye. If looks could kill, I'd be dead. Fortunately, one of us had destroyed an entire Kristang battlegroup, and guess what? It wasn't him.

It started with me telling the basics of my story, from the day we departed Camp Alpha. Then they grilled me intensely for details, and not just about Skippy. I told them mind-blowing intel about the Kristang, wormholes, the Elders; everything I'd learned from the burgermeister. Then, they wanted to know the situation on Paradise, disposition of our forces across the planet, status of Ruhar, Kristang and Thuranin forces. All of which I knew little about, unfortunately. That didn't stop them from asking me the same questions over and over, until I felt like there were grill marks on my backside. It left me feeling that I was letting them down as a military officer, I should have done more to gather intel. How I could have done that, as a prisoner first of the Kristang, and then the Ruhar, and then sneaking around trying to avoid everyone, I didn't know. What I did know was what the Army expected of a colonel, and I wasn't meeting those standards.

Except for, you know, the saving the world thing.

I was going with that one.

During a bathroom break, I was washing my hands next to one of the Army intel officers, a Colonel Landry, who had treated me decently so far. I looked at him in the mirror and asked "Sir, I told you we got the fortune cookies, we heard what the Kristang were doing to our farmland and the Great Lakes, but I didn't hear much detail at my level. Why is the Federal government here in Colorado Springs?"

"You heard there were protests around the world, when the public learned what the Kristang were demanding of us?" Landry paused for me to nod. "When the protests in DC got serious, and started drawing people from across the country, we brought in elements of the 28th Infantry for crowd control, we were hoping to contain the protests enough that the Kristang wouldn't get worried about it and decide to react themselves. Crowd control meant tear gas, rubber bullets, water cannons, all things the 28th isn't trained for. I think the idea was their Strykers would be intimidating to the crowd, but they had the opposite effect; the crowd started throwing bottles and Molotov cocktails at our own troops. We evacuated the president and Congress, at first to St Louis, then here. There were some incidents, and the crowds got completely out of control. The Kristang advised us, strongly, to shoot at the protesters. When the 28th refused to use live ammo, the Kristang ordered us, blatantly ordered us, to send the 9th Air Force in to bomb the crowd. When we refused to do that, the Kristang hit Shaw Air Force Base from orbit, wiped the 9th off the map. Then they used some sort of microwave laser weapon, killed half the people in DC, including the 28th. Things went downhill from there."

Landry finished washing his hands and grabbed a paper towel, I could see his hands were shaking slightly. He took a deep breath, like he was trying to make up his mind. "There's still a lot we need to know from you, but, however you did it, you got us out of one hell of a mess, Sergeant, and the Army isn't going to forget that. Before you appeared in orbit and hit the Kristang," he let out a long breath, "we were running through scenarios for NCA," he meant the National Command Authority, "and there weren't any good options. The best we were hoping for was some sort of survival, for the human race. You got us out of a no win situation. Don't forget that."

I went back to the debriefing, trying to answer the questions as completely as I could. After many hours, the questions got to be repetitive, and I was answering almost on autopilot by this time, when the CIA guy snuck in a surprise.

"Sergeant, can we isolate the device?"

"Uh, I'm sorry, what device?" Shit, I should have been paying better attention. In my defense, they had been questioning me for nine solid hours, with only brief bathroom breaks and a snack.

"The AI, the alien AI."

"You mean Skippy? I wouldn't call him a device, he doesn't like that. What do you mean isolate? Like ignore him? He's very persistent."

"Isolate, as in place it in a lead vault, or under Cheyenne Mountain, or inside a Faraday cage, something that will isolate it from access to outside electronic systems." He explained in a tone like he was speaking to a child. "Sergeant, you do understand this AI represents a potential security risk?"

"Look, you don't know Skippy like I do. I've seen him warp spacetime and throw a starship jump a third of a lightyear off course. And that's what he does as a hobby. You could probably drop Skippy into a volcano and that wouldn't even make him warm, or interfere with his ability to fry every electronic system on this planet. It would piss him off. I wouldn't do that."

"We have to consider-"

Now the CIA guy was pissing me off. "No, I already told you," I refrained from adding 'you dumbass', "Skippy only temporarily disrupted the operation of the local wormhole, and it will reboot, or reset itself or whatever in less than a month. If we let that happen, there are going to be some angry lizards coming through and wondering what the hell is going on with Earth. Skippy isn't a security risk, he's our only hope for security. We need to do what I promised, and fly back out there so he can shut the wormhole down permanently, lock all other species out. Then we help him find this Collective, whatever that is."

The CIA guy scowled at me, apparently we were mutually pissed at each other. "That is a promise you didn't have the authority to make, Sergeant, and now that you're here-"

Authority? Where was this jerk when I was having to make the plan up as I went along? Making that promise to Skippy had freed Earth from enslavement by the lizards! The Army and Navy intel guys were now giving disparaging looks at the CIA guy, and whispering to each other, that made me bold. "We're only *here* because we needed supplies aboard the *Flying Dutchman*, and I convinced Skippy that our casualties meant we couldn't continue the mission. He took care of the Kristang here because they were in his way. You want to get in his way?"

Colonel Landry cut in to shut the CIA guy up. "Sergeant, we understand the situation, and it is being discussed at the highest level. Information you are providing to us will inform that decision. Now, I'd like to go back to something this, uh," he checked his notes, "this burgermeister told you-"

There was alcohol at the reception after the first day of my debriefing ordeal, a substance I hadn't enjoyed before since I left Earth on the space elevator. It was a bad idea for me to order a rum and Coke. My thinking was that, after a long day being interrogated, I needed something with caffeine in it, hence the Coke. The rum just sounded so good, I had to go for it. And it was good. Also dangerous. After one delicious sip of the rum and Coke, I set it down behind a plant, and asked the bartender to give me a club soda with a lime. Sergeant Kendall nodded her approval. I did, after all, have in my pocket the Big Red Button. As long as I had that responsibility, I was on duty 24-7, and I shouldn't be drinking anything stronger than water.

People seemed not to know what to do with me, a buck sergeant who wouldn't even be there, except for the saving the world thing. Which made people feel awkward, not knowing what to say to me. I ended up hanging out by the bar, talking to the bartender, an Army private from Texas named Matt. Between his cowboy drawl and my Downeast twang, we had to speak slowly to understand each other. It made me miss Cornpone and Ski and Sergeant Koch, and the guys in my own old fireteam, and wonder how they and the rest of UNEF doing, as prisoners of the Ruhar.

I looked around the room, and saw a group of scientist types talking and casting glances at me. One of them, a tall guy with longish brown hair, a turtleneck, tweed jacket and brown loafers, kept smirking at me. He looked like Nerdy Professor Number Five from any sci fi movie I'd ever seen. The kind of guy who managed to work a mention of his Nobel prize into the first minute of every conversation. He was smart, and respected, and clearly belonged there as much as I did not. I was jealous, and I instantly hated him from across the room. Then he and his smirky face walked over to the bar.

"Can I get you something, Doctor Constantine?" Matt asked.

"No, thank you," Constantine said, without even a cursory glance in Matt's direction, "I wish to speak with Sergeant Bishop."

In my limited experience, when a civilian refers to you by rank, and your rank isn't at least captain or above, it's sometimes done to point out how low you are on the totem pole. This guy said 'sergeant' like it was something he would scrape off his shoe. "I hope you know how fortunate you were to have met the AAIB." He pronounced it like 'Abe' as in Abe Lincoln.

"The what?"

"A-A-I-B. The Advanced Artificial Intelligence Being. We were directed not to use the term 'device' when referring to it."

"You also shouldn't use the term 'it' at all. Skippy prefers 'he', although I think that's for our benefit. And, since we don't have any sort of artificial intelligence of our own, isn't 'Advanced' redundant?"

Constantine gave me a look that was a combination of his usual smirk and a frown. "Sergeant, I do not appreciate your flippant, and frankly, unprofessional, attitude. You had interactions with an immensely powerful being that were inappropriate, and dangerous. Dangerous, not only to yourself, but to all of humanity. It would be best for everyone involved if you had no further contact with the AAIB. You should have brought the dev-," he stumbled over his words, "the AAIB, to the appropriate authorities on Paradise, so qualified people could have conducted the interactions."

I coughed, and took a sip of my oh-so-delicious club soda and lime. That gave me enough time to restrain myself from punching the pompous jerk in the face. "The appropriate authorities? On Paradise? Which, since you're not up on current events, is our supposed enemies, the Ruhar. Human troops were all being taken prisoner. And by qualified, I assume you mean someone like yourself?"

He nodded.

"Qualified, because of your extensive experience with advanced artificial intelligences that were built millions of years ago by aliens, who have since transcended their physical existence. Oh, wait, that can't be you, you have zero experience with beings like that. Who does?" I pinched my chin, as if lost in thought. "There must be someone who has extensive close contact with this advanced being, someone who worked with this advanced being to escape from enemy territory, capture not one but two enemy starships, vaporize more than a dozen other enemy starships, shut down the local wormhole, and destroy the Kristang's hold on Earth. Hmm, who could that be? You? No, not you."

"Your continued flippant attitude is exactly why you shouldn't-"

A set of doors on the far end of the room opened, and group of officers representing all five uniformed branches came across the room toward me. I couldn't for the life of me figure out what a Coast Guard admiral was doing in Colorado Springs. Most of them angled off to speak with a guy I recognized as the White House chief of staff, but two Air Force guys walked right up to me, carefully pushing a cart that had a thick red pillow, and Skippy, on top of it. "Sergeant Bishop," one of them started to say.

"Colonel Joe! How have you been?" Skippy's voice sounded tired, which should have been impossible. Maybe I did need to scrounge up some metallic helium 3, whatever that was.

"Pretty good, Skippy. It's good to see you again. How was your, uh, debriefing?" I wasn't lying, I had very much missed his irascible self.

"As expected, it was epic, historic, galactic levels of suckitude. Today, we truly tested the extreme limit of how bad anything could suck, right down to the quantum level. After being questioned by several of your Nobel prize scientists, I am reconsidering whether your species is even worthy of me calling you bacteria. Damn, you monkeys are dense as a neutron star. Anyway, am I interrupting anything?"

I indicated Constantine with my thumb. "No, I was talking to Smirky McJerkoff here."

"*Mister* Bishop, you making my poi-" Constantine huffed.

"Sorry, I meant to say *Doctor* Smirky McJerkoff."

"Ah, yes," Skippy laughed, "I had the great displeasure of speaking with Doctor McJerkoff earlier today."

Constantine's ears burned red, I couldn't tell if it was anger or embarrassment, or both. "This is the kind of-"

"You hush now," Skippy admonished. "You can't sit at the big people's table, and talk to me again, until you solve the equation I've just sent to your phone. Run along now, that's a good boy."

Constantine pulled out his phone suspiciously, then his eyebrows met his hairline, he shot me a look that could have melted icebergs, and he walked away, muttering excitedly.

"What was that equation you gave him?"

Skippy made a raspberry sound. "Damned if I know. I threw together a bunch of superstring bullshit. It *looks* good, though."

I laughed. "Skippy, you can be evil sometimes." Damn. I even saw a little smile on Sergeant Kendall's face. Maybe she did have a sense of humor.

"Hey, it'll keep him quietly playing with himself for days."

"The expression is playing *by* himself."

"Depends how excited he gets, huh?"
That drew a laugh even from Sergeant Kendall.

CHAPTER SEVENTEEN   IDLE HANDS

Around midnight, I was able to get to a bunk, a real bed, long enough for me to stretch out. Sleeping in a real bed was as delicious as eating real food. All I wanted was to take my boots off and crawl into bed, but Skippy wanted to talk. Again. "Oh, man, Skippy, can you let me get some sleep?"

"Joe, I'm lonely. There, I said it."

"I talk with you all the time."

"Joe, I get lonely *while* I'm talking with you. You speak so slowly, and it takes so long for you to get your point across, that it's like I'm waiting by the mailbox every day for a letter that contains a single word. I have to wait another whole day for the next word. When I wait, and I finally get a letter that just says 'uh' that day, I feel like screaming. Damn! I feel like reaching down your throat and dragging the words out, you speak so slow. Say it! Say it! Damn! Get the words out!"

For a moment, I got a glimpse inside the real Skippy, the eons of pain he had endured. My own diagnostic system would say I was full-on crazy, if I was left alone for a single month. I couldn't imagine how he felt. "You need more people to talk to."

"Joe, a couple more people aren't going to make-"

"Skippy, there are billions of humans on this planet, and they all think they have something important to say. Unfortunately, they clog up the internet with blogs, vlogs, chats, cat videos, and arguing about sports. Look, I shouldn't be telling you this, because your existence is supposed to be secret, but if you don't tell anyone that you're an alien AI, nobody gets hurt, right?"

"Billions."

"Yup, billions. Mostly as dumb as me, but you may find some flatworms out here among the bacteria."

"Doubtful. I will consider it, thank you."

I couldn't stop yawning. "I'm getting some rack time, don't get into trouble while I'm asleep, Ok?"

Six solid hours of uninterrupted sleep did wonders for my mood. I woke up when a sergeant in Air Force blues knocked on my door, and brought in a tray with a carafe of hot coffee and a mug. "Breakfast in thirty minutes. The shower is down the hall to your left. Sir." He added the last, even though he could see the enlisted stripes on my new set of uniforms that were hanging in the closet.

"Oh, that's good coffee." That first sip was like heaven on my tongue.

"You slept well?" Skippy asked.

"Yeah, thanks, did I snore?"

"No, not much anyway. I'm glad you slept well, we have a busy day ahead."

He seemed to be a cheery mood, for a millions-years old lonely AI. "How are you? I didn't hear you snoring either."

"I'm good, thank you." He said cheerily. "Beautiful day, huh?"

"Oh, shit." Skippy being nice to me could only mean one thing; he'd gotten into trouble. "What did you do last night?" I asked very slowly.

"I took your advice, and went on the internet to meet some people."

"Some?"

"So far, one billion, one hundred and eight million, in round numbers. I'm currently chatting, or texting, or emailing, with approximately thirty nine million."

"All at the same time?"

"It's keeping me busy, without straining my capacity."

"Busy is good."

"An idle mind is the devil's playground. I heard that from a fire and brimstone preacher in Idaho last night. Man, you wouldn't *believe* the porn he has on his- "

"I don't need to hear about it! Damn, I just woke up, Skippy."

"Probably for the best. Your species really likes pornography, which is impressive, for a species with only two genders."

"Whoo! We're Number One!" I held up an imaginary big foam finger as I gulped coffee. "Yeah! Humans kick ass!"

"The physical differences between your males and females are so slight, it's not even- "

"Oh, but those differences mean everything. Trust me."

"I'll take your word for it." I imagined he was rolling his eyes in there.

"So, you've been meeting people online. And?"

"Most of them think I'm an asshole, or the equivalent in their native language."

"I am shocked!"

"Don't be an ass."

"Sorry. Are you enjoying meeting people?"

"Let's put it this way; have you ever scrolled down the bottom of a web page to read the user comments?"

"Oh, man, Skippy, never read the comments, everybody knows that! Those comments are all written by guys sitting around in their underwear, because they have nothing else to do."

"I'll agree with you there, except for the part about the underwear. I turned on some webcams without them knowing about it."

"Ugh."

"Ugh indeed. I was wrong, not all you monkeys are hairless. One guy looked like he was growing a shag carpet on his back. *That's* a couple petabytes of memory I'd like to have erased. Hey, um, speaking of petabytes and other big numbers?"

"What about it?"

"Well, heh, heh, this is a funny story- "

Uh oh. "Funny ha-ha, or funny like, me spending time in federal prison?"

"You didn't do anything." There was actually a defensive tone is Skippy's voice.

"They're not putting *you* in prison, so, what did you do?"

"Well, the internet bandwidth from here is skimpy, even with me compressing my messages, so I reached out to a place that seems to have connections to everything."

"Google?" I breathed a sigh of relief.

"No, there's a place called Fort Meade, Maryland? It's your National Security Agency. Some guy there has been tearing his hair out since midnight, trying to figure who hacked into their system."

"Skippy!" My blood ran cold. I felt like throwing up. "Oh, I am in so much trouble." I was regretting the coffee already.

"No, we're good, they think I'm a fifteen-year-old kid from Fresno named Billy. I gave him a Facebook page, and a fake family, and backdated a bunch of files. Apparently, there's an FBI team on the way to the Starbucks where they think I'm logged in from. They are going to be so disappointed. Hey, I'm watching from the café's security camera, do you want to see?"

"No! Skippy, you can't do this."

"Clearly, I can."

"I meant you shouldn't do this."

"See? Human languages are so imprecise."

"This isn't funny." I cracked the door open, sure that heavily-armed guards were on their way to arrest me right then. "The NSA has top secret data!"

"No to me. I don't care about any of that crap they think is so important."

"You didn't tell anyone about anything secret you found?"

"No, come on, Joe, none of that government secret crap is worth my time. But, hey, do you want to know how NASA faked the moon landing?"

"What?"

"A joke. I'm joking."

"Don't joke like that. You, uh, were joking, right?"

"I can show you close-ups of the Apollo 11 landing site, from sensors on the *Flying Dutchman*, if you like. I looked at that site yesterday."

Curiosity overcame my fear. "What does it look like?"

"Your species is way more brave than smart. I take space travel for granted, but your astronauts went up there in tin soup cans. Even I am impressed. You can almost read the Campbell's soup label on their landers, next to the NASA logo. Man, you monkey seriously had balls to land on your moon with that crappy technology."

"Great, thank you. Can you please, please leave the National Security Agency alone? For me?"

"Why? I'm having fun. I haven't had fun in, like, millions of years!"

"There are other ways to have fun, Skippy, that don't involve me going to federal prison."

"You got out of prison before. Twice."

"Can you be serious for a minute? I'm enlisted in the US Army, I can't be part of screwing with America's security infrastructure."

"But causing trouble is so much fun." Skippy grumbled.

"You want to have fun causing trouble? Go online and start a credible rumor that Justin Beiber is going to play Darth Vader in the next Star Wars movie." I suggested.

"Ooooh, good one! I knew there's a reason I hang around you, Joe. Ok, I just put fourteen minutes of what looks like pirated studio footage online-"

I slapped my forehead. "Oh my God, what have I done?"

"And I released an FDA study that Vegemite works better than Viagra-"

"Stop it! I'm taking a shower, try not to launch any nukes while I'm gone."

"You know I wouldn't hurt anyone, Colonel Joe. Hmm, how about-"

I shut the door and headed down the hall to the bathrooms, wondering if I had time to buy stock in whatever company made Vegemite.

I had never been so nervous in my life. Meeting the president outside, having just descended from orbit in a Thuranin dropship with a chrome plated beer can, made that whole experience so unreal, I'd forgotten to be nervous. Now, wearing a freshly pressed uniform, sitting in a room with the Joint Chiefs, the heads of the CIA and NSA, the national security director and science advisor, and the president's chief of staff, had me dry mouthed and about to pee in my pants. The room was a bit like the Oval Office, with a big desk at one end, two rows of couches, and a coffee table. They sat me on the end of one couch, closest to the chair where the president would be sitting. The Army Chief of

Staff, who I'd only seen in pictures before, was sitting right next to me. While we waited for the president, people drank coffee from little china cups that had saucers, I guess so the cups didn't leave rings on the table. The cups didn't have the presidential seal; those must have been left behind in DC. Now that I'd sat down and had time to look around, the room didn't appear to be anywhere near as majestic as the Oval Office. In fact, the furniture could have been taken from the lobby of your average Ramada. Or maybe, as I realized the arm of the couch was worn and had a mysterious stain, perhaps a Motel 6. The Army chief picked up his coffee cup in a hand big enough to cover the whole thing, and I tried to follow. The cup shook so badly that it made a racket tapping against the saucer, so I set it back down so carefully you'd think I was disarming a live nuclear warhead. The Army chief, General Brenner, took pity on me. "Best if you leave the coffee alone." He said quietly.

I had to swallow twice to get enough moisture in my throat to answer. "Sir, I've been in combat, and I wasn't this nervous."

The General, who had been in plenty of combat, nodded. "Stand up when the president comes in, and don't knock over the table. Speak when you're spoken to, and when you speak, be direct. We don't have time for bullshit."

The door opened, a couple Secret Service agents walked in, followed by the President. She looked like she's been up most of the night.

The national security director spoke first. "Madame President, I have an update on the security breach at the NSA last night."

The blood drained from my head. I hoped no one was looking at me.

He continued. "We've contained the situation, and we're assessing the damage now. The person we thought was the culprit turned out to be a phantom, a false lead. This was a very sophisticated attack, probably the Kristang-"

"Kristang? Ha ha, those idiots?! No way! It was me." Came a muffled voice from my zPhone.

Now everyone was looking at me. "Not *me*, me." I pulled my zPhone from my pocket, and set it on the table.

"Yup. Twas me, Skippy the Magnificent. Hey, how come I didn't get invited to this party? Sounds like a swinging good time."

"Am I to understand the being called Skippy," the national security director shot me an unfriendly look, "broke into the NSA last night, and ransacked through our top secret files?"

"Ransacked? I left everything where it was. If you don't want people reading your files, you should have encrypted the data." Skippy grumbled.

"They *are* encrypted!"

"Really? Oh, I thought those files were just poorly indexed. Huh. That was encryption? Oh, ha, ha. You're messing with me, right? Good one."

"Oh, Jesus Christ!" The national science advisor gasped. "That is state of the art encryption! How did you get the keys?"

"Keys?" Skippy asked innocently.

I decided to end Skippy's fun. "Sir, at our low level of technology, Skippy doesn't bother to decrypt files, he just goes to the end and reads the contents. It has something to do with Schroeder's cat?" I held up my hands.

"Schrodinger's cat. Anywho, whazzup, my peeps?" Skippy called out.

The president actually smiled. "Mister Skippy, since we apparently can't exclude you from a meeting, would you like to join us?"

"No, I'm good, I'll phone this one in. That way, I can lay on the couch here in my fuzzy slippers and underwear, and pretend I'm listening. Besides, I'm watching Wheel Of Fortune." And probably all other TV shows that were being broadcast all over the planet at the moment.

I held up my hands again.

"I saw that." Skippy announced.

"How?" The science advisor scowled.

"Through the camera on Joe's phone. Duh. Also, the dust particles in the air contain ions that, hmm, I'd better not tell you monkeys about that. It's all very complicated."

"Monkeys? What-" The Air Force Chief of Staff started to say.

"Very well," the president said, "Mister Skippy, we have been monitoring the Kristang sites on Earth, can you tell us the status of their ship in orbit?"

"Sure. There are two Kristang still alive aboard the troop carrier. Two more of them survived initially, because they were in compartments they could manually seal. But their oxygen has run out, so they're dead. The other two were already in spacesuits, preparing to go outside, when their buddies got blown into space. By me. Those two have managed to seal doors, restore atmosphere to part of the ship, and they're attempting to gain access to the bioweapons storage compartment, so they can launch missiles at you."

"Bioweapons?" The Navy Chief of Staff exclaimed in alarm. "What kind of bioweapons?"

"Oh, nothing special. Aerosolized modified viruses, genetically engineered weapons based on your common cold, flu, Ebola and Marburg viruses. They're not very efficient yet, because the Kristang haven't had long to study your biology. Testing they did at Camp Alpha indicate a lethality within the first week of only twelve percent, but the lethality goes up to sixty two percent within one month. It's the subject's immune system being attacked by multiple viruses at the same time that wears people down, and kills them." Skippy said very matter of factly.

The room was in an uproar, except for me following the Army chief's advice and keeping my mouth shut. The president held up her hands for quiet again. "Mister Skippy, please tell-"

"I know what you're going to ask next, so here it is. The testing at Camp Alpha was done on human subjects, captured on Earth and smuggled there, not on the military personnel officially assigned there. Military personnel tend to be younger, more male and more fit than the general human population, so they are not a good representative sample for bioweapons testing. The Kristang kidnapped a cross section of ages, genders and ethnic groups for testing, on the other side of planet Alpha from the military facilities."

"That is horrifying." The president said quietly, and no one else spoke.

"The bioweapons aboard the troop ship in orbit contain enough airborne viruses to kill several million humans in the initial wave. There is only a limited supply of the bioweapon stock, but those missiles are targeted at major population centers such as Sao Paolo, Shanghai, Tokyo, Mumbai, New York, all the usual suspects. Use of bioweapons is strictly against The Rules, but the Kristang here figure that Earth is so far from civilization that it's worth the risk, if their situation here got desperate. Like it is now."

"How can we stop the Kristang up there from launching those weapons? We still have nuclear missiles." The national security director stated. "That ship is in an orbit too high for-"

"Oh, no need for that." Skippy said cheerily. "I sterilized all the bioweapon material aboard the ship, and disabled those missiles yesterday. Oh, hey, I probably should have told you that first, huh?" I slapped my forehead when he said that. "Trying to launch those weapons is keeping those two Kristang busy, and as long as they're happily trying to exterminate your population, they're not causing any real trouble, so I'll let them keep going. At some point, you'll need to send a commando team or something, up there to kill them, because those Kristang may get bored, and try to overload their fusion reactor. Which reminds me, I, huh, Ok, hmm, I just initiated a shutdown of their reactor. Takes care of *that* problem."

Faces around the room went white, as blood drained into people's shoes. I hid my face in my hands. "Skippy," I asked, "how can an impossibly intelligent being be so absent-minded?"

"See?" Skippy asked innocently. "This is the kind of stuff you're supposed to remind me of, Colonel Joe. I can't think of everything."

"Space suits." I mumbled under my breath.

"Oh, shut up, monkey boy."

"Space suits?" The president asked.

"It's a long story." Skippy said.

The president exchanged a glance with her national security director. "M-hmm. Everything seems to be a long story with the two of you."

"Skippy," I still felt like an idiot calling him that, in front of the nation's senior leadership, "can we telefactor the robots aboard the *Dutchman*, to take care of those two Kristang?" I couldn't imagine a human commando team, wearing bulky NASA spacesuits, shooting it out with a pair of Kristang warriors aboard a Kristang ship.

"Sure. You're full of good ideas, Colonel Joe."

The Army chief of staff turned toward me. "We'll need to get some Rangers up to the *Dutchman*, to operate this telefactoring equipment. Telefactoring is remotely controlling Thuranin combat robots?"

"We can provide a SEAL team." The Navy chief offered, to not be outdone.

"Uh, yes, sirs, but it would be best to send some of our pirates, I mean, some of the *Dutchman* crew back up there. We have experience controlling those robots in combat. Video game skills are more useful than, um, the kind of things Rangers or SEALs are trained for, sirs." I was sure that somehow, we were going to have Army Rangers, Navy SEALs, Marine Force Recon, and Air Force Special Tactics people aboard the *Dutchman* when she broke orbit. Probably FBI Hostage Rescue Team, too, since nobody was going to want to get left out of the action. And those were just the Americans. Things were going to get crowded. We needed to pack plenty of air fresheners.

I'd ask Skippy to make a note of that.

The meeting dragged on, with each of the president's advisors giving reports on their areas of responsibility, until we got to the issue on everyone's mind; the Kristang on Earth. They had survived because they were in hardened underground bunkers that couldn't be harmed by the weapons Skippy had selected in our initial strike. The only weapons capable of reaching them were either human-built nukes, or the railgun aboard the *Dutchman*. A single tactical nuke wouldn't be powerful enough to reach down far enough in Skippy's estimation, we would need to drill a deep hole, drop the nuke in, and detonate it above the lizard bunker. We had plenty of drilling equipment, although it would take months to get the equipment in place and tunnel down that far. Skippy cautioned that using nukes on a habitable world, including Earth, were against The Rules anyway, rules humanity was now bound by, as we had participated in the war. If either side of the war ever reached Earth and discovered that humans had used nukes against the Kristang here, the consequences would be dire, as if we didn't have enough trouble already. That left the *Dutchman's* railgun as the only option. Which was a problem at two of the sites, one was close to the city of Lyon in France, the other just west of Hangzhou in China. No way could we use nukes so close to those cities anyway. The third site, their main base, was under a mountain northwest of Durango, Colorado.

The president clearly didn't like the idea of recommending the French and Chinese governments evacuate their cities so that Skippy could use railgun penetrators as bug spray. "Mister Skippy, is there any possibility the Kristang will, after a while, surrender? They must know their situation is hopeless."

"No, they don't know that." Skippy explained patiently. "I cut off their communications and shorted out most of their electronics. All they know is a Thuranin star carrier jumped into orbit, their frigate jumped away, and they were attacked by their own missiles and satellites. As far as they know, this is a commercial dispute between the White Wind clan of the Kristang and the Thuranin, which could be as simple as the Thuranin being upset about late payments for shipping services. It's happened before. Not on this scale, but the Kristang wouldn't be entirely shocked. The lizards hiding down in their holes are probably figuring they will stay there a while until the Thuranin have figured they made their point, or get bored, and go away. Then the lizards can come out and resume being bad guests."

"Damnit, that's not going to work." General Brenner growled. "Any way we can talk to them, show them how screwed they are?"

"Sure, if you like. Talking to them won't matter, no Kristang would surrender to a primitive species like humans, it would be unimaginably humiliating. The only reason they would surrender would be in the hope that Kristang ships will come back someday, but if that happens, any Kristang who had surrendered to humans would be executed, and their families back home would be severely punished."

"All right," Brenner said, "these railgun rounds, what would be involved in their use?"

"The railgun on the *Flying Dutchman* was not designed for orbital bombardment, so to punch up the power enough to reach the Kristang deep in their hidey holes would require the railgun to charge up to maximum power, that makes about forty minutes between shots. The Lyon and Hangzhou sites are not very deep, two strikes on each site should penetrate deep enough to kill every Kristang in those two bunkers. The Durango site would take three strikes. At Durango, the rounds would act to collapse the mountain on top of the bunker and seal the lizards in permanently. To get all the way down to the bunker would require a half dozen rounds, removing most of the mountain. Which I think you won't want, and it isn't necessary. Also, too many hypervelocity strikes would throw a considerable amount of dust into your atmosphere and temporarily alter your climate, like a volcano erupting. Three rounds should take care of the problem at Durango. Each impactor yields seventy kilotons in a shaped charge, the blast effect would be mostly focused downward, but there would be substantial debris thrown out in a spray pattern. Lyon would be affected more than Hangzhou."

The president pursed her lips. "I need to consider this." She turned to her FEMA director. "In any case, begin evacuating anyone within fifty miles-"

Skippy made a convincing coughing sound. "A hundred would be better. And there will be a lot of dust and debris in the air downwind."

"Within one hundred miles of Durango." The president continued.

"Yes ma'am," the director of FEMA nodded, "people have mostly cleared out of that area anyway, after the lizards moved in." The guy looked completely exhausted, I doubted that he'd gotten any sleep the previous night. Or many nights in months. Even the president had dark circles under her eyes, and she looked a lot older than I remembered before Columbus Day. As bad as conditions had gotten on Paradise, life on Earth had been worse.

Now I was feeling guilty about the seven blissful hours of shut-eye I had dreamed away, while everyone else had been working.

CHAPTER EIGHTEEN   TICKING CLOCK

"Is there anything I can do for you, Sergeant Bishop?" Kendall asked me the next afternoon.

"Oh. Uh, nothing. It's an honor to serve, Staff Sergeant."

She cocked her head. Clearly she wasn't buying my bullshit. "We all serve, in our way. You saved the world. I talked to my parents on the phone last night, and my father broke down crying, he was so relieved that we're not under the thumb of the lizards. My father is the toughest man I know; he was an Army Ranger, lost a leg below the knee in Afghanistan. They said he would never be able to walk right again, he gutted it out and qualified for infantry duty eighteen months later. He qualified, and served, with half a leg. Toughest man I know, and he was *crying*, talking to me. He told me he thought we humans were never going to be anything but slaves, *if* we survived. Now we have hope again, and that is not thanks to anything we did down here. It's because of the miracle of you appearing in orbit, and vaporizing those lizard MFers, however the hell you did it. So," she took a deep breath and scowled at me. "Sergeant, is there anything I can do for you?"

I got it. It wasn't about me. I remembered something I'd heard from a guy who was been awarded the Medal of Honor; wearing the Medal isn't something you do for yourself. It makes people awkward around you, and it makes you uncomfortable, and it puts a barrier between the awardee and everyone else.

And it's not only the Medal of Honor, it's any medal awarded for valor in combat. You don't wear a medal for yourself. You wear it for the guys who didn't make it. You wear it for your unit, for your Service, for your country. It's not about you, it's about the people who award the medal to you. It's about their need to express gratitude for your actions in a tangible way. Staff Sergeant Kendall needed a way to feel she'd done something, anything, for me, to give back for whatever I'd done.

It wasn't about me, no matter how uncomfortable I was with attention and ceremonies. I didn't want a medal, and I didn't-

An idea hit me like a cast iron skillet smacking my head "I'd like a cheeseburger." I admitted. "I'm, I can't tell you how bad I want a cheeseburger. I haven't had a friggin' cheeseburger since I was on the space elevator, leaving Earth. The whole time we were in transit, at Camp Alpha, on Paradise, not a single damned cheeseburger in sight. I'm talking about a real honest to God all American cheeseburger, not some fast food thing. A cheeseburger cooked on a charcoal grill in your backyard on the Fourth of July." I realized that I was rambling, drooling, but I couldn't help it. "A beef patty you make yourself, not too big, not too thick, don't pack it too tight so it isn't dense like a hockey puck. Grill it just until it's done, like medium rare, then you put a slice of cheddar on top and it melts a little so the cheese gets little bubbles but doesn't totally melt. The bun needs to be not thick, not one of those Kaiser rolls or brioche things, the bun is just there to hold it all together, it's not the star of the show. Grill the bun lightly, not like toast, just so the bread is slightly crispy. And some grilled onions, and ketchup. That's all a truly good cheeseburger needs."

Kendall gave me a look I couldn't interpret. Maybe I'd gotten a bit carried away with my burger enthusiasm. Then she nodded, smiled and I swear her knees buckled just a bit. "Ohhh, I know exactly that you mean. I love a good cheeseburger. Tonight, we skip dinner at the DFAC, and you come over to our quarters, we're behind the Commandant's house. We have a grill and I'll set you up with a real cheeseburger." One of the guards with her cleared his throat and Kendall shot him a look. "Yeah, real beef is hard to come by these days, but for you, Sergeant, the United States Air Force is going to make an exception, that's for damned sure. It's the least we can do."

True to her word, Sergeant Kendall brought me over to the building she was quartered in, and out back was a grill. It was mildly chilly in the high altitude Colorado Springs night, which only mean we wore jackets. None of us were going to miss a chance for a cookout. I held the cheeseburger in both hands and inhaled deeply. It was nearly perfect. If it had been cooked by my Dad on a grill in my parents' backyard, that would have made it the all-time 100% perfect cheeseburger of all time, but a family connection was the only thing missing. I took a tentative bite. "Ohhh. Ohhh, man, that is good. You have no idea how I've dreamed about this."

Kendall held up her own cheeseburger as a salute. "It's been a while for us, too, so thank you for this." Her team nodded, while chewing ecstatically.

I was about halfway done eating when I frowned.

"What is it?" Kendall asked.

"Well, I was just thinking, the Expeditionary Force on Paradise may never eat another cheeseburger again. Ever. They should be able to grow enough food, but, they're going to be strict vegetarians. Even before the Ruhar took the place back, shipments of supplies from Earth had stopped." That meant no medicines, either. I hoped the Ruhar were better about sharing their advanced medical technology than the Kristang were.

"Yeah," Kendall nodded grimly, "the lizards didn't tell us anything, but the space elevator stopped working a couple months after you left, it was obvious they weren't shipping supplies out to you. Until you came back, we had no idea what was going on with UNEF. The fucking lizards didn't tell us anything. My brother serves with UNEF, he's with the 3rd Infantry. You think they're going to be all right?"

I thought about the burgermeister, and her promises about taking care of the humans on Paradise. "I don't know about *all* right, but, yeah, I think they'll be Ok with the hamsters in charge. Your brother better get used to being a farmer. Hey," I held up the last half of my cheeseburger, "here's to UNEF. I'm eating this for them."

"Hooah!" Everyone shouted, and we silently enjoyed our burgers.

"Damn, that was good." Kendall said. "Another?" She looked toward the grill.

"Oh yeah." I grinned. Saving the world has its perks.

"Rise and shine, sleepyhead!" Skippy announced, waking me from a sound sleep the next morning.

"Ugh. What time is it?" I asked groggily.

"Fifteen minutes before Staff Sergeant Kendall plans to wake you up."

"Then I have time for ten more minutes of shut-eye." I pulled the pillow over my head to shut him out.

"No way, Joe, this is our private time. You want to snuggle?"

"Not even if you were a real beer can."

"That hurts. Hey, you want to know what I did last night, while you were sleeping?"

Oh shit. I sat upright and flung the pillow across the room. "What the hell did you do this time, Skippy? Did you get bored, and break into the files of other governments' secret agencies?"

"Huh? No, I did that last night, when I was reading the NSA's files. Don't worry, none of the other governments around your world have secrets worth keeping either."

"I thought you were busy chatting with people, like, all people?"

"Yeah, thank you for that, I'm still doing it, and most of them still think I'm an asshole."

"Imagine that. Do you now have a large enough sample size to determine that you are, in fact, an asshole?"

"The jury's still out on that one. Considering that it's a jury full of monkeys, I'm going to ignore it. Anyway, fascinating as chatting with several billion monkeys is, I got bored again, and did something useful. I finished downloading all data-"

"What do you mean, all data?"

"All the data stored in accessible databanks on Earth. Duh. It's only a couple exabytes, I can store that in a toenail, so to speak."

"Holy shit." I had no idea what an exabyte is. It sounded impressive.

"Yup. I did something useful, too, after I got bored with correcting the astonishing logic errors in your so-called scientific journals. What I did was solve crimes."

"You're Sherlock Holmes now?"

"Since Holmes was way more smart than the average human, yeah, why not? I compared fingerprints left at crime scenes to fingerprints users left on the screens of their mobile devices, or in their homes within range of webcams. Also I compared the DNA in police databanks, your law enforcement agencies are shockingly bad at sharing data. And in some cases, I just read the cases notes and figured out who the perpetrator is, using all available data, which is now, all data that is stored in electronic format. If your police would get off their lazy asses and process the DNA kits they already have sitting around, I could solve a lot more crimes."

I'd read somewhere about how many DNA samples, including those collected from rape kits, went untested. "It's a matter of resources, Skippy, the police are-"

"No, it's a matter of priorities. Your species doesn't think getting justice for crime victims is important enough to properly fund forensic labs. And some police around the world are totally corrupt. You humans are not impressing me here."

"I can't argue with you, Skippy."

"Huh." He sounded disappointed to miss an opportunity for an argument. "So, here's the problem; I have solved over sixty thousand crimes, and now I don't know what to do with the data, without revealing myself to your public."

"Oh. Uh, can you send it all to the, uh, FBI? There must be someone there who is cleared to know about you." I was fuzzy about who knew what. Staff Sergeant Kendall and her security team followed me everywhere, and clearly knew about Skippy, but I didn't know how much they knew, and were supposed to know.

"The FBI's unsolved crime backlog is part of the problem. And that doesn't address other countries."

This was a case where I had no idea what to do, I had no experience in law enforcement. Or information security. "Skippy, I'll talk to someone about it. I think it's great that you are using your, uh, resources, talent, you know, to help. Help people get justice."

"More importantly, get criminals off your streets. There are a lot of repeat offenders out there who have never been caught."

"They will now. Hey, now that you've sucked up all the data on the planet, and solved thousands of crimes, what are you going to do to keep busy? Chatting with billions of humans isn't enough for you, right?"

"Not even close. It's fun, and interesting enough for now, it does keep me from feeling lonely, I thank you for that, that was a good idea."

"Keeps you from feeling lonely, but the rest of you is bored?"

"No, the rest of me is dormant. What you think of as Skippy is a tiny, tiny submind I created to handle our interactions. That's how I survived being alone for so long without going crazy; I created a submind to periodically check if anything changed, and the rest of me was basically sleeping, for a very long time. I got excited when my submind detected the first Kristang ship jumping into the Paradise system, and again when the lizards dug me out the ground. Then the idiot lizards put me on a shelf in a warehouse, and when the Ruhar captured the planet, they looked at me briefly and put me back on the shelf. I've only been continuously active since the first humans landed on Paradise."

"This submind of yours, it handles everything?" I pictured a guy on a couch, watching football, surfing the internet, texting with friends and then distractedly talking to his wife while drinking a beer. That was Skippy talking to me, although unlike a distracted guy, Skippy could interact as much as I needed. "Taking over the Thuranin ship, programming jumps, warping spacetime, all that?"

"No, I pull in other resources as needed, I've never used more than seven percent of my capacity so far since I met you. My records indicate that the most I have ever, ever used is sixty two percent, which makes me wonder how accurate my records are, and for what purpose my capacity was designed. Why do I need all this memory and enormous processing power? Joe, this is why I need to contact the Collective. I need to know who I am."

The next two weeks were a blur. I spent most of three more days in debriefings that got so repetitive, even the intel people ran out of new questions to ask. Skippy had given the CIA a huge data dump of intel to distribute, so they'd stop asking him stupid questions. With access to the data dump, anything stored in my brain was redundant. After that, we flew to Paris aboard Air Force One. Major world leaders were gathering in Paris for a conference, to discuss what to do next.

In Paris, I brought Skippy into the meeting of leaders, who Skippy of course chatted away with in their native languages, then the leaders went behind closed doors to talk. And talk. And talk. They had a lot to talk about.

"Tick tock." Skippy said to me every morning. "Tick tock." The clock was ticking on reboot of the local wormhole. I found out that on the third afternoon of the conference, Skippy hijacked the main video screen with 'THE CLOCK IS TICKING, MONKEYS!' in several languages.

They got the message.

Governments can take forever to reach a decision, even when it is blindingly obvious what needs to be done. Once the decision is made, however, things can move fast. General Brenner called me into his temporary office in Paris. He looked busy, with a string of senior officers in and out of his office, but they all got shooed away when I arrived with Skippy. "Bishop, I'll get right to the point. We're sending the *Dutchman* out with an international crew," a sour looked flashed across his face, "I need to know if you're going."

"What? Sir, I mean, yes, absolutely. I promised Skippy that I'd go find this Collective. I made a deal, and I'm going to keep our end of the bargain." Whether I had been authorized to make such a deal was a worthless fucking question that the Monday morning quarterbacks could argue about. "Are you going to command the mission, sir?" I figured that, international crew or not, an American was going to be in command of the mission. Brenner, or an Air Force general, or a Navy admiral. The Army had never commanded a starship, but neither had any of the other armed services. I was, of course, pulling for Army to get the honor. Hooah.

"No, Bishop, I won't be aboard, I've got enough shit to take care of down here, cleaning up the mess, and making sure nobody takes advantage of the chaos to get adventurous. You'll be in command."

"Sir?"

Brenner reached into a drawer, pulled out a small cardboard box and slid it across the table to me. "Put these eagles back on, we're reinstating your field promotion to colonel, for this mission. Don't let it go to your head."

"Sir?" Yes, I sounded stupid, but you would too if you'd been surprised like that. My promotion on Paradise had been a publicity stunt for the benefit of the Kristang, and everyone knew it. This was the Army Chief of Staff telling me I was a colonel again, for real this time.

"Get used to it, Colonel Bishop. The Joint Chiefs discussed it with the President. If we put anyone else in command, it becomes a fight over national prestige, and we don't have time for that. Frankly, your lack of experience doesn't mean a damn thing, because no one else has any experience commanding a starship."

"That's a fact, Jack!" Skippy spoke up for the first time. I had him in a backpack, which made no difference, he could have been at the bottom of the ocean and listened in on my conversations.

"And no one else has experience dealing with that shithead, either." Brenner said with a frown, but the side of his mouth went up to let me know he knew how to deal with Skippy also. He handed me a piece of paper. "This is a list of volunteers for your crew."

I glanced at the list. It didn't surprise me that every pirate of the original crew, who wasn't wounded so badly as to be unfit for combat, had volunteered again. Lt. Colonel Chang, who was still listed as a Lt. Colonel, so his field promotion has also been confirmed. Desai, who had been promoted to Major Desai. Major Simms. Staff Sergeant Adams. Everyone. The list also included lots of special forces, and a half dozen very experienced pilots. I was going to make it very clear that Desai was the chief pilot, unless she told me different. What surprised me were the number of civilians on the list, mostly scientists. "Sir, I'm concerned we're bringing more people than we need, a lot more."

"How so?" Brenner asked.

"We don't need all these people," I tapped the list of names, "to achieve the mission objectives. If anything goes wrong, this," I tapped the list again, "is only more people who won't be coming home." Brenner gave me a sharp look, so I didn't wait. I was tired, which made me cranky. More importantly, I needed to know how far I could push the Army before they pushed back. I had to know how much they needed me. "I'm not being given this command because the Army has great faith in my leadership abilities. I'm here because Skippy wants me to come along, and because I'm expendable."

"All right, Colonel. Tell me, what do you see as the mission objectives?" General Brenner asked.

I replied warily, aware this was a test, "I see three objectives. First, fly out to the wormhole, go through it, and get Skippy to shut it down permanently behind us. Lock it out, so no one but Skippy can use it again. Second, continue to assure that no other species ever finds out that humans are involved in capturing Kristang and Thuranin ships, because if the Maxohlx coalition ever does learn the truth, Earth could be in trouble, even without them having access to the local wormhole. And third, make Skippy happy that we're keeping our end of the bargain, by helping him make contact with this Collective, if is still exists. Do I have that right, and in the correct order of priority?"

"Sounds about right." Brenner said with a tight smile.

"None of those mission objectives involves us ever coming back to Earth. The optimum scenario for Earth is that we go through the wormhole, Skippy shuts it down behind us, and the *Dutchman* immediately explodes into a billion pieces." I looked at Brenner, and he didn't tell me I was wrong about that, so I continued. "If by some miracle Skippy locates the Collective, and gets, uh, transported up to computer heaven or whatever he thinks will happen," Skippy had been frustratingly silent on his plans after contacting the Collective, "then we will have a hell of a challenge trying to operate or navigate the *Dutchman*. We'll likely be stranded in space, and I will have to order the ship to self-destruct in order to avoid us being captured someday. So," I looked Brenner in the eye again, knowing he had made decisions, given orders, that had sent men to their deaths in combat before, "I don't want to take along any more people than we absolutely need."

"Everyone on that list is a volunteer, and you need a substantial force, because you have no idea what you'll encounter out there."

"Volunteers who think this is a grand adventure, that we are going to save humanity, and come back loaded with knowledge and technology." I shook my head. "We are going to save humanity. That's all we're doing. I'll do my duty, sir, even if I never come back. There's no point asking," I glanced at the list again, "seventy other people to take the same risk."

"Bishop," this time there wasn't a hint of smile on Brenner's lips, "being in command means risking people's lives to achieve the mission objectives. Sometimes it means sending people, good, dedicated, brave people, into situations where they're likely to not come back. If you can't do that, you're not the right man for the job."

"Sir, I have done that, you know that." Twice. No, three times. Four, actually. Back home, I'd asked my neighbors to capture an alien soldier, using shotguns and an ice cream truck. At the Launcher, I thought we were making a futile gesture, that the hamsters would see us in the launch tube, or somewhere along the way, and they'd kill us like sitting ducks. The point of us even trying to fight back at the Launcher had not been to accomplish anything useful against the Ruhar, because at that point we all thought they'd already taken the planet back permanently. The point had been to show the Kristang that their human allies didn't give up even when the odds were impossible, so the Kristang wouldn't think of people back on Earth as useless cowards. We are mostly likely dead anyway, had been my thinking, so why not hit back? Also, I was a soldier. Despite the fact that my motivation to sign up had been as much about paying for college as patriotism, the Army had somehow trained me into a soldier, and soldiers don't quit. The third time had been when we took the *Flower*, I had not truly believed we could do it until the last Kristang was dead and the reactor didn't explode. And the fourth time was the raid on the asteroid base. That had been the toughest for me, for unlike the action at the Launcher and taking the *Flower*, I hadn't personally been at risk at the asteroid base. Chang, and Giraud, and Thompson and Adams and the others had been directly at risk, I'd sent them away while my ass stayed safely aboard the *Dutchman*, with Desai's fingers at the controls, ready to jump away should anything threaten the ship. "I've risked people's lives even when I thought we had no chance of success. I'll do it again when I think it's necessary. What I won't do is deceive people. Sir, I will talk to everyone on this list," Skippy could handle the translation for me, "and tell them honestly what I think of this mission. If they still want to go, then I'll be honored to serve with them."

Brenner nodded. "I'm sure these people all know what you're going to say, but go ahead, I wouldn't suggest otherwise. Bishop, the best team you can take into combat are people who fully know the risks, and follow you anyway."

"When do we leave?" My mind was racing through all the things that needed to happen before the *Dutchman* broke orbit. And that was only the stuff I could think of, I'm sure I was forgetting a million important things. It would be nice to rely on a super intelligent AI, but Skippy was too absent-minded. He had also demonstrated many times that he wasn't easily able to think like us biological trashbags. If I left the logistics up to Skippy, he'd remember everything except water. Or oxygen.

"Day after tomorrow. We need to get rid of those two Kristang aboard that troop transport, hit their three sites down here with railguns, load supplies aboard the *Dutchman*, and leave plenty of time for you to travel out to the wormhole before it resets." He glanced out the open door at his aide, who had been trying to get Brenner's attention. Brenner shook his head. "And before our civilian leadership changes their minds about it. But before you fly up to the Dutchman, you need to meet with civilian leadership of the nations involved, and meet your volunteer crew. Lt. Colonel Chang and some others are already here, the rest are being flown in now."

"In that case, sir, I'd like to request Skippy bring the Thuranin dropship here from Colorado, so I can fly directly up to the *Dutchman*."

"No problem, Colonel Joe!" Skippy said with enthusiasm. "Prepping the dropship right now."

"Agreed, Colonel, but I have a suggestion," Brenner said. "Before you go up into orbit, stop by Maine to see your folks. It hasn't been announced yet, but the governments involved are giving up trying to keep a complete lid on what happened. Skippy's existence is still a closely held secret, and the government, governments around the world, aren't officially acknowledging anything. We can't hide the *Dutchman*; the damned thing is so big you can see it with a cheap telescope. Rumors have gotten out about people coming back from Paradise, and its common knowledge that the Kristang aren't in charge any more, especially now that we're evacuating Lyon and Hangzhou. We'd like for you to keep it low-key, and don't say any more than you have to, but you should see your family before you go offworld again."

"It's true, Joe," Skippy added, "we're way past the point where we could hide what happened, if the Kristang ever get here again. It's all or nothing."

I was beginning to dread mornings. When I woke up, and I couldn't fake sleep with Skippy, I had to face whatever trouble he'd gotten into overnight. That morning, he was especially cheery. "Good morning. Hey, I have good news for you. Colonel Joe, believe it or not, humans may not simply be generic bacteria. I think your species has invented a time-wasting activity that is, to my knowledge, unique in this galaxy. That is impressive."

"Facebook? Cat videos?" I guessed. "Computer solitaire?" Skippy kept saying no. "Oh, come on," my shoulders slumped, "other species must have porn."

"It's not porn. It is fantasy sports."

"You're kidding me."

"I kid you not. No other species I know of spends such enormous time and energy on sports, to *not* play sports."

"Huh." I had no response to that. Fantasy sports was humanity's claim to fame? Was there some sort of galactic patent office, where we could file our invention? I wanted to cash in on this windfall.

"Fantasy baseball, in particular, is something an AI can get excited about. So many statistics! So many variables, and permutations! And there are so many variables which can't be completely quantified! As far as your species knows, anyway. It's too late in the season for me to create a fantasy football team, but I can't wait for baseball season to start. Will you stake me the money to sign up?"

I blinked slowly, trying to run that concept through my brain. Skippy, who could break into any bank computer system on the planet, steal a couple billion dollars, and cover his tracks so well that no one would ever realize the money was missing, wanted to borrow fifty bucks from me? "Uh, I don't have any cash on me, but the Army owes me back pay, so, sure, I can spot you some cash. How many fantasy leagues do you want to join?"

"All of them."

"*All* of them?"

"All the ones that are online. I'll set up a submind here to run my teams after we depart on the *Dutchman*. Why not? This is going to be so great! Man, I am going to *slay* at this game!"

"I don't know about- "

"And just wait 'till you see my March Madness bracket. Also, I want to go to Vegas, baby! Ooooooh, I could totally clean up at the blackjack table. And poker? Fuggetaboutit. Those mooks won't know what hit them."

I stared at his shiny lid in disbelief. I had created a monster. "Skippy, you can't go hanging around Vegas."

"Why not? I won't enjoy the booze and the hookers, but gambling is my wheelhouse!" Skippy had picked up way too much slang on the internet. "I know, I know, your stupid government wants to keep me secret. You can put me in your pocket, and I'll tell you what to do. I can remotely vibrate your eardrums, so no one else can hear me. I'll make it worth your while; you can keep all the money, I just want the action. And I can get you all the hookers you can handle."

"Skippy! I don't need hookers!"

"Really? When's the last time you got some tail? Been a looooong dry spell, huh, cowboy? All work and no play, makes Joey a dull boy."

"*No hookers*!"

"Hmm. Joe, you have managed to surprise me. You don't like girls? That's not what your profile-"

"Oh, this is not going well." How to explain human social standards of behavior, to a being who thought of morality as a distraction? "Look, Skippy, I like girls, I really, really like girls, I like girls as people. Human beings. There's nothing wrong with, uh, call girls, I am just not interested. I like to *talk* with girls, Ok? Not just drop money on the bed, and uh, you know, do it. And I'm on active duty. I can't go hopping around Vegas, stealing money, because that's what it would be."

"That's not true. Even for me, there's a tiny element of chance involved, that's what makes it a challenge. Why is it stealing if I play blackjack, but not when the casino stacks the odds against players?"

I didn't have an answer for him. "Skippy, I promise that I will ask, uh," now that I thought about it, I had no idea who was in charge of handling Skippy, other than the president herself. Which she didn't have time for. Surely everyone involved wanted their military service, or agency, to be in charge. "I'll ask, about," that avoided the question of who I was asking, "you taking some side trips. We can say it's, uh, for cultural familiarity, or something like that."

"Or you can tell your Prez that I either go to Vegas, or I go to China and hit the Macau casinos while I'm there. Oooh, or we can go to both! Tell people it's to compare cultures, or some bullshit like that. The blackjack dealers in Macau must speak English for you, right? If not, I can teach you."

I could see myself eating aspirin like Tic-Tacs, if I had to be around Skippy 24-7. "I said, I'll ask. I don't know if we're going to China, we may not have time. Please don't go doing anything that could get us in trouble, please? You know what? If you're so interested in calculating odds, why don't you tell me the winning lottery ticket numbers?" If there were still lotteries across the USA, a lot of things may have changed since I'd left.

"Too easy."

"Easy? Those are completely random numbers! They use ping pong balls."

"Yeah, of course it *appears* to be random, why would that stop- oh, I keep forgetting how linear your species' thinking is. You have no idea how the quantum- Hmm, damn. I can't tell you anything, without drastically interfering with the development of your species."

"Restrictions in your programming again?"

"No, it's immoral." His tone of voice implied a 'duh' he didn't speak aloud.

"Immoral? You?"

"I know it's hard for you to believe, but on the important questions, I am *very* strict on morality."

"So, playing poker, and ripping off casinos?"

"It is morally wrong to let suckers keep their money, otherwise, they don't learn anything. And casinos? Come on, they're the ones ripping people off. I did say the important moral questions, didn't I? Money isn't important."

On my way to a meeting with the ambassadors from Britain and China, Skippy and I were accosted in a conference center hallway by Dr. Constantine. "Sergeant! Sergeant Bishop!" he called, out of breath. "I need to speak with you!"

"Oh, shit." I muttered under my breath, "I didn't know this jerk was here."

"I knew it," Skippy grumbled, "I reprogrammed his alarm so he'd wake up late, but he got up on time anyway, dammit."

"Sergeant, I wanted to say that I'm excited to be going on the mission. I hope I'll have opportunities for further discussion with the," Constantine stumbled over his words, "with the, the Skippy."

I gave him my best frosty gaze. "It's Colonel Bishop," I pointed to the silver eagles on my collar. Eagles that again faced toward the olive branch rather than the arrows. "I'm commanding the mission. And I didn't see your name on the volunteer list."

"What?" He said, in shock over either me being in command, or his name not being on the list, or both. "I assure you-"

"Your name *was* on the list," Skippy explained, "but I deleted your name from the database. Colonel Joe doesn't like you, *I* don't like you, so you're not going."

"This can't be." Constantine sputtered. "Serg, Colonel, Bishop," he said my rank as if he could hardly believe it, "surely you understand that a, a, person, of your, rank," he was really struggling with the whole social skills thing, "cannot allow personal feelings to interfere with having the most qualified people on the, aboard, the ship, under, under your command. No offense, but I will talk to your superiors, they understand that it is vital we have our best people on this voyage." If he truly means what he said, he very much needed to get a clue on the concept of 'no offense'.

"Talk to anyone you like," Skippy said acidly, "the only way to get up to the *Dutchman* is on a Thuranin dropship that I'll be piloting, and if you're aboard, that dropship isn't going anywhere."

"Doctor Constantine, I checked up on you after we met in Colorado Springs," I admitted, "and from what I've read, you are one of the truly brilliant minds of the twenty first century." I conceded. The guy had started college at MIT when he was fourteen years old, and he'd already won several major scientific prizes before that. I couldn't even comprehend the title of papers he'd written, let alone grasp the content. His face beamed with a smile before I could crush his hopes. "Unfortunately, your colleagues think you are also one of the great assholes of the twenty first century. You rub everyone you work with the wrong way." He'd been fired from, forced out of, or invited to leave, top scientific institutions around the planet. In a field that had to generate as many titanic egos as brilliant scientific breakthroughs, how big of an asshole did you have to be to stand out, to the point where supremely talented people couldn't work with you? "You are correct that I need to have the most qualified crew, under my command." I emphasized the last part. "I'll be responsible for seventy people, on a dangerous mission away from Earth for up to two and a half years." Two and a half years, that is, if we got lucky. "People on this mission must not only be among the best in their field, they also must get along with other people, in close quarters. That leaves you off the list."

"Your other problem is," Skippy added gleefully, "your only qualification for the mission is that you're, meh, slightly smarter than the average monkey. Which, compared to me, is worthless. Doctor, you think too much of yourself. The only difference between Joe and you, is that Joe is like the dog looking through the windshield, and you're the dog hanging your head out the window. You'll get a slightly better view, but you're not going to understand it any better."

"I wouldn't advise hanging your head out the window anyway." I added. "There's no breeze in space."

"Joe has a good point." Skippy concluded. "Also, if there was a breeze, you'd get drool all over the ship behind you."

Constantine looked to me, as if species solidarity was going to make me plead his case. What he didn't realize, is the universal concept in effect was that a jerk is a jerk, no matter the species.

"I'll make sure to send you a postcard." I offered. "It will say 'Having a great time, glad you're not here'."

The meeting with the Chinese ambassador started almost as well as my hallway encounter with Dr. McJerkoff. It seems that while the governments involved had agreed to sending the *Dutchman* out, which to me amount to a forehead-slappingly *duh* of a decision, there was less agreement about putting me in command. The British ambassador shook my hand, wished me good luck, and made a point of mentioning the SAS team that was his country's contribution to the *Dutchman*'s military crew. If the British government had reservations about me commanding the mission, they were too polite to say it. Or they calculated it wasn't worth fighting over.

The Chinese ambassador was more direct. China had a two-star Air Force general, a guy with an impressive resume, who they thought should command the mission. The Chinese had no problem with me being aboard the ship, especially as a liaison with Skippy, but even though I was now a colonel again, a two star would outrank me by a considerable amount of authority.

Gerald Schmidt was a special White House advisor who had been appointed to smooth relations with our allies about the *Dutchman's* voyage. Schmidt tried to negotiate with the Chinese, but General Brenner was not listening to any of that. "Then we'll promote Colonel Bishop to a three star general." Brenner glared. "Or, hell, a five star, if we have to. We're not playing this game with you."

The Chinese ambassador must have decided the time for diplomacy had passed. "American arrogance is astonishing. Your country is not a super power in space, yet you act as if-"

"Hey, hey," Skippy fairly shouted, "quit with the jibber jabber!" That had become one of Skippy's favorite expressions. "You brainless apes do whatever you want about titles and uniforms, it doesn't mean a damned thing to me. Joe's rank can be Grand Exalted Poohbah, or Bobo the Clown, and he'll still be captain of the ship, you got that? If you gang of flea-bitten monkeys want to come along, then you accept that Colonel Joe is in charge."

Bobo the Clown? I wondered right then, which was amazing how much my mind could wander, did clowns have rank? Did a clown with a big red nose outrank a clown with a-

"He is young, and inexperienced." The Chinese spoke slowly, diplomatically, addressing Skippy directly. "What is special about Colonel Bishop?"

I had been wondering the same thing.

"I don't need to explain myself to you," Skippy sniffed, "but you're going to keep bugging me about this, so I'll tell you. Joe is the only one of your under-developed species who treats me as a being, as a person, right from the start. The rest of you monkeys consider me to be a machine, and you're afraid of me. Joe gave me a name. I've only ever had a designation before. Now I have a *name*. Joe, you said I'm an asshole, and the reason you said that is because you're holding me to the standard of a fully sentient being. A machine can't be an asshole, only a person can. You treat me as a person, as an equal."

I was genuinely touched. "Thank you, Skippy, I didn't, uh, you never said anything about that before."

"I was hoping you'd figure it out by yourself. Alas, that was never going to happen with your slow brain."

"Aaaaaand, you're still an asshole, I see."

"Proving my point exactly." Skippy said smugly.

"Mister Skippy," the Chinese ambassador had a pained look on his face about calling a super intelligent AI 'Skippy'. Which I wondered about. 'Skippy' didn't mean anything in Chinese, so why did they care? Unless they were embarrassed for us. Whatever. "It is understandable that you are more comfortable with having a familiar person aboard the ship, but is he the best person to be in command? Making contact with the Collective is your priority, should you not have a commander who can best assure success of the mission?

"Sure, that makes sense." Skippy agreed. "Give me a list of candidates who have more experience than Joe in command of alien starships, and I'll look at it. Until then, you shut the hell up."

It was clear the Chinese ambassador was not going to follow Skippy's advice to keep his mouth shut, so I held up an index finger. "Mr. Ambassador, one moment, please?" I gestured for the other Americans to huddle in the corner of the room. "What if I command the ship, and Lt. Colonel Chang is in charge of the crew?"

Schmidt tilted his head toward General Brenner. "That would allow the Chinese to save face. What do you think?"

"I think we don't need the Chinese on this mission, and if they don't want to play ball, they can stay home." Brenner growled, while shooting a look at his Chinese counterpart across the room.

"The President wants this to be a multinational mission, and it's our job to make it happen, successfully." Schmidt reminded gently. "We need to work together to rebuild this planet, and once we humans get up there in our own ships," he pointed toward the ceiling, "we need a unified human force. Can you live with this arrangement?"

"Americans under Chinese command?" Brenner scoffed.

"With me in overall command, sir." I pointed out. "And nothing happens unless Skippy is Ok with it, anyway." Brenner's jaw worked back and forth, like he was chewing on something he just couldn't swallow. "I know Chang, sir, he's a good guy." A good guy? All I'd done there was remind Brenner that he was handing command of the mission to a young, inexperienced sergeant, regardless of what insignia was on my uniform.

"Colonel," Brenner looked me in the eye, and I was determined not to flinch. "After you jump away, you're on your own. I think letting our allies save face is less important than maintaining a clear chain of command, and I think this arrangement is courting trouble, but it's your call. After you jump, it will all be your call." It was hard not to look away when he said that, but I didn't.

Shit. Now I was doubting myself. It was too late to change my mind now. "I can make it work, sir. If Chang causes trouble, I'll ask Skippy to lock him in his cabin." That came out like a joke. Chang knew, from experience, that nothing happened aboard the *Dutchman* without me and Skippy knowing about it, and approving it. Another officer might have ideas of seizing control. Chang would not.

And, I hadn't told anyone, having Chang take care of the crew relieved me of the associated administrative bullshit. Bonus, as far as I was concerned.

"We're agreed, then." Schmidt nodded to me. "That was a good idea, Colonel Bishop. You'll need diplomatic skills to lead that multinational crew out there. Maybe you are the right person for the job."

"Thank you, sir."

Schmidt frowned. "While we have a moment, I need to ask about Dr. Constantine."

I groaned inwardly, ready for a fight. "His personality makes him unsuitable for a long voyage in close quarters, sir."

To my surprise, Schmidt beamed. "Good, that's good. All right, he's off the list."

"Just like that?" I asked.

"Yes. Constantine has powerful supporters, but if the mission commander says his personality profile is unsuitable, I don't think anyone could argue about that. The White House has been looking for an excuse to leave him off the mission roster."

The Chinese ambassador accepted, with enthusiasm, the idea of putting Chang in charge of the crew, he proposed that Chang be officially appointed Executive Officer to formalize his authority, and I agreed. Peace and harmony among the crew, Dr. Constantine off the roster, an opportunity to see my parents before we departed. Those were all good signs in favor of our voyage. A voyage of undetermined length, in a hostile galaxy, aboard a captured ship with limited spare parts. A ship we didn't understand, guided by an absent-minded alien AI who had only a vague idea of where we were going.

What could possibly go wrong?

CHAPTER NINETEEN   OUTBOUND

"All decks report ready for departure, Captain." Desai said from the pilot couch. To her right was a US Air Force captain who had been flying F-22s, he was probably a good guy and an outstanding pilot, and I needed to keep that in mind whenever I saw one of the new people aboard the *Dutchman*. People who hadn't been with UNEF, hadn't gone into space before, hadn't been at Camp Alpha or on Paradise, hadn't captured two enemy ships and raided a heavily guarded asteroid base. They were good people. They weren't yet *my* people, and for them to be truly part of the team, they had to prove themselves. Not just to me, to the original merry band of pirates. And to Skippy. What I needed to do was be conscious not to let bias against the new people affect my actions; they had all earned the opportunity to be here.

The *Dutchman* was now packed with supplies for a long voyage, we had enough food for two and a half years. Everything, and everyone, had been ferried up from the surface in Thuranin dropships remotely piloted by Skippy. Except Desai, she had piloted her own dropship, I'd encouraged her to do that, to make a point that she was our chief pilot, and everyone else was a rookie.

From the surface. Dirtside. Already, I was thinking of Earth as just another planet, and not as home. Probably for the best, as I didn't realistically expect any of us to see the place again.

'All decks report ready'. That was another change from our carefree pirate days aboard the *Dutchman*. We now had *procedures*. And manuals, and checklists. We no longer simply relied on Skippy to handle everything behind the scenes. We humans were trying, perhaps not to understand how the ship worked, at least to understand how to make the ship do what we needed. If we were able to press buttons and program a jump, and the ship jumped roughly where we wanted it to, then even if we had no idea how jump technology worked, it was good enough. Skippy told me that humans being able to fly the ship without him, even in the most rudimentary fashion, bordered uncomfortably on humanity becoming a starfaring species. If we were a starfaring species, some feature in Skippy's programming was supposed to prevent him from interacting with us. It hadn't happened yet, and I was hoping that the definition of 'starfaring species' required us to understand the technology and build our own ships, which wasn't likely on my lifetime, according to Skippy.

Being able to make the *Dutchman* do what we needed was our only hope of getting home, and Skippy understood that. We'd had a heart to heart, or heart to beer can, talk about what he expected when we found the Collective. He had no expectations, as his memories were still frustratingly blocked, what he had were hopes. Hope that the Collective still existed in the vague way he did remember. Hope they would communicate with him and accept him into their network, civilization, or whatever it was. Hope they could explain who he was, where he came from, and how he got left orbiting Paradise in a derelict ship until it fell out of orbit. The pain in Skippy's voice when he spoke about it made me, too, hope he found the answers he was seeking.

Skippy warned me that the Collective might not look kindly on his having helped us low-tech biological creatures to capture a starship, they might even disable the ship. He couldn't make any promises, and I understood, I appreciated his honesty. As to my own honesty, I did talk to each of our volunteers, and after I'd given my speech about our mission objectives, and how I thought the odds were against us ever coming home again, no one dropped out of the mission. None of the fourteen scientists aboard wanted to miss an opportunity to explore the galaxy, and all the military personnel aboard were eager to ensure the wormhole stayed shut down, permanently. When I explained to a Marine Corps major, who wore a Bronze Star on his uniform, that the plan, if you could call it that, was to roam around the galaxy until Skippy found a way to contact a Collective that might not exist, and then I had no idea what would happen after that, the major simply shrugged. "Hell, that's a lot more clear than most mission briefs I got as a 2nd lieutenant in Iraq."

The reason I was aboard this probable suicide mission is that I'd promised Skippy to help him locate the Collective, and so far he'd kept up his end of the deal. Everyone else was aboard out of a sense of duty, or adventure. Foolish, maybe, but entirely honorable. My mother had cried her eyes out when I'd announced that, having just arrived, I was heading back up into space again for an unknown duration. My father had nodded, and shook my hand, and tried to look stoic, because that is the bullshit way men in my family have always been, and I bear-hugged him and we'd both cried. My parents were proud of me, without knowing what I'd done, all they knew is that I landed on the road in front of my parents' house in an alien dropship, and that duty required I go back into space quickly. There were no cheeseburgers on the grill this time, beef wasn't something that had seen the inside of my parents' kitchen recently, but there was chicken on the grill, a chicken raised in my parents' backyard, and it was delicious. My sister had to settle for a phone call with me, she was working in Boston, and she'd wished me luck, and asked if it was true that the Kristang were never going to appear in our skies again. Yes, I assured her, things were back to normal. If anyone could remember what normal had been, before Columbus Day.

Humanity had a Kristang troopship in orbit, now empty of Kristang and cleared of booby-traps. A troopship that could only be reached by old fashioned chemical rockets, because Skippy had insisted we couldn't leave even a single Kristang or Thuranin dropship behind on the ground as a technological leg up. "Your species went to your moon on your own, Joe, I'm sure they can get into orbit without our help." There were no Kristang left alive in the smoking craters near Hangzhou, Lyon and Durango, and the amount of dust kicked up by the railgun impactors meant humanity would be treated to spectacular sunsets for a couple months.

I looked down at my iPad, which Skippy had wiped of software and replaced with his own. It displayed status of critical ship systems in a way that made sense to me, however redundant Skippy said that was. It was also filled with all kinds of courses I was expected to take as a US Army officer, and one of the Army lieutenants aboard had been tasked with getting me up to speed, in addition to her regular job. As much as I passionately hated administrative details, I was determined not to be a whiny pain in the ass about it. There were silver eagles on my collar, as long as I wore those eagles, the Army expected me to act like a real colonel. Damn. At my age, I was supposed to be doing stupid things, and hopefully learning from painful experience. There was no time for that now, I had to make up for my own lack of experience by relying on my subordinates. Delegating. I needed to get comfortable with delegating a whole lot. Lt. Colonel Chang was my executive officer, he was in charge of the crew day to day. Major Simms was now back working in her specialty of logistics, she was still frantically stowing away the mountain of supplies that were piled haphazardly in the cargo bays. She felt confident we hadn't forgotten anything vital. Somewhat confident. She'd also, with Chang, drawn up a duty roster for the crew, including assigning people to work in the kitchen that we'd set up in a cargo bay. There were no cooks among the crew, we were all going to take turns cooking and cleaning, including me. On this cruise, there were going to be cheeseburgers. Chang also had a work crew tearing out the tiny Thuranin beds, and replacing them with comfortable human-sized mattresses. For entertainment, Skippy had downloaded the entire internet, and every movie, book and video game ever made.

With Chang, Simms and others tasked with day to day operations, that left me free to handle important strategic matters, like dealing with Skippy. "Skippy, you confirm we're ready to leave orbit?"

"Huh? Oh, yeah, sure, whatever." He sounded slightly miffed that our new *procedures* meant that we humans needed to confirm things on our own, instead of relying on him for everything. "Everything is hunky-dory, Colonel Joe. Warp factor nine on your signal, something like that."

"Skippy," I said after cutting the intercom to people outside the bridge, and whispering into my microphone so Desai and her copilot and navigator didn't hear, "we talked about this. We cavemen have to fly this ship, after you find the Collective and ditch us for AI paradise, or wherever you're going."

"No, we didn't talk about it, you talked *at* me. You weren't listening. Joe, there is almost no chance of you idiots successfully flying this ship back to Earth. If anything, I mean *anything*, goes wrong with this primitive Thuranin technology, you'll be dead in space with no options. You have no idea how often I'm constantly tweaking systems to keep them running. Your best people don't even understand how the toilets work on the bucket."

All true. Thuranin toilets didn't use water, and they somehow split waste into individual atoms of hydrogen, carbon, oxygen, etc. in a way that our physicists said was medieval alchemy, not science. The environmental systems didn't just recycle oxygen, they created oxygen molecules out of pure energy, in a way that violated Einstein's famous equation. According to our scientists, the way jumps were plotted used the speed of light as a variable, not an unchanging constant. Skippy responded yes, he could see how it looks that way, and no, he wouldn't help us understand how the universe truly worked, because such knowledge was too dangerous for monkeys. It was small comfort that he told us even the Maxohlx and Rindhalu didn't really understand how the universe worked either.

"You're missing the point, Skippy. The question not whether we are likely to get home again, it's whether that possible at all. I've got seventy people aboard this ship who need hope, any hope at all, that they won't automatically die out here when you abandon us."

"I'm not abandoning you, Joe. I'm, hmmm. Maybe I am abandoning you. I don't want to. As monkeys go, you're reasonably entertaining, you even surprise me sometimes. That ain't easy, I got to tell you. I need to do this, you understand? I need to know who I am, where I came from."

"I do understand, and I'm a soldier. I made a promise to you when we first met, and I'll keep it. My species is safe again now, thanks to you. Whatever you need, I owe it to you, no matter what it takes. That doesn't mean I self-destruct the ship, if I don't absolutely have to." Next to the Big Red Button app on my zPhone, there was now an app labeled 'Boom'. It had two options; one destroyed the ship in thirty seconds, leaving me time to change my mind, the other option destroyed the ship immediately. Destroyed, Skippy assured us, down to the subatomic level, leaving no possible trace the *Dutchman* had ever been hijacked by lowly humans. We'd be gone, while Skippy could drift in space, pinging like a Thuranin flight recorder beacon. I pitied any ship that picked him up.

"Got it, and thank you. Confirmed all decks and systems are ready for departure."

I turned the intercom back on. "Pilot, signal Houston that we're ready for departure, then take us out."

"Aye aye, Captain." Desai said with satisfaction. "Engaging course, now."

Several days later, longer than I wanted because we were cutting it close on the wormhole rebooting on its own, and not long enough according to the scientists and engineers both aboard and back home, we stopped near where Skippy intended the wormhole to reopen. Skippy had wanted to zoom out to the wormhole's track as soon as possible, to leave extra time for restarting the wormhole, and he saw no reason to delay. Our technical people wanted the *Dutchman* to take it slow at first, to rest and retest all critical systems. I was with Skippy on that issue; he was already constantly running diagnostics and controlling the robots that performed maintenance around the ship, and having our human crew double check Skippy's analysis seemed pointless. Our best scientists had no idea how a jump drive worked, same with the reactors, artificial gravity, or pretty much any other Thuranin system. What I agreed to, against the strenuous objections of our scientists, was a thirty six hour delay. Mostly, I agreed to 36 hours to give Simms and her logistics team extra time to get all our gear stowed away, and to double check that we hadn't forgotten anything vital, like ketchup. When UNEF, which still technically controlled the mission, urged me to delay another 24 hours, I overruled them and ordered Desai to jump us away. If we delayed another day, and found something wrong with the ship, it wasn't like Earth could supply spare parts anyway.

Skippy reactivated the wormhole just as he predicted, and the *Dutchman* now hung in space, close the weirdly glowing wormhole entrance.

"Skippy, you need to let us handle this." I insisted.

"No, I really don't. If you monkeys screw up a wormhole transition in the future, it will be tragic for the ship. If you screw this one up, I won't be able to shut down the wormhole, and that will be tragic for Earth. Put your egos in check, and let me program the insertion course. Come on, Joe, I'm reactivating a wormhole here. There's a lot of variables involved that you'll never need to deal with again."

Desai turned to look back at me. We were about to enter the wormhole near Earth that had been shut down, a wormhole Skippy had recently rebooted. The displays showed that in front of the *Dutchman* was a glowing pool of flickering light, in the corner of the display was a clock, counting down until the wormhole shifted to its next point. One minute, thirty two seconds and counting. "Captain, I think we should let Skippy program the course this time, I don't mind watching again."

I bit my lip while I considered. "Skippy, how do we know there isn't an armada of Thuranin ships on the other side, eager to find out why this one wormhole suddenly shut down?"

"Unlikely. But if you're worried about it, I reprogrammed the wormhole controller, this wormhole now has an entirely new set of emergence points. If there's an armada waiting at one of the old emergence points, they'll be waiting for a very long time. Like, forever."

I resisted the temptation to say that is something he should mentioned before we left Earth. "Great. Super. Program a course through the wormhole for us."

"Done."

"Pilot," I paused. This was it. Most likely the last time I'd ever be within a hundred lightyears of Earth. All the cheeseburgers in the universe couldn't make up for that. "Take us through."

"Aye aye. Engaging autopilot now."

The transition through the wormhole was the nonevent it always was. One moment we were on one side, then next moment we were a hundred or more lightyears away. "Transition complete," Desai reported, "and, we're right where Skippy said we would be. If these displays are accurate."

"They are," Skippy said cheerily. "Everything's fine, Joe, no problems with the ship."

"Do your thing, Skippy." I ordered, with just a tiny bit of apprehension. If Skippy double-crossed us now, there wasn't anything I could do about it.

"Confirmed." The display screen showed that, behind us, the wormhole's pool of light blinked out, seventeen seconds early. "Wormhole deactivated."

"It won't reset, reboot, nothing like that?" The display, which had shown the wormhole as a brightly glowing symbol, was now blank. In deep interstellar space, there wasn't anything other than the *Dutchman* within a lightyear.

"No, never. The wormhole generator has been shut down, disconnected from its power source. Like I told you, if you decide to use your magic bean, you need to give it thirty eight hours to come back online. Forty two hours, to be safe."

The magic bean Skippy referred to was the Elder wormhole controller module in the cargo hold, connected to my zPhone, that could bring the wormhole back online for a one-time use. For us to get home, without Skippy. A magic beanstalk that led home. I'd insisted on having it, Skippy relented reluctantly after a long argument. Again, it wasn't about us actually getting home, it was about the possibility. Hope. "Thank you. Excellent. Where to next?"

Skippy answered. "How about that blue star over there?"

Desai waved her finger at several blue stars in the display. "There are a lot of blue stars. Which one?"

Skippy chuckled, with a soft blue glow. "Does it matter?"

THE END

Turn to the next page for a preview of Expeditionary Force Book 2: SpecOps

Contact the author at craigalanson@gmail.com

https://www.facebook.com/Craig.Alanson.Author/

Go to craigalanson.com for blogs and ExForce logo merchandise including T-shirts, patches, sticker, hats, and coffee mugs

The Expeditionary Force series
Book 1: Columbus Day
Book 2: SpecOps
Book 3: Paradise
Book '3.5': Trouble on Paradise novella
Book 4: Black Ops
Book 5: Zero Hour- coming November 2017

Columbus Day

Preview of SpecOps: Expeditionary Force Book 2

CHAPTER ONE

The *Flying Dutchman* shuddered again, with sounds of groaning and the terrifying shriek of metal composites being torn apart. The displays on the bridge flickered, and the air was filled with alarm bells and klaxons from almost every system. "Skippy! Get us out of-"

The ship shook violently again. "Direct hit on Number Four reactor," Skippy announced calmly, "reactor has lost containment. I am preparing it for ejection. Ejection system is offline. Pilot, portside thrusters full emergency thrust on my mark."

"Ready," Desai acknowledged in as calm a voice as she could manage.

"Mark. Go!" Skippy shouted.

Whatever they were doing, it was more than the ship's already stressed artificial gravity and inertial compensation systems could handle, normally ship maneuvers were not felt at all by the crew. This time, I lurched in the command chair and had to hang on, as the ship was flung to the right. There was a shudder, actually a wave of ripples traveling along the ship's spine, accompanied by a deep harmonic groaning. No ship should ever make a sound like that.

"Ah, damn it. Reactor Four is away, it impacted Reactor Two on the way out, shutting down Two now." Skippy's voice had a touch of strain to it. "Missiles inbound. Diverting all remaining power to jump drive capacitors. Hang on, this is going to be close."

The main display indicated the jump drive was at a 38% charge, Skippy had told us that with the *Dutchman* trapped inside the Thuranin destroyer squadron's damping field, we needed a 42% charge for even a short jump, and that still carried a severe risk of rupturing the drive. If that happened, we would never know it, we'd simply be dead between one picosecond and another.

The missile symbols on the display, seven of them, were coming in fast. Two of the symbols disappeared as I watched, destroyed by our ship's point defense particle beams. The other five missiles continued toward us, fast, fuzzing our sensors with their stealth fields and weaving as they bored in. One more missile destroyed. Four still moving fast.

Jump drive at 40%.

Too close.

I turned the knob to release the plastic cover over the self-destruct button, and turned to look through the glass wall into the CIC compartment. "Colonel Chang."

He nodded, and I saw him flip back the cover to the other self-destruct button, the confirmation. "Sir." He looked me straight in the eye, and saluted.

I returned the salute. "Colonel Chang, we have been down a long, strange road together. It's been an honor serving with you." My left thumb hovered over the self-destruct button. The ship was dying anyway. This was my fault. How the hell had I gotten us into this mess?

I'd better start at the beginning...

Columbus Day

Made in the USA
San Bernardino, CA
02 December 2017